IN THE EYE
OF THE STORM

*   *   *

ELLIS STRAKER, *star captain*. Whether facing exile or striding a warship's bridge, Straker's will cannot be broken, his resolve to fight Yamato cannot be swayed.

JOHN OUJUKU, *star captain*. Call him "hero," "outlaw," "corsair," or "pirate," the Black Dragon only wants to be the Shogun's worst nightmare.

MICHIE, *daughter, wife, mother*. Beneath her dutiful mask, Michie will defy even the Emperor himself for those she loves.

DUVAL STRAKER, *weapons engineer*. Yamato stole his name, his mind, his honor. Now Duval must sacrifice everything to regain what his enemies have taken.

GANESH RAMAKRISHNAN, *psi mystic*. He can prove that the ultimate weapons are the human mind—and the human soul ... and he's for sale to the highest bidder.

*

Please turn this
YAMATO: A

D0465464

YAMATO

"Science fiction adventure of a truly galactic scale. Plenty of action, adventure and intrigue. A great read!"
—**William C. Dietz**
author of *Warworld*

"Kudos to Ken Kato. YAMATO is space opera for moderns, with the power to please those who ordinarily don't care for space opera. It pulls you in and does not let you go. Its characters are richly drawn, its plotting intricate but tight, and its far-future science and technology have the feel of reality. . . . Doc Smith and L. Ron Hubbard never produced anything to match YAMATO."
—**John Dalmas**
author of *The General's President* and *The White Regiment*

A RAGE IN HEAVEN PART 2

"Amazingly well done."
—Bill Baldwin
author of the Helmsman series

"A rousing space epic . . . both a precursor of the future and a metaphor for the past."
—Peter Albano
author of the Seventh Carrier series

"The book is so full of incidents, exotic settings, quirky characters, and fast action that it quickly achieves not merely suspension of disbelief but absorbing interest. Its nearest historical analogue is the duel between Tudor England and Spain, and in science fiction and fantasy it recalls the work of David Eddings and L. Ron Hubbard."
—*Chicago Sun-Times*

YAMATO

A RAGE IN HEAVEN PART 2

KEN KATO

WARNER BOOKS

A Time Warner Company

WARNER BOOKS EDITION

Copyright © 1990 Ken Kato
All rights reserved.

Questar® is a registered trademark of Warner Books, Inc.

Book design by H. Roberts
Cover design by Don Puckey
Cover illustration by ROYO

Warner Books, Inc.
666 Fifth Avenue
New York, NY 10103

 A Time Warner Company

Printed in the United States of America

This book is the second volume of a two volume set, originally published as a single volume in hardcover by Warner Books.

First Printed in Paperback: August, 1991

10 9 8 7 6 5 4 3 2 1

For James Clavell
who certainly asked for it

My thanks are due to my parents, and to all who have read, corrected, translated, revised or criticised this work prior to publication, or who have contributed suggestions to it, scientific, literary or inspirational. I should like to mention by name: Ishihara Shintaro for the spirit of *pachinko*, Kawasaki Kiichiro for digging up and bringing home, Ninagawa Yukio and Akimoto Matsuyo for the spirit of *Genroku*; Chris Clarke of UCL observatory, Stephen Boyle and his stellar database; Takahashi Masae for herself; Lillian Chia for her "uranographie Chinoise," C.J.R. Lord of Braybrooke; Steve Turnbull and Yamamoto Tsunetomo for the spirit of *bushido*; Martyn Brain for IBM contact, Gerry Santoro and Steveley-san for cosmic views, Dr. F. Richard Stephenson of JPL for novae and the heavenly mansions; Nakadai Tatsuya, Tsutomu Yamazaki, Kurasawa Akira and Tanaka Tomoyuki all for the fox spirit of Nagashino; Ohno Yuji for the music of the spheres, Iwasaki Kazuaki for his visualisations; in England, Blackwell's for hospitality, Tom Robinson in memory of fine days in Tokyo and Hiroshima and better ones to come in the Big Apple—and finally to Mary Judah.

Particular thanks are due to two men in New York, agent Richard Curtis and editor Brian Thomsen, for the spirit of *nazukeru*, and to my dear friend in London, David Wingrove, magnanimous in victory and brave in defeat, for the spirit of *go*, our intellectual martial art.

Atari!

CAST

Four Traders

Ellis Straker

Trader captain, grade-one psi-talent and astrogator. Born A.D. 2396. Appointed commander of the nexus ship *Dwight D.*, A.D. 2421. Cruising in quest of profit in the disputed region of Known Space between Yamato and Amerika called the Neutral Zone.

Duval Straker

Chaos theorist and weapons engineer. Ellis Straker's brother, younger by two years, graduate of RISC. Sent into the Zone aboard the *Thomas J.* on an illegal trading expedition, his mission to ship-test a new species of weapon.

Jos Hawken

Commodore. Ex-Navy, now private trader. Leader of the expedition. With his brother Billy Hawken, outstanding agitator of the Expansionist faction to promote Amerikan trade in the Neutral Zone.

John Oujuku

One of Hawken's captains.

Thirteen Power Brokers of Amerika

Alia Kane — Expansionist President. Past opposition to the policies of the Henry clan meant that she spent many years under house arrest. Her election to power in the turbulent year A.D. 2411 caused the overthrow of Lucia Henry's power and the ending of the pro-Yamato policy.

Lucia Henry — President, A.D. 2407–11. A pro-Yamato President, now confined in internal exile to suppress a return to power of that faction.

Stratford Henry — President, A.D. 2362–2400. Original dynast of the powerful Henry clan who have run Amerika during most of the century. Father of Lucia.

Halton Henry — Vice-president, brother of Lucia Henry, and schemer for power. His betrayal of his sister opened the way for Alia Kane to gain the presidency.

Conroy Lubbock — Chief ally of the President and leading influence on Expansionist thinking.

Reba Lubbock — Daughter of Conroy Lubbock.

Jiro Ito — Ex-ninja, confidential messenger for Conroy Lubbock.

Pharis Cassabian — Adroit spymaster and manipulator. A more extreme Expansionist than Conroy Lubbock.

Timo Farren — Pharis Cassabian's intellectual companion.

Ganesh Ramakrishnan — Psi-savant and psientific theorist. Founder of the Liberty ashram.

BOOK *1*

23RD YEAR OF KANEI/A.D. 2425

Sending my dear,
Back to Yamato,
I stood in the dark of night,
Until wet with dawn's dew.

Even when two go together,
The autumn mountains
Are hard to cross.
How will my lord pass over
them alone?

Princess Oku
A.D. 661–701

AURIUM

Begins: rticular chemical elements make possible advanced industries: aurium and ARGENTIUM. Both are
transuranic elements found in the island of isotope stability in an extension of the periodic table beyond the
Actinide series. Argentium has atomic number 125, and
aurium 126, the principal isotope being Aur-310. Both
are super-heavy, super-dense stable metals with very
complex chemistry. A third super-heavy metal, PLATIN-
IUM, makes up the tri#

. . . HACK INTERRUPTED . . .

#Vela supernova of 13,000 B.C. exploded giving rise to
the Gum Nebula. (The next nearest remnant is the
CRAB, at 4,500 lys.) Cold ejecta has entered Known

Space, and several planets exist that were terraformed from debris originating in the Vela exp#

. . . HACK INTERRUPTED . . .

#la Pulsar (0833-45). The Vela pulsar (2CG-263-02) is an SNR (supernova remnant), like the Crab Nebula pulsar, only somewhat older. The associated nebula now covers 30—40 degrees of the sky seen from Old Earth. The pulsar emits high-energy gamma rays. It has an approximately 90 mS period, a rate of slowing of $1.5 \times 10(-5)$ sec/yr. The pulsar itself was originally identified with a 24th magnitude star appro#

. . . HACK INTERRUPTED . . .

#ospecting in the NEUTRAL ZONE in search of "blue gold." The systems of SADO and OKINAWA both have rich super-heavy element deposits which are being rapidly and exclusively stripped whilst the demand for aurium and argentium continues to increase. Unfortunately both elements exist only in tiny amounts and are formed under physical conditions so vastly energetic that they are only found in matt#

. . . HACK INTERRUPTED . . .

#he key to several crucial processes. Both are used in the manufacture of PLEX, the light material that is universally used for its strength, durability, and versatility in building. Ship hulls and city domes are made almost exclusively from plex. Both are used in the basic DOVER process that allows terraforming and the transmutation of water, carbon dioxide, and energy plus trace elements into synthetic foodstuffs (fats, sugars, carbohydrates, and proteins). Both are also used in the transport technology that allows NEXI to be created and permits GRAVOMETRIC machines, like ships' gravity/acceleration force compensators, to operate. A radioactive isotope of argentium is used to power a new class of sh#

. . . HACK INTERRUPTED . . .

#generate defense fields. These remarkable strategic materials are found in very limited quantit#

. . . HACK INTERRUPTED . . .

#the only place where atomic nuclei so heavy could have been forged: Class Sp. XIa supernova remnants. Being stable, they do not decay radioactively like other transuranic isotop#

. . . HACK TERMINATED.

1

THE PALAWAN SYSTEM, N.Z.

"Unidentified ship bearing green two-oh-nine azimuth ten on the forward scanner!"

The shout from the helm galvanized Captain Kondo Izumi. His stomach began to clench in anticipation, and his eyes moved eagerly across the forward screens. Seeing nothing, he quickly punched up the scene to starboard, promising to have the monitor operator disciplined if he had made another false call.

The other ships of the outward-bound *kin kaigun* aurium fleet powered in on a steep orbital approach path. The Palawan system had a bright A0 primary star, diamond blue, a fast-burner fifty times as luminous as the Sun. Vega, that's what the *gaijin* call it, he thought, and it possesses a big gravitational field that moderates the nexus exactly as expected, making the passage easy.

He saw that the ships were steady, staying tightly formed-up in their convoy to starboard during deceleration, Admiral Kurita in his flagship, *Musashi*, and twenty-six other ships, big and small, burning the giant retro-engines that would brake them into the system, shedding velocity at between a hundred and two hundred gees to bring them down from the 0.9 cee they needed to transit this nexus. It was sobering to reflect at such times, Kondo thought, that if the gravitational compensators failed, everything within the plex hull would instantly be pressed into mush by the braking forces. If.

The bridge of the *Kogyo-Maru* was in operational lighting, a sullen red lit only by the screens and the spangle of stars that glared through the overhead blister. Kondo Izumi strode across the bridge and leaned against the rail, until his line of vision to the forward scanners cleared the obstruction of the helm console. Balanced there, he waited, watching for the appearance of the *gaijin* pirates.

Still nothing.

May the gods castrate the monitor operator if he's wrong this time, he thought, angered by the shout.

Kondo was unsettled. The alarm six hours ago as they came out of the nexus had skinned his nerves, and this new disappointment was sharp in his throat. He realised he would have to endure longer in purgatory before a real chance to show his samurai spirit arose. But when that chance did occur, it would be glorious. Of that there was no doubt.

The *Kogyo-Maru* was a remarkable vessel, a unique ship, with extraordinary qualities, new to Kondo and untried by all aboard. The thought of her powerful concealed armament filled him with impatience. He looked up through the plex blister at the primary star and damned the lookout once more; to the helmsman he muttered, "If he's wrong again, I'll have the knife to his topknot, Noma-san."

"It's a clean system, Captain-san. It's hard to make a mistake now the nexus's properly cleared."

Noma Shimei made his reply deliberately soothing, sensitive to Kondo's brittle temper. A bluff man, craggy-faced but with heavy brows, he was also a capable first officer, highly experienced at handling a nexus ship and its esoteric apparatus, which was why Kurita had insisted that Kondo enlist his services.

"No. He's tired," Kondo said. "And not properly mindful of his duties as a samurai."

"Takano is keen. I know his family. He has good blood." Noma turned suddenly to a loitering fifteen-year-old cadet. He bellowed, "You there! Boy! Go to the main scanner bay. Find out what Takano is shouting about."

"*Hai!*"

Cadet Takano's record was not without blemish. Naturally awkward, he had been the last of his watch to get to stations when the *Kogyo-Maru* had come bursting out of the Celebes nexus. After the initial deceleration was complete the master at

arms had handed him the punishment pill and nodded at him
phlegmatically to swallow it. Takano had then gone to the airlock, suited up, and shot himself into space, and there, seventy
feet above the ship and directly visible to the whole bridge,
secured himself to the communications gantry, knowing that he
must remain there without sleep for twenty-four hours, straining
his voice on the comms channel, singing "I Did It My Way"
endlessly over and fighting the steady loosening of his bowels
brought on by the laxative pill. It was immensely humiliating
for Takano but caused great hilarity among his all-male crew-
mates.

Of course, he had fouled himself audibly within the first hour,
after which they had switched him off, but he had had to remain
singing on the gantry for the full punishment period, then clean
out the suit to the master at arms' satisfaction. Perhaps it had
been more than Takano's aristocratic dignity could take, as the
captain said. As they had come blasting into the Palawan system,
his alert had brought all hands to stations and inconvenienced
everyone at a critical moment. But somehow it did not seem like
Takano's way.

"Yes, Captain-san, Takano is a good man."

"That good man made fools of the entire crew last night,"
Kondo said stiffly. He underlined his point, placing the flat of
his hand deliberately on the rail before him. "I *must* have my
ship perform to the utmost limit, Noma-san. That means a disciplined crew. And a lesson for those who are slow to commands.
You know this is no ordinary ship. We cannot afford slackness."

Noma scratched his head. "Yes, Captain-san. Of course
you're perfectly correct. I've never sailed any ship like this
before."

"No one has, Noma-san."

The *Kogyo-Maru* was a vessel of five thousand tons, a four-
engined nexus freighter deliberately rigged to look much older
than she was. Her dorsal hull strake had been extended with
sliding plex blisters that made her high-charged, and her thrust
plates were emphasised with bulky strapping that ran from stem
to stern and gave her a ponderous appearance.

But she was not ponderous. Her balance was superb. Her
center of gravity was set more forward than the placing of her
hull indicated. Beneath the mid-line she was smooth and hand-

somely swept back, so that she cut through orbital maneuvers like a fast battle cruiser.

The seven beam weapon ports that ran along her side were flush, disguised by integral ray reflection shields and internally opaque at all scanner distances. And behind the ports were powerful pieces of offensive weaponry. She was Admiral Kurita's brainchild, laid down to his specific design, his answer to the Amerikan and Chinese and Korean pirates who were coming increasingly into the systems of the Neutral Zone.

Kondo's thoughts turned to the extraordinary man who was his admiral. Ever since the debacle at Niigata, Kurita had worked hard to erase the stain on his honor, but the indictment of his subordinate had required more than just carefully chosen words. So while Kondo had languished in confinement, Kurita had used his connections in Kyoto to petition Prince Sekigahara, the Emperor's brother.

Unhesitatingly the prince had secured a command for Kurita, whom he respected both as an admiral and as a man. Kurita had been placed under Baron Harumi, to lead a squadron of ships against the Chinese, and at Hainan Kurita had repaid the imperial trust that had been vested in him. He had triumphed and had returned covered in glory, yet even in the midst of his victory, when another might have basked in the praise of his Emperor and set his sights on higher things, he had not forgotten the disgraced Kondo.

During the long months awaiting his appearance before the tribunal on Edo, Kondo had been a broken man, his career shattered into a million shards, his status as a samurai hanging by a silk thread, but Kurita's evidence had been irrefutable, his support magnificent. Kondo recalled the day he had swept into the court wearing the sash of the Order of the Chrysanthemum to speak on his behalf. His bearing and humility before the *bakufu* daimyos had dazzled the judges. They had acquitted him, and Kondo remembered how he had burst euphorically from the courtroom, blemishless once more, uttering a catechism of thanks to the gods who protect star travelers, and slamming his forehead into the dust at the feet of the admiral.

But the day after, Kondo had discovered that he was no longer vice-admiral of the Yamato Guard. Despite the verdict there was to be no reinstatement, no pension, and not a single word of explanation. He had been discharged from the Emperor's service, without honor and without a future.

He had wandered the Home Worlds like a Buddhist soul in purgatory until the admiral's agents had come upon him one night in a pleasure house in Yakiyama, insisting that he follow them to the apron at Kure. He had been astoundingly drunk, spent out on despairing carousals and cheap *sake,* vulgarly rude and sword-happy. He had rejected them, *ronin* style, but they had ducked him in the mama-san's ornamental carp pond until he became reasonable, and had taken him red-eyed to a secret meeting.

He had been incredulous when Kurita had shown him the *Kogyo-Maru* in her secret hangar. He had been utterly astonished when Kurita had assigned command of her to him. "You'll master her, Izumi-san," he had said with dark humor as they stood under the gilded chrysanthemum figured into the ship's nose. "I want a man who's hungry for the task and you're the hungriest man in Yamato. You'll take her with the next aurium fleet to the Neutral Zone and you'll seek out the Amerikan pirates. To those *gaijin* curs the *Kogyo-Maru* will seem the perfect victim. To their eyes she'll be an old and fat freighter, holds stuffed with a dense aurium cargo, massy, wallowing helplessly, hog-backed, without speed and lightly armed. And the scum will be drawn to her like rats to a *shoben* sluice. But look at this!"

Yes, Kondo thought now, remembering how Kurita had kept faith. The daimyo's condemnation on Sado might easily have cut my topknot, not to say my belly, had it not been for the admiral. I owe him my life. He's given me a chance to redeem my honor, to prove that I'm neither incompetent nor a coward. May the gods help me do my utmost to repay the trust of a great admiral.

His thoughts were brought swiftly back to the present by the urgent beating to quarters over the comms channel. Crewmen were swarming to their stations, but below he saw the cadet whom Noma had sent after Takano. He was cupping his mouth and shouting back at them excitedly.

Kondo felt his hopes surge. Then he too saw it on the screen.

At first he could not be sure, then his eye latched onto the gray speck. "Make a signal to the *Musashi,*" he told the ensign at his side. "Unknown ship bearing: azimuth red one-four-one; range: two-one-oh-five-decimal-four *ri.*"

The ensign spoke into his pickup, transmitting the signal, and drew a fast response from the *Musashi*. Kondo exulted at the message: *plan cherry blossom.*

Here, in the outskirts of the Vega system, interplanetary space was a clean, fathomless black. Low gas and dust levels made it easier to maneuver without abrading the ship with millions of submicroscopic particles and vestigial gas pockets that taxed the shields and dissipated energy. Here was the chance to sully its transparent beauty with Amerikan wreckage. This place where the ether was infinitely clear and frigid was surely a most fitting place to settle the blasted hulk of a General Dynamics ship. He would send its arrogant remains into an endless hyperbolic orbit, plummeting forever into the cold blackness that lay between the stars. May the gods grant that she's Amerikan, he prayed. Kondo unsheathed his ancestral sword and closed his right hand upon the corded fish-skin grip.

"By the gods, the Emperor, and Yamato!" he said solemnly as he raised it above his head, once for each article of his faith. All over the ship, his officers did likewise.

Look at her, sniffing at us like a prowling shark. Come on, *same*, let's see your teeth!

Think like Miyamoto Musashi, the Sword Saint. Think as the warrior you are, Izumi-san . . .

She can't be a Yamato ship. If she was a smuggler, she'd be shy of us because of the fines Edo would impose as soon as she was identified. Nor can she be a regular freighter—nobody jumps nexus points in the Neutral Zone without being part of a convoy these days. She can't be Kan, not here. So . . .

What else?

Only an Amerikan would be working up towards home this far out, ignorant of the newly made nexus points at Matsui and Taiseiyo Tokai, unaware of the great chain that could carry a ship towards the Boundary. So . . .

Hai!

My prayers are answered! She is an Amerikan ship! Probably loaded with thieves' booty, and no doubt red-handed with the blood of Yamato settlers. Is she from one of the Kalifornias? Too far to tell yet. Either way they're pirates. Either way they'll pay for their crimes now with their lives!

"Ready starboard shields," he ordered tersely.

As the ship on the scanner steadily resolved itself into a three-engined trader-warship looking like a hammerhead shark, a long aerial was extended along the *Kogyo-Maru*'s lateral line, generating confusing signals, the images of a near-critical engine failure.

It was a deception the crew had practiced often, and at which they were smoothly skilled.

Hidden from the enemy by the ship's ailing signals and sunk in the drone of false noise, the real power of the ship was waiting to spring upon the pirates. Already, Kondo felt the *Kogyo-Maru*'s acceleration falling off. The compensators groaned and creaked, complaining at the extra resistance. The shields flamed at the bows and he felt the slight pebbling as they passed through Trojan-point debris. Moments later he looked to see how much the remainder of the *kin kaigun* had pulled away. The *Kogyo-Maru* was gradually falling back. A wounded animal limping after its herd.

"Let the engine failure commence!" he shouted to the men on the consoles.

The compensators suddenly juddered as their pent-up energy was released. The effect was spectacular. It was as if the upper port engine had blown out. It was as if it had overheated furiously, then failed, and drones were sent edging along the maintenance wells as if to begin stripping it down.

Kondo watched the prowler carefully for a reaction. She seemed to edge a point or two closer. Yes, you barbarous pigs, come closer. You see our one balanced engine straining to give us one gee and you imagine we're bursting our hearts to get away from the shark!

"Run out emergency booster motors and rig for close order maneuver."

Noma passed on the order urgently to the officers of the watch, knowing that the frantic activity inside the ship as the drones tried desperately to repair the defective engine would be scanned by the stranger and interpreted as a bid to outrun them. He ordered more men aft to increase the illusion of panic. The other ships of the *kin kaigun*, now strung out half a million miles ahead and to starboard, were also accelerating. Steadily they began to pull away. Escaping. Abandoning their weakest to the predator.

Still the lone nexus ship approached, on an interception course, with no sign of her slackening. Her hull was stealthed out in a blanket of radio black so that the ship was hardly visible. No call sign or corporate device could be made out in her muted emanations. Nor was there any identification jack on her hull. That *proved* she was a pirate.

Kondo watched the ship grow larger. As she came closer, her aspect changed, she showed her hull in UV and visible wavelengths, and he realized that the pirate planned to cross her bows and capture her with grapple fields. Then he'll come round abaft and run with us, stealing up on us with his better maneuverability. That's when the ultimatum'll come, he told himself savagely. And that's when they'll see they've cornered not a lamb, but a lion!

As the marauder came to within two thousand kilometers, Kondo's high-penetration scanners began to resolve the men aboard. They were heavily armed, he saw, and five boarding parties were crammed into the central deck airlocks. He expected the forward-firing beam weapons to loose a ray across their bows soon, and to hear the hated order to surrender on all hailing frequencies. Only then would he respond.

He turned to the ensign. "Are the drones clear of the wells?"

"Yes, Captain."

"Are you ready to cut free?"

"There's a man at the bulkhead, Captain."

"Let go the instant I command."

Below the bridge, on the orlop, fourteen beam weapons were being manned behind the reflective screen-proof layer. Harmless holos of cowering passengers were being broadcast in their place. All the guns were small antipersonnel lasers. Their blisters were masked by two long holos of deck activity, wonderfully real like a ship's interior and indistinguishable. Kondo knew that the numbers of men he had sent up and down the ship would have been enough to give the impression that the *Kogyo-Maru* was commanded by an inexpert captain. The apparent chaos of her decks was carefully rehearsed.

Two shots from the pirate's forward beam weapons crackled out, pluming the airwaves with pink noise as they seared into the weakened shields. The accuracy of the beams impressed Kondo and he saw Noma look away from him wordlessly. He knew that the man thought him reckless, and his tactics overly flamboyant, but for all his skill in ship-handling Noma was at heart a shrinker from action. He could scent caution about the man like a bad smell. He thought of the Sword Saint's words:

"In the Way of Strategy, those who study as warriors think that whatever they understand in their craft is the Void. This is not the true Void."

As the two enemy beams fed energy into the shield, it tested the hardness of the fields. Instead of remaining rigid, it began to deform, bending inward at the bows. The shield was soft and flaccid. Within a few minutes it could be penetrated and the shriveling energy of the beam brought to bear on the plex hull itself. The plex would stand up to it, but the silvery liquid crystal motes suspended in the plex, the motes that allowed the hull to change color and reflectivity, would begin to burn and the plex would either "fail black" and heat up in a huge white-hot patch, or worse, "fail clear" and permit the beam to go straight through.

The hands in the *Kogyo-Maru*'s nose began to panic as the other vessel bore down on them. It looked certain that the beam would intensify as the ship closed, the shield would continue to buckle, and a hull contact would be made. Some men scattered, others shook their fists defiantly. Then, at the last moment, Noma ordered the single engine cut to bring their acceleration to a dead zero.

The beams stopped.

"Close down shields!"

The *Kogyo-Maru* broached. Waited, shield naked and apparently helpless. The pirate flashed across their bows, beam-sighting laser after beam-sighting laser drawing patterns on their hull, frighteningly close. Every detail of her threatened under bright arcs as she circled. The gleaming muzzles of her armaments were twitching and she could easily have loosed off a staggering blast that would have fried the inside of the *Kogyo-Maru* instantly.

The sweat stood out on Noma's hairless head. He stared at Kondo, disbelief in his eyes.

"Cut compensators!"

"Captain-san! What are you thinking? Can't you see they have us at their mercy?"

"Cut compensators, damn you! And prepare to open all channels."

"Captain-san, please!"

But Kondo's attention was riveted on the pirate. Slowly she came around so that the ships were abeam, separated by no more than a quarter of a mile.

"Closer, you bastard! Closer!"

Noma's complaint was doubled. "Captain-san! Order the firing, I beg you! Before they come astern!"

Kondo's eyes were unseeing. His ears unhearing. The pirate was so close, undoubtedly coming astern—just as he had gambled.

"Captain-san!" Noma's voice was hoarse. He grabbed Kondo's arm, but he threw him off.

"Order our weapons to fire before it's too late! Please, Captain-san!"

"*Enough!*"

Then the critical moment ended as their target passed out of the arc of fire. In the monitors he could see the arcs glinting on their helmets and gloved fingers, see their ears, the enemy's faces burned dark but originally fair. No Mongoloids these, but Caucasian peoples. Of the three figures on the bridge none was dressed in clothes fit for a captain, but the foremost wore a dark blue cross-belted coat trimmed with white piping and a broad white collar that stood open under his golden beard. The man's lieutenant hailed from the other ship as she came about; the guttural order was sharp and uncompromising, delivered in bad Japanese.

"What ship is that? What ship is that? What ship is that? Identify yourself."

Kondo replied immediately, his voice strong despite the tension in his belly. "*The Princess Nukuda,*" he lied, "rare earth trader, out of Shikoku. I am Captain Murano Shiro, carrying the daimyo of Bizen to Osaka under the protection of His Imperial Majesty, the Emperor of Yamato. Whom have I the honor to address?"

Two small beam weapons down among the engines and a pair of *yubi*—swivel guns—mounted high on the tail were all that the *Kogyo-Maru* could train on the pirate now. In the terrifying silence the surge of low-level static in the comms channel filled the bridge. The rest of the *kin kaigun* had passed beyond full-resolution scanner range, and there was suddenly the immense oppression of being alone and friendless in the wilderness of space.

Inch by inch, it seemed, the other nexus ship moved across their stern and came round so that her beakhead lay a few hundred yards off their starboard quarter.

"Captain-san, stand off from them. They'll see the holos for what they are and realise we're fooling them," Noma warned. "The animation will begin to loop and they'll see it repeat!"

"They're not close enough." Kondo gripped his courage in both fists.

"Look! They suspect something!"

Kondo wheeled on him, hissing, "That's no naval ship. They're pirates! Greedy bandits who live on what they can catch. They want to take us, not destroy us."

"What if they open fire and fry us?"

"They want to take us as prize!" Kondo's voice raged at his subordinate. "Damn you to the nine hells! Where's your spirit, *hinin?*"

Noma was suddenly sobered by the insult. He seemed to realise that his cautiousness had been seen as cowardice, and his jaw jutted. "I'm only thinking of the ship, Captain-san."

"Don't think. Just do as I tell you."

Kondo's mind tried to bury the distraction. His heart hammered and his *bushi* spirit soared as he tried to bury the knowledge that the moment he had dreamed about had come upon him. Soon he would know whether he could afford the reckless luxury of sitting shieldless at point-blank range. And soon he would discover how the *Kogyo-Maru* and her crew would behave in their first real action.

"Come to me," he whispered through gritted teeth.

Simulated beam weapons stood visibly unattended in their transparent blisters, but under the holos, out of sight of the enemy, real gunners were poised at real beam weapons. Kondo watched the pirate ship drift inexorably into position with the smooth motion of an automatic tea house shoji. Her captain would want to put her in the most threatening place he could—abeam as close as possible, so that all his nearside guns were trained on the victim's vitals. A pirate would trust to no code of honor. To him, the Covenant of Shipping would mean nothing; he would want to come alongside and secure umbilicus tubes and send boarding parties thundering into the *Kogyo-Maru* to disarm all opposition before he came himself. To do so he would have to get into bed beside the *Kogyo-Maru*—naked.

Kondo heard indistinct orders being shouted aboard the pirate as the sound detectors listened in. What language was that? He saw that the chief of the rabble, the great gold-bearded brute, was so sure of himself he had scorned helmet and fighting gear. When the man put his hands to his mouth, the same arrogant gruff hail rang out across the comms channel, again in pidgin Japanese. "Order your people to put down their weapons and assemble in the aft mess, lying on the floor with their hands raised, Captain Murano. We're coming aboard. If you resist we'll fry you all."

Yes! The swagger! The temerity! The unmistakable insouciance of the man. They were English scum, the same that had almost closed up the spaceway into Europa through the Baltic chain.

Kondo raised his hand. He closed one eye, and with his thumb he mentally obliterated the mocking figure as he would a dung fly on a windowpane. Down below, at the head of the gun deck, the gunnery captain raised his hand also, and when Kondo brought his arm sharply down, the other did the same.

There was just enough time for the pirate to realise that it was not a sign of acknowledgement but an order to fire. Seven head-bursting explosions of light tore across the vacuum between the ships. The *Kogyo-Maru* shook under his footing and heeled as the energy hammered from her cells. Momentarily the hull of the pirate was obscured by an intense aura of brilliance over which her bridge and tail fin thrust like the head and tail of some monstrous dragon, then the plex snapped into transparency—a fail-clear!

As the light play began to die, Kondo steeled himself against the reply, but none came. Furious shouts on the talkback told him that his gun crews were ready. Then his heart leapt as he saw the devastation they had wrought. The pirate's gun deck had been burned away. Instead of five airlocks along the side of the ship, packed with boarders, the whole of her side between channel wale and lateral line had been turned into a smoldering mass. The load-bearing members of her frame were like the rib cage of a blasted corpse, arclight spilling across the debris from above where human fragments and the wrecks of gun mounts and umbilical tubes lay hideously mingled. Atmosphere swirled from the airlock doors, and a shout from his own deck told him that the pirate's power cells were cracking and splintering, their protective coverings burned away.

Before the light echoes of the blast died in their eyes, his own boarding crews had begun screaming like berserkers. Transformed, they jetted from the airlocks, armed and lusting for the fight. A fourfold grapnel field was flung towards the enemy, binding the stricken ship in a powerful tractor lobe. Teams of men on fore hull and tail were cutting into their victim with meson projectors, others trying to blitz their way inside the burned-out airlocks as the charred corpses drifted out.

Kondo was suddenly filled with the sweet knowledge that whatever happened now he had carried the day. He turned to his men and raised his naked blade, shouting, "*Banzai!* For the Emperor and Yamato!"

A tremendous wail of answering war cries went up across the talkback, and the assault began.

Umbilicus tubes with special adhesive termini and meson ring cutters were slammed across from lateral line to lateral line, and men poured across them, seething out like ancient warriors, *katana* clamped in their fists. The cracks of blasters could be heard, and the pirate rabble were smashed back before they had time to regain their senses. Then the *Kogyo-Maru*'s samurai were bursting across the interior, hacking and slashing, until the transparent belly was awash with blood and strewn with convulsing bodies.

Some of the pirates bolted through unsealed bulkheads, others found themselves cornered and leapt from intact airlocks into space, and still others swarmed into the nose, prepared to make a stand or crying pitifully for mercy. Kondo himself crossed with the second wave, cutting his way into the enemy's bridge, towards a looked-for duel with her captain.

But he was too late. The man was dead, a lifeless mass of gray entrail looped out beside him, his lower jaw blasted off bloodily, and his shaggy blond beard with it, now raised aloft as trophy by a delighted samurai.

Kondo saw that battle had become rout; it was, he knew, the point when, if left unchecked, desperate courage soured to fanatical savagery. He cut it short, watching which of his men came down latest to his order. Such men, he knew, were always the cowards, the least obedient, those with the brittlest minds, men who needed most watching, and whom he would be rid of as soon as he could. He sent them off the smoldering ruin, back aboard *Kogyo-Maru,* and the rest speedily into the cargo bays, to search out captives and whatever booty should be discovered before the gutted vessel lost its atmosphere.

2

In his magnificent cabin aboard the *Musashi*, Admiral Kurita laid aside his log feeling hugely gratified. Kondo had carried out his orders to the letter and demonstrated the power of the *Kogyo-Maru* to lure sea thieves to their deaths. The single-minded courage of her captain had been quite superb. Kurita felt certain that had he given the task to any other subordinate, the execution would have lacked that particular edge of daring that was Kondo Izumi's gift of rebirth. It's true, he thought, congratulating himself. The plucking of Kondo from disgrace had been a master-stroke, and of course he had performed his duties with that special eagerness encouraged by his difficult position. In another's hands the *Kogyo-Maru* might have proved less than worthy, but the unfortunate pirate had met a man for whom there could be no release from torment, except through death or glory. Certainly the value of a man so fortified by the spirit of *bushido* was impossible to overestimate.

Kurita was about to open his cabin door when he saw the silken robe woven with the subdued steel-gray barred-spiral device of the *kempei*, and immediately his pleasurable thoughts abated.

"Admiral-san," the *kannushi* priest said, his voice rising questioningly. "If I might please beg a moment of your time."

He was *metsuke* Fukuda Ikku, a man of bird-like frailty whose skull-like face was pinched and unsmiling. About the ship and on the bridge and in the sight of the men, he habitually wore the hood of his office and carried the *o-gohei*, but in private quarters there was only the pious shaven head shining like a jaundiced moon. The *o-gohei*, a stick carried like a short inverted spade but with four flagged plates cascading down from either side of the blade, was once simply the *gohei*, the Shinto symbol

of divinity, but when dignified with the honorific "*o*"—
"great"—it became much more. It was the rod of power and
authority presented to *metsuke,* the inspectors general of the
cultural police, the *kempei.* These powerful men were appointed
by the *toshiyori,* the five elders who did the Emperor's bidding,
but acted independently of the general staff. Their function was
"to conduct surveillance of vassals, great and small, to report
to government on infractions, deviation, and subversion, and to
maintain cultural integrity within Yamato and all the territories
of the Empire."

Fukuda had come aboard with an Imperial rock melon, the
symbol of the Emperor's personal gratitude, and he had brought
with him a terminal full of imperatives. He had been appointed
to carry his mission into the Co-prosperity Sphere, for the glory
of Yamato, to safeguard men's spirits and the Way, in the Emperor's newly gained systems across the Zero Degree Boundary.
Kurita knew his reputation and hated the cleric with such de-
testation it was hard for him to reply civilly, but he managed to
make his voice coolly formal. "*Ohayo gozaimasu.* All is well
with you, I trust? Please, come in."

"*Ohayo.*"

The admiral's cabin was luxuriously appointed. All the stern
accommodation aboard the twelve-thousand-ton flagship was fit
for the highest-ranking officers of the Empire, for their families
and their extensive staffs. Every effort had been expended to see
that the greatest convenience was provided for. In a voyage that
would last two months, and which might be intolerably crude
or confining to an aristocratic state official, a premium had been
placed upon comfort. They dined using the best real porcelain
and pairs of real bamboo *hashi. Sake* was liberal and of the best
quality. Real wood embellished the quarter galleries and private
cha-no-yu chambers. Real first-grade handmade tatamis and actual cedar and rice paper wall fittings gave the illusion of a Kyoto
villa, their shoji sliding open to reveal mural holos of breath-
taking seascapes or contemplative gardens. And because the
officials who ventured across the nexi on the Emperor's errands
and the *kannushi* of the Imperial Court were notoriously unused
to the sensations of transit, the futons were triple thickness and
expensively appointed with silken quilts stuffed with down
plucked from the breasts of year-old geese. Even so, Fukuda
Ikku and his coterie of zealots had strayed from their quarters

repeatedly, to accost the crew and interfere with the working of the ship.

Kurita went down on one knee and bowed, his twin scabbarded swords jutting back from the left side of his sash, cutting edge upward, as tradition demanded.

Uninvited, Fukuda Ikku folded his legs under him, kneeling in the admiral's place, raising his fingers to decline a shallow receptacle of *sake*. "The barbarians: how many are there?"

"Twenty-one."

"Why have you had them brought on board your ship?"

Kurita politely put his knuckle to his lips and coughed, trying to conceal his resentment at being examined. Fukuda was exceptionally skilled at asking questions. He obviously relished the sense of power it gave him. It's the same with all physically weak men, Kurita thought with sudden penetration. Don't they always try to compensate for their lack of stature or girth in other ways? And isn't it the sexually constrained who are the worst? Have you ever in your sixty years had a woman? he asked the old man silently, watching his soulless eyes search everywhere but his own. Never! And if you had, how would you have performed? I can see you as the novice you were forty years ago, white-faced and straining to shoot your seed into the belly of some seminary whore. It was overzealous offal like you who drove the Emperor's son mad with your excesses and started the trouble on Kyoto. Filthy-minded priests twisted tight with lust and perversion. Wasn't that the truth of it, for all their piety? Down on the raw floorboards, or in the dust, copulating under the Emperor's all-seeing eye. Peevishly surrendering to your animal lust and taking a peasant woman by force. Ah, I'd give plenty to know how you performed when your spirit craved the flesh! Was it the head priest's slavering mouth? Or the anuses of prostitute boys from the local pleasure house? Or perhaps you were the victim—the buggered runt of the seminary? That would explain the serpent of hate which writhes in your hollow chest. There are many ways a man dies inside—what was it that snuffed out your spirit?

"These prisoners are my responsibility," he said, keeping his voice neutral. "They are Europan pirates, and the laws of Earth Central and the Code both require that I execute them for entering what is now Yamato."

"Ah! Thank you, Admiral, but I asked you why they're on

board the *Musashi*. Why were they brought from the *Kogyo-Maru?*"

"Since it is by my authority that they will be executed, it is only proper that they be brought before me. I shall explain to them their crimes so they may understand them before they die."

Kurita made a final gesture that should have stopped further inquiry, but Fukuda Ikku seemed suddenly alerted. He tried another attack.

"Of course, they are worthless individuals who have surrendered, but they have a purpose. Is it not your duty to make their deaths shout an example to your men? Are you not familiar with the precepts of *bushido?*"

"I know my duty, Fukuda-san. And my understanding of *bushido* is my own affair." He regretted that as soon as the words had left his lips.

The *metsuke's* eyes traveled slowly to his. "No, Admiral-san. Your understanding of *bushido* is my concern also."

Kurita felt the muscles of his stomach knotting. He tried to deny it to himself, but realised that he was experiencing something he had not felt since he was a young man—a spasm of cold-blooded fear.

"The beheadings will be witnessed by the men, Fukuda-san," he said guardedly.

"It has, quite naturally, occurred to you to execute them as a warning to others, but—please correct me—you will kill them for *piracy?* That's an example to no one. Unless you suspect that there are those among your crew who are liable to turn pirate themselves."

Anger rose in Kurita. "The crew of the *Musashi*—all my crews—are loyal to the last man!"

The other smiled insipidly. "Ah! Your obligation to them is such a marvelous example. It is good that a samurai has faith in his subordinates. But you miss my point, for there is a much more glorious example to be made, a greater loyalty to be tested—to a principle much higher than obedience to the Emperor's statutes."

Kurita's fists had bunched and he carefully relaxed them. He had divined the direction in which the priest's octopus words were leading, but he knew he had to oppose Fukuda Ikku, to show him that here, in space, the admiral must be absolute master. Still, the strangling tentacles of the Shinto *kempei* were many. He must contain his impulses. It was madness, he knew, to gratuitously make an enemy of one of the *kempei*'s most exalted and ruthless instruments.

"Do you not agree?" Fukuda Ikku was asking. "Do you not hope, as I do, to inculcate some understanding of the Way in all men, however worthless, before they die?"

Kurita bowed his head humbly, feeling nothing but disgust and revulsion inside. "Within *bushido* alone have I lived my life. The Way is sacred to me."

Fukuda Ikku's words sharpened as he felt the resistance in Kurita. "I ask you: shall we behead pirates as common criminals?"

"That is the law."

"The law. And what of the Emperor's edict? That law says that barbarians shall die by crucifixion."

Kurita felt the grip of the octopus tighten about his throat. With an effort he raised his head. "It is a matter of practicality. We cannot properly crucify men aboard a nexus ship, but we can behead them. Unless you would have me carry them all the way to Sado?"

"You are a warrior commander, Kurita-san. You think like a man of action." The priest's smile lingered, then suddenly his aspect changed and his tone grew subtle. "I've heard reports of your gallantry in the great battle against the Kan. Did you not command a squadron bearing the *mon* of Prince Sekigahara? And was it not your own vessel that carried the banner of the Heavenly Throne from Lui Te-shan's vessel? They say it was ripped and urinated on by their officers when they were ordered to do so by the prince. Defiled until its vile symbol was made invisible. What men will allow defeat and then do that? Only non-men. Because we secured victory, the chrysanthemum standard, emblazoned with the symbol of our Emperor, suffered no blemish, not a sword in the whole fleet was broken, not a single Kan troopes entered any Yamato vessel. When men act honorably and according to the will of the gods, they are protected and favored. Are they not?"

Kurita stared into the bloody dregs of his wine, despising the priest even more as he remembered the horrifying truth of Hainan. The Chinese had been a fearsome enemy: when they took the planet of Hainan, they had skinned the Yamato garrison commander alive, stuffed his skin with excrement, and sent it as a trophy to Peking, and when news of the outrage had reached Kyoto, the Emperor had been persuaded to act. The Yamato fleet had surprised the Chinese in orbit, surprised them utterly.

With the enemy unprepared and in confusion, the battle had been over in half a day. The Chinese Blue Dragon and Red Lion squadrons were smashed and routed. The remains of the Golden Palace squadron, under Admiral Cao Yung, had struggled away—a mere thirty ships, badly mauled, seeking the chains of Zhanjiang, or falling crippled into the huge green oceans of the reconquered planet. On Hainan's main island fortress, dusk had decayed that day over a scene of absolute devastation; the sick sea for miles around had been stained with blood and strewn with the broken bodies of crashed ships, and of men. And through it all the shuttles and air-cars of fanatical Shinto priests had plied with sword and blaster, personally chopping down the surviving enemy. When night settled, the ghastly flare of the citadel's burning had continued to illuminate the carnage, sending tongues of flame towards the sky so that the work of the gods could go on.

Kurita felt the tensions within him polarise. Maybe the priest's right, he thought with dread. Maybe my belief is failing. He knew suddenly why men clung to the Way, for without the Way the world was too terrible to contemplate, a chaos of evil, a catalog of inexplicable atrocities. He remembered how his own victorious ships had made for the Weizhou Dao system, where he, along with the other admirals, had received the grateful thanks of Prince Sekigahara. The ceremony of victory had been celebrated there with the officers of the *kempei*, under a magnificent pavilion bedecked by the purple blooms of almond trees and accompanied by the thundering of giant battle drums and the chanting of Confucian monks, and at the word of the prince each ship of the fleet had fired a salute that lit up the sky brighter than daylight. They had lost seventy thousand men and more than twice that number sullied by wounds; the Kan had lost two hundred fifty thousand.

Fukuda Ikku's voice came to him, insistent and cold. "The purpose of the execution of barbarians is not to dignify the condemned, but to put fear into those who are witnesses."

"Excuse me, Fukuda-san, but I will have no crucifixions on board my ship," Kurita said, rising to his feet. His words were hard and final. He had made his decision. The next move was the priest's.

The *metsuke* regarded him silently for a moment, then gathering his robes he rocked back on his heels and stood up.

"I shall pray that you see fit to alter your resolve."

He went to the cabin door and without turning back left the admiral alone with his choice.

_____ *3*

The next day a compromise was agreed.

And the priest was allowed to address them, holding out before him a great scroll with golden stoppers and great tassels, and it seemed to the admiral that Fukuda Ikku's eyes never once strayed to the parchment, but roamed thirstily over the faces of those upon whom he broadcast his words.

"Hear me, now, men of the Way, samurai and priests, officers of state and of His Imperial Majesty's ships, technicians and soldiers, men of every condition, quality, and degree, whose attention to this will result in the purification of your minds."

The *Musashi*'s assembly area was formally hung with silken banners, and all the secular splendor of state was displayed for the occasion. The entire complement of the *Musashi* was paraded below. Five hundred men knelt in rank and file in their color-coded coveralls, the samurai of the first class, and behind, those of the second. Above them were fifty more in ascending rank, seated on collapsible stools along the quarterdeck, and above them all Kurita, the admiral. Five captains from the fleet's other ships flanked him, including Kondo and the *Musashi*'s captain, Takashi. Then came the commander of assault troops, with his lieutenants at his side and a line of fully armored soldiers. The ship's lesser officers dressed the rostrum, the astrogators, the engineers, and, ranked behind, the gunners and surgeon. Even the merchants and other passengers and the Emperor's revenue officers with whom they dealt were assembled. Last came the scientists, the Dover chefs, and the cadets.

Fukuda Ikku's voice grew incisive. "You are hereby warned to declare and manifest the things you have seen and heard of any person or persons, alive or dead, who have defamed or acted against the Way; or who have cultivated or observed the filthy laws of the barbarians or of the *sengokujin;* or who have perpetrated any crime of cultural impurity. Do you know any who say that the Emperor is not the true descendant of Amaterasu? Or the true Son of Heaven? Have you heard any man or woman deny that? Deny the purity of *bushido?* Say that the Way of the Warrior is not virtuous? Or that the shrines of Shinto, wherever they may be, are not holy and inviolate? Or who say or affirm scandalous libels against the sacred office of the *kempei* or its officers? Or who assert that the Three Imperial Treasures—the Jewel of the Moon, the Mirror of the Sun, or the Sword of Lightning—that the Emperor possesses are not the true relics of Nihon? If you do, then I command you to speak now!"

Twenty *gaijin* prisoners were shackled in a miserable line below the rostrum. One had died of his wounds overnight and had been dispatched through the toxic-waste chutes before news of the death could be communicated to the *metsuke.* Facing the English-speaking barbarians now were the Emperor's own officers. There could be no denying the visible authority of these men: Fukuda Ikku, their chief with his purple robes; Hishikari Noburo, his studious companion who carried the *o-gohei.* It was he who had spent years examining and censoring the library of the Imperial Court itself, excising unwholesome histories that did not accord with the New Truth. Kurita knew that Hishikari's obsession with *sangokujin* heredity was total; he prayed that neither Kondo nor any man would be foolish enough to admit that their ancestry was tainted with Korean blood. Beside Hishikari sat Suzuki Tokuji, and to his left Wada Zengo, the recorders. Both were cowled and sinister.

Kurita boiled with indignation. He had made a compromise, but he had not given permission for this. Fukuda Ikku had agreed to the beheading, and in return for that concession he had asked to deliver his sermon, to address the men on the evils of impurity. Surely the admiral could not deny the sacred office that small thing? Even an admiral who regarded the common laws above the wishes of the Emperor? Kurita had let the insult pass. Fukuda Ikku might be beneath contempt, but he was also above the law.

Kurita watched the proceedings with an immobile face, unwilling still to focus the malign spite of Fukuda Ikku's fanaticism on himself or his officers. That much he knew was expedient. But doubt raged in the private quarters of his mind. One part of him wanted to put an end to the priest, the other part was sure he was giving in to weakness. Men must be punished for what they do, not for what they are, he told himself, and he replied, equally angrily, that surely what men did *made* them what they were.

No one moved, and Fukuda Ikku lowered his scroll a little, growing more intimate with them, his gaze dwelling in turn on the officers and merchants.

"And if anyone here knows of any person being children or grandchildren of a barbarian already condemned by this office, let him come forward. For those vile offspring are disqualified and may not make use of any office, or bear arms, or wear silk or fine cloth, or ornament themselves with silver or gold, stones or pearls.

"And is there a man here who knows of any once-condemned person who now possesses confiscated or forbidden goods? Furniture or apparel, jewels or credit? If so, come forward!"

This is outrageous! Kurita thought, suddenly awake to what was happening. The *metsuke* was delivering no sermon, he was conducting an exercise in terror. But still Kurita dared not move to intervene.

Now Fukuda Ikku leaned back, angry with them. His shrill voice blasted them with threats now, rushing like a torrent.

"If you have knowledge and, after the period of amnesty, will not speak and still hold your spirit obdurately, know that it is greatly to the burden and prejudice of your family. You shall have incurred the sentence of exile and exposure, and you shall be proceeded against as an abettor of impurity. You shall be denounced, denied *seppuku*, separated from the Empire and its colonies, cursed by all, and spat upon by *hinin*. And upon your heads, and upon the honor of your families, and the memory of your ancestors, shall be loosed the corrections that befall all who deny the Way.

"Loathsome is the man who abjures the Way! May he be

afflicted in living and dying, in eating and drinking, in working and sleeping, and may his body suffer pain without respite. May his days be evil and few. May his children be orphaned and his wife and swords be used by *hinin* overseers to dig dung. May his family remain in disgrace and may none help them. May they be turned out into the streets and trampled down to die in want.''

Fukuda Ikku stared at them, filled with a terrifying power. He saw the light emanating from his hands and feet, felt the fear in the *kami* that appeared before him. Incense sticks burned, perfuming the air. The *gaijin* were goaded back and forth at his command, dressed only in *fundoshi* loincloths, men and women alike. They were made to kneel down, bound, so that their heads might be shaved. Water was cast over them as the sentence was read. Hishikari's voice rose shrill above the bowed heads before him, terrifying the captives who suffered it uncomprehendingly. Then his hand was thrust out and the *o-gohei* pushed into each face so that each was turned away.

''See how they flinch from the symbol of divinity?'' Hishikari demanded.

The *gaijin* stared at one another unable to understand.

''They are without value!''

The incense sticks fumed, the long robes swirled, as the officers of the *kempei* passed now among the crew. Fukuda Ikku raised the *o-gohei* above the crew now, reciting a list of impurities.

''Your admiral will bring his ships into the system of Sado in thirty days. Half that time shall be your period of amnesty. If you know, or have heard of, any Koreans who eat the flesh of dogs or who continue to speak the Banned Language—come forward! Which among you falls short of his duty? Come out! Yes! Which of you has unsatisfactory thoughts? Yes! I promise you will not suffer serious penalty if you admit it now. Step forward! Come out, obediently!''

Kurita remained fixed to his camp stool, mesmerised by the mounting wrath of Fukuda Ikku's oration. He wanted to act but he could not. He knew he must order the *metsuke* to stop, but something powerful smothered his will, making him listen to the insistent words. Below him, the men's mouths dropped open as they contemplated the rapturous questions. Fear warred within their minds but their spirits were captured. Kurita raged inwardly as he watched his crewmen wrestling with the terrible urge to make an admission. Then he felt his hatred rise up and burst the invisible bonds that held his own mind fast.

"Enough!"

"Admit your imperfections! Do not wait for others to denounce your crimes! Confess! And it will be the better for you!"

"Halt! I command you!"

"Confess! I am waiting!"

Fukuda Ikku was deaf to Kurita's words. Blind to his presence. As he swept down the central aisle the *Musashi*'s crewmen ground their foreheads harder into the flooring. He walked, sure of his power now, erect and bigger than he had been, hands opened before him menacingly until he was beside the airlock. The ecstasy flowed in him unstoppably as he approached the climax of his work.

That morning he had ordered twenty-one steel crosses made. He had suggested the craftsman could hang the crosses in the main egress airlock and cover the airlock port with a silk banner as part of the formal dressing to conceal what he had done.

Ah, yes! Look how they revere the Spirit of the Way, the familiar voice said inside Fukuda Ikku's mind. Their respect does them credit, but who can deny that they are all lost to the Way? Tell them they are to witness the deaths of impure creatures.

He told them.

Tell them they have the chance to show the Emperor how they glory in the destruction of impurity!

He told them.

They are simple men, and simple men are weak, prey to all manner of deviant thoughts. They must be helped to confine themselves to the Way.

He cast boiling water over the English.

"See how they shrink from the Way! See how it eats their flesh!"

He stalked along the line of kneeling prisoners. They began to wail, imploring him for mercy in the vile English tongue, caught up in the horrifying power of the ritual, and as they showed their fear so the samurai who held them increased their grip.

Ah! How their animal spirits cry out to me. But how they fail to understand their shortcomings. It is impossible for a *gaijin* to have worth except by the purifying elements of pain and fear. Though their bodies are tainted clay, we shall purify them with death and return them to the state of dust from which they came!

He threw back the silk covers, revealing the shining crosses within, and the stink of stale airlock air swirled out, making men groan with understanding.

"Only suffering can destroy the stain within men," he shouted.

"Bring the captives! Attend the gas valves!"

The order rang out from the chief maintenance engineer who had been induced to prepare the punishment. Three hands ran to obey.

"*No!*" Kurita grabbed the arm of the first man and threw him back, his face contorted. To allow the captives to be attached to the steel crosses in the airlock and the oxygen partial pressure progressively altered to enhance the agony as the *metsuke* wanted was not something he had agreed to. He had to stand up. Whatever the cost. Whatever the risk. He had to.

"I will not allow it!"

Fukuda Ikku turned on him. "You cannot prevent due punishment."

"This is not what we agreed!" Kurita shouted.

"Stay where you are!" Fukuda Ikku's fingers clawed out. "No man may interfere with the Emperor's will. No man here will allow that!"

Kurita halted, a thousand eyes locked on him. His way was barred by his infantry captain. "Araki! Step aside! I order you! Honjo, you will prepare for a beheading! You there, Sergeant! You will decapitate the prisoners now! Move!"

No one flinched. The men's eyes were riveted on the hem of the *metsuke*'s robe.

"Move, I say! This is mutiny!"

"They will obey only the word of the Emperor! Take him!"

"No!"

For an interminable moment all were frozen in a terrible stalemate. Kurita saw that he had lost. He went for his sword, then the universe crashed sideways and he was carried off his feet.

The ship's deck had canted hard over, sending men toppling down or scrambling for a handhold. Over the talkback, klaxons wailed a priority failure warning as the *Musashi*'s frame quivered. The huge ship jolted, then jolted again, her decks convulsing like an earthquake before she quieted. The symptoms were of an imminent and incapacitating stabiliser fault. Immediately Kurita realised what had happened and he thanked the gods.

In the confusion, Kondo came from the shadows under the deck arch. He drew his sword and advanced on Araki. "Obey the admiral—or I shall execute you! The rest of you, get to your stations! Now!"

Instantly the confusion of men in the assembly area threw off their doubts and dispersed, driven by the familiarity of orders and suddenly awakened from the terrifying spell that had been cast over them.

Kurita tried to order his thoughts, but his mind raced feverishly. He damned his own foolishness. Incredible how Fukuda Ikku had spellbound everyone with his sorcery! And thank the gods that Kondo had had the strength of mind to get to his terminal on the bridge and call up a training simulation of main stabiliser failure condition one. *What a mistake I made! I was disobeyed by my own men. It was mutiny until Kondo slapped them back to their senses. The way the* metsuke *bent them all to his will was truly amazing. I felt it myself.* Kurita's spine chilled at the thought. *Even the psi-talents were hypnotised by him. But how can I oppose him now? I can't placate him—the affront was too much for him to ignore. How can I stop him?*

He seized his panicking thoughts and savagely bent them to the present. At all cost, the initiative Kondo had gained must not be lost.

"We must carry out the beheadings immediately," he told Kondo. "The quicker the better."

He knew his authority depended on it. Fear spurred him, crept into his voice as he fired his orders to Takashi, the *Musashi*'s captain.

Hands were rushing to action stations, unaware as yet that the emergency was only a simulation.

Kurita ordered that the twenty captives be brought to the airlock. The English were hauled to their feet and marshaled quickly into line. Some began to pray, some to struggle, others to defecate.

Kurita searched out Fukuda Ikku. The *metsuke* leaned drunkenly against the bulkhead, his whole body racked with a strange seizure. His eyes were rolled up white and his lips curled back, flecked with foamy spittle. Kurita struggled to understand. It must be the sickness of the Void, he thought, horrified. The same that sometimes afflicts Zen astrogators awakened from their trances after a difficult passage. Then Kurita saw what he must do.

He sent a man to begin the beheadings. Then he steeled himself, seized Fukuda Ikku, and shook him until the pupils of his eyes looked once more on the living world.

"Come to the airlock!" They must die, he thought. "Here! Execute them with your own hand!"

He closed his grip over the priest's fingers and clamped them to the handle that fired the explosive bolts on the egress hatch, holding it there, unmoving, until the executioners were clear.

The inner door sheared shut. Warning lights flashed orange above them. Kurita heard the interlocks impact with a deep, smothered thud, then the gas valves were squealing, super-pressurising the lock, the indicators climbing to maximum.

A computer-generated androgyne voice repeated auditory warnings with enthusiastic urgency. *"Please be careful! Airlock pressure is very high! Please check with your superior now! Please be careful . . ."*

He jammed the priest's palm against the handle, and the outer hatch blew off, and the headless corpses, empty egress suits, helmets, and steel crosses were jerked altogether off the floor and wall pegs and out into the stream of exploding air. They soared up for a sickening moment until their tangled limbs hit the hatch rim and were snapped through.

Kondo watched the twisting bodies tumbling in space, the severed heads like sport balls, then he stared at the vacant eyes of the *metsuke* and knew that the admiral had done his duty excellently. Fukuda Ikku was shaking, the hollow husk of the man who had addressed them minutes before. The admiral had been magnificent: what courage it had taken to stand up to the *metsuke* at that moment!

"Have Captain Takashi see to the airlock personally," Kurita told him, his voice infinitely weary now.

"Yes, Admiral-sama."

"And—thank you, Izumi-kun."

"Honjo, take Fukuda Ikku below and confine him to his cabin. Have the surgeon sedate him."

"Hai!"

Kondo felt his burn of satisfaction fade. He saw that Kurita had pitted himself against an implacable enemy.

"What have we done?" he asked.

Kurita shook his head hopelessly. "We have a *kami* by the tail, Izumi-kun." The suffix "kun," more informal than "san," was customary aboard nexus ships after an emergency; the looseness of it emphasised their differences of rank and celebrated the triumph of the team over whatever had caused the problem.

"Yes."

"I don't know what can be done with him."

"You've locked him in his quarters and had him sedated, sir?"

"Yes. But I can't keep him confined there forever."

"You'll have to, Kurita-sama, at least until we reach Sado."

Kurita wiped his mouth, then he took his hand away and nodded. "Yes, I can do no other. But then what? When we reach Niigata I'll have to release him."

Kondo swallowed hard. He knew well that the *metsuke* would demand revenge for his humiliation. The thought of the impeachment that must greet them when they returned to the Home Worlds turned his bowels to ice. He looked around him at the few men who remained in the assembly area; all were intensely occupied, working furiously at whatever tasks they could find. They had been deeply scared by what they had witnessed.

"Did you see his eyes, Izumi-san?"

"Yes. They were—without life."

"He's mad. You know that?"

"Yes."

The admiral's voice dropped. "Do you know what we must do?"

The terrible thought broke over Kondo like an ocean wave, followed by another, more sinister consideration. He blanched. "You can't mean that. Unless—"

"What are you thinking?"

"I dare not say."

"I order you to tell me what you're thinking."

Kondo clasped his hands together as if in prayer. "I asked myself what we would do if—if we discovered that Fukuda Ikku was *possessed*."

Kurita stared at him, unable to believe his ears. *"What?"*

"What if it could be proved that his mind had been taken over by an evil *kami?*"

"Those are dangerous thoughts, Kondo-kun."

Kondo seized his arm. "Yes. But thoughts that might explain a lot—and perhaps solve much more."

Kurita's eyes widened as he began to understand the implications of Kondo Izumi's words.

"Think of it, Admiral. If an inspector general of the *kempei* was possessed by a demon."

"Ai-eee! That's meddling with unspeakable things. Can you imagine the upheaval that would follow if it were to become known that so exalted a functionary of the Emperor had been possessed by a demon?"

"Precisely."

"You're suggesting I make that *known?*"

"No! That would certainly destroy you." Kondo's face was taut with anxious hope as he pressed his plan. "But as a threat, what better lever can there be to control Fukuda Ikku after he's made planetfall? Tell him that if he wants revenge, the price will be his own exposure. I'll back you. And I'll see to it that other witnesses do likewise. We can easily—manipulate—the ship's log. It's the only way to contain him."

Kurita closed his eyes. When he opened them again, he said, "I agree. I'll put it to him just as you propose. Such a threat might deflect him—it might conceivably save our skins—but it won't contain him. He'll find some other way to slake his thirst for blood. And may the gods help them all on Sado."

4

SADO

Michie saw the ceremonial water gate and squeezed her father's hand. Her precarious side-saddle seat on the white horse was made even more unstable by the sleekness of her silk kimono, and she almost lost her parasol. The *torii* of Nikko, she knew, had stood here for fifty years, its two huge timber legs as red as crab flesh and rooted in the tidal mud, its crossbar curved up like a sword blade and roofed in grass-green tiles. The ebbing tide of the Great Lake had left an inch of water, making the mud of the inlet a mirror, and the reflection of the *torii* rippled as she watched, delighting her.

Dedicated to the ancient goddess Ama no Uzume, it had been erected shortly after the terraforming of Sado had stabilised, marking the planet as one destined to become part of Yamato. It had stood unchanged since the days of Bashi, the Shinto *kannushi* priest, who had come with the first settlers more than half a century ago. He had dedicated his life to building the Nikko shrine.

The shrine was built from massive timbers, polished cedar walkways jutting above algal green mud that flooded with warm, clear lake water twice a day, and twice a day was a mass of worm casts and lungfish and tiny freshwater crabs with eyes on stalks. Above the shrine complex, tiled roofs glittered like new steel, and within, incense smoke curled up ceaselessly, blackening the rafters. At night, a thousand lanterns would bob and dance in the breeze, and the shattered image of Sado's huge red moon would lie over the water, but now the primary star that acted the role of Sado's sun was almost directly overhead and the shrine was a cool refuge from the brilliance outside. On the land beyond, trellised blooms hung about the cliffs, brilliant climbers garlanded the leathery trees, and aromatic shrubs loaded the air with their perfumes. Nikko, her father had told her, had been built to mirror the ancient flower gardens of Old Japan where for hundreds of years the Japanese people had gathered decorations for their ceremonies.

"Are you nervous, my daughter?" he asked her.

Michie nodded and searched out her father's hand. He was leading her horse, watching for the priests amid the rioting flowers. She looked out also and sighed at the beauty of it. Bright sun had baked the mud to a crust away from the walkway, sending the crabs and lungfish into their burrows, but its rays were kept from her by the bamboo and paper parasol which he held delicately over her shoulder.

On the far side of the neighboring *han*, square rice fields of new green stretched to the foothills of the Kanto-sanchi range; behind them the rocky outcrops were planted now with pines, and small streams cascaded between mossy hummocks. She thought it a fitting landscape and knew that her father had been right to insist on this place, and on a small gathering in the shrine, despite the wishes of her mother.

How her father had shown strength! A quiet resolve, persuasive and encouraging. He had swayed her mother and brought her round to see that this must be the only solution.

Kenji caught her looking at him. His kindly eye strayed to her face and he grunted amiably.

"You have been completely dutiful, Michie-san," he told her proudly.

"Thank you, Father."

"You seem to have no regrets."

"I have none, Father. It is my duty."

She thought of her brother's opposition, but banished it from her mind instantly.

"I hope your mother reminded you about constancy? I'm sure she did. They are her most precious words, treasured up in her head for thirty years. She received them from her own mother's mouth—after it was found that a handsome but foolish young samurai called Hasegawa had begun to find her beauty irresistible. She has been a faithful adherent to those high principles of duty ever since, even though the man she married never deserved such devotion."

Michie protested at her father's modesty, dwelling on the sentiments her mother had passed to her in the quiet of her bedroom the night before.

"My dear little dove," she had said, tears glinting in the corners of her eyes. "The gods know that you are our own flesh and blood, but it is my duty to instruct you as my mother earnestly charged me. Who else will tell you what it is becoming for you to do and what to avoid? Neither must you forget the things your father has told you, since they are all wise and most precious, but there are things no man can tell you. First, take care that your garments are decent and proper, and do not adorn yourself with finery, for that is a mark of folly; remember that a courtesan may be taken for a lady, but never must a lady be taken for a courtesan. When you speak to servants, do not hurry your words from uneasiness, but remain calm and deliberate. And when you walk abroad, do not carry your head overly erect, for that is a sign of ill breeding and shows your people that you do not care for them as you should. Always show a modest countenance; have no shame, nor arrogance; do not paint your face like a *maiko* girl, but that your husband may not dislike you, adorn yourself, bathe and take exercise twice daily." She had drawn closer then, enfolding Michie's hands with her own. "Listen, my daughter: in this life, it is necessary to live with prudence and circumspection. You must treat your husband with respect at all times, then he will respect you. Do not cross him in manly matters, or he will secretly despise you, and when the day comes to ask of him that which you desire, he will spurn you. Beware that in no way should you commit the treason against him called adultery. See that you give no favor to another, for this is to fall into a pit from which there is no escape. According to our law, you shall be thrown into the street and despised by peasants, and the stain will spread to all your family and your nobility and your honor of birth. And remember that even though no man sees you, nor your husband learns, still *the* kami, *who are in every place, see you*. You shall be maimed or struck blind or your body will wither or you will come to extreme poverty for daring to injure your husband.

"My dear daughter, whom I brought into this world, see that you live in peace and tranquillity and contentment all the days of your life. See that you do not disgrace yourself, that you do not stain your honor, nor pollute the luster and fame of your ancestors. And though I remember the day when your husband-to-be first came here and I would not have him enter our house, I now bless you both, so that the gods may prosper you and your marriage."

The grove of trees parted as the horse came round the last bend of the road. She felt a fluttering within her as she heard the chanting of the monks, growing louder as she neared the shrine. What will the daimyo say when he finds that his permission has not been sought? she asked herself. The daimyo's permission was not requested, even though strictly it might be expected in so complicated a case. Katsumi had not taken the announcement well, nor after that the oath his father had demanded of him. Kenji had announced his final decision after careful thought and expected his son to render him the filial duty he owed by swearing to treat Duval as a racial Japanese.

"But this will not reflect well on the family, Father."

"Nevertheless, that is my choice. Swear."

"I cannot swear to acknowledge him as I would a samurai husband. The shame is too great for me!"

"I am your father, and you will do as you are told!"

"I also have a duty to Nishima-sama. A higher duty."

"You will do as I say! Swear to me that you will acknowledge him as 'adopted husband.' "

"I cannot!"

So it had gone round and round. Everybody knew that it was the custom for samurai families to arrange the marriages of their children, and it was the children's duty to accept their parents' choice. In almost all cases, marriages were samurai-samurai, the first rank usually marrying the first rank, and so on. And it was expected that the wife would go to live in the family house of the husband. But not in this marriage. This marriage was very different. Michie was aware that her father's decision was unique.

But then not everyone married normally. Occasionally a rich member of the commercial classes would attempt to marry their sons into samurai families, because the offspring of such a marriage would be samurai, and the samurai family would sometimes agree for money. Although the social status of samurai was paramount and highly prized, their incomes were a fixed proportion of the income of the *han* where they belonged. Often the lower classes, those of technicians, slave-farm owners, and traders, commanded high incomes. Only samurai family heads who dwelled in the impoverished fourth and fifth ranks would consider this option; it was unheard-of for a prosperous *han*-holding family of the upper second rank, such as the house of Hasegawa!

But even so, this was not the basis of the objection Katsumi was making. Even rarer than transclass marriages were the cases of "adopted husbands," when a family took in a man for their daughter. In such a case, the man's surname was erased from his family records as if he had never existed, all his filial duties, or *giri*, were transferred to his wife's family, including his surname, and he was accepted on the same terms that a wife would normally be accepted into her in-laws' home. What had enraged Katsumi was that this practice was carried out by families who had succeeded in raising only daughters and were therefore without heir. The choice of Duval as adopted husband, Michie knew, had been a severe slight to Katsumi.

"The marriage will change his surname," her father had said in conciliation. "He will be one of our clan. And because his personal name is impossible, I have decided that from the marriage day he will be called Zinan—second son."

"Does that make him one of us?" Katsumi had said bitterly. "It's as if you believe that we can all be who we want to be. That we can alter our state at will. That is contrary to all that's sacred in our society, Father."

"What is most sacred is that sons obey their fathers!"

"And everyone the law!"

And that was another consideration. The legality of the marriage was uncertain. There was no specific statute against marriage to a *gaijin*—since Yamato had been effectively closed to outsiders for generations and since nobody would dream of marrying a *gaijin* even if it were possible. There had been no need for such a law. Michie understood that her father had chosen this course because an adopted husband was bound to his wife's father and his business by bonds of *giri* closer than any other tie. Her father was quietly doing his duty to Lord Nishima by advancing the weapon project and at the same time clearing his debt of honor with the man who saved his life—and hers. He was breaking no specific law, but perhaps there were those who would not approve—Nishima-sama included. Like all daimyos, Nishima-sama was accountable to the *bakufu* on Kyoto, of course, for whatever went on in his domain. He could be replaced at any time, and because of that he had to be careful. But what Nishima-sama did not know about, he could not very well object to. By not informing him, Kenji was doing his duty by protecting him; by swearing Katsumi to accept that plan, he was swearing him to secrecy. But Katsumi had not sworn, nor would he.

A small knot of women were gathered at the door, maids and servants and others wearing kimonos in pastel shades. Beyond them was a group of laborers, who knelt and bowed their heads as she slid carefully from the saddle, staring at the fine silk wedding kimono she wore.

Her head felt hot inside the heavy marriage wig, an object made of real human hair woven into a traditional style, lacquered stiff and stuck with long, decorative pins.

Her father led her on his arm inside the shrine, where light filtered sparingly onto the polished floor with wisps of incense rising. It was cool and clean, austere after the flowers. She looked to her kneeling mother and searched her face, saw that Katsumi was not beside her. Then she was filled with sobriety as she gazed upon the great golden *gohei*. She walked to the front and stood beside the official go-between and before the priests and smelled the incense and tasted the salty sea air in her mouth, and the minutes were strung out like pearls, hardly passing.

The recorder came forward. "On this penultimate day, in the second month of the twenty-third year of the Era of Kanei, in the shrine of Nikko, we receive Hasegawa Michie, daughter of Urawa no Hasegawa Kenji; and Zinan, this son of unknown parents, to be married in accordance with the imperial wedding statute . . ."

Michie repeated the words of the oath with solemnity beside the man who had come into her life and won her and who had taken the Way for her, so he could be her husband. I know that Zinan can truly become like us now, she prayed. May the gods destroy me if I lie, if he lies. And I know he loves me as much as a man ever loved a woman. When my father came to him with thanks for his life after the struggle on the fiery mountain, he offered him his pledge. "What shall I grant you?" he asked. "You have only to name it." I watched him playfully appraise Kenji's favorite horse, and then his long sword; I saw the smile on his lips as he stole a glance at me. He must have seen the look in my face. And then he boldly said, "I ask only permission to marry, for there is a woman I want." And my father, who is a good man, nodded and drew himself up. "One life for another? That is fair and just. But will this one that you desire be an appropriate choice?" Zinan looked to me then, and he said, "Yes, Kenji-san. I can say that." He was right. Whatever he may have done in the past, he is not a *gaijin* now. He truly may become one of us. And I will do my duty by him.

The shrine was completely silent as the vows were asked of them. He promised to protect her and she to serve him, come what may in life and unto death. Zinan, her husband. Michie, his wife. The witnesses were hushed, but into the silence the sounds of air-cars circling closer rose, drowning the official recorder's words as he began to speak again.

"*Kokoni osuwari kudesai . . .*"

He beckoned them forward and they knelt. He placed a

band of gold on each successive finger of her heart-side hand, removing it each time, then he slid it finally onto her third finger.

"I, Zinan, give my body to you, Michie, as your loyal husband."

"I receive it. I, Michie, give my body to you, Zinan."

"I receive it."

The recorder placed his hand over theirs, which were entwined, making the moment solemn. "I join you in marriage in the name of the Emperor and his sacred laws."

She looked to him as if for the first time and saw that his face was filled with adoration. Unhooded, she had taken his ring, the universal token of a man and a woman joined, and the recorder said, "You are now made one."

He kissed her, his eyes full of colors, so that she caught her breath with shock.

The tumult outside the shrine grew louder. The clangor of war gear and shouted orders and the whining engines. She turned, and saw her husband turn also. Then the screens of the shrine parted, and in the glare of the cool interior flooded with unmuted sunlight. Outside, her brother, proud and armored—Katsumi at the head of two ranks of armed men. All heads turned; the recorder raised his hand and man and wife walked hand in hand toward the light, uncertain, for what had been witnessed and made Nishima-sama could now unmake.

Kenji shaded his eyes, rising from his contemplation, and in the brightness fifty swords were pulled from fifty sashes and were laid before their owners, who knelt in two lines. Then Katsumi knelt also, and they went in procession, followed by their pages, by Kenji and his wife, walking the gauntlet of samurai which Katsumi had brought from the daimyo to salute them to their marriage bed.

5

He warned Yao to treat the test with respect, remembering that terrible day in his first year at the RISC lab at Lakeside when the compression chamber had lost stability and a half-ton singularity had bubbled out towards Nate Smith, the mathematician, and killed him.

With so many people gathered here now, Duval had plexed off a space ten feet around the testing pit, but there were few who could bear to stand closer. The field reactor was working now, the static field surrounding them spiking their hair like iron filings on a magnet and making their skin prickle. The field was intense, rushing from the open maw of the test chamber as its heavy door was irised open periodically. And above it the great black power skeins looped evilly.

"Everything is almost ready," Duval announced with satisfaction, walking back towards the assembled dignitaries. It was the same everywhere when weaponry was developed. As the climatic moment arrived, the pace of work heightened, illustrious visitors were invited, and the testing was done with great ceremony. Necessary witnesses were those connected with the factory, the purchasing authority, and the state. It was a tradition that Kenji insisted must be observed.

Duval paused appreciatively, enjoying one of the few moments when his attention was not demanded by some practicality. The industrial councilors of the *han* were here in full uniform. Visitors from Niigata and Kanazawa had honored him in their regalia, and the *hatamoto* and other officials representing the military, resplendent in their martial uniforms. Even the local judge and the secretaries of his legal bench had come to enjoy the occasion and the lavish entertainment that was to follow. To be seen in the company of the daimyo was an opportunity too good to miss.

Nishima himself stood on the raised plexed-in gallery that had been built for the most important visitors; Kenji and Katsumi were both at his side. They gazed up at the heavy machinery that stood idle now above the buried chamber, and down at the field reactor. Michie waited proudly with the ladies, the wives and mothers, and the young children, close to the big factory office doorway, away from the noise and the field and the danger of explosion. He saw Masae-san there, engaging the formidable Fumiko-san in conversation and gesturing towards the daimyo.

Duval was being questioned closely by the samurai. He explained how the pit had been made, how the six biggest chambers—those of the prototypes—had been lowered in one by one using the massive waldo that hung from the frame. They were placed vertically, he said, not too close to one another, muzzle end uppermost, and their lower ends bedded in plex "sand." Then they had lowered in refrigerated argentium tubes, this time further from the accelerator point, then filled the pit with more plex granules, and finally they had made up the rest of the space with a variety of equipment, mostly monitors and transducers, so that the behavior of the chambers now buried up to their filter heads could be thoroughly investigated. Six technicians had spent the morning tamping the plex sand down with stamps, not too tightly, and Duval had supervised, dampening the mixture with ordinary water at intervals, but sparingly, so that not too much moisture was allowed to seep in around the carefully positioned chambers.

"Of course, the top of the pit slopes this way," he told them, sweeping his hand across it and speaking up at the daimyo's party. "At its highest it must be lower than the injection hole so that the initiator particles can be fired in from the accelerator, and lower still as the distance from the accelerator increases. Relativistic effects alter the spacing of the pulsers as the particles approach light speed. The initiation will come via this vacuum chamber here and flow along these field line channels. You can see the way they branch. Each branch leads to its own individual chamber."

"What's that man doing?" the daimyo asked, indicating the technician who stood on top of the pit. He was delicately adjusting valves on the channels with a torque reader and a small pair of ion keys.

"Two hours ago the channels were heated to drive off gases

and harden the vacuum, Excellency. His responsibility is to do this evenly by means of small heater elements in each section along which the stream will flow. He's simply testing the integrity of his work. Remember that the particle stream is of such high energy that any collision with stray gas molecules in its path will produce cascades of gamma radiation. If this is above a critical figure, it will affect the fields.''

"Ah! And these small gratings you've placed in each channel?"

Katsumi answered. "If you will permit me, Excellency. As the particle stream begins to focus, the grating will be phased open so that the stream can be collimated.''

"Of course. Yes. I see that.''

"Excuse me, Excellency," Duval shouted up. "It's ready. With your permission I'll begin the test now.''

He climbed the ladder swung up onto the top of the reactor and crossed it, heading for the control room. He was tired. For the past day and night he had been on his feet unceasingly, checking the field figures with which to charge the test. And his obsession with secrecy in this had driven him to hide his procedures, especially from Yao.

At first, the mixing of units had been a problem, so ingrained had the Amerikan system become in his mind during his own training. He had laboriously learned from his men the Yamato equivalents—the *shaku*, or Japanese foot, which was slightly less than an Amerikan foot: 11.930542 inches. Ten *sun* made a *shaku*, and ten *bu* made one *sun*. A *rin* was a tenth of a *bu*.

"The dimensions of the chamber are fundamentally important," he had patiently explained to Yao, who had struggled to calculate the form equations of the chambers using the Japanese system, which differed from the Chinese system he was used to. "Above all there is the interfocal distance of the concentration chamber. That's essential. We must get it right.''

And Yao's openness had betrayed him again. His eyes had gleamed and his lips pursed. Someone—Katsumi, Duval guessed—had charged him with learning the key secrets. But Yao was a poor spy because he had become a good friend; he had helped him build the facility, he had been the man who had stood and given a speech on his behalf at his shoulder at his marriage feast, and Duval had asked himself, How can I lie to him now?

So far he had given Yao all details freely and without deceit. But these were techniques already well known to Yamato's military engineers, and to Koreans and even to certain Chinese. The compression chamber secret was different. It was what lay at the heart of the gun's practicality, what permitted it to be used with reasonable safety, what permitted greater accuracy when the gun was fired, and, ultimately, what lengthened the effective range of it.

The problem had kept him turning in his sleep knowing that soon he would have to divulge his secret to the enemy. But then he had realised his error. Where was this enemy? No man who worked for him at Hasegawa Industries was his enemy. The household of the *han* were, none of them, his enemy. His new family? How could they be his enemy? Even cold Katsumi and the haughty daimyo were simply acting as functionaries of the state. All their moves had been sanctioned and prescribed by circumstance. It had been their duty to imprison him and the others. And afterwards, had they not shown incredible clemency to mere *gaijin?*

The daimyo had been right: Jos Hawken had been guilty of breaking the laws of space. He had deliberately provoked Yamato, which, in truth, was the conqueror of this Zone and had the right to use it as it pleased. Who did the Amerikans think they were to interfere?

"What's the matter, Zinan-san?" Michie had asked him tenderly that night as they lay on their futons. "Is the heat keeping you awake?"

He had sighed. "That and an unquiet mind."

"Perhaps I can help."

"Perhaps."

And he had told her and she had listened, and all the while he had remembered Horse's stubborn and suspicious mind and his accusations, and he had asked himself what kind of man could keep himself so stiffly apart from others and reject the hand of friendship as consistently as Horse had done. Only a barbarous Amerikan, a stupid, self-gratifying egotist, blind to the way of purity and discipline. Without refinement, without subtlety in his language, or place, or tradition, how could he know? He could never learn.

In Amerika there lay a deep and insane spirit which held on to its people and never, never let go. Left to itself it slept, but once stirred up it awoke and roared out with ferocity as it had over Hiroshima and Nagasaki on Old Earth so long ago. It was a crazy spirit. And manic. And it seized people and caught them up blindly. He could only see it now because he had been separated from Amerika and all things Amerikan, and by chance had come to see as an outsider sees. No wonder the rest of Known Space saw Amerikans as they did, as men possessed by a desire to free mankind, convinced of the rightness of their crusade, single-minded in their unbalanced beliefs. Always they spoke of rights, but never of duties.

The insight had chilled his heart. There was something awesome about that knowledge, and he wondered how much of the crusading freedom spirit was dormant within him. He watched Michie: the night's blue-blackness fired her hair, the silken surface of her body was dark and magnificently arousing against the white futon on which she lay. He felt himself harden as he told her, "Do you know that if Amerikans see a racial Japanese in Amerika, they assume he's a spy?"

She had laughed at that.

"And are there many Japanese in Amerika? Fumiko told me that the Amerikans are all ugly—hairy with huge noses and bad smells. But you are Amerikan, and you are quite the most beautiful man I have ever seen."

"I was Amerikan. And your eyes are a wife's eyes." He kissed her forehead. "In Amerika there are many strange people. A great variety. In Amerika they think variety is a good thing."

"Do you think variety is a good thing?"

He placed his hand flat on her stomach, his fingers splayed, his touch infinitely soft. "Since we married, I've wondered many times how it might have been for a Yamato scientist stranded on an Amerikan planet. I don't doubt that, had I been a racial Japanese and arrested on Texas or Maine, I would now be doing much the same thing." She placed her hand over his, and he lightened his words. "The difference is that I would have found it much harder to adapt to Amerika."

Michie's teeth showed white in a smile.

"Then maybe variety is a good thing."

"Yes. Maybe."

He held her for a long moment then, watching the *hotaru* fireflies dance in the garland of jasmine flowers that surrounded their window. The air was heavy with fragrance and filled with the high-pitched sound of *semi* singing in the trees. Then they made love, unhurriedly, until the futons were damp with their sweat, and the huge limb of Sado's bloody red daughter world rose up over the mountains.

Afterwards, they had lain together until their hearts stopped hammering, and he had told her what really troubled him.

"Surely you can still make working guns without the dimensions that are so special?" she had asked at last.

"Yes."

"Then do so. Give the daimyo adequate guns, but deny him magnificent guns."

He had sighed. "I can't do that. Because I love my profession. I have my pride. Don't you see? I have a duty to science and I owe my best to my work."

"You feel you must live up to that?"

"Yes, I do. But those who entrusted this knowledge to me— and who therefore saved my life—are Amerikans. It would not be right to betray them. To give their secrets away would break the oath I swore when first admitted to RISC. I can't do it."

She thought for a moment, then said, "I know a way."

He lay back, smiling at her words; it was as if she thought there could be a simple solution. "If you do, then tell me."

"Your science was learned in another life, an old life. And in that life you were true to it. But now you have a new life, on a new world. You must be true to that also. Tell no one how to make the special chamber, *but make it all the same*. Order many ingredients that you do not need as a blind, use sleight of hand. Cover your actions, and design your equipment so that it falls to pieces if anyone tries to get inside it. That way you will make your fine guns, but the secret you will have kept to yourself."

He had made up his mind then, giving in to his vanity. They would be *superb* guns! The best he could make. Long projectors and a way of imparting spin to the singularity to improve its endurance. Ten miles must be possible. Must be. A more powerful field, more concentrated, and with a flash-over of longer duration. Yes, and a more tightly wound propagator so that the singularity would go further and faster and straighter. It could be made smaller and more compact, the initiator rods condensed and turned back on themselves. Lastly there *would* be self-destruct catches, just as Michie said there should be, a globe shield of thin plex containing every important part, arranged to consume itself in a confined and stationary singularity if its integrity should be violated. The guns would bear his name—the Hasegawa Zinan gun—and no one would know but him how it was done, and when asked how, he would lie . . .

Yes, he was tired, he decided as he stood by the test control bench. Tired, but only through lack of sleep and the gyrations of this crazy double planet, and this was the great moment he had been waiting for, the one he had anticipated in his dreams for five strange, difficult, rewarding years. A buzz of delighted expectation tingled in him.

The equipment was ready, its power humming, its temperature exactly stabilised. The watchers waited as the compensators came on, bending the light paths across the test range, twisting the scene like something seen in a distorting mirror. Duval began the initiation sequence by driving the main console. When he withdrew control, a gush of golden light and heat, like liquid metal, radiant like the sun itself, glowed inside the transparent channel and flowed, splitting at each branch into three, four, then five incandescent streams. He stepped forward as it sprang to life, raising the field strength to 5.52 *yukawa* at the filter heads, and he saw how the smooth flow of light reached the testing pit and disappeared down into the five chambers.

It had been a long time since he had done this, and never had he supervised a test solo, let alone with equipment he had virtually designed and built himself, but his intuition had not deserted him. The equations that steered his actions were solid. They defined the precise moment to close off the particle flow and concentrate it by pulsing the field. More automatic choices were made, this time differential alternations to the internal field in the prototype chambers, then again to reverse the effects, and finally one piece of destructive testing, one containment being deliberately ruptured so that the probes could pick up data on the behavior of the distorting singularity.

As the power was cut, the equipment died, its vitality spent. He went down to the lab floor, looked up, and saw a hundred faces looking on, silent and engrossed, so he held his hands out to them, like a showman might, to tell them that the show was over, and there were nods of appreciation and a discreet round of applause.

The pit was opened and decontaminated. At the sight of the

men in orange flexiplex removing the packing from the pit, people emptied from the facility and went out into the yard, where tables had been set up for the dedication ceremony.

Katsumi walked with him. "His Excellency is anxious to see the weapons perform. When may I tell him they will be ready?"

"It's difficult to say until more work has been done, Katsumi-san."

"You know that he's losing patience. The fortifications at Niigata and Hitachi are nearing completion. Of course, we have possession of one whole gun and certain parts from three of the guns salvaged from the Amerikan wrecks, but a large battery is planned."

"I hope our new weapons will soon be ready."

Katsumi nodded shortly. "Good. It is the daimyo's hope that he may have the weapons in place at Niigata in time to protect the next aurium fleet."

"Protect it from whom?"

Katsumi seemed surprised at the question. "From pirates, of course. Amerikan pirates."

6

A week later, Duval prepared to meet Kenji and the daimyo at the proving ground. A dozen weapon mounts were lined up along the wall. Before them was the newly mounted barrel of the *Thomas J.*'s singularity gun recovered from the apron at Niigata, still a malevolent matt black and still with the marks where he had destroyed the end stops to use it to smash into the ship's strongroom. The sight of it turned his thoughts again towards his brother. He touched the boss of the gun with his fingertips, felt the black smoothness that after five years of development work now looked so obsolete.

He drew his hand back suddenly. It was as if an electric charge from the gun had tingled his hand. Suddenly he knew, he had sensed, that Ellis was alive.

Where was he now? Could he be one of the pirates prowling the space lanes of which Katsumi had spoken?

He tried to put the painful thought away, but he knew that if Ellis had survived he would surely come back to Sado. Strange that he should feel this anxious excitement. There had been a great sense of loss at their parting; perhaps this was its counterpart at Ellis's return. He considered Katsumi's words for the fiftieth time, then he examined his feelings and saw a greater deception.

"It's because I am changed now," he said aloud, feeling afraid at the traces of regret that came with the declaration. Anger stiffened him. Go home, *a-ni*, he said silently. Go home, elder brother. For the brother you once had is long since dead and buried. This is my home now. I am Zinan, a new man. A married man. Reborn on a new world, in a new life, with a new name. And of the other there is no trace remaining.

Beside him, his technicians worked amid the machines and tools and laboratory benches making more parts for the proto-types. They whispered anxiously, wondering at the illustrious party that had arrived and laying bets on the performance of the weapons. The guns had almost reached the stage where they could be mounted and powered up.

"Wen-yuan, Dae-woo, Watanabe-san—you must take off the rim and break the seals before you take out the cores," he had told his men the day after the machining. "Then, if everything is satisfactory at my inspection, your teams will go ahead on the actuator insertion. For the largest gun that will take a day and a half. You'll work in teams of two until the job is done."

"Then we'll be ready to assemble the barrels?" Yao Wen-yuan had asked.

"Yes! And be careful to collect the spent casings you remove. They'll be useful in future."

He had checked each gun carefully to see that the cores had remained straight during machining, and he had supervised the mounting of each one in the great compression lathe. Then he had set the plex tools that would cut out the bore, each barrel descending fraction by fraction, under precise control onto the cutting tool. The tool, geared to a mill, was forced round at hundreds of thousands of revolutions per minute until, twelve hours later, the bore was completely reamed.

"We must remove precisely the right amount of metal to accommodate the windage," he had explained, moving an ancient laser micrometer across the cut-away diameter of the demonstration hologram. "A bore precisely one plus pi-to-the-minus-four times the diameter of the event horizon of the singularity being projected is the ideal."

"So sorry, but what is this for? And how do you arrive at that expression?"

"Excuse me for not explaining myself more lucidly, Watanabe-san," he had said, and launched into a long mathematical derivation at the chalkboard. "See? Quite simple."

They had smiled and nodded, not really following his leaps of logic, so he had checked the sums over again slowly before pushing on. Peering minutely at the *hiragana* symbols used in chaos math, searching for the mistake he knew did not exist, but which he had to search for to save his colleagues' face.

He had worked meticulously over the weapons, his teams duplicating his work on the components, and he had seen them grow jealous of their parts of the project and the importance of the segment they were given to work on. He had smiled inwardly at that, for this was how it should be. They had learned that the esteem of the master and his trust in them were expressed in this way, and to them all his praise was of the highest importance.

Next he had shown Mori-san how to install the vent—a hole narrower than his little finger that would connect with the implosion chamber. It was the means by which the singularity was propelled into the projector on firing. He specified that each be tilted back towards the cascabel at pi-by-three radians, the most convenient angle for the injection.

Yao Wen-yuan had come to him full of woes. "We'll never be ready in time!"

"Don't worry."

"I'm not worrying!"

"We'll soon be finished."

"But we have yet to prove the weapons, Zinan-san!" Wen-yuan shook his head.

"Leave that to me. We can't prove an unfinished weapon," he had replied with satisfaction, polishing the best of his prototype barrels on its elegant black snout.

"She's perfect now! Perfect! What more can there be? Hasegawa-sama demands that we are ready before the daimyo comes here again on *kin-yo,* the agreed day. He says Nishima-sama's patience is at an end."

"One thing remains."

"Not a big thing?" Wen-yuan had said, resigned to the fact that the weapon-making would never end.

"The most important thing of all."

And that afternoon he had done it, proudly incising the maker's mark, the fallow deer, and his name, on every base ring.

Now four of the five big guns were set up on the benches of the covered test range, a two-mile-long plex shed with high transparent roof echoing to the sounds of men and machines. Each barrel was a masterpiece of polished chrome, weighing five hundred pounds without its mounting and a waldo hung overhead to move them. The fourth weapon, the best of them, was in its mount, feather light to the touch because it had been so accurately counterbalanced, but still with massive momentum. Charged and ready, it stood beside the weapon that had been salvaged from the *Thomas J.* and restored to action. Both weapons were hooked up to massive black power cables.

Kenji met the daimyo in the administration block, and they walked towards the range together with a dozen stern-faced *rikugun* officers of the Yamato Guard who followed Katsumi. When Duval asked them to inspect the unmounted guns, the daimyo's irritation overflowed.

"How long before the weapons may be fired?" he asked rudely.

"In due course, Excellency. Please excuse me."

"Answer my question precisely."

Duval felt an unexpected shaft of anger at the daimyo's curt impatience. Yes, he thought darkly. There's much more to making a singularity gun than you first imagined when you brought me here. Much more. But you'll not hurry me, and I'll give you what I promised you and more. "I beg your pardon, Excellency. I can discharge the weapons immediately if you wish."

Kenji intervened. "Please, Nishima-sama, if I may explain —" He raised a placating hand, outlining the targets that had been erected down the vast shed exactly one mile away. The biggest was in the form of a huge cast ingot of plex a yard square and two hundred yards in length.

"You intend to fire at those targets?" the daimyo asked, screwing up his eyes. It seemed to Duval that Nishima was unable

to believe that the weapons could project that far, much less
work on the target.

"When I first started the project, I was asked to demonstrate
the performance of my best gun and to compare it with the gun
from the *Thomas J.* in a straight contest. In those days there
were those who believed I could not be trusted to render my best
skills to the Emperor's service."

The daimyo's sidelong glance was condescending. "Let us
hope his doubts were groundless."

Katsumi regarded the mounted weapon appraisingly. "The
first gun seems impressive, Excellency."

"It is," Duval agreed.

"Perhaps we should proceed." Kenji moved to the daimyo's
side.

He grunted. "Yes, demonstrate the weapons. Show us that
your skill is all that you claim, Amerikan."

"*Hai!*" Duval nodded briskly, unsettled by the daimyo's manner. The way he had called him "Amerikan" had been deliberate, and he was clearly preoccupied with some weighty matter.
That made him dangerous.

"Before I demonstrate the guns may I ask you all to retire to
safety."

The daimyo looked about him. "Safety?"

"It is usually unwise to stand too close to unproven weapons,
Excellency."

"Unproven weapons? I told you they were to be ready. Today.
Now."

"So they are, Excellency. Ready to prove. As you can see
the weapons have not yet been fired. I thought it would be best
to—"

"You thought to wait until I arrived?" The daimyo's manner
froze still harder.

"It is customary in Amerika to give the customer guarantees
that what he is buying will work."

"Guarantees are implicit."

Duval indicated the plex-screened viewing gallery that had
been erected fifty yards away. "May I request that your distinguished party retires to the gallery?"

Katsumi began to lead his officers to the rear, but stopped
when he saw the daimyo was not moving.

"You will come too."

"I cannot." Duval made a gesture of apology. "I made the weapons. It is I who must test-fire them."

The daimyo laced his arms together. His suspicions were aroused and he watched Duval steadily. "Then we shall stand with you."

"That will not be practical—"

"I said, we shall stand with you."

Duval blew out a breath. "As you wish, Excellency."

Katsumi and the others began to gather again uncertainly, their cap insignias glinting as they looked to their lord with sidelong glances, detecting the mistrust in him. Finally the daimyo said, "You seem ill at ease, Amerikan. Explain to me the real reason why we should not stand here. Why are you insisting on firing the weapons yourself?"

Duval's pride overcame him, but he trod warily, facing the daimyo with coolness. "I have faith enough in my own skill. I can assure you that in service these guns will perform properly."

"Then why do you suggest that we retire? Do you think I am afraid?" The daimyo looked to his officers imperiously.

Duval stared at the floor. "Of course not, Excellency."

"Tell me: have you made unsound weapons? Are they unsafe?"

"It is merely that a singularity weapon, any weapon, no matter how well made, may be dangerous. That's what a weapon is for. This is the first firing." Duval met the daimyo's eye insolently. "And, were it not for one small fact, I would welcome your standing beside me as I fire the first round."

"One small fact?"

"I've made a powerful prototype, many new components, many innovations. The weapons are powered to their limit and will be operated to the limits of their components, perhaps beyond. Consequently, if there is anything I've overlooked, I want it to show on this first test firing. With me standing here. I don't want any one of my team to pay for my mistakes. In Amerika it's a traditional saying that the inventor of the airplane pilots the first flight."

The daimyo looked flintily back and Duval saw that his certainty had deserted him. He enjoyed the moment. He allowed a slight smile to play over his face as he explained quietly, "If we stood here, and the gun malfunctioned on proof, it would turn us all nicely into butcher's offal, Excellency."

The daimyo's response was sharp. He barked an order to Katsumi, who ran up and came to attention before him, then he turned back to Duval. "I have made it plain to you that your function is to manufacture singularity weapons for my batteries. How dare you jeopardise your life unnecessarily? This man will prove the weapon."

"But, Your Excellency, it is my duty—"

"Silence! Your duty is to do as I order!"

Duval made a gesture of concession. The blood had drained from Katsumi's face. He turned and saw the development team regarding him with little respect.

"Katsumi-san is not technically compet—"

Nishima rounded on him furiously. "Weapons are weapons! Tell him what to do."

Duval's eyes were fixed on the daimyo's own. Then he shook his head slowly. "I must apologise humbly, Excellency, but I cannot allow Katsumi-san to prove my weapon."

Nishima's anger grew and his fist closed over the grip of his *katana*. "You will do as I say!"

"With respect, Excellency, I will not. I must be sure that the gods intend Yamato to have my skills."

Nishima halted, bottled his threat, seeing suddenly that nothing he said could counter Duval's twisted Amerikan logic. "Very well. Retire!"

Duval watched them go, feeling the sweetness of his victory as they trooped towards the viewing gallery. His team buzzed with anxiety but he calmed them, saying nothing about the modification that only he knew had been strapped to the new gun. He motioned his crew away to safety, spitting the dryness from his mouth. Everything he had told Nishima Jun was true, everything except one detail. There could be faults. His life was hostage to that, to his skill and his conviction, as was only right. Then why had he lied about the modification? Why had he set a fifty percent power margin, over and above his safe firing limit?

It was a reckless, foolhardy action. Had some part of him secretly wanted to goad the daimyo to stand here beside him and blow them both into Shinto hell?

No. It would have been very easy to have manipulated the man's dignity to that end.

Then what was it? And why, when Nishima had retired, had

he felt himself sweating? He knew suddenly that the modification was enough to carry the prototype's performance beyond that of the Amerikan weapon. If successful it would open up a whole new area for advancement. It also made the outcome a true gamble: a disaster—*or the reward of making known what was previously unknown.* He had told the daimyo the whole truth when he had spoken of the gods. That single massive discharge would in one firing prove the weapon, the theory, and also the weapon-designer's destiny.

The end of the range house was being opened. Grav compensators clicked on, distorting the interior of the test range in a fish-eye manner, like an image reflected in a mercury droplet. The all-clear sounded. He sent his team away to the gallery, then, alone, he stood behind the weapon he had built and put out his hand to the firing levers and took a deep breath. Like a man looking down from a high building, he felt an irrational impulse. It would be so easy to turn it on the viewing gallery and end everything now. He mastered himself and pulled the firing triggers.

The concussion was terrifying. The cold argentium tubes delivered their charge, and the explosion flung the gun and its mount back against its recoil springs and ripped him to the ground. As the gun crashed back, smoke blew around him. For a few seconds he was enveloped in it, then he saw his development team running towards him. He stood up ecstatically, deafened by the roar, finding his notes and throwing them up through the air like a madman.

The gun was intact!

In the distance, vermin pigeons that had leapt from their roosts as the sound thundered down to them fluttered out, flying crazily through the compensator fields. Far away in the paddies beyond, slave rice planters straightened and looked up. He looked to where the daimyo stood, saw Kenji raise his hand and wave it in congratulation. He ordered the weapon repowered immediately, this time with the modification bypassed. They brought fresh argentium tubes out from their floor recesses, their interiors maintained at a steady low temperature to fight the chemical instability of the special isotope mix. Then the team were dismissed to safety.

Why the hell was it smoking?

Again the gun bellowed and bucked. Another great plume of smoke filled the air and drifted thin above him. All was well. They repeated the repower, faster this time. And a third angry blast roared out.

Duval began to feel the ringing in his head, the peculiar gun-drunkenness that stretched time and made everything euphoric and unreal. He felt as though he had been clouted hard on the ear, slightly concussed, but paradoxically able to aim the weapon the better for it. He handled the argentium tubes with infinite care, set the power catches until the range was correct, sighted the target, and laid the gun's azimuth.

The shot threw the gun back violently with another ear-shattering roar. Further gouts of lightning and acrid smoke spewed out from the muzzle, and Duval watched the pads of burning liner arc to the ground leaving smoky trails. He moved to the side so he could follow the propagating singularity. The cameras downrange showed that the singularity had carried just over the target.

He ordered a repower and fresh barrel core and moved ten yards away to the *Thomas J.*'s gun, checking the sighting once more. It was intact except for the mechanism that recored the barrel for rapid firing. It was already charged up and ready to fire, but he altered the gun fractionally to the left with a twist of the mount adjusters before firing it off. This time the cameras showed that the singularity had blipped out short of its target. A plumstone appeared and continued towards the target like a giant bowling ball. It struck with tremendous force, but the plex target was as unmoved from its anchorings as if the iron object had been made of ultra-light helithene.

He felt the urge to destroy overwhelm him, just as it had that day on the apron at Niigata. The plex targets became real, his memories vivid. He urged his technicians to double their efforts each time they repowered and replaced the core, shouted at the crews ferociously, exhorting them in savage language, willing them to work faster against one another, to compete.

They had never seen him like this, but they did his bidding, restoring each of the weapons to firing condition within half a minute. With the next two shots the target was penetrated, the range found. Then they scored hit after hit. It was too easy: a sitting target, no movement to compensate for, no variables. His hungry singularities began to lance the plex into pieces, and he saw exultantly that his own was the deadlier. He had created one of the most precisely destructive weapons ever made.

First the target was eaten away, then the anchoring ramp, then the steel backing screens punctured neatly, but Duval continued to fire, now with his own gun, now with the gun from the *Thomas J.* After two dozen shots, the barrels were almost too hot to touch. The air tasted of burned liner. His technicians were running with sweat. A dozen shots more, delivered as fast as they could fire them. Still he shouted them onward, and they saw how he was touched by a *kami*. Angry, yet not angry. Time passed, but its passing did not reach him. Nothing diminished the passion and intensity of the attack. The target that had once been the epitome of durability was reduced by the test to a splintered block of gray shards, but still he urged another repower and another and another, until all fear and all grief and all anger and all hatred were pouring from him, on and on and on and on, until there was no more will and no more breath and no more strength in the technicians' arms and legs with which to feed the guns and the terrible flame within their master.

As they fell to their knees, he took up the tools and the argentium tubes himself, threw off the hands of those that tried to stop him.

"Enough!"

Then the officers of the Guard were hurrying towards them. They saw the glaze in his eyes, the stark rawness that lingered there, and they knew they had witnessed a man who was prepared to push himself to the utmost limit to demonstrate his skill.

The daimyo looked at the new gun with awe and fascination. From the very first shot he had been profoundly impressed by the demonstration, by the range, the consistent accuracy of the shooting, the power of the singularity to destroy. The anxieties of the morning rose up in him again as he faced the Amerikan. He had been half expecting, half hoping that the demonstration would prove nothing. After so many delays it was not unreasonable to suppose that the results would not justify the expense, that the experiment would prove a costly and inconclusive failure, but the Amerikan had done all that he had promised and more. Such a pity that the prize must soon be lost, he thought. Duval is now a real asset and not simply a potential one. How unfortunate it has taken so long to manifest itself. How cruel the turn of events back in Kanazawa.

"That was magnificent shooting, Amerikan. I congratulate you."

Duval's eyes were staring through him blearily. Kenji took his arm, wiped the sweat and grime from his face, his own breathing fast and excited. "Do you hear that, Zinan-san? Such guns! Who would be our enemy now?"

The daimyo watched his host's delight grimly. If we had a hundred of these guns, fully finished, with loading and charging and coring functions completely automated, we might subdue the entirety of Known Space, he thought. But this is hardly a start. Is there still time? *Is there still time?*

"Hasegawa-san, you will immediately put your facility into full production. By this time next year, I want a hundred of these weapons in my possession. No delay is to be tolerated. No expense is to be spared. Do you understand?"

"Yes, Excellency. Thank you. It's a great honor, but perhaps a *hundred* singularity guns in a single year is too many for our small facility to produce."

"Then you must build another. I will pay whatever is necessary. You will start tomorrow. Today. Now."

"You do us too much honor, Excellency."

The daimyo motioned the *han*-holder aside. "Can it be done without the Amerikan?"

Kenji seemed not to understand the question.

"I ask you: can the facility operate without the Amerikan? Have your men learned enough?"

"I—I don't know, Excellency."

"Then find out. You have a year to make those guns, Hasegawa-san."

But the daimyo knew that he did not have a year. That very morning he had learned from his council that Fukuda Ikku, imperial *metsuke* and inspector general of the *kempei*, was preparing to put out his hand in search of impurity. To begin its quest the office wanted first to examine the captured Amerikans, and the name "Duval Straker" was at the head of their list.

7

"KABUL BASE"—A SECRET LOCATION IN THE NEUTRAL ZONE

The Yamato Guard had come here and found their base and all was destroyed.

Oujuku stood on the blasted crete and stared at the fire-blackened ruins two hundred yards away, feeling the pain in his leg and tasting the bitterness of yet another disappointment. Behind him, the landing party stirred uneasily, watching the purple undergrowth and straining to listen for dangers despite the wind.

"So. The sonsabitches've found us out," he said.

"We've been betrayed!" Pelgar Rosen, his second-in-command, came to his side. "They must have learned from those who we left for dead at Okinawa. From Ramirez or Esterhazee."

"Yeah, and maybe it was just bad luck!" Frane said. The belligerent Ohion third officer threw down his cap. He and Esterhazee had been close. "We've got bad psi, I tell ya!"

"Shut your mouth, Frane. The captain don't allow that kind of talk."

The shuttle crew fanned out across the mountain shelf. A cold wind howled in the peaks, driving small clouds westward, giving movement to everything in land and sky.

Oujuku shaded his eyes and looked from the base to the *Lexington*, to the *Valley Forge*, then back to the base again. This had been his secret stronghold, the place he had code-named "Kabul Base" because of the drabness and the deep valleys and the towering white peaks that stood over them. Behind, the land was clothed in dust, rising steeply—god-awful with the sun sinking low, casting the shadow of the mountain across it. A rock stood at the entrance to what had been the underground complex, and not far from this place a frozen waterfall of pure crystal that he had first washed in almost two years ago. This place was hard to find unless you knew what you were looking for.

They followed him warily toward the ruin, pushing through twisted metal, their sensors fluttering. Kabul Base was to have been their base of operations: a secure port where he could replenish his ships and stockpile the booty they had meant to take from Yamato ships. But now their stores were stolen, their provisions spoiled or carried off; there was only snow and charred metal and the threat of ambush. Kabul Base was known to the enemy, and so it was useless.

"Are you a'right, Captain?" his thick-spoken shuttle coxswain asked once more.

Godblind yah, Frane! he thought uncharitably, wanting to savor what the enemy had done, the better to decide on a fit way to get them back for it. The deep wound in his calf muscle raged, echoing the disaster that had befallen them at Okinawa. Three months had passed since then and still the leg had not properly healed. He hated it because his men thought him a cripple and because it reminded them of the bloody failure. *His* bloody failure.

"Get the landing party back aboard. Let's piss off out of here."

"Aye, sir!"

They sat meekly at their controls, the huge windshield buffeted by snow flurries, waiting for him, watching him limping up into the shuttle. The leg burned as he stepped up the ramp.

Frane hesitated. "Captain—"

"Get about your tasks," he shouted, his voice rasping hoarsely.

The new loss infuriated him. The shame of it. *This piss-burning poisoned leg!* He'd have to have the bastard off if it didn't improve in three days. He strode inside and heaved himself into a seat smartly, knocking away Cao's helping hand, unwilling to fill their eyes with any more of this goddamned crippled-captain sideshow.

He looked at their faces and saw they were all troubled and lined. None would meet his eye. He knew they could not lightly put aside this new setback. He read their thoughts: Betrayal. Fuming anger. Above all, disappointment. Ramirez and Esterhazee again. Stupidity! Ramirez. Wanted to be a hero. Ramirez, the comms expert, was certainly dead, his brains splashed out by a sniper, but Esterhazee might have been alive.

Oujuku folded his arms to stop his hands going to his knee. An analgesic might stop that blood-pounding ache. Oh, no! Suffer and smile, you sonofawhore! Put your mind to something else.

There was another explanation. What if Ellis Straker had been taken and had talked? No, surely not. Not Ellis. His men, then? But Ellis alone knew the full extent of the plans; he alone knew the location of Kabul Base. Ellis would have died before telling anybody. And he wasn't indiscreet in marking up his visualiser log.

So it was Esterhazee. Fucking Esterhazee. The rat-faced little scum-bucket. Maybe not . . . maybe they cut his balls off first. Yeah, think about that, John, and save your recriminations up for them that can defend themselves to your face.

When they reached the *Lexington,* the shuttle swung inside the hangar deck. He climbed out with gritted teeth, looked for and found the furtive way the rest of the crew regarded him. None of them would hold his gaze and that angered him more, and the anger showed and made them more evasive still. He cast about him with his jaw tight as a fist and his lips protruding, and went below to his quarters. Immediately he broke out a bottle of mash, but there was no comfort in it and no spirit to light up inside him. He could not put out of his mind what he had seen in the faces of his crew.

At the outset he had promised them riches beyond imagination. "You all heard of Mitsubai? That's the chief *zaibatsu*—a kind of Yamato mega-corporation. It means 'secret trade.' And this is its symbol—" He had held up a *kanji* that looked like a bunch of fishhooks. "Mitsubai is the outfit that contracts and ships most of the aurium out of the Zone. Now, how many of you guys wants to become a corporate raider?"

They had grinned at that, but so far there had been struggle and toil and death. Twenty-five of them had fallen in fighting, five more to ship accidents, and two taken by local fauna. And the remainder had seen neither credit nor a single flask of Mitsubai's heavy compounds with which to redeem their promises.

That had been the original plan: take enough to buy the men who had been grounded on Sado, finally discharge the debt that

Jos Hawken had run up in the marooning. But what to do now? The Amerikan they had picked off that Yamato ship had changed everything. The isotopist had given him plenty to think on.

Still, a promise was a promise, but Okinawa aurium was better spent on Liberty than at Niigata, whatever Ellis Straker thought about it. They would have to talk it over.

He remembered how they had seen it in the raw, tons of it, stacked in spherical ingots, in the metal vaults of Aurium Terminal on Okinawa. After Sado, Okinawa was the biggest super-heavy element shipping point in Known Space, and like Sado, pretty poorly defended. Nobody had dreamed of interfering with the place before. But it was rich: aurium and argentium *and* platinium, plus a few exotic decay nuclides—long-lived radioactive fusion products that were associated with the supernova wreck of the Gum Nebula. All in all, it added up to something worth hanging around for. But the mission had misfired and they had got away with none of it. *As a leader, he had failed them*.

It had been a sorry debacle. He had bluffed his way into orbital stack around that unlivable hole of a world using captured ID interrogation equipment and intended to land at break of Okinawa's short seven-hour day, and storm the metal vaults, but the party under Jerry Dyson's command had made their landing prematurely at 0300 UT, in pitch-blackness, using full suits, and they had been forced to follow up. Then their four shuttles had been rumbled by a patrol ship; and the high-security compounds had been alerted before they had even scrambled out of their vehicles.

It had been chaos! Caution and order had flown away. Totally disoriented, they had assaulted the dome complex in a screaming panic, searing down the defenses, running and shouting like madmen, careless of life and limb, into the guard fire that had peppered them randomly from the blackness. Crashing about because of the shitty gravity. Utter indiscipline. Utter, uncoordinated, piss-boiling chaos!

Incredible, but the shooting had died away.

It turned out to be Taito, a town the size of Harrisburg, maybe twenty, twenty-five thousand ·inhabitants, almost all of them Mitsubai Aurium Terminal workers and their dependents, because this place was nobody's idea of paradise. Under plex-dome cover, dust like gray talcum everywhere, filthy mineral flats and blue-green algae scum and poisoned, acrid air. Like

Biak a real terraforming gone wrong. It had been emptied by the alarm. The townsfolk fled before them, panic-stricken, crying in their terror of the Mongol horde that had come out of the night, but the three shivering prisoners the Amerikans grabbed had told them of the vaults and the fabulous treasure they contained and so they had swarmed through the narrow streets, their mission coursing with undeserved good fortune, riding unhindered on the back of surprise.

"You know how to breathe ammonia, fellah?"

The question had taught one of the captives to speak a little English.

"Okay. You know what this is? It's a meson cutter! We'll blow your fucking dome wide open, y'hear me? Now move!"

Oujuku smiled bitterly at the memory of it. What a nonsensical miracle. They had taken him there, and there had been ion interlocks on the vault. By psi alone, by his own eerie inner certainties, he had guided them to the very place where the wealth of Known Space was concentrated. Tons of argentium! Great big, assay chop stamped pure 99.9999% refined bars. One for each day of the year—and there were five hundred fifty-two and one-third days in Okinawa's year. Three fortunes for each Amerikan raider. Bars stacked six feet high in the main vault, filling the space completely. It had gleamed like moonbeams under their torches, astounding everyone who gazed on it, because it was without doubt the greatest single repository of argentium in all creation.

But in the queer tension before a psi-storm, when the claustrophobia inside a suit is thick enough to curdle milk, a man's mind can easily slip away from reality, and then argentium seems like some other, baser substance, fresh-poured lead or bright iron.

He had forbidden them to touch any of it. Trusting his own mind, he had been sure that another place was nearby that contained the same immense hoard—*but of aurium*.

And so it had been! In the Mitsubai warehousing by the apron they found the unattended strongroom bursting with it. Their glee had been unutterable—Rosen and Frane and Zaratini and Cao and his own brother, Frank—all his lieutenants had run their hands over it, capered and gawped, seeing the stuff and the super-heavy cast spheres—metallic blue in tint. They had stared with the eyes of wonder at those pawnbroker balls, those golden goose eggs that could buy the future of Known Space. Next they had turned their gorged eyes on him and he had exulted in the knowledge that he had delivered them here and that his promises to them were thereby fulfilled.

"Didn't I tell ya? Didn't I? *Didn't I?* Eh?"

Then the Mitsubai guard had come to their senses, and the sounds of personnel carriers grinding into the complex was raw. The craven garrison had composed themselves and returned, seeing their four shuttles and understanding how pitifully few they were, and as the guard came on to repossess their treasury, the astonishing vision had vanished. Their surprise was exhausted. They would have to go.

But it was the whole point that they take this stuff away!

He had felt strong and charged with confidence, unbreakable and unstoppable, but how his followers had read the omen differently. Huddled in that queer light, amid an immeasurable wealth flashed blue by damaged lighting panes, those deep superstitions had flared up in them.

The many awed voices had spoken out in their paralysis, the repairman turned pirate and the stevie looking for excitement, and the nexus hand who'd become a corporate raider because it sounded real smooth.

"I don't like it!"

"They're coming after us, John!"

"We've gotta get outta here!"

And that awed voice still: "But look at it! It's a dying man's dream!"

"Captain, we'll never get away with it. It's too much. They'll hunt us down wherever we go!"

"Remember, it's Yamato we're stealing from."

"Oh, Jeezus! We're going to die!"

"We can't take it!"

"Come on, let's get gone, Captain!"

And he had risen up in a mighty fury at them. His voice had filled with power and flame. "Listen to me! I have brought you to the treasure house of the *universe!* Follow me, until the job is done! Because if you leave without anything, you can blame no one but yourselves!"

His rage had shaken them. The spell of fear had abated. They had activated the waldos then and begun to shift Mitsubai's monstrous eggs down onto floating pallets, running them out to the waiting shuttles, knowing, because he told them so, that if they were to leave it here, then that sonofabitch Emperor would use it to trouble the last outposts of freedom.

"Do you want them to come into Amerika to pillage your own people? Rape your wives? Smother your babes?" An egg of vast weight had swung in the waldo fist. "*This* is the pay they give their samurai."

Then the firing had intensified. There had been an almighty explosion, and he had let out a groan and staggered in a sudden faint. And they had seen the air jetting from the hole in his leg and the flame within him guttering.

Those foolish stevies and adventurers and repairmen had abandoned the treasure to pick him up. They had slapped a pressure pad on him and carried him to the shuttle and took him away, still their captain, and still much more precious than any Emperor's load of scrap.

"Take the aurium and leave the man. Surely I taught them that much?" he said, sick at their misplaced loyalty. "And tan their hides for it, because our mission is to rob and to plunder, and not to care a damn for anyone, least of all a fool who gets his leg slit open.

"Godblind me! *Why do I feel so weak?*"

Oujuku stared dispiritedly into the mirror. The man he saw before him was a sorry piece of loot, black skin peeling. A mane of dready hair, elfed up in a headband that was stiff and caked with dust. There was a line of jigger lumps on his neck; where he had scratched at them to get at the burrowing ticks they were skinned raw. He stripped his shirt off and examined his chest, then the muscles of his upper arms and the smooth forearms also knotted with muscle where he had worked alongside his people in building Kabul Base. When his heart moved in his chest, each beat sent a pulse of pain down his thigh and into his calf muscle. It was hard not to give in to the urge to have treatment, but he had his Naturalist principles to stand by. No medication. The natural way, for good or ill. But the microfauna of Known Space was so diverse now, there were always evil strains of something appearing, something the medics couldn't handle. It would be a hell of a thing to die of a cut on the leg!

Sullenly he looked inside himself, finding a pervasive fatigue there, like the sour dregs of a water tank swilling in his belly.

I did fail them, he said silently. They look to me alone for their future. Mine is the driving force. But there's not a lot remaining within, and nothing I can do to stop the soreness growing in my eyes. And I don't look like I ought to—not like a captain. That I must do, at the very least.

He took another belt of mash and wondered suddenly on which planet his heart would beat its last, how many beats it still contained; then he was ashamed of the thought. It was the first time in all his life he had asked himself such a question. He stoppered the flask and vowed never to ask it again.

But listen, he thought, slamming the flask back in its place in his cabinet, it's only me, John Oujuku, that's carried the burden of hopes and fears for a hundred volunteers these past few months. Only me that's filled them with dreams and hassled them on, never asking anything in return except a bit of faith. And they've followed me gladly and without complaint, suffering trustingly, some even dying, because I'm their leader. Their captain. And it wasn't fear or compulsion that made them do it, but free will and trust. Be worthy of them, John, you sorry bastard! You hear me?

When a knock came at the door, he was ready for it. Pelgar Rosen, his tall, unsmiling second-in-command, came in, surprised that her captain was stark naked. Oujuku was wet shaving his cheeks and chin. His hair was combed and had been trimmed back short.

"Well?"

"I'm sorry, I thought—"

"What did you think, Pel?"

"I—the helmsman wants to know if you're ready to light out, sir."

Oujuku's reply was distorted by his shaving. "We must find ourselves a new place to lay up, but I'm undecided as yet. What would you do, Pel?"

"Set up another stronghold down the chain, maybe Tuamotu."

"Not further down? To Tahiti or Raiatea?"

"Seems to me, sir, preying on nexus traffic's our only hope of profit now. Unless we make some hits, we'll start to run out of vital stores. Lube, for example. We'll have to find plexoline somewheres—we really have need of a new base where we can refit properly when necessary."

"Where do you think it ought to be?"

"A new place remote from Yamato. So's we're not displaced again."

Oujuku looked up and shook his wet hair so that droplets flew from it. "I want none of that, Pel. We're here to do a job of work. We'll keep close by our quarry."

"If you say so."

"I say so. In any case, the fall is coming on in Liberty and I mean to hit a rendezvous that's been agreed for November of this year."

"Oh?"

"Yep. There's a man who, if he can, will meet us at a pleasant little dustball between Upolu and Savaii. A man we owe plenty."

Rosen's face lit up as she realised whom Oujuku meant. "We're to meet Captain Straker at Apolima?"

"Yep."

"Will you tell him about the isotopist?"

"I'll have to, though it'll break his heart."

Oujuku shrugged on a fresh shirt. His kit was newly broken out, laid out on his strap hammock. He would change into the kit he had sworn not to wear until they had something to celebrate.

"Help me with my boots, Pel."

Rosen took hold like someone shoeing a horse and eased the boot on. The right was easy, the left impossible even when Oujuku sat down on the lip of his strap. They gave up.

"Shall I fetch the surgeon?" Rosen asked, too circumspect to make direct comment over the gash. Oujuku flexed his ankle so that the calf was laid open from top to bottom, and the flesh all around was swollen. It had slashed badly when a jagged lump of steel had spun off in the firefight. Now it was full of yellow pus and smelled nasty.

"Surgeon? No! The bastard's too happy to put a man in a unit. I've got an aversion to synthetic parts being attached to me. And, well, they say it leaves you woozy for a week."

"It's the easy way to get fit. You're a Naturalist, aren't you?"

"Bodies were meant to heal naturally. Don't you know never to trust a ship's doctor? When he took the poison out of my leg, the sonofabitch nearly killed me. He'll have my leg off quick as a wink and then what'll I say to Ellis, hopping around with one half of a white leg?"

Rosen was unamused. "C'mon, sir, they got black below-the-knees in the freezee."

"I'll not waste good limbs on a little-biddy flesh wound, and that's flat."

"I booked you in. It'll kill the pain."

Oujuku straightened instantly. "Hey, do I seem to you to be in pain?"

Rosen shook her head. "No, Captain, but the impairment—at least take a course of sepsin."

"I told you, I don't hold with medication. I need a clear head, and there's a better way. One I learned from Ayrton Rodrigo. Open the cabinet. You'll find a tub of yoghurt there. Bring it to me."

The yoghurt had been thrown away, and in its place was a mass of maggots. They had been rotting inside the tub in the cabinet for a week. Oujuku took out half a dozen pale-colored grubs with the tip of his knife and grinned. "A blow for a blow, that's what Ayrton used to say, eh, Pel? Come out of there, you little beauties!"

He placed a dozen maggots into his palm and then one by one onto the place where the suppuration was worst. They wriggled and quickly dived into the wound.

Rosen watched with absorbed horror at Oujuku's side.

"Pick the smallest for their appetites. See? When they come out of the air, they have a mighty taste for pus and dead flesh. It's their meat and drink and what makes 'em grow fat. They'll clean me up for sure. I can feel them doing me good already."

He clapped a wad of cotton torn from his old shirt over the wound, tied it round, and forced on his boot again, feeling hugely pleased with himself. He danced a reggae jig for Rosen's benefit, ending on a clap and a stamping flourish.

"You see?"

Rosen's face was green and Oujuku clapped her on the back with a full-bodied clout. "Well? Shall we get on up to the bridge?"

"Yes, Captain," she said. "Anything you say."

8

THE APOLIMA SYSTEM, N.Z.

It had been an uneventful planetfall, and it was good to be back on a low-grav planet in a G-type star system, good to see the primary westering red at the ending of each day. But each night there was a rage in heaven the like of which he had never seen, and it made Ellis think of his brother and the real reason he had come to this rendezvous.

Apolima was cataloged as uninhabited—surprising, since it was hard against the Yamato Boundary, but perhaps less surprising when it was realised that Apolima was utterly without all exploitable resources except one: physical beauty.

This part of it was delightful. The night was calm. *Constitution* was in standing orbit with *Lexington,* directly above the place they had code-named "Providence," and the shuttles were drawn up on a sand beach. A score of wood fires burned there among inflatable tents as Ellis stepped down. There were no clams here, but they were going to have a clambake anyhow.

"Ellis."

"John." They clasped forearms. "Any news?"

"Not good. C'mon, have a bite with us."

Ellis sat down with a roast kale fowl to learn of Oujuku's doings. It had been May by the Amerikan Central Calendar when Oujuku had left Liberty with seventy-three men and women in the *Lexington* and the *Valley Forge.* Provisioned for a year, they had got offplanet before anyone could stop them with a countermanding order from the Security Council. By June they had reached this world, and after refitting had headed for the systems Oujuku had surveyed on his reconnaissance the previous year.

Oujuku grinned as he recounted how they had sighted the Okinawa system. "We attacked Taito in July. That's where I got this."

He pointed to the leg. The bulbous muscle of his calf was knotted with scar tissue, but seemed not to impede him now.

"You were almost killed, they tell me."

"That's aright, Captain," Cao growled protectively. The man's shipboard slang seemed strange, and Ellis remembered the terrible day Cao had first seen Harrisburg, how he had sat with him in the bar after the news of Janka's death. Then the man had shown outstanding qualities.

"I hadda carry him out the Mitsubai strongroom myself, he was so heart-set over them eggs."

"I fucked it all up," Oujuku confessed disgustedly. "Suit puncture. But I swear it'll take more than a chunk of tin to put me down for good."

Ellis poured more beer into his mouth and ripped the white flesh from a kale-fowl breast. "You got away with their aurium, then?"

Oujuku shook his head ruefully and told the tale, the bright firelight flickering across his face. Despite the failures, Ellis thought he seemed utterly at peace with creation, except for one thing.

"Bewitched, it was! In my palm and my fingers closing over it, when *pssht!* Hell, there was probably too much to shift. And we weren't exactly the best-disciplined hit squad there ever was. It won't be the same next time."

"Next time?"

"Sure! I'm resolved on it. Broke but game. Give me credit for that at least."

"Pity about Okinawa. Some of it might have made the ransom—for the maroons."

"Might have." Oujuku stirred uneasily. "I was meaning to tell you . . . about something."

"What?"

"Oh . . ."

After a pause Oujuku stood up and walked barefoot towards the tide line. Ellis picked up his order satchel and went after him, knowing that what was to be said was for them alone.

Waves lapped gently there. Out of range of the beach fires the sky was brilliantly dark and spangled with stars, and the tremendous vivid veil of the Milky Way spanned the heavens. One star in particular, an intense blue-white point, riding at forty degrees elevation in the north, was vastly brighter than all the rest, magnitude minus six or seven, its light reflecting on the water. Ellis looked at it unhappily.

"The supernova terrified my people at first," he told Oujuku. "Half of them just knew it was their home primary, though that's impossible."

"I confess it weighed heavy on my own mind for a while. Wondering what system it was. *What* it was."

"And when you located it as Nagoya?"

"I worried again."

"A bad sign, you think?"

"Ain't nice to see any star go suddenly nova, and if the system's cataloged as inhabited . . . it's unthinkable. But listen, I don't believe it was a supernova."

"Well, it wasn't a nova, Ellis. Too big for a nova, and I don't have Nagoya's primary down in my catalog as a cool Main Sequence-plus-white-dwarf binary, which is what they always are. Mass transfer's the mechanism—"

"John, I didn't say it was a nova."

"Then what? Check it out. The classic type-one supernova was 1054 Taurus, eighteen hundred and forty parsecs away. The 'Crab' reached magnitude minus four as seen from Earth. That's equivalent to, let's see, five plus m, plus five-log-ten of . . . there you go: minus fifteen-point-three. That's about a hundred and fifty million times as bright as one standard sol. The event at Nagoya was smaller. It'd show as minus fourteen or so otherwise."

"So it's a small supernova."

"No."

"No? Why not?"

"Because they don't happen that frequently. Forty or fifty novae per year per galaxy, sure, but very few supernovae."

"And it's in Yamato. So it's suspicious."

"Correct. Look, this is the furthest any Amerikan has penetrated towards Yamato, and what do we find?"

"Yeah."

"The light from that whatever-it-was took forty-nine years to get to here, John. It's still lit up at peak. That peak is five times ten-to-the-thirty-four watts of radiation. Nothing, not even a supernova, can keep supplying that kind of energy for more than a year. Ergo, the thing blew less than fifty years ago."

"You think they kept us out of Yamato, with that sonofabitch edict and all, to stop us finding out about Nagoya?"

"I wouldn't put it past their government."

"But why? I mean, so what?"

Ellis continued to stare at the sky. Like Oujuku, his astrogator's instincts had been greatly disturbed by the apparition and what it might portend. It blazed like a diamond, a jewel bright enough to cast a shadow, and because it shone in the black of a moonless night, it was even more impressively luminous.

What was Nagoya?

Before the last jump it had been invisible, then, after the transit, he had seen it blasting out as bright as an uncharted white dwarf in the Apolima system. He had immediately embargoed the computer records on that location hoping to hold off speculation until he had figured out what to do. He had said nothing to Angelo, his co-astrogator, or to Bowen, but the following day they had come to him to demand he level with them.

Novae did not suddenly appear in space; they were unstable binaries—all crews knew that. And Ellis had had no better answer for them. The stellar sciences, as Ganesh Ramakrishnan had acknowledged, were by no means exhausted. Long hours of study had taught Ellis that the stars were as variable and sophisticated as the members of the plant or animal kingdoms. Even the Main Sequence stars in their pedestrian courses of evolution sometimes behaved according to a far from predictable plan. The Earth ancients believed that in times of earthly crisis odd things happened in the sky, for it was a mirror and in it all things were reflected. How right they were.

The thought reminded Ellis of crucifixions and the forgotten roots of his religion. There had been a report of a new fixed star coming into the sky unannounced two and a half thousand years ago, the one the three wise men had seen.

"Doesn't it send a shiver through you?" Oujuku asked, troubled. "My crew have asked me how we'll report it. What we'll tell them back in Amerika. What do you think I should say to them?"

Ellis studied the unwavering spark, deeply shocked by the message he knew it carried. He quoted Rorenzo: "*Ask rather what earthly matter can be of such importance that a new star must herald it.*"

"Huh?"

"Never mind."

"You're not going all bookish on me, are you, Ellis?"

"What, me? No, to answer your original question, I think we ought to swear both crews to secrecy, bind everyone to it."

Oujuku stared at him, hard. "Why?"

"I don't know yet."

As they walked, Ellis told him the startling news he had received at Harrisburg whilst he had gone through final preflights aboard *Constitution*. In that communiqué Hawken had told him that Halton Henry had been executed for his crimes and that Okubo had been ignominiously sent out of Amerika after an attempt to have the new VP shot down in the street, but there had been another report enclosed, recounted in harrowing and despairing terms. It had come from Cassabian on Peking, and told of an infamously bloody massacre.

The Dowager had, on the Feast of the Wall, ordered the assassination of the Korean leader and the entire pro-Yamato Cabinet. The mob in the capital had had their own ideas about how to react.

Oujuku was stunned. "So the running dogs of Peking have fallen on their neighbors."

"All Koreans, of whatever rank, indiscriminately butchered on Peking alone. Tens of thousands until the Yangtse itself ran red. Cassabian admits he was completely unprepared for it. Up until the very day he was continuing political marriage negotiations with the Dowager. They even had to fortify the embassy against the murder gangs that roamed the streets when it turned into a general riot against foreigners. It's said he barely escaped with his life."

The killings had plunged Amerika's position into doubt once more, changing everything. As Oujuku's oaths against the atrocity subsided, Ellis took from his satchel the hard copy he had been waiting to give him. Sweeter news, but needing explanation.

They walked along the lapping water, hearing the boisterous carousing of the crews at their barbecue fires, shouts and laughter and the strains of vambo and E&L music on the sound systems. Oujuku concentrated on the documents in the flickering glow, finally grunting scornfully.

"This is all bullshit!"

"Better than we might have hoped for." The hard copy was passport confirmations, letters of marque, and a permit signed by the chairman of the Security Council; accompanying them were copies of the financial arrangement Ellis had bargained out.

"Better, you say? Then you're a poor judge of a stinking deal!"

"You're wrong, John." Ellis kept his face stern and lowered his voice. "We're backed by powerful factions now, you and I. Otis le Grande's put credit into our voyage—without him I couldn't've raised a crew. Capital's come from Cassabian too, and there's the money I took from Okubo. Our mission may not be official, but we're watched for, and our dealings will be closely followed at home."

Oujuku thrust the hard copy back at him. "You're fucking crazy! Jeezus God, the President's seal comes at a helluva price! With so many ways to cut the apple pie, we'll be lucky to come out with a bite."

Ellis felt his anger rise unstoppably. "Look further than your nose, John. There's more to this than the credit involved!"

"Is that a fact?"

"Sure. Don't you see? There's no alternative."

"No?" Oujuku squared with him. "We could choose piracy! Then what we do is totally to our own advantage!"

"Come on! This is a better way. We're Alia Kane's instrument of policy. If I've read her intentions correctly, we have permission to punish Yamato just as we see fit, so long as when we come home we turn a profit, and so long as we turn half of it over to her."

"Sheeee-it!"

Oujuku's face set in a mask of grim mistrust, and Ellis went on. "Because we're financed by private subscription we're unaccountable to the Security Council. That means we bypass Lubbock's—the VP's—authority. We're free to conduct a private war, with profit at its center, and free to take from Yamato anything we can shift."

"And if we fall into Yamato's hands?"

"The President'll deny all knowledge of us."

Oujuku spat. His voice dropped scornfully. "That's a real balanced deal you've got us there, Ellis. You begin to sound like Hawken. The government risks nothing and gets half. What do we get by alliance with Alia Kane?"

"We keep our asses when we get home. Total amnesty. Protection. And leave to walk about in Lincoln as rich men."

"Ha! I can nexus-hop to a pretty fine planet up beyond the Europa chain—Suisse—and live there just as happily!"

"Never more to see Amerika or your wife?"

Oujuku's defiance stood firm. "She can easily be sent for, or brought out by a contract man at a price. Yeah, and anyone else who wants to visit me."

"And how will you spend your credit on Suisse? What will you spend it on? Get a big ranch? Get a Bristol air-car or two? Buy yourself some friends? Hell, John, you don't ski and you don't even speak French!"

Oujuku grunted, and Ellis saw that his tantrum had blown itself out. They sat down and he came again with his plan, more coolly now. "Our duty is to Amerika. We're all moths flying round the President's flame, and the Security Council is the window through which we can fly in. Those fifteen people watch after Amerika as if it was a lover, jealous of everything—mostly one another. Think! We want credit and revenge, and, after that, status among our own kind and the knowledge that we kept the Emperor's greedy hands off Amerikan liberties. That's what the new star foretells for us. We'll carry home enough of Yamato's ill-gotten glory to bankrupt her economy."

"But a clear half of all we take, Ellis! It's fucking usury!"

Ellis picked up several small white cockleshells from the sand. "Don't imagine the government's motive is avarice."

"Oh, yeah?"

"From each pound of aurium we bring home, they'll take a sixth for the maintenance of the Navy fleet at Harrisburg." He threw a shell away. "And another for the shafting of Yamato's plots in Korea; and a twelfth to loan to the independent Korean leadership; and another twelfth to help the insurgents in Hainan." The last shell he held up significantly. "D'you see now?"

"Alia Kane confided all this personally to you, did she? You who's spent the last God-knows-how-long being a guest in Camp Worth, and almost had your ass freezeed by her?"

"Yep. I spoke with her directly."

Oujuku levered himself to his feet, shook his head. "Oh, yeah! They use the Probe on you, or something?"

"Jos Hawken is very well connected."

"Yeah! Jos Hawken is!" Oujuku's voice was edged with steel. "But you said you spoke *with the President herself!*"

"You better believe it."

"I don't believe Hawken. And I've got my own schemes that won't cost me a bloodsucking." Oujuku stabbed a savage finger toward the zenith. "There's *Constitution*—Hawken's ship. Built to his specifications. I think he's using you, Ellis."

"He has talent in that line. Also the services of the finest ship designers in Amerika—which means the finest, period. But *Constitution* is mine."

Oujuku took a deep breath. "Can you satisfy me that Jos Hawken isn't still working you like a puppet?"

Ellis's chest swelled up. "Is this a puppet you see standing here?"

"I don't know. But I don't believe you. Or you've not told me the whole story yet. Hey, Ellis! Aren't we confidential with each other anymore?"

The pause between them dragged out, tormenting Ellis until he felt he must break it.

"I was sworn to silence."

"I knew it! And we're sworn to be straight with one another."

"Okeh, Jos Hawken never had a part in any of this. If you want to know the reason, then I'll tell you: I was in love!"

"In love? You?"

Ellis caught Oujuku's surprise, and the angry part of him got hot. He gestured at Oujuku dangerously. "Yes! Me! In love! And I married—in spirit—just as you did in body and soul."

In the light of the fires, Ellis's face was as hard as iron. The words spilled from him, telling how he had come to love the secretary of state's daughter, how he had pursued her and played a dangerous game under Conroy Lubbock's nose. He finished, stilting his words, and sat down again on the powdery ground, his head in his hands.

Oujuku was shaking his head in wonder. "You *crafty* sonofabitch!"

"She was married to Kurt Reiner, the Halide heir, in St. Anthony's before I left Liberty. With Alia Kane in attendance, and a guest list like Who Knows Who. And my son was in that bride's belly." He lifted his head, staring at the painfully bright point in the nameless constellation. "You see that star? It shines for my boy. It's his star. But when he's born there'll be a better bed for him to sleep in than the one this nexus rat could give him. There'll be wise men enough around him. And the President herself will be his godmother.''

The waves lapped slowly on the gently curving, shallowly sloping beach. Some of the fires had burned down to embers, some of the people were stretched out, ankles crossed, elbows out from their ears. Others had crept away into the darkness. Some told likely tales, still others laughed at them. Happy crews with an adventure ahead of them and no cares about tomorrow.

"I want my brother, John."

"I know you do."

"Are you gonna help me or hinder me? I must know which, because with you or without you I mean to get him back."

Oujuku sighed. "You can't now."

"I can. There's not a man alive that can't be ransomed out of Yamato if the price is right."

"No."

"Listen, if—"

"No, Ellis. No!" Oujuku laid hands on him.

"Why no? Explain."

"Just this: I've had a little news of my own. News you won't find a whole lot to your liking."

Oujuku shouted for Frane, who went on his errand, reporting back with another of Oujuku's crewmen. Despite the way the man's cheeks had caved in with the loss of his teeth, Ellis recognised him immediately.

"Good God, aren't you—"

Oujuku cut in. "I hoped to be able to spare you this, Ellis, but you won't be put off," he said, then he turned to Horse. "Tell Captain Straker the same tale that you told to me."

"Okeh."

Ellis listened silently but with mounting dread as Horse recounted his story. He spoke about Chi no Tsuki and Sado, and how he had been imprisoned by Nishima Jun. Then he spoke of his working in the argentium refineries, but this was only preamble to a more shocking tale. When he told of his visit to the *han* of Hasegawa, his march to the great volcano Fuji-san, and his subsequent escape offplanet, Ellis felt hollow inside. He was unable to speak.

Oujuku questioned the isotopist some more, then dismissed

him. When they were alone again, Oujuku said, ''We picked him up when we took a trader bound for the Marquesas chain. He was working his passage, calling himself a German isotopist, looking to get to Europa, and eventually, so he says, to ship for home. I heard his story some two months back just as you've heard it now.''

''He's lying!''

''No, Ellis.''

''He's lying, I tell you!''

''Why would he lie? For what reason? Eh?''

Ellis's mind boiled with impossible explanations. The shame of it! It couldn't be true. Not Duval. Not his own brother—making secret weapons for Yamato? A big thing going with a Japanese woman? No, it was Oujuku's lies! All Oujuku. He'd put the man up to it! Yes.

''You've set me up—''

Oujuku leaned back, his face showing his compassion. ''It's no setup. You know the isotopist. You know he went to Sado four years ago. He's got no reason to lie.''

''No. I don't believe him.''

''All right, maybe you'll believe this.'' Oujuku pulled out the ring. Its gold glittered in Oujuku's palm. It was the same ring Ellis had once passed to Chambers. ''It went from Jon Chambers's hand to your brother, and from him it was taken by Horse in their struggle on the volcano, and from him to me. You'll have to face it, Ellis: your brother's made a fool out of you.''

Ellis twisted the ring over and over in his fingers, burning with humiliation. By God, how could Duval have done it? According to Horse, they had not tortured him or put him to the Probe. He had given up his priceless design skills freely.

''I can't believe it,'' he whispered, knowing it was a lie.

''He's made fools of us all''—Ellis tried to shut out Oujuku's words but they came at him like relentless daggers—''and he'll do so again.'' Oujuku spoke flatly, but he could not keep the reproach out of his voice. ''Once Sado and Okinawa and Dozen and all the other ports along the Boundary are fortified with singularity guns, we can kiss goodbye to any more raids. We'll be reduced to scavenging orbit ships and thieving nickel-'n'-dime traders and running like shit from the Yamato Guard—''

''Jeezus, that's enough!''

''I'm sorry, Ellis. But you had to know.''

Oujuku walked away, went back to his bonfire, and Ellis let him go. His plans were in ruins.

And his soul was in hell.

SADO

The daimyo's apartments were in darkness. Nishima Jun lay on his cushions, his satisfactions over the work of fortifying Sado temporarily driven from his mind by a maddening sexual itch. It took all his willpower to turn his mind away from the deliciously illicit liaison he had entered into six days ago.

The supple young body of the Taiwanese girl. Her full lips and black eyes. The wispy hair of her pubis. The fire of her *sangokujin* blood. Her resistance. How he had delighted to break that down, to smother her protests, to threaten her and then promise her, to take her and enter her and sate himself, and then to order her not to run away, not to tell anyone. Or her family would all suffer.

He wanted her again—such a delight—once, twice, three times a week. Oh, the smell of her. He could take her daily. Twice daily. "Wei," he whispered, pronouncing the syllable of her name slowly, repeatedly, enjoying the way it sighed across his tongue.

What if she tells? What if she has my bastard? he asked himself, suddenly disturbed that he could be proud at the idea. That would show Fumiko. If ever she found out. If ever. But that's why I spilled my seed outside the maid's love tunnel. I must be careful. It's too dangerous these days. A man must be oh-so-careful! Because fornication with a *sangokujin* is not the way a daimyo should conduct himself. It is contrary to the Confucian ideal, and only death and disgrace can come of it. No one is immune from the *kempei* now.

His thoughts went brooding out over the night's darkness, across the sculpted roofs of the city to the place where the *kempei* had installed itself, and he knew he had made a serious tactical mistake. He could not afford to have them know of his weakness. No, that would upset everything.

He heard footsteps through the wall behind him, but no challenge from the guard. The shoji slid open, Fumiko came in, and the attendant closed it after her. She approached him, put her hands together, standing so close that the folds of her long robe touched his oiled swept-back hair.

"This heat!"

"Does it keep you awake, Fumiko-san?" His reply was ice cold.

"Don't you want to go to bed?"

"I'm not tired."

She faced the spray of willow fronds that arched from a fine porcelain vase. "A marriage bed is not only for sleeping, Jun-chan."

He drew in a loud breath and moved away from her, but continued to stare out of the open window. Oh, how the sound of her voice drained his desire. *Wei.*

"The law commands men and women to—"

"I know what the law commands."

"Then why don't you obey?" Her voice was hope-lorn.

He tried to smile. "What would be the point? You are barren, Fumiko-san. We both know that."

"But I've completed another application. I've received permission for an operation. Three nights in the medical center on Kyoto, if you will only agree. A new womb and ovaries. The gods have favored me, the donor is samurai. It's certain to be a success. Please, Jun-chan, can we make love tonight. For my sake?"

"Not tonight."

Her words hardened, cut at him as she turned away. "You're the one who's afflicted. You have no love of duty in your heart. You're not a real man."

Always the same. Blaming him. If only she knew. If only she had seen the copious seed that had gushed over the belly of the maid. Potent seed. He had been stiff enough this afternoon. Poor, clever, studious, barren Fumiko. Couldn't she understand that no transplant could make her desirable. To use another woman's ovaries was merely to be a bearer of counterfeit genetic currency. He would never desire her. He would never give her a child.

"Go to bed, Fumiko-san."

But she had already begun to leave the room.

He lay back, rubbed at his eyes. He was tired, but he had to unknot the problem before he surrendered to sleep. Go over it again, he told himself. Once more to get it clear. From the beginning.

The first ominous sign of trouble had come when the *kin kaigun* had landed. News of Fukuda's arrival had preceded his appearance in Kanazawa by two weeks, wild rumors carried across the continent from Niigata that had inflamed the whole planet like a disease. Immediately a committee of samurai worthies had formed and he had agreed to meet with it, ostensibly to prepare a welcome for the distinguished *metsuke*, but the true function of the meetings had been otherwise.

The coming of the *kempei* had long been dreaded by the *han*-holders who were already established in the Co-prosperity Sphere, and would be greeted frostily by many of the samurai who had pioneered it. In all the years since the conquest never had they been subject to the control of the *kempei*. In all those years Kyoto had respected the status of the worlds beyond the official limits of Yamato. As a matter of practicality the men who were the source of the Emperor's wealth were spared the spiritual policing so necessary inside Yamato itself where mixed bloods and secret *sangokujin* had to be rigorously controlled. But over the years the inspectors general had been able to build up an irresistible pressure on the Emperor's government. They had used their unearthly influence on the shogun, who in turn had approached the Emperor, and so the hand of the *kempei* had reached out across the nexi and come at last to Sado.

Nishima recalled with sour regret the way he had recognised the threat the *kempei* posed to his own temporal powers. He had seen a way to accommodate the office, and to deflect for the moment the fears of his *hatamoto*, but the committee of worthies had been right about giving the office a single grain of rice and expecting them to be content with it.

Fukuda had virtually requisitioned the grand house across the main square, next to the shrine, and decided that it was best to call to question first the famous Amerikan interlopers—especially those that had become integrated into the fabric of life on Sado.

The orders had been read out and notice given that the Amerikans were suspected of impurities and must come to account for themselves. They were sent for and searched out in all parts of Sado, and proclamations made, upon pain of confiscation and exile, that no person should keep secret any *gaijin*.

At first, Nishima had done nothing. He had taken no steps to protect his investment, deciding that discretion might be a more effective policy. He had sent Hasegawa Katsumi to speak with his father about the weapon-designer, and to reassure the family, but nothing more. After all, wasn't he now an adopted husband? Hadn't he taken marriage vows and been doubly confirmed in his spiritual purity by absorption into the highly respectable Hasegawa clan? The man had a new name. He applied himself assiduously to his work. He was confined on the *han*. With luck, Nishima had thought, it could be years before the *kempei* came to Chiba.

But Duval had been betrayed. By whom, it did not matter. A servant, a priest, one of his own men, another of the Amerikans who knew where he was, had learned of his work and chosen to point the finger at him . . . Whatever the means, the *kempei* had found out about him and he had been taken.

At this point Nishima had pressed his daimyo's privileges. As proconsul to the *bakufu* he had certain rights, could make certain small demands. He had indulgently explained about the new guns. "A matter of the utmost strategic importance, Fukuda-san. I'm sure you understand?"

But the *metsuke* had stared back unmoved. At their second formal meeting, Fukuda had been at pains to clarify his position. "Your Exalted Excellency may be the tool of government, but please remember that our office is the instrument of the Emperor himself."

"Of course, and we agreed that all *gaijin* should be exposed. But this man is not a *gaijin*."

"Agreed?" Fukuda had echoed, leaning back without any hint of his former amity. "I was not aware of any agreement between us. The term '*gaijin*' includes so-called adopted husbands and all those who cannot trace their ancestry to Old Nihon through the paternal line."

"Please excuse me!" he had cajoled, pricked by Fukuda's

inflexibility. He had swallowed his pride again. "How can that be? This man is an adopted husband. He's given up his identity completely. His old life is over, his former self is dead. He's as good a Yamato citizen as I am."

"Indeed?" Fukuda had paused significantly until the debating point was both scored and acknowledged. "I salute Your Excellency's noble efforts on our behalf, but I must point out that accurate measures of depth of belief and sincerity of conviction are quite impossible. However, that small and worthless skill in inquiry that a *metsuke* such as myself possesses must now be applied. If the gods allow it, an interesting outcome may result."

He had sighed, humbling himself further. "But surely this one man, who may do His Imperial Majesty great service? Surely he could be overlooked?"

Then the *metsuke* had laid the closely written scroll open to his inspection, passing a hand over the names. "It is the Emperor's will that all—*all*—herein proscribed shall be brought captive to the city of Kanazawa and committed separately to prison cells to undergo examination."

"And if you should find him pure, Fukuda-san?"

"Ah." Fukuda's smile had shocked him with its ugliness. "If he was found to be pure, then we should release him. But who amongst the living is really pure?"

"I'm gratified, Fukuda-san," he had said, readying himself to leave. "Gratified, and so pleased we understand one another."

Nishima's eyes continued to dwell on the house whose plex annex had become a prison, one cell of which held the man who remained the key to military victory. It's too bad, he thought, scratching at his scrotum vigorously. I tried. But the Amerikan's survival is probably no longer an issue. He's served his purpose now; his gun secrets have almost certainly been learned by his team. I pray to the gods that that's so, because I'll wager a ball of aurium to a bamboo cup that he'll never get out of that house alive.

He examined his fingernails in the muted light and a frown clouded his face. "Wei! You filthy young whore," he muttered, suddenly realising about the prickling at his groin. "She's lousy. And the disgusting little *sangokujin* has made me lousy too!"

10

"Do you believe in the divinity of the Emperor, Duval Straker?"

The inspector general, a small, gray man in purple robes, knelt on a slightly raised rostrum. To his right sat another, Hishikari, a severe, heavy-browed man in his late forties, in a black kimono decorated with gray barred-spiral galaxies as a repeated motif, crossed tightly at the neck and stiffly winged at the shoulder. He was silent, staring down at his papers. To the left, Wada, a younger man in plain brown, taking notes with practiced ease into a five-finger keypad as they spoke, and in the shadows at the side, seated against the wall, a big man in a loose black *haori* robe. Another, whose name was Suzuki, was concealed behind a black lacquer and mother-of-pearl screen.

On the low table, which was spread neatly with a cloth of white silk, stood a small replica of the *gohei*, an ink block and brushes, some hardcopy sheets, and a half-unsheathed disemboweling sword. Alone in the center of the table was a scroll containing the *metsuke*'s imperial mandate.

"I ask you again: do you believe in the divinity of the Emperor?"

"Yes."

"Witnesses say that you do not."

"What witnesses?"

The man seated to the inspector general's right spoke. "Many good people offer themselves to our service. A person needs only a clean heredity to help our office discover error."

"Who informed on me?"

"It is our rule never to say."

"Tell me who alleges I am impure now."

"We do not break rules. We adhere to our methods."

"What is the specific charge?"

"It is our practice not to divulge that."

"Then how may I defend myself?"

"It is not for you to prepare defenses, only to answer our inquiries with the whole truth."

"Do you believe in the divinity of the Emperor?"

Duval's thirst raged, blood pounded in his head, and the light from the translucent walls pierced him. He had been confined in absolute blackness for a long time. How long? Three months? Six? Nine? It was impossible to say. The trailing of the inked brush over the sheets fascinated him, the sound plucking his nerves raw. He watched the soft light sharpen on the semi-revealed edge of the *seppuku* knife, glinting at him as the questions were repeated endlessly, the same questions put to him time after time until he longed to answer them with other words.

On the striking of a large, distant gong, a new question.

"Tell us about yourself."

"There is nothing to tell."

"Every man has one story to tell."

"Some have more than one," Hishikari Noburo said.

"Can you read Japanese?"

"Yes."

"And write?"

"Yes."

"How many *kanji* do you know?"

"I don't know—four, maybe five thousand."

"You know what this is?"

"Of course. It's a writing brush."

"Take it."

"Why?"

"Take it with you to your cell. A lamp will be allowed. You will record for us a full confession of your life. Every detail, exactly as you recall it. Not until that is done and we have examined it will you be brought before us again."

"And if I refuse?"

"You will not refuse."

*　　*　　*

He ached all over.

He could not tell if it was night or day. He might have been here a month or six months or a year, but there was no way to tell, no regularity about the appearance of rice and water or the times when that intense, blinding blue lamp was lit for him. No natural light penetrated to the hot, humid cell, but still the flies found their way in through the ventilators, attracted by the stench in the corner.

His ears were sharp to the sounds that came from beyond the seamless door, muffled sounds, as if the feet of the guards were bare to deaden their noise. They had ordered him to make no sound, and they had beat the soles of his feet to insensation when he had disobeyed. No one spoke outside, though often he could hear them faintly, passing by. No human sounds, except a distant coughing, a wretching, or the screams that trailed away beyond another muffled door.

How long before they came to beat him again? The dread kept him awake interminably until his mind grew as heavy as aurium and his thoughts melted into chaos. Am I ill? he asked himself, unable to understand the incredible lassitude that filled him. Am I dying? Have they drugged the water? Have they given me a disease?

He lay back, imagining the room upside down, that he was falling. He dreamed that he was dreaming fractured dreams on the frayed and fetid tatami that served as his bed. He felt the need to relieve himself, but he could not get up, could not will his legs to lift him. He had written the confession after the third beating, filling the sheets with every item of his past that he could recall, and after that they had come and collected the sheets but left him in his corner. He felt the pressure in his bladder, but he could not move and he could not raise the effort to halt the unmistakable series of relaxations in his belly. He tried to hold his muscles shut, but it was too late, and he felt the hot urine flood his groin and the smell was rich and dark and uric, but he could do nothing except lie there and tell himself that it did not matter because it was not real and that the nightmare was only a nightmare.

* * *

When he was called again into that intense light before the *metsuke*, they told him quietly that they had read all the sheets he had written. They were seated as before, and they told him their names as before, and examined him and commanded him to explain for them certain Zen *koans*, or riddles, which he could have responded to at one time with ease, but somehow as he addressed the words he found his mind wandering, and they gave him some water so that he could continue like a man and not caw like a crow. He thought of Helene di Barrio and the rest. A great many, he knew, would be able to make nothing of a Zen *koan,* other than to call it a half-assed piece of mystical bullshit.

Then they demanded in thin, flat voices, "What is the sound of one hand clapping?"

"The sound of the wind from nowhere."

"Where is this nowhere?"

Duval said nothing.

"Answer."

"If I must answer, then nowhere is the place the darkness goes when the light is turned on."

"Do you believe in the divinity of the Emperor?"

"I do." It was true. In one way, Mutsuhito *was* a god.

"Ai-ee!" The one called Suzuki exploded with anger. "You're lying, trying to save your life. You know that if you answered as you truly believed, you would die."

"I want to die."

"What were you taught as a child?"

"To believe in logic."

"Nothing else?"

"To believe there are many ways, all valid. To believe in the fundamental rights of mankind."

"*So desu ka?* Truly? You were forced to believe these lies?"

"In Amerika there is no compulsion to believe."

"Then where did you find such chaotic ideas?"

Duval swallowed, aware that he was being maneuvered into a trap of self-condemnation. He said, "My childhood was poor. Deficient in all kinds of learning. Which was no fault of mine."

"But as an adult you did not correct your errors? Why was that?"

"In all my days in Amerika, no one questioned me as you have."

"There are many errors in Amerika."

"The minds there are never silent."

"*So desu ne.* I agree. Who commands that?"

"It is the Way of Amerika."

"An impure way!"

"A different way."

"In Amerika there is no understanding!"

"There is no *bushido*."

"Therefore, there can be no honor."

Silence.

"You and the other Amerikans allowed yourself to be captured in battle. This is the real reason why you are now so obedient to the Way. You are dead."

"This is not so."

He began to shiver, his teeth chattering together like ivory dice.

"Explain!"

"The people first imprisoned by the authorities were freely exchanged hostages. The people who were brought down from Chi no Tsuki were marooned. I was not captured in battle. I was arrested several days after the battle whilst trying to obtain food."

"Then your status is that of a thief."

"Attempted thief."

"There is no such status as attempted thief. Yamato law does not concern itself with motives, only behavior."

"Then I am not a thief."

Fukuda stirred, his purple robe crackling as he adjusted a fold in the sleeve. "It is not our purpose to inquire into your status in law, only your state of purity. You may know that it is not possible for a man to become a *go* grand master unless he begins to play the game regularly before the age of five. So it is with the Way."

"I had no control over where I was born."

"The fact remains: you spent a quarter century in total ignorance of the Way."

"Not in total ignorance. There were some writings on *bushido* available. The *Go Rin No Sho* is a book found in many libraries in Amerika in English translation."

"Do you know how much you have revealed your ignorance by that remark? Japanese is much more complex and subtle than any barbarian language. Japanese cannot be successfully translated into any barbarian language. It is impossible to render an ancient classic like the *Go Rin No Sho* into English."

"Some people in Amerika learn to speak Japanese, just as I learned."

"You learned this as an intellectual exercise?"

"Partly."

"Yes or no?"

"Yes."

"Was it not to distinguish yourself from those who willingly remained ignorant?"

"We did not consider ourselves ignorant. Amerikans think there are many ways, and that all ways are valid."

"You behaved and believed according to that philosophy?"

"I behaved and believed as everyone around me did."

"*Wakarimashita!* Ah, as a sheep does?"

"As people do."

"Yet you say there was no compulsion of belief in Amerika?"

"It is the law in Amerika to guarantee all men and women certain fundamental rights and freedoms."

"Such an idea is dangerous and repellent. Law and order of this kind is an attempt to pervert the natural order!"

"There is a saying in English: no man is an island. It means that we are none of us isolated. We are all affected by the context in which we live."

"Then you admit that you did not behave and believe of your own free will."

"How could I?"

"So you were acting contrary to your culture's imperatives."

Another asked him, "Were there never days when you had doubts? Never days when you preferred not to endure the foolish ideas of rights without duties?"

"There were no days like that."

"Were you taught about the Way?"

"Not formally."

"You had a word for racial Japanese?"

"We called them Yambos."

"Do you believe in the divinity of the Emperor?"

"Yes."

"Open your eyes."

Hishikari consulted the sheet, adjusting it to the light. "I read your history and I ask myself this: what can account for the recent change in your convictions?"

Wada Zengo, the recorder, explained. "We find as the honorable ancients found before us that the mind of man is as a clay vessel, malleable at the first throwing upon the potter's wheel, but as a man ages so the vessel is fired. The form is imprinted indelibly and may no longer change."

"And when pressure is applied," Hishikari added unsmilingly, "the vessel shatters."

"And yet you say you changed, Duval Straker," Fukuda said. "And you did not shatter."

"My beliefs are as changed as my name, which is Hasegawa Zinan."

"*Masaka!* It is no matter to change a man's name."

Wada said, "All criminals maintain aliases."

"I am not a criminal."

"And alibis."

"I am not a criminal!"

Hishikari slapped the signed sheet before him. "Is this your alibi, Duval Straker?"

"It is the truth, as you asked it of me."

"Strange, then, that it does not accord with the confessions of certain other Amerikans."

"What?"

"They condemn you."

"That is their fear talking."

"Do you have no fear?"

This time he did not answer.

Then Fukuda asked, "Did you agree to become an adopted husband of Hasegawa Michie only that you might be allowed to live?"

He stared at them, his anger suddenly stronger than his fear or his exhaustion, but the mention of his wife's name sent shivers of panic through him.

"If you will only tell us the truth, you will be set at liberty."

"I have told you the truth."

"Are you sorry for the infractions and offenses you committed in Niigata against the imperial government of Yamato?"

"By the gods it was nothing to do with me!"

"Why did you make no mention in your confessions of your Japanese heritage?"

"What are you saying?"

"We have carried out a genetic test and found you to be half Japanese."

"Impossible. There's been some mistake."

"I warn you again to tell the truth."

"Probe him!" Hishikari demanded.

"Must we Probe you?"

He knuckled his eyes, his mouth was dry again.

Fukuda renewed his question, his voice cooing now, redolent with regret that such action was necessary and unavoidable. "Must we?"

"Yes!" Hishikari shouted.

"If only you would be frank with me and make a sincere confession."

"I have told you everything."

"Oh, wicked half man. Show him what is coming."

* * *

They had recruited *hinin* and Koreans for their stainless-steel shop of terrors, and some who enjoyed watching the pain brought up in others.

An electric branding rod glowed red in its stand, and liquid crystal tattoo inserters and other implant instruments. This place was where the *han* administration office had once IDed slaves, but now its function had been taken over by the *kempei*. Through the window, he recognised the horrible twisted figure of Jeff Smith hanging unconscious from a punishment frame, his marked body suspended upside down. He had been there some time: the blood had pooled in his head, making his face purple, and rivers of dried blood patterned his body. It was not possible to tell if he was still alive.

They took him past a side room, where Kentwell Harper's naked body was bound to a bench, his head confined in a hood, his nostrils plugged with cotton, his throat packed, and water was being dripped into his mouth through a funnel. Next door Kai Boscovitch's feet had been smashed with hammers. Her face was a hideous yellow. As they dragged Duval into the room, a pail of water was thrown over her, rousing her to groans. The steel frame below was bloodied, and she screamed at the sight of her broken legs, unable to stop.

A Shinto priest stood at Boscovitch's side, with the *gohei* held up before him.

"Help me! Oh God, help me!"

"*Doshi mashita?!*"

"Help me!"

"*Yorokonde.*"

"I'll do anything." The victim screamed again, her eyes popping, her breath pumping. "Anything!"

"But the truth is what we require."

"The truth . . ."

"She's fainted again, Hishikari-san."

"Here's another. He is special. You will Probe him."

"Yes, Hishikari-san."

They made him look at the Probe, secured his ankles and his wrists, gagged his mouth, levering his teeth open so that the packing filled his mouth like a horse's bit, and twisted it tight, then the cage was put over his head, the mechanism clicking as they turned the machine on.

Where are you, Michie? he thought, his brain beginning to blind with terror. Are you thinking of me?

And then the true agony started.

11

Michie had not hesitated to steal either the heirlooms or the air-car. She had finally broken free from the confinement her family had imposed on her at Chiba and come to the city of Kanazawa to do what she could. Night and day she had lingered outside the daimyo's residence with her petition, but the guards would not admit her without authority and she had not dared to reveal her identity for fear that her father's searchers would find her.

She had fixed her hopes on Katsumi. Surely her brother must help her. Surely he would fix her an interview with Lord Nishima. But when she asked after him, they told her the honorable officer was far away in Niigata.

Friendless, the city was a changed place. A dark pall of fear had fallen over it. Well-to-do samurai doors were barred against her. Few dared listen to her pleas, and those who did professed themselves as helpless as she was, or took the opportunity to remind her of her father's foolishness in ever thinking to marry her to a barbarian. Some even tried to trap her, to send her back to Chiba. So she had fled.

She had sold the conspicuous air-car for a robber's price and got herself lodging at an inn in a bad part of town. Here technology was either banned or shunned. The town was a mass of semitraditional-style shanties all tumbled one upon another. She had dressed in the white false silk of a low-class widow, but her bearing and mannerisms constantly gave her away. The fawning servility of the lower orders had evaporated here. In their own territory and with no samurai to watch them they were tough-bodied and flint-eyed and their language stung like salt in a wound. She endured the whispers of the street. The *ikki* women thought her mad. They gossiped acidly at her misfortune and speculated at what had given her delusions of samurai status. She could not really be samurai—could she? She bore unflinchingly the stones of *hinin* children who made faces at her and danced out their parents' superstitious hatred insolently in front of her. And the stinking drunks that encountered her at night pressed themselves on her when they saw her fine looks, making foul suggestions and pawing her until she showed them the razor-edged short sword she kept concealed in her robe.

There had been talk. Her father's people had heard the rumor. Yukiko, her maid, and two of her mother's servants had laid hands on her to bring her away, but she would not surrender herself, telling them that they should help her rather than hinder her, but they only repeated what her father had said. So she had pulled out her *aikuchi* dagger and threatened to spill her own blood if they did not let her run from them.

So she had come at last in utter desperation to the domicile of Wataru Hoshino.

"Please, Wataru-san! You must help me!"

"Come in, Lady. Come in."

He had made a place on his floor for her and offered her green tea and noodle soup, which she would not eat, and apologised for his humble home, smiling toothlessly but compassionately, until her tears dried.

"What can be done for you now?" he asked, facing her across his low table, stroking the long, graying head of his old dog. The heady stink of dog permeated the room, and dog hairs were stuck into the weave of the tatami. Through the slightly parted door, on the other side of the street, she could see a tattooed *yakuza* delicately stripping the insulation from a humming 550-volt power cable with a knife, prior to making an illegal tap.

"You know that Zinan-san is imprisoned," she said.

"I heard the proclamation, Lady."

"I must try to save him."

He patted the dog's head and clasped his hands together. "In your heart you believe that to save him now is too much to hope for."

"No!" Her face was white, drawn with anguish and lack of sleep. "I can't believe that. I must not believe that. They are going to crucify him, Wataru-san. Do you understand? *They are going to crucify my husband.*"

"Hush, hush."

"Wataru Hoshino, you are an honorable man. You have been a soldier. You must help me or I shall die by my own hand!"

"Quiet, now, Lady. Listen to yourself! Are you not a daughter of the Hasegawa clan? I will help you. Take courage. And plan, as your father would plan, to think how you might make the *metsuke* change his decision. But take care also for your own life. Those black priests will see your devotion only as the taint of the *gaijin*."

She nodded rapidly, recognising the wise counsel of an old man. "I must find a way to see Fukuda, explain to him that Zinan is a true subject of the Emperor, that our marriage was real. But the guards he has posted on his door will not admit me."

Wataru put up his hands. "No, Lady! You must not go to Fukuda Ikku."

"But if any man can reverse the decision of the tribunal, surely it is he."

Wataru's eyes clouded. "There is nothing you can offer him that will change his mind."

Michie reached inside her robe and took from it a leather bag. She opened it and spilled a glittering assortment of super-heavy nuggets across the scarred wood: aurium, argentium, and small, green-tinted nodules of native platinium. "Look! These can be his ransom."

"I don't think so, Lady."

She went on breathlessly in fervent hope. "But I have been

told that Fukuda's rapacity is boundless. Doesn't the *kempei* finance itself through confiscation? These are not conterfeit, they are completely genuine and worth exceptional credit!''

''Then, for your own sake, Lady, do not show any of them to Fukuda Ikku.''

''But—''

Wataru was shaking his head. ''I have seen the *metsuke*'s like before. And in Niigata the men who came on the last *kin kaigun* told me about the time his zeal was unleashed on board Admiral Kurita's flagship. No, Lady, he is a complete fanatic. You cannot bargain with him. If once you show him your pretty nuggets, he will take them. Then he will be forced to commit you to his prison to cover his theft.''

''But how, then?''

''We have few allies in this battle, Lady.''

''Even Katsumi is in Niigata.'' Her mouth twisted with bitterness. ''All of those who I thought were my friends have deserted me. I could hardly believe their cowardice.''

''Don't fault them. They are scared. You must see that when the Amerikans are used up, the *kempei* will begin looking for others to indict.''

A canyon of silence opened.

''So Zinan-san must die?''

Wataru's head lifted on his shoulders. ''Do not lose hope.''

''Do you think he will escape?''

''He's imprisoned alone and well guarded in a prison with plex walls. He cannot escape. But—''

''Yes?''

Her eyes were luminous with tears; her whole being hung on what the old man was about to say.

''I know one thing, Lady. Your brother, Katsumi, is certainly not in Niigata.''

Then he told her what she must do.

*   *   *

The city square was in darkness as she ran through it. The sculptured roof of the daimyo's residence stood out starkly against the star-peppered sky, and the wooden edifice of the *kempei*'s punishment stage was eerie and empty. At the gates she was stopped by the guard, who looked at her *ikki* garments and denied her entry.

''Go away, woman! You cannot come here.''

The guard was armored, a soldier but not a samurai, with pocked face and tattered beard.

"How dare you speak to me in that manner?"

"Go, woman, before we set the dogs on you." The other, a man of slighter build and shorter ways, thrust his torch into her face. "Go!"

She stood her ground. "I am the sister of Hasegawa Katsumi. I must speak with him."

The first guard shifted his weight and peered at her, apparently unconvinced, but when he spoke, his mode of address had altered. "The man you name is not here, Lady."

"Don't lie to me, soldier."

"He is not here, I tell you."

She produced a nugget of bluish metal and held it up so that it reflected the torchlight brilliantly. "This says that Hasegawa Katsumi is dining with the daimyo tonight."

The slighter guard took the nugget and examined it, spitting on it and polishing it on his cotton sleeve. He looked about him and weighed the stone in his palm—there was no doubt it was aurium.

"I'll inform Hasegawa-san, Lady."

"Quickly."

He vanished and reappeared moments later with Katsumi, who was furious at the disturbance. He seized her roughly and brought her inside, out of earshot.

"Michie-san," he whispered fiercely, towering close over her. "Are you mad? What are you doing? Don't you know that our father is here in Kanazawa, combing the city for you? Where have you been?"

"I want to see the daimyo."

"Don't be stupid. That's impossible!"

"Katsumi-san, I must see him!"

He shook with anger, plucking out a hair and holding it at her. "Don't you *understand*? By the gods you are that far—*that far*—from getting us all impeached by the *kempei*. Thank the gods I've found you. Now your father can put you in hand."

"You didn't find me! I found you!" Her voice rang out in the timbered interior, then grew intense, pleading. "You must help me, Katsumi-san. If ever there was a time a sister needed her brother's help, it's now. Do not deny me, please!"

"Help you? What for? So you may find a way to get the Amerikan out of prison. You'll get us all killed and dishonored."

"He is your brother-in-law. Where is your duty?"

"I warned you at the very first not to look at him, Michie-san. But you disobeyed me."

"Hypocrite! Don't give me your lies. You brought him to me in the first place. And now, for fear of the *kempei* you deny all. Bring me to the daimyo, or I'll denounce you to the *metsuke* as a secret worshiper of the Christian God!"

"Sister, control yourself!"

She inclined her head and set her words in a deadly threat. "Take me to Nishima-sama, or I will do exactly as I have said."

All around faces appeared at corners. Doors cracked open. He hurried her deeper down the dimly lit corridors, to the heart of the residence, a quiet flagged quadrangle with moss rockery and stream, then he stopped again and implored her, his hands curling in the empty air at his breast. "Think carefully, I beg you. I have been to the daimyo once already, and I have heard his answer. He'll never back down. And if he did, what could he do? He has no authority over the *kempei* prison. Even he is powerless to save your—"

"Take me!" she shrieked, and the sound echoed like a *katsu* shout in a Zen temple.

He clapped his hand over her mouth and led her away to a great, carved wooden door, guarded by two sentries, who snapped to attention as they saw Katsumi's uniform. Neither looked at Michie, but gazed ahead, allowing the daimyo's principal lieutenant to pass. Inside, Saionji Hidemasa, the daimyo's chief *hatamoto,* was at his station.

"Excuse me. Is Nishima-sama within?" Katsumi asked without ceremony.

Saionji, a man in his forties with eyeglasses and a shock of sleek black hair, looked up slowly from his reading, appraising the grime-streaked woman who stood beside Katsumi. "He is, Hasegawa-san. So sorry, but you can't go in. The *metsuke*'s with him. Excuse me, but who's this?"

"Thank you." He looked dangerously at his sister, but when he turned for the exit back into the courtyard, she refused to follow.

"Michie-san—"

"So sorry. We'll wait," she blurted out.

"As you wish, woman." Saionji shrugged and sucked a tooth. "So sorry, but His Excellency may be quite some time. May I inquire the nature of your business?"

"So sorry. It's confidential."

"Very well."

Michie stood with her eyes downcast; Katsumi stood with his back to the secretary. His intense embarrassment that Saionji should see him thus exposed showed in the color of his face, which was reddening. He seemed to be waiting for Saionji to offer some slight, but the secretary merely unfolded the wires of his spectacles and looped them over his ears, allowing disdain to be suggested by his indifference.

Was Wataru-san right? she wondered. Was the inspector general so terrible? Should she throw herself on Fukuda Ikku's mercy when he appeared? What sort of man was he? Surely a man personally entrusted by the Emperor would have compassion. For the sake of her husband she would throw herself at his feet, beg him to reconsider, and the daimyo would add his voice to hers and Zinan would be saved.

The daimyo's door opened and everyone bowed low, holding their bows. Michie was surprised to have seen Fumiko standing at his side. Nishima-sama was subdued, almost reverential before the tiny man in purple.

She steeled herself, not daring to look up. This was the moment. If she was going to fall at the *metsuke*'s feet, it must be now.

As she raised her head, the daimyo looked up suddenly, seeing them for the first time, but his expression was so full of displeasure that she froze.

"What's she doing here?" he muttered furiously, touching Katsumi's sleeve, then he swept past with the *metsuke*, his wife conversing banally with him.

As the echoes of Fumiko's nasal tones died away, Saionji said to Katsumi, "So sorry, but I warned you that the lord was extremely busy tonight. Would you like to stay a little longer? I'm sure he'll be back presently."

"Thank you, but we'll leave now."

He grabbed her arm but she fought him off. "No! I won't go!"

When Nishima returned, he ordered Katsumi and his sister immediately into his sanctum. "Explain yourself, Hasegawa!"

"Excellency, I'm sorry. My sister—"

The daimyo turned his anger on her. "What are you doing here? Don't you know that your family's worried about you? That it's dangerous for you here?"

"I—I *had* to see you, Excellency," she stammered, terrified to be confronting him this way. "It's about my husband."

"What of it? He's under arrest. I can do nothing for him."

Fumiko came in, eyeing her coldly.

"Please, you must save him. For your own sake, Lord."

"What does she mean, Jun-san? Speak up, child."

"The weapons. It's the weapons. Zinan told me that he has kept the secret of how the gun is made in his head. Without knowledge of the general equation of state for the form of the compression chamber the facility cannot make others. If he dies you will not impress His Imperial Majesty with your work, and he will not order you back to Yamato."

The daimyo's eyes flashed to Katsumi. "Is this true?"

He made a helpless gesture. "I don't know, Excellency. It might be."

Fumiko watched her husband sit down on the tatami heavily and begin to stroke his moustache. Though they knelt to lower their heads below the daimyo's, Fumiko seethed with anger inside. You're a fool, Jun-san, she thought. Why didn't you stand up to Fukuda Ikku like a samurai of the first rank? Now we're both trapped here on this vile colony planet forever. I'll never see Kyoto again. Never. I hate you, Jun-san. I hate your weakness and your pride and the way you treat me. You think I don't know? I have eyes to see and ears to hear, and I am not a fool. God knows how many days and nights I've endured your humiliating me with your filthy *sangokujin* whores. Must I endure it forever? The Emperor will never have you back in Yamato until Prince Sekigahara, who aided you in your murder of Prince Kono, is dead. But Prince Sekigahara is not yet thirty years old, and his life is charmed in war. You will die, Jun-san, and I will die long before he does. You knew the new weapons were our only hope, and yet you let Fukuda Ikku take the Amerikan away. And tonight, instead of working for his release, you humbled yourself before that stinking little jumped-up priest. Don't you care that we're marooned here beyond the outermost edge of civilisation?

"Do you know why the inspector general was here tonight,

Michie-san?'' Nishima was saying. He was calmer now; regret edged his voice. ''Tonight I asked him for your husband's release, but he refused me. There is no legal way I can countermand him.''

''Then please try to find some other way. I beg you!''

''Hasegawa-san, take her to her father. She must understand that she can do no good here.''

''Yes, Excellency. Come here, Michie-san!''

Fumiko stepped forward. ''It would be better if you left her to me,'' she said. ''I know how to calm her. It's a woman's comfort she needs, not harsh words.''

The girl was shaking as she allowed herself to be led from the daimyo's rooms. When they were alone, Fumiko said, ''Tell me, child, how do you know that the Emperor would be reluctant to recall his daimyo from Sado should my husband desire that?''

Michie looked up at her, suddenly speared by the realisation that she had revealed her knowledge about the daimyo's past, but she seemed no longer to care. She said, ''I saw long ago that Nishima-sama's appointment here was in effect an exile and that he wanted the singularity gun as a means to recover the Emperor's favor.''

''That's very perceptive of you, Michie-san.''

''I know also that the Emperor sent him here because he committed a great crime, but at the same time he did a great service for His Imperial Majesty.''

''And do you know what that crime-and-service was?''

''No, Fumiko-san.''

The young woman's perfect oval face stared up at her unsettlingly, paining her unbearably. She might have had a daughter like Michie-san if she had not wed a man unwilling to give her permission for a transplant in twenty years of fruitless marriage. Jun-san has ruined my life, she thought as she watched those grief-reddened eyes. It is time he was made to pay.

''I will tell you the daimyo's crime,'' she said imperiously. ''Then, if you so desire, you may use that information to persuade him to help free your husband.''

12

THE OKINAWA SYSTEM, N.Z.

Ellis stood on *Constitution*'s tall tail fin at peace with the world, arms laced together, deep in contemplation. The morning on this idyllic world was cool and pleasant: the K-type star of this system low on the eastern horizon, lost in a great tangerine haze. Mists clung to the edges of the forest clearing in which they had set down. The plex underfoot was still wet with dew, undried as yet by the sun and smooth under his boots. Here and there on the broad wing, huge patterned moths shivered for warmth—green triangle wings, powdery mantles, feather antlers, thorn legs, and amethyst eyes. So beautiful. Each one the intricate handiwork of evolution. They had been blown out of the forest on the fetid breath that the jungle exhaled nightly, and Ellis wondered fleetingly how many countless millions of them were scattered as bird bait over the endless tracts of broadleaf in Okinawa's southern polar continent. Beautiful but wasted, unseen by any human eye. Wasted like the rain that fell over an ocean. Wasn't it strange that it rained at sea? A glitch in the efficiency of nature. An unknowably idiotic phenomenon but one that no terraformer had thought about bettering.

He took another turn about the tail plane, and his thoughts focused down on practicalities once more. His eyes followed the experimental stealth aerials. A new radio black dipole, four-stranded, twisted right to left, attached to a strange horn-like transmitter device, quite unlike anything he had seen before. The Yamato trader they had taken it out of had been rigged with it. "Ninja," the comms officer had called it, said it was brand-new and he didn't know how to switch it on. He ran his fingers over one of the dipoles where it was half-wave loaded. It had been his intention to renew the stealth equipment as necessary with a totally new rig, but he decided against it. After so long away, a man grew to know his own stealth gear, how it performed in space and under different magnetic conditions, how much it would take, where it would fail, and where it would go beyond spec. He had learned from Ayrton Rodrigo how to get the best from it, but this new Yamato stuff was reengineered and highly refined. Using it, a ship could be virtually invisible. And what had been built for shipping that wanted to avoid pirates could also be used by the pirates themselves.

Thoughts of Ayrton turned to thoughts of his brother. Horse's words haunted him now, shamed him with images of Duval sitting comfortably on some Sado *han* with a wife and his own research lab, making weapons for the enemy, *being* one of the enemy. After all the moments he had imagined Duval's peril, all the nights spent in Camp Worth worrying over the problem of his release like a dog at a bone; the defiance, the risks he had taken—and for what? It had soured him more deeply than anyone among Oujuku's crew, or his own, could know. The samurai had taken Duval bodily: that he could understand—for that he could almost forgive them man to man, could conceive bargaining Duval's release in civil terms. But they had cast a spell on his mind, the foul priests had suborned his spirit, and, by God, for that they must now pay.

But slowly, and by degrees, with planning and plenty of forethought he would descend on the Emperor and take from him due compensation. A brother's ransom it would never be, but he would take a million in credit from Yamato for each ounce of Duval's body weight.

Since the time he had assembled his crew around him, Ellis had worked on them like a hammer on white-hot metal, forming them to his principles. He had quietly told Tom Brophy and Leah Glass, his second-in-command, that leadership was an art he'd like them to learn.

Both were like Bowen, capable of being brought on. It was born in a person, but leadership could also be encouraged by good policy, and in combat it was essential that the team hauled together: "Make yourself respected by your sections. If they don't like you, then you have to use fear, and fear is a poor substitute. But either way, respect they *must* have for you. In punishments, an officer's anger has no place. In all cases, first have the problem put right by the wrongdoer as far as it can be done. Allow no disrespect against your subofficers and take a crack against one of them as you would against yourself. Trust your people but demand as much of them as you think they're capable of delivering. Beware of those with too much mouth. Give them small secrets and follow those secrets to see who betrays you, because when a big secret is to be trusted, you need to know where it will end up. Always remember that in a fight situation five fearless volunteers will always outperform ten fearless volunteers and one coward.''

In the days and nights of their passage, his principles had seeped into the flesh of all the people on board, armoring them more securely than any plex hull. And although they knew that they were just one hundred seventeen in number, they had faith that the captain's plan must succeed—whatever it was.

The Okinawa *kin kaigun* was expected to form up in convoy in several months real-time. Meanwhile the *Constitution's* crew had made excellent progress on Okinawa. They had taken five small ships on the planet, stripping them out: equipment, cargo, personal effects—everything they could want. They had arrested the grounded ships with little opposition, each time releasing their crews and demolishing the pillaged vessels. No blood, but inordinate fear, and fear was a contagious disease.

The trackless idyllic southern continent of Okinawa had been their base. It was the place where the ore was mined and refined, vast open-cast pits where Mitsubai's immense machines had penetrated the planet's skin. The refineries were heavily guarded.

The filthy, dusty heat of the equatorial belt with its ammoniac fumes and its one-hundred-Celsius-plus temperatures was where the Mitsubai terminal was that Oujuku's crew had attacked. The dome town of Taito sat on the stinking gray wastes of the equator itself. Ships leaving the high-gravity planet loaded with superheavy cargoes needed as much grav assist as they could get, and Okinawa's fast-rotating equator provided a slingshot to ships needing to get into orbit. It also gave rise to vast Coriolis forces that wound up deep atmospheric depressions and flung typhoonicanes across both temperate zones a thousand times a year.

A spur of land connected Okinawa's two landmasses, and a monorail link ran down the middle of it. That too seemed invulnerable to attack.

"Best of luck, Cao."

"O-keh, Captain."

Cao's tight smile had flashed in the blackness of that awesome night, the whites of his eyes yellow in the sodium glare: he was embarking on the most dangerous course of all, and alone. And all those who watched him depart wondered at the mission he was to try, knowing that if the Okinawa authorities should catch a *sangokujin* saboteur near their railroad, he would be skinned alive.

After that, Pel Rosen had landed a shuttle full of goods in the southern continent: survival commodities and gifts to offer the escaped slaves who were known to inhabit the less easily policed areas. Near a steep cliff they had found a sizable cave and hidden equipment containers in it: tools and a stock of plex, a readied shuttle, stores, suits, spares, listening gear, and new and expensive weaponry—enough to blow Yamato out of the Neutral Zone.

Then they had taken their task force northward. The Yamato astrogator from Rakahanga had told him much, that the *kin kaigun* was expected on the Taito apron in a short time, that her commander was Admiral Kihei, and that the metal would not be waiting in Taito for fear of another raid, but would be transported at the last minute by rail.

"Attack Amerikan ship make alter habit of Yamato," the astrogator had said. "They know two Amerikan ship here. Maybe come down, but no danger in Taito. Maybe hold metal until admiral bring ship planetside."

"How can we attack Taito after Captain Oujuku's attempt?" Brophy had asked after they had put the astrogator down. "It'll be like a hive of wasps."

"We're not going to attack Taito," Ellis had said.

"Then where, Captain?"

"All in good time, Tom."

At length, they made camp within sight of the coast exactly at the mouth of the Kin River, at the very narrowest part of the isthmus, and waited for Oujuku's ship. There, in a clearing near the coast, they materialised from the forest, the chameleon-skinned ship blipped a sudden bright yellow on her underside surfaces to acknowledge contact. Ellis discovered that Oujuku's party had come close to disaster.

"Twenty-eight've died so far," Oujuku reported. "A virus."

Ellis feared the deliberate microbes which had been introduced onto some worlds. Sometimes they were too sophisticated or just too simple for the atmosampling filters to catch, and without blood conditioning they were often fatal and provided a practical barrier to unwanted visitors. He saw concern lay heavy on Ouju-ku's mind and probed him. "A planetary welcome bug, you think?"

Oujuku shook his head, shrugging off the suggestion. "The epidemic's past now, but the fight's gone out of the rest of my crew. Most of them want home. They figure a promise that failed their dead shipmates might just as soon fail them."

"And you?"

"I'm human too, Ellis."

"Be careful your people don't catch onto that."

Oujuku did not smile; he scratched at his arm. "We're few, and growing fewer. Another blast of fever and we're broken as a raiding force." Then, seeing Ellis's eyes upon him, he admitted, "Two of my brothers died—Zeh and Joseph. Zeh in a half-assed attack I would never have mounted had I been there with him. Joseph of that piss-boiling fever. And the surgeon that freezeed him didn't outlive him by more than four days."

"I'm sorry, John."

"Yeah."

"And a real good officer was Joh."

"Yep."

Ellis studied him again, seeing him bottle his grief, remembering Oujuku's bluntness when Horse's report had been made. "Then we'll have to punish Yamato for three lost brothers, eh? And put heart in the crew for the job."

"Yep."

13

Three days later, Ellis received the message he had been hoping for. The comms channels were insecure, and so a prearranged signal had been arranged and watched for. Smoke smudged the

top of a hill nearby, and he went secretly a short way along the
coast, alone in one of the surface skimmers they had brought to
take the news. Then he had consulted with Oujuku urgently.

"You came by skimmer? Are you crazy? What about the
wake? The surveillance satellites Mitsu operates can resolve a
pinhead on the surface. Why've we been keeping under the
trees?"

"Relax. It's overcast, isn't it?"

"Optically, yes."

"Their infrared resolution's poor. And besides, we're not the
only living things on the continent. They have settlements and
there's the escapees. That's why they're troubling themselves to
mount surveillance in the first place."

"Yeah, to target strikes on anything suspicious. Keep the
vermin down, eh. Us, like."

"Fact is I laser-blinded the one that passes over here mid-
mornings. By the time they check it out and send a vehicle for
a look-see, we'll be gone. And we're looking out too."

Oujuku's temper rose. "Ellis, you and I agreed no unilateral
action. You don't get final cut on this mission without consul-
tation."

"O-keh, o-key. Calm it. What's the reason you brought me
out anyway?"

"Well, I'll tell you. I had rumblings. Prickly back. It's time
we did something about the morale around here. Some of them're
scared, I think."

"You want to give the people the old one-two?"

"Tricky, Ellis."

"We'll do it after you brief them on the mission."

". . . a'right."

That night, in the *Constitution*'s open cargo bay, the captains
laid their carefully rehearsed plan before both crews. They gathered late and the atmosphere was broody, cut by the sultry heat
of the night. Oujuku smoothed the big visualiser clear in front
of him. He punched up a map of the isthmus and began to poke
at it with the tip of a pointer.

"The land bridge runs north-south. This is us here—the north
part of the south landmass, latitude minus seventy-one degrees
or thereabouts; along this track we've reconnoitered. Here"—
he stabbed at a spot on the middle of the equator—"is Taito.
A place some of you people might just recall. And this is the

rail link. At the other end is their number one refinery at Kin. Both terminals are now strong and well defended. But you can see that to bring their stuff up from the south and send it into orbit, they must first load it at Kin and rush it overland to Taito. This they do on monotrucks, following the *kinto*, along thisaway.'' He touched a button on the pointer and scored a red line between the two ports.

Leah Glass raised a hand. ''Excuse me, Captain, but I can't figure why they use a monorail to take refined aurium north. I mean, if it was massive trucks of ore, yeah, but refined stuff? There's escaped slaves kicking around in the southern jungles, so why not just put it on an air-freighter, and zip, straight off to Taito?''

''Their own security regulations,'' Oujuku answered patiently, pleased by the question. ''They built the rail link after an air crew mutinied and tried to heist a squillion credits' worth of the stuff offplanet. They don't want to tempt anyone else into that kind of thinking.''

They looked at one another, some making low whistles.

''What about the slaves? Don't they want to give their ex-masters a hard time?''

''They don't have weapons. And not much they can do with aurium in a jungle in any case.''

Ellis listened to Oujuku explain further and watched him finally stab the middle of the line and leave the pointer hanging there, suspended by the field. It was time to intervene. He scanned the faces of the mingled crews, saw them lit variously with greed and the promise of a fight, willing and unwilling, seeing with pleasure the eagerness in some as they crowded in on him. He noted most those that seemed least hungry for action, then, just as he and Oujuku had prearranged, he stepped back.

''C'mon, Captain Oujuku,'' he said, acting his part with relish. ''It's a tough request for your people. Are we gonna pick twenty candidates and hope to overcome a thousand guards? I know which of my people are up to it.''

''So your people are capable, and mine're not, that it?'' Oujuku replied with mock rebuke. ''You think your crew's hot, and mine's a pack of shipneys?''

Ellis leaned in on him. ''I'll tell you this, John. Any of my crew would cut your throat on an order from me, despite the fact they like you and respect you.'' The eyes of the hundred who clustered around them stood out in disbelief at what they were hearing. The attention of the last of them was nailed to Ellis as he continued, "It's to fight Yamato that we've come here. Yamato aurium is our aim. Tons of it, yep, and argentium too! And things like this!" He drew a nugget of native metal from his waist pocket and rolled it in his palm. "Big and blue and heavy as hell. And there's more where that came from. Spherical ingots the size of a grapefruit that burn with an electric fire, each sphere worth a million. Enough to make everyone here rich as the Mitsubai daimyo's bastard.

"What title does Mitsubai have to it? That's a philosophical question I want you to think about. Who does the aurium really belong to?"

No answer came.

"Fact is the Zone was made an independent territory by unanimous treaty over four hundred years ago—*in perpetuity*—and that means forever. They talk of a Co-prosperity Sphere, but the truth is they annexed the Zone by force, and they did it to provide their industry with the means to mount a massive invasion of Amerika."

They stirred uncomfortably.

"Until now, they've been forced to use subversion within Amerika, to stimulate rebellion and to threaten us with troop-massing operations. We've always been able to halt their plans because we've prevented them from completely destabilising us at home, and because they have to come through the nexus points of the Boundary worlds where we can concentrate our firepower. But they won't give up. The culture they have made their religious ideal was forged during five hundred years of civil war. They treat the *hinin,* the lowest class of their own people, like filth—the word means 'subhuman.' They honor samurai like minor gods, and they have an unshakable belief that they're superior to the rest of mankind. You've seen the way they herd their slaves like pigs. You've seen the way their soldiers scorn death. You've seen the way they're obsessed with rank and with duty. But they *can* be beaten."

Nate Allen, Oujuku's expeditor, shouted an oath and some of the crew smiled, then Ellis's face clouded and Allen remembered himself again.

"We're not slaves. We're a free people who know about duties *and* rights. We don't believe the universe is fixed and that our fate is immutable; we believe we can affect the outcome of events! And that is our strength!''

''Yes, sir!''

''Yeah! We can handle it.''

''Hey, you're making sense, Captain!''

''We're with you!''

''Remember, he who attacks carries the day, and he who thrusts at the enemy's softest place will be the victor. How can we fail when right and justice are on our side?''

He saw them fill with belief, some shouted out, others whooped and made agreement, and all the while he and Oujuku were looking them over, sorting out the ardent from the fainthearted, knowing by their attitudes which of them were only carried by words and which were at heart fit to take on the most dangerous part of the mission, and which again were fit to put in charge of the ships and shuttles they would depend on for escape.

Ellis grew serious now, seeing it was time to draw them back from an excess of encourgement, and he began to put to them the opposite view.

''There's not many of us. Twenty of us can be spared to go on the strike. Twenty only. Ten from the *Constitution,* ten from the *Lex.* I have to make that choice: this is a wilder planet than it seems down here at the pole and fraught with dangers. Thank God, then, that we're not alone in our mission.''

''You bet! God's got to be on our side!'' Patrick Navajo shouted.

''Yeah!'' someone else assented.

''Amen to that,'' he said. ''But I have somebody else in mind, as you'll find out.''

Then Ellis pushed through them, clearing a way before him until he had reached the open cargo bay doors. He jumped down from the ramp, cupped his hands to his mouth, and brought in the armed, silent crew members who had been planted in the fringes of the forest as sentries in lieu of the guard fields that would have given their position away. He brought them in and made them sit all together and called again into the darkness three times in a loud voice and they waited and watched until their eyes deceived them with expectation.

After a space they heard movement in the undergrowth. Oujuku hissed at one of his men who reached for his Wesson, and stilled him. In the gloom the palmito leaves parted and a squat figure in black garb ran crouching out from the darkness.

As he approached, the arclight picked him out and the crew began to shout his name and yell out because few had thought they would see him again.

"Cao!"

At his back was a host of Mongoloid warriors who came out one by one and waited, some crouching down, some standing with spears and with bows. Only one came forward and Cao presented him to Ellis and to Oujuku with great ceremony.

His code name was "Kuwa"—"Mulberry"—headman among the Okinawa *gurentai* of *hinin* and escaped *sangokujin* slaves, whom he had turned into a small bandit force. There was nobody in the Neutral Zone who hated the samurai more, nor knew their habits on this planet better.

14

The next day, the mission was finally prepared, weapons issued, battle suits passed out to those that were chosen and to their newfound allies. Use of the shuttles was ruled out by the possibility of emission surveillance, and the difficult ground made land vehicles impossible: it was going to be a long march. Cao interpreted tirelessly to discover from the *gurentai* what was best to take and how precisely the land would be against them. The first day's trek inland was arduous, the second and third more so, and at certain places *gurentai* scouts were dispatched ahead, pathfinding and leaving a trail of subtle signals by ripping leaves and snapping jungle stems. Silence was imposed on the rest as they walked. Stealth was their watchword.

All morning they climbed higher into a land filled with the chattering of monkeys and exotic birds, scaling the mountains that stretched east-west like a spine down the isthmus, Ellis swearing that they would find no rest until they had broken the back of the land. Some time before noon local time on the fourth day, Oujuku called a halt. The *gurentai* chief pointed to a thickly forested hill lying a mile or two off the track. Its peak rose above the general lie perhaps a hundred feet, and Ellis agreed that now they should take the weight off their backs for an hour. Although it was approaching the hottest part of the day and the sun had burned away the morning mists long ago, leaving the day clear and bright, the trees hereabouts were lofty and full of shade and the red earth beneath was moist and cool.

Oujuku came over, his ebullient face gleaming with sweat.

"I've spoken with Kuwa. He says there's something he wants to show us. Will you come?"

Ellis felt the ache in his thighs. The climb had been steep and growing steeper as the morning wore on and as the climax to the pass neared. He slumped against the bole of a tree and charged his mouth with water from the recirculator tube, swilling it round his teeth before swallowing. The distraction unsettled him.

"Hadn't we better rest now? And keep our minds on the business in hand?"

Oujuku put his chin back, balked. "It's worth it, Ellis."

"I've eaten enough of the local game, and I have no great taste for more of Kuwa's forest lore."

"It's no hunt, Ellis. I've got something to say to you."

Ellis sighed and found his feet.

"All right."

"That's right."

"I'll swear you were born with the energy of the devil."

"Energy conquers all. And that's a fact."

"Okeh," Ellis admitted, realising it was probably important. Reinvigorated by the thought, he picked up his Wesson, gave instructions to Nate Allen, and followed. "What is it? Sighted a settlement?"

"Better."

"I can think of nothing better at this particular moment. Except maybe a strap hammock."

Ellis followed the two *gurentai* who took them along the spur and to the ridge that led to the hill. After a deal of walking Oujuku thrust out his hand.

"Look! There!"

"What?"

"Don't you see? Near that tree?"

"John—*this is a fucking jungle!*"

"C'mon! There. There! Look!"

"What is it?" Ellis followed the line. A glint of light, a straight line abhorred by nature even more than a vacuum. It was clearly artificial. He took the glasses. A massive span stood across a clearing, a plex structure, slender, die straight, supported by gossamer uprights. "Yes, a plex span. What is it, a road?"

"A bridge."

"I swear I'll—"

He stopped, looking at the line that stretched tantalisingly between walls of living rock.

Oujuku clapped a hand on Kuwa's shoulder. "Looks like our hosts are right, eh, Kuwa?"

"*Hai,*" the *gurentai* leader agreed gravely.

Ellis raised an eyebrow. "Great. A bridge."

"Yep. Coming up the rock?"

They threw off their suits and climbed to the best vantage point fifty feet above, seeking handholds and footholds where they could pull themselves up the rest of the way, until they came to the highest part.

Oujuku was first into the rough slit trench at the summit where the view burst upon them spectacularly.

"Jeezus, Ellis! Would you look at that!"

Despite himself, Ellis absorbed the panorama with an inrush of breath. The quiet moment that followed was heightened by his bodily tiredness, a moment of soft peace and silence, filled with the green smell of the forest tops and the echoing cackles of rude-faced monkeys and other strange creatures. In the distance the cordillera stretched away magnificently. To the west they could see the faintly shimmering White Jewel Ocean, to the east another ocean, blue and infinite. It rent their eyes with its color and shimmered vastly.

"That's not just any bridge," Oujuku said. "That's *the* bridge. The one that carries the rail link. The one they use to carry the aurium up to Taito. Not many miles from here is Yomitan, the midpoint of the link. Kuwa says that's where we'll get our information."

15

They turned north and marched another short day until the forests subsided, to be replaced by tall knot grass, tracts of open land which had been cleared by burning. Kuwa insisted on greater care and secrecy, knowing that they approached Yomitan, and after consulting with him, Oujuku suggested that they go to a more secluded place along the link. Up close, the scale was apparent. The rail link was much smaller than he had expected. Small tunnels only eight feet in diameter bored through the rock outcrops.

"It's like a mine train."

Oujuku nodded. "Makes sense, if you think about it, I guess."

They doubled back and looked for the protection of a dry riverbed, following it some distance until the luxuriant forest came up around them again. Then, as they were passing along a gravel bank on an eastward bend of the river, they heard the noise.

Ellis ordered silence. What was it? The link causeway was narrow here and overhung with big trees that followed the watercourse. Instantly the whole raiding force fell unseen into the shadows under the rail embankment.

The rhythmic noise came again out of the gray plex rail: diffuse, light-pitched, murmuring like children's voices, then the sound grew plainer and Ellis picked up his glasses and saw the vehicle sliding smoothly round a distant bend. He estimated its speed as cautiously slow, maybe forty or fifty mph, probably to give the track-check scanners time and reduce the risk of a mishap on this difficult section.

"It's now or never," he muttered, almost despairing that their timing had been so misinformed as to jeopardise the whole mission.

The horn sounded like a lure in the distance. On maximum magnification he made out five sleek trucks, coupled one behind another, each burdened with two one-ton flasks. The guards rode in special open carriages, seated back-to-back, staring outward. At the head a gun with its crew of three mounted on a special truck followed by a carriage of twenty armed soldiers, then the traction car. At the tail another gun truck. Each guard carried a quartered rifle blaster and a bandolier of power tubes around him, staring out at the land under tight discipline.

When Ellis looked towards the southern horizon, he saw with amazement that another train followed on some miles behind with a further seven trucks, separated by more soldiers, and a third of six trucks. He silently calculated that together they must contain more than *thirty-six tons* of refined aurium bullion.

A soft blasphemy escaped Nate Allen, who hugged the ground beside him.

"Radio black those suits," Oujuku told them grittily.

The first train came on unaware of the men that crouched under the riverbank ahead of them. He prayed that surprise would be advantage enough to overcome the guard, but there was little time to deploy.

The trains continued to approach. Oujuku sent a dozen men scampering over a bend in the road with Cao, a further dozen working back one train length, and the rest up ahead with him. Ellis took the remainder, six *gurentai,* Kuwa, Jenkins, Allen, and Brophy, with him forward another train length. He pulled Kuwa down behind the stem of a plantain tree.

"Tell your people I want no shooting until the train stops," he whispered, his voice a rasp, his hands making explanation. "Do you understand?"

Kuwa nodded, his suit camouflage blending perfectly from moment to moment with the dappled light. He turned and passed on the command, dispatching his people to hidden locations on each side of the track, then he drew out his blaster. This time it was no practice, it was for real; the rifle was set to cut and to kill, a big punching Esandubya, a full six pounds and a half in weight. He knocked off the safety and crept out of sight.

Ellis's heart thumped and he breathed deeply to calm himself. Somewhere in the distance he heard the sound of rushing water. It mingled with the rail sounds, filling his head with music. He picked up a branch as thick as his leg and dragged it across the

track as if it had fallen there from one of the trees. Then, me-
thodically, he primed his blaster pistols, charging them with
power tubes from his belt and adjusting the set to maximum.
The clicks as he rotated the lever seemed to echo through the
forest.

Twenty yards away, Allen grimly loaded his meson cutter
with a tube and began to carve out a slice of the plex track.

The horn sounded, the vehicle began to brake, slowing as it
detected a fault on the track. The train came on at a walk, the
guards blithely unaware of the true danger ranged about them,
and their officer stood up. When the lead gun truck had come
to within five yards of Ellis, it stopped and the officer jumped
down. Ellis leapt out in front of him, Wessons in hand.

The officer pulled up sharply.

"*Konnichi wa!*" Ellis greeted him, his eyes deadly on the
man's own.

"Aggh?"

The officer's face contorted. The incredible challenge had
stunned him. He recovered himself immediately, but before an
order could escape his mouth a beam slashed out of the forest
and across his throat and he crashed to the road at Ellis's feet.

Then all hell broke loose. Once, twice, Ellis squeezed his
triggers, blasting the nearest two samurai back into the arms of
their comrades. Instantly the answering reports of other blasters
came out of the forest. More heavy weapons, impaling the infantry and showering the track with severed foliage. The samurai
guards, panicked by the sudden ferocity of the fire that assailed
them, tried to scatter, but the raiders surged across the track and
cut them off, preventing them from falling back.

Another volley of burning rays sliced into them. Two samurai
fell. A third fought on, smoldering, until shafts cut into his
shoulders and back. When the guards got off their replies into
the shadows, it was at random. Then Ellis felt himself wheeled
round as if by a giant hand slapping his pelvis.

Jeezus, he thought, that was too close! He looked down and
saw the burn holes plucked in his suit. The reflections zinging
off the track had blown one of his belt tubes. The guards' blasters
could fire a tight beam with enough energy to penetrate a battle
suit at four hundred yards, and their burning power was instant
death at this range, except that at the moment of the ambush
they had been set up to deliver spray fire. At close quarters the

virtue of this was that they could blind and incapacitate as well as kill when fired into an ill-defined group of men.

Blood began to trickle from somewhere on his head and cascade into his beard, but he ignored it. Three samurai guards were advancing on him, the desperation on their faces grotesque. He cut them down with the last of his tube, making his blasters useless.

All around now the road was a struggling mass as raiders came crashing from the undergrowth and into the guards, slashing and stabbing beams with their new weaponry. There was no time to reload with fresh tubes, and the raid was degenerating into a terrifying hand-to-hand fight. Through a blur of red, Ellis saw men stumbling closer to the edge of the track. Their feet clawed for purchase on the crumbling earth that overhung the riverbed by ten or fifteen feet. Jenkins darted from his cover with his side arm and plunged into the blinded men, rending them. Those closest to the drop began to topple, crashing over and rolling helplessly into the green pools below. Others were forced down until a dozen were kicking and flailing in the shallow water.

Ellis flung a hand over his face and brought it away sopped with blood. It trickled from him so that it seemed there must be a big gash on his head. He groped out for a rifle blaster instinctively. Then more guards were on him again.

Ellis's anger hammered in his head. He pulled the trigger, knowing that if the gun had been abandoned because it was empty he was a dead man. It jerked and chopped a huge swathing beam into the first man's rib cage, notching him so that he went down immediately. The next trooper flung himself on Ellis and struggled to use his sword. A *katana* lunged at him but he deflected the blade down so that it passed between his thighs. Then he drove his fist into his assailant's face, knocking off the man's unlaced helmet. But he was now unbalanced himself and falling to his knees. He staggered back, fingers reaching wildly, and the third, a man with no breastplate, came at him wielding the butt of his firearm like a club. He rolled away from the initial blow as the man tried to dash his head open. His fingers found the chin strap of the plex helmet that had rolled within reach. He swung it up, launching it with desperate strength into his attacker's way. The sharp brim bit into the man's fingers where he gripped his weapon and it fell from his hand. It was enough to buy Ellis the split second he needed. He tore his knife from his belt, gripped it ready for the upthrust, remembering what his combat instructor had taught him about killing: that a man's ribs are shaped like a louver, that a down-stab jags off the bone, but an upthrust slides in.

The man was defenseless before him now. All he needed to do was hug him close and dispatch him, but he saw the stark fear in the man's face. He was not a guard at all, young, hardly able to grow a beard—probably the operator. In that moment there was a change in the sounds around him: the solid rage of battle resolved itself into a hundred separate noises and fell away from his ears.

Through the blood, the man Ellis gripped seemed suddenly to be so like his brother, Duval, that at the last instant, instead of the kill, he doubled his fist and knocked the wind from his opponent, then he kicked him down, furious at his own weakness.

When he looked up, he found that the remaining guards were fleeing back along the track. The *gurentai* were expending their last tubes, crouching in their strange way, their rifles held flat and horizontal, their middle fingers hooked awkwardly under the trigger guards. He called them back.

Two hundred yards away Oujuku's force had already triumphed, and the rest of the guards were in rout.

Ellis felt exultant. A wave of intense triumph beat through him as he realised that they had actually won. He felt the blood course down his cheek and drip onto his shoulder, the burning points on his thigh and hip where the tube had blown dug into his flesh, a distant discomfort, but he felt no pain. Only numbness and elation.

It had all been so *easy!*

A vast treasure. A staggeringly vast treasure. *They had just taken an aurium train.* Just like that. Here, on a gray plex track in the middle of a polar rain forest, was more wealth than had been raised in taxes in the whole of Amerika since Alia Kane's inauguration. It was awesome. Immense. Impossible to comprehend.

"They'll be here soon."

It was Oujuku, slinging his gun.

"In God's name, John, we've *done* it!"

Oujuku grinned evilly. "It's not ours yet."

Yomitan was close by, and the garrison there would turn out

immediately the first survivors reached it. At worst, there might be an airborne patrol riding down on them within the hour and a thousand troops combing the forest before nightfall. While Nate Allen's work had cut the track, the two following trains would not be coming through. They had already slammed into reverse and were gone, guards and all.

Ellis and Oujuku took stock of the situation.

"How many dead?" Ellis asked.

"A few. Theisen and Kennedy for sure. Pollack's burned pretty bad."

"Kuwa's boys?"

"Ten maybe. And a dozen hurt bad. You can't say they lacked enthusiasm."

"We have to get off the track."

"Which means unloading this lot now."

"Thirty-six tons?"

"Jeezus' sake! There's more than we can carry."

"Half the job's to take it, half to keep it."

"We can keep some of it, by God!"

"Each of those flasks weighs around a ton. There should be —uh—twenty spheres in each one. That's seven hundred and twenty in all. Aurium's around three and a half times the density of lead, more than twice that of uranium. Each ball weighs about a hundred pounds apiece."

"We'll bury what we can't move. The main part we'll take into the forest. Fifty pounds per man. Absolute max. Tell your people only aurium. Cut the spheres in half. Leave anything else."

"Is there time to sort it and bury it? They'll surely find fresh-dug earth."

"We'll have to get on with the job of cutting the spheres and burying the rest. There's the ideal place!"

"Where?"

"Down there." Ellis pointed to the stagnant pools. "Bury it under the riverbed."

"Yeah! And we'll shatter the rest and dump the pieces into land-crab burrows for them to discover. Maybe disperse a few spheres into dust along false trails. That should hold their detectors up a while."

Ellis's fingers searched through the blood-matted hair at his temple.

"Let me see that." He submitted as Oujuku satisfied his curiosity. "Not much: a cut no more'n an inch long. And no depth to it. It's pretty well cauterised."

They got to work with the meson cutter, spilling out the contents of the flasks across the track, rolling the grapefruit-sized spheres down the banks, digging out trenches, and sinking the spheres into the green water pools. They blasted a few spheres to dust, which scattered and settled all around. The *gurentai* looked on, at first with cool amazement, preferring to collect their own trophies from the dead guards. To them, neither aurium nor argentium was of the least account, weapons being their prized booty. They menaced the wounded and the captives, declaring that they would take their victory payment in the traditional way—in ears and noses and genitalia—until Ellis told Kuwa this was no way to hurt his ex-masters, who loved aurium better than life itself, and that if the *gurentai* would help in the rest of the job, they could have all the small arms the *Constitution* contained.

*   *   *

It took them five arduous days to recross the mountains and come back again, through rain and wild weather at the tail of a typhoonicane, to Akarie Ue, the place where they had arranged to meet with their shuttles. But there was no sign of them.

Instead, a Yamato Guard frigate cruised overhead, and Ellis looked up at it, heartsick.

Nate Allen voiced the great fear of them all. "If the shuttles are taken, then we're blipped, Captain. They'll torture them and learn where our ships are hidden, and the *kin kaigun* will be in strength on the Taito apron by now!"

"C'mon, Nate. This is no time to lose heart. We've got to keep trying."

Oujuku railed against the disappointment, then his temper cooled. "At worst, if our shuttles are taken, the Yamato commanders must have time to search them, time to Probe the crews, time to mount their counterstroke. The *Lex* and the *Constitution* have both got pretty good stealth measures operating. And that big bird has got a whole goddamned continent to comb. If we're lucky, we can still get to our ships."

"The enemy haven't found us yet," Bowen stated. "Guard frigate or not."

"Yeah, but as soon as we break comms silence they'll be down on us like a ton of aurium. We going to walk to the ships?"

Ellis added more hopefully, "Look, if the shuttles were late coming here and arrived to see that vulture buzzing the area, they might just be lying low. Have you all got so little faith in your shipmates?"

They wasted no more time in idle speculation. Oujuku led three scouts west to check out the number two zone, leaving Ellis to comfort the remainder with encouragements. He told them they were sitting on a treasure that amounted to only one tenth of the haul they had taken, but that was still an immense prize. And that as soon as they made the ships they were as good as offplanet and through the nexus.

Two hours into the dusk Oujuku returned in the shuttles, and by nightfall of the next day they had regained their ships. As they slotted the craft aboard, everyone wanted to know exactly how the enterprise had gone. Powerfully Ellis lifted the five-inch aurium sphere from his pack and bowled it heavily across the decking.

"Oh, pretty well."

They erupted with cheers. Against his own orders the boss had carried twice the limit—one hundred pounds—across rough terrain, and he had got it back successfully.

That night they divided the spoils, paying off Kuwa in the way he wanted—blasters and as many spare tubes as they could give him. They ate a festive meal. The local meats imparted flavors the Dovers never made, and they started to drink and to sing in the way all hunting parties had done since the dawn of time.

Doones started it off. Bosco joined in, then a third, Jenkins, the top gun with a voice like a bassoon. Together they raised a dozen verses, and while the crews caroused, Oujuku and Ellis consulted together to unburden their minds.

"You know that I want to take my ship home," Oujuku told him. "I've half a mind to overfly Taito with our guns blazing, to show them we don't give a good goddamn about them."

"And you know that I want to stay in the Zone—to prove as much."

"Then our partnership must dissolve."

"I wish you good psi, John. Will you carry our share home with you?"

"I sure will. And I'll invest it against your return."
"It's a deal. Now let's get the hell out of here."

16

SADO

They came out into the Sado daylight to the beating of gigantic
war drums and the ghostly blowing of the *shakuhachi*, and the
mass of people confined beyond the high bamboo lattice fence
wondered what could be the reason that these terrible *gaijin* were
feted in so important a fashion when they were only here to die.

Duval walked on in procession, sweating under the weight of
the heavy punishment collar and the iron chains they had attached
to his wrists and ankles. He felt a sudden faintness; fear daggered
him. Where was Michie now? Was she here among the crowd?
Was she imprisoned? Was she about to go through the same
terror that he had suffered? He had not dared to ask after her,
even via the arcane *komuso* monks who appeared to offer him
only support. He allowed himself to trust no one, fearing that
any questions might precipitate her arrest. The residual paranoia
left by the Probe had paralysed his mind, but the monk had
unknotted his terror, and the dread and loathing had passed
slowly away.

Pray for my rebirth, Michie-san, he asked silently. Pray for
mine as I pray for yours. If only I could see your face. Once.
Just once more. But no, an answering voice said. Don't wish
her here to see your degradation. You must wish her far from
this hell. Imagine her far away and happy and free. You're
together in spirit. The thought of her safe deliverance will give
you strength to acquit yourself like an adopted son of the Hasegawa clan should.

He stared ahead towards the market square. The open graveled
square had been transformed. A scaffold that was a hundred feet
long and thirty high had been erected in the punishment grounds

off the Square of Perfect Harmony, surmounted by dozens of crosses, one for each of the accused. Some of them were inverted, others made in spread-eagle form. The monstrous punishment ground was fronted on one side by the towers of Kanazawa's castle-like ramparts, and on the other by the daimyo's residence, the veranda of which now formed a part of the upper tier. Forty steps led up to the stage on which the *metsuke*'s rostrum was placed. Opposite was a rectangular space towards which they were being led, and all around were the huge timber tiers of the theater that had filled with the ranking samurai hierarchy of Sado. Down below, a crowd vast enough to have emptied the city waited, all the low classes without official entitlement to a surname: merchants, technicians, clerks, industrial workers, and land workers—everyone except *sangokujin* and the *hinin*.

The special cedarwood stage for their "trial" had taken many weeks to craft. The sounds of hammering and hewing and sawing of timber had penetrated even to the dark quarters in which he had been imprisoned in these last few days since their bodily sufferings had abated. It was like a deliberate taunt, magnifying their terror.

Duval was revolted by the eerie pomp of the rite and the way it consumed reason and displaced all that was good in men's minds, how it had been designed to make a vile spectacle of the intimacies of death.

When the sessions of interrogation and torture had stopped, and the severity of their confinement relaxed, he had called it mercy. But his flood of relief had been stemmed by the realisation that this was not mercy, merely a time set aside for reflection, a span in which a man might be tempted to surrender himself utterly to the Void.

The words of the sacred *Kensei*, the Sword Saint, Musashi, had been repeated to him: *The spirit of the Void is nothingness. The Void is unknowable to man. But by knowing that which exists we come to know that which does not exist. Men of this world do not comprehend. They imagine that which they do not comprehend must be the Void. It is not. That is only bewilderment.*

Through all that time *komuso* monks had visited him daily, soothing him at first, then urging him, as one friend might urge another, to meditate. They had been patiently deaf to his protests that he was a son of the Hasegawa clan and should not be treated like this. Even so, the *komuso* had interceded on his behalf. They were not like the priests of the Black Brotherhood, but Zen monks of the order of *Fuke-shu*. They wore dark blue kimonos tied with a red sash, and high-blocked *geta* sandals, and were never without their hardwood *shakuhachi* flutes, which they could wield with the defensive skill of a sword master when attacked; but their strangest piece of apparel was the *tengai*, the woven reed basket that covered the head and protected the monk from worldly identification. Their efforts had brought him light and food and then a short period each day in the high-walled yard to exercise alone. Lastly the rule of silence had been withdrawn and he had been permitted to associate together with the others.

"A woman can't trust her eyes and ears," Helene di Barrio had said wonderingly on that first day of greeting.

Duval had embraced them, but Jeb Womak had searched the blank walls, full of suspicions. "Yeah, they'll give us this and then take it all away again."

"I guess they're making their judgements now," Juli Dexter had said ominously.

"It's their rule." Duval had understood the procedure. The *kempei* ensured that their victims were watered and well fed, that the injuries captives had suffered in the torture chambers or under the Probe were sufficiently healed prior to their coming out for judgement.

"We're soon to go for trial."

"Wouldn't do to crucify a cripple, would it?" Torven Jones had grinned sourly. They had taken out each of his gravestone teeth to teach him humility.

"Yeah. These bastards have taken care to keep us alive—or else how could they murder us?"

"The *kempei* are not allowed to kill us, according to their law," Duval had said, his voice laden with irony.

"Oh, sure!" Davey Marks had snorted. "Except maybe in a great big public ceremony, to show the poor bastards who're watching how high their power stands. That's their way."

"Still, we're safe until then."

Duval had been assured by the *komuso* that the *kempei*'s own rules forbade killing within their prisons, that the office was merciful and just. He had debated the matter from his nightmare bed, asking how they could justify the weeks of terrible torment they had inflicted, the physical and mental pain, the repeated tortures. The *komuso* had explained earnestly that what they had suffered had not been *repeated* tortures. Unlike other less enlightened authorities, the *kempei*'s rules allowed torture only once, and therefore he had suffered only one torture. One torture *continued* over many sessions. That was the Way and the measure of their duty. There could be no repeated amputations and reculturing of limbs, no conscious dissection under medical control, no sadistic Chinese practices; in fact, most modern techniques were disallowed, except the Probe, and that was a purely mental agony.

He had told the monk about it. "Mind rape, they call it in Amerika. I feel as though my brain has been turned inside out and picked over by strangers. When I first came out, I felt completely worthless. As if my most personal intimacies had been tampered with. I couldn't face myself. It's a disgusting device."

"I will help you to heal yourself."

"You cannot."

"I will try."

There had been sessions of deep meditation during which the monk had relaxed him and rebuilt his confidence. Duval had told his shipmates what he had gleaned from the *komuso* about the *kempei*. "Since they can't kill us themselves, they'll have to hand us over to the civil authorities for execution."

"That's a real fine distinction, Straker!" Matt Kaiser, Horse's closest friend, had been set to work as a slave overseer in the aurium mines. Prosperous and married to a Taiwanese slave, he had been making the best he could of his life until the *kempei* arrived. Now his thin red hair was all gone, but the wounds on his face were as livid as the hatred his captors had stored up in him. He had spat. "Does it matter to somebody like you?"

Duval had bridled at that. "What do you mean by that, Matt?"

Kaiser had looked away. "To a collaborator."

"I'll tell you: to me the *kempei*'re guilty of crimes against humanity. They're trying to wash the blood from their hands with legal niceties. I'm saying that I'm beginning to understand how they think."

"You think maybe their Shinto consciences plague them? Like yours maybe?"

"You got something against me, Kaiser?"

"They say you married into a samurai family, yeah, and even took their religion!"

"And you took their credit!"

"Credit? You got a nerve. I *earned* it honestly, Straker. In the mines. Every day. Toiling and sweating. What was *your* pay for?"

Di Barrio had got between them and calmed them. "Hey! You're both married men, anxious for your wives. Beating up on one another won't help."

"Yeah. Don't give 'em the satisfaction. They're spying on us." Dexter's single eye roamed the walls. She thrust a finger up insolently at the sightless socket of a surveillance lens.

"See there, they're always watching us," Jeb Womak whispered, pointing.

Then Horner spoke softly to Duval. "Haven't you heard the rumor? It was your brother's interference that brought us all to this place, Gunner."

His mouth fell open. "My brother?"

"You mean you don't know?"

"No. Tell me."

"The word is that Ellis joined up with John Oujuku to bring off an incredible heist. They landed on Okinawa and busted out a whole heap of refined bullion. They've stirred up Yamato like a nest of Mexikan hornets, smashed Mitsubai's finances, and spread panic throughout the Zone. It's even said that the Empire's economic stability had been shocked, that the loan rate is twice what it was last year. Believe me, Gunner, they're angry as hell."

Duval had let out a whistle, stunned by the news. "Which is why we're going to be scapegoats?"

"Some of us believe so."

"And you?"

Horner had shrugged. "As for me, I think they'd do it anyway. Seems to me that the supreme and untouchable *kempei* does what it wants. The Emperor thinks an O-type supergiant shines out of the *metsuke*'s asshole. He takes no notice of the *bakufu,* or any other level of Yamato's government, much less your brother's doings."

Then Duval had sunk back against the wall and there had been silence until Dale Seeback's feather-light singing voice had floated up, sweet as an Irish flute. "The Emperor's got us in his grip—"

Answering voices had given the refrain. "*Fly, men, fly!*"

"The Emperor's got us in his grip—"

"*Who's a fool now?*"

"The Emperor's got us in his grip, but through his fingers we shall slip."

"*With heart and head and hand and hip, Who's a fool now?*"

Duval had watched the old song cheer them, whilst above, shuttered windows had opened and shaven-headed acolytes had goggled out at the crazy *gaijin*, mystified that there could be laughter in such a place. The song had made them think of the old days, made an Amerikan crew of them again, but despite the first smiles to light their pale faces in a year, they had all known, deep in their hearts, that none of them would slip from the Emperor's fist; each had understood that those that were deemed pure would be flayed through the streets and then sent into Yamato to be chained in slavery; those that were deemed impure would be nailed to crosses to die. Duval had known then with great certainty what his own sentence would be.

A month later, the *komuso* had brought him news that a proclamation had gone out, warning the citizens and people of Sado that the judgement was to be served in the Square of Perfect Harmony, and that all must lay aside their toils or their leisures and attend to hear the sentences solemnly announced. Those of the populace who attended would be granted intercession at the shrine of their workplace, the monk had said in his fervent way, adding at Duval's asking that those who failed to attend would be chastised.

Last night they had all gone without sleep, *ashigaru* soldiers incessantly marshaling and drilling them in the prison yard so that they were set in order and given instructions where they must walk and who must follow whom. Then, in the waning hours of night, Wada Zengo had arrived with a squad of men. They brought out the punishment collars, the white *hachimaki* headbands, and rough pajamas like judo suits but striped in broad red, the color of the criminal. All was meticulously cleaned and made straight. Hishikari had passed the headbands out to the prisoners personally and with great reverence, telling each one that the *hachimaki* would hang one day in the rafters of the great warrior Zen temple on Kamakura, as immortal reminders of their correction. All bore the red sun of Yamato in front and ancient black ideograms intended to be read in the Chinese reading: Earth, Water, Fire, Wind, and the Void. The punishment collars were painted red and intended to demean and to humble the wearers.

At dawn they had been breakfasted on rice, raw fish, and a cup of rice wine. A shower of rain had quenched the dry earth and gone away again, and, two hours later, the great procession was begun, marching a crooked mile through streets packed with people, headed by a column of soldiers in full armor, carrying long ceremonial bamboo pikes and the long flags of the various *han* of Sado strapped to their backs. Next came a cadre of the Black Brotherhood, attired in black kimonos, with white obis round their middles. Following them a dozen pages carried the barred-galaxy standard of the *kempei* and, after it, the Standard of a Thousand Gourds, to represent the *rikugun,* the military power of Yamato, all flanked by guards in charcoal gray and moss green.

Duval moved forward at the solemn pace the cruel ceremony dictated. Now he saw the *hatamoto* take their places in the procession, headed by Nishima Jun, a distant, upright figure, clad in his formal kimono of midnight blue, and deviced with the three-leaf *mon* of his clan. Along the far side of the Square of Perfect Harmony Duval saw the ladies of the nobility ranged at balconies and windows overlooking the scaffold, peach pastel in their finest kimonos, and fanning themselves under multicolored parasols. Today had been proclaimed a great public holiday, but the buzz of gaiety and expectation was fueled by a dark and seething fear that he saw keenly in their faces. Every spectator, no matter what his rank or station, knew that though this day they watched the procession from afar, tomorrow they might be walking in a similar one themselves.

Duval walked as if in a dream, flanked by the basket-headed monk and another, younger monk, who watched and prayed continuously in droning rote verse. Around him were raised the horrific effigies, as big as life, of those of his shipmates who had perished when they had first come ashore, or who had died since, and whose names the diligent inquiries of the *metsuke* had brought to light. Horse's rice-straw image was there as were those of the men who had been killed on Chi no Tsuki. They were raised up on poles, dressed in the same fashion. Also, there were coffins of red lacquer containing the remains of Kier Rider and Jim Collier and Denzil McFadden, whose obstinacy had killed them in the *kempei*'s cellars, though publicly it was said that they had died of fever.

Each Amerikan was accompanied by two *komuso*—monks who, like his own, prepared them for death as they walked. Each prisoner's collar was linked to the others before and behind by an iron chain as they walked. The uncontrollable Juli Dexter had been manacled and gagged to stop up her shouts. Behind her, Matt Kaiser mouthed the Lord's Prayer, his eyes burning red as coals. Those that had wives and children that they cared for went quietly, knowing that their families were hostage to fortune, hoping with good behavior to save them.

The tri-vee cameras followed them as they went, capturing the moment, beaming it to every receiver on the planet, and soon to every planet in the Emperor's domain. Duval suddenly saw the fallacy of his last hopes. My skills will save me again, he had thought. Surely Michie-san has told her father that I retained the secret of the singularity gun. Surely Kenji-san must have passed that on to the daimyo. Surely the daimyo has struck a bargain with Fukuda Ikku. He must have. Yes, he must have. He's not the sort of man to give in so easily. But what if he hasn't? And what if the *kempei* wants to demonstrate revenge for Okinawa more than they want singularity guns? I'm trapped, he thought, looking around. Trapped. It's insane. I'm letting them lead me to my death. Without complaint. Without a fight. Is that what a sane man does?

Panic rose in him. His eyes searched to left and right for a way to escape, but there was none. To the rear the procession snaked on with the representatives of each samurai family walking two-by-two in their distinctive gear, followed up by a column of brightly armored horsemen. On each side double ranks of pikemen stood shoulder-to-shoulder along the way, holding back a pressing mass of people. Every window was full, every gallery also. People fringed the rooftops and clung to any high vantage point they could find in every building except the daimyo's residence itself.

The rumor swept before him that this was the brother of the pirate who had raided Okinawa, and heads turned as he came into the square. At the first sight of them a huge shout went up.

He saw the shiny black crests of warbonnets, like stag-beetle horns, the signs and symbols of mounted officers riding ahead, making a way through the massive crowd, the sun glinting on a drawn sword as it was waved.

As he breasted an alley he smelled the tang of woodsmoke from a chestnut vendor's fire. Dread boiled up in his belly. He remembered the kamikaze ship that had smashed into the *Thomas J*. The terror of impending death he had felt. The face of Iwakura imploring him. Then the deep memories of the fanatical crucifixions that had happened on the park-world came upon him. They had played in his mind in that dark cell, haunting his unguarded moments. And he had confessed it. They had written it down.

The death of his mother and the way he had been helped by his brother to buy the education his intellect deserved . . . His mother had been a strange woman, loving but very secretive. His father had never treated her well and had disappeared soon after her death. The park-world crucifixions had been around that time, but he had been too young to understand. And in those days of mild warmth between Amerika and Yamato, when Lucia Henry had been President and the government had played Yamato's tune, there had been a huge cover-up. Only later, when Alia Kane had exposed the iniquities of her predecessor, had he seen the tapes and seen his mother's body hanging there.

The *kempei*'s command to confess all had made him dig deep inside himself, deeper than ever before. He had confessed too to believing their genetic report on him. Half racial Japanese, they had said. Father's side. There was no doubt. He had not known anything about it. Hadn't there been an official visit to Liberty by the Emperor and a huge entourage? And the touble between his father—Ellis's father—and his mother . . . it might easily have been. Easily.

He had signed that declaration, but they had smiled, delighting in the special terror he had for the sudden rootlessness it gave him. Once a man's past was taken from him, he was nothing, a confused wanderer, a man with no certain rock on which to build his identity.

He stumbled then, but his *komuso* took his elbows and helped him up. He stiffened, but they pulled him on until they reached the timber stage. There the prisoners were urged forward to climb the steps and take their places for the solemnisation of the proceedings, and he suddenly saw himself as others must have seen him, cringing and being carried forward as a coward. Something unbearable squeezed his heart. Will you stand up, or will you be led like a beast, Duval Straker? Choose! But look how Juli Dexter battles them every step of the way; she gets nothing but bruises and only rouses the crowd further with her resistance. So is that courage, or cow stupidity? Isn't courage nine parts stupidity? Isn't that what Ellis used to say? And the last part was what? *Defiance!* He heard Ellis say it clearly. Show the world you defy it and it runs like a kicked dog. Dare to do as you please. Lift your head up! Go boldly, and be proud!

He felt the tight fist in his breast loosen. He shrugged off the hands that held him, climbed unaided. His shoulders went back. His head lifted. And courage did fill him, driving back the terror as he mounted with the others into the prisoners' dock.

A huge gong clashed and reverberated. Silence was called. The great banner of the *kempei*, as big as a nexus ship's tail fin, was broken out on a tall mast, rippling across the most impressive square on Sado. A huge silken rectangle on which the golden image of the *o-gohei* was represented, fluttering for the cameras. Then a tiny form in flowing purple garb mounted his high podium under that immense banner, and soon the goggling crowd was silent, bowing, down on their knees in a full kowtow, hushing children and straining all to make sense of the piercing words ringing out of the speakers.

"By the authority of the Emperor, the Imperial Office of the *kempei*, and of the Council of the Supreme and General Bakufu of Kyoto, according to the precepts contained in the Instructions of Nikko, I do hereby declare this judgement made."

Fukuda began to read out the sentences. He came first to those that were dead or escaped, dealing with them at length, discussing the baseness of their crimes. As the man spoke Duval watched the mood of the people change; a great stirring in the crowd began, swirls of ill temper rising up like a wind passing across a rice field, ruffling the sea of heads as their feet shifted and shuffled. He could feel their indignation grow into hatred; their voices raised in ritualistic answer responded louder each time. One by one, the vile effigies were taken up and imprisoned in cages, each to be absurdly lectured at and shown in ridicule to the baying crowd.

Then a gate in the dock opened and Dean Jarvis, the *Thomas J.*'s chief armorer, was hauled up.

"Gunner, can you understand it?" di Barrio whispered suspiciously. "What's the *metsuke* saying about him?"

"It's a very old form of Japanese. But he said that Jarvis secretly urinates on the graves of samurai and that the *o-gohei* weeps and sheds blood for shame at it."

"The devils," di Barrio said. Her thick brows set close over her eyes. "What the hell was all that truth shit about, if they were going to condemn us on lies anyway?"

Jacob whispered. "I was on Panay in 'oh-two when the *kempei* took a buddy of mine on the evidence of whores and thieves, and the year after Captain Lennon was taken for straying into Yamato itself."

Di Barrio nodded grimly. "I heard they took him to the Castle of Himeiji, the *kempei*'s fortress on Kyoto. They Probed him like they Probed us and stripped his mind bare like a maple tree in winter."

"They're insane," young Cadet Philips mumbled.

"No, Cadet. They took him for his ship, and all her cargo and above two million in credit. That was how Fukuda Ikku got his first fortune—by plain robbery!"

"And they call us pirates!" Chambers said.

Horner scratched at his chin. "The money I had stashed up! Jeezus, it makes me sore as hell."

Mario Agasi grinned tightly, full of false bravery. "That brother of yours'll punish 'em now, eh, Gunner? They got no answer to men that's aboard nexus ships. Free men curdle their blood!"

"No man'll save us now," Jeb Womak told him balefully. "We'll be locked up till we die."

"You think that's what'll happen to us, Gunner?" Jacobs asked hopefully, not daring to face the other possibility. "That we'll have to wear these stinking necklaces forever, and all?"

"We'll know that soon enough."

Horner pointed to the crosses waiting at the execution ground. The road to it passed under an arch on which was built an old guard tower at the northernmost corner of the daimyo's residence. It was next to the kitchens and now served as a loading hatch for rice. The deliberate withholding of technology from areas of life where it was not strictly necessary was a major part of the Yamato ideal. The *han* system of agriculture and industry tied the population closely to a patch of ground where they could be controlled absolutely. Despite the spread of Dover technology, rice was grown manually, harvested manually, and transported by road to the cities to be cooked in the old way. Only food handled in this way was considered properly edible outside the ruling classes or the military. The cities themselves were built almost exclusively from traditional materials; only samurai of the first and second ranks and a few technicians and *han* retainers were permitted to deviate from these rules, and then it was a scrupulous matter of necessity. It had never seemed odd to Duval that Buddhist nuns rode donkeys in the square or that ox carts were often to be seen standing under the arch and rice sacks being hoisted up by simple pulley into the house of a planetary ruler of the twenty-fifth century.

Now the same arch was dressed with soldiers of the daimyo's personal guard.

"Look at those ugly bastards in brown. Trust the daimyo's men to get the best view of the killing."

"They'll be severe on us," Jeb Womak said. "Don't doubt it. They all fear what Ellis Straker can do, and they want us for examples!"

Philips's voice quavered. "What became of them, Captain di Barrio?"

"Who, Cadet?"

"Captain Lennon and the other one?"

"They got away, don't you fret now. And they both got home and went on the broadcasts. Saw one of them on a gossip show when I was at Harrisburg one time. Just like you'll be doing in a year or two."

"You think so?"

"Sure."

"Yeah, and if Lennon hadn't escaped, we might not be getting nailed up now," Kaiser whispered fiercely. "He was my hero as a boy. He was the only reason I signed up."

Young Philips swallowed hard, staring at the crowds.

Di Barrio leaned across. "They'll not crucify you, son. You're too young. Plenty of work in you yet. It's the old gals like me they want to get rid of. Folks set in their ways. They know there's no hope of keeping this Amerikan down. Now, get your chin up, Cadet."

"Yes, Captain."

A hush swept across the Square of Perfect Harmony as sentence was made on the armorer: to receive three hundred lashes and condemned to serve on the Imai *han* as slave if he survived. He was led out of sight by another way. Juli Dexter was next to be dragged out. She fought like a wild thing, mouth still gagged, nostrils flaring, her single eye vicious. Her headband came off again and she knocked down a guard, but her hands were bound to the yoke around her neck and her struggles soon subsided.

"What's he saying now, Gunner?"

"Crucifixion."

"God help her."

Agasi's "Amen" was echoed a dozen times among the remaining prisoners.

Next, Cadet Philips was brought out and told he would be taken to serve in a Zen monastery for the rest of his life. He also was led away. Duval strained to watch the way he went, disappearing behind the staging and reappearing briefly before being clapped astride a donkey and conducted under the arch towards the *kempei* prison. It was at this place at the corner of the daimyo's residence that he had lost sight of Juli Dexter a second time. He had passed under the guard tower arch and had been taken right instead of left, towards the execution ground instead of the prison. Already part of the crowd was breaking away from the main body and trying to get through the bottleneck to congregate in the spots that gave the best view of the crosses, but the soldiers forced them back. On the far side, partly obscured by the residence, the crosses were visible, too many of them to give any hope to those that awaited sentence.

Another was led up before the *metsuke,* then another and another in strict order. One by one the rows of kneeling prisoners were emptied. Nausea rose in him at the sight of those vacant places. Then the next man was called, the first of his own row. Spaczynska and Mathias and then Roberts went up, then Shamir and soon van Heever. Beside him Helene di Barrio was pulled to her feet. She turned and offered her hand in a final gesture and Duval took it. For the first time he saw fear sparkle in di Barrio's eyes.

"God love you, Helene."

"And you, Gunner."

Then the gate was opened and di Barrio went out to receive her sentence of death.

17

Wataru Hoshino climbed into the ox cart and stood up to get a better view, but what he saw dismayed him. Things had come to a pretty pass. It wouldn't have happened like this in the days of the last Emperor, he thought. Not in those days, when this planet was a truly new world and the only samurai in it were heroes—real men, soldiers and pioneers that blazed the path and knew the Way, not like those that followed them, jumped-up bureaucrats, half-witted administrators, power-hungry monsters like Fukuda who twisted Japan's ancient and honorable culture to suit their own cravings.

"Get down, old man!"

The shout made him turn in anger and brandish his fists at a lumpish, flat-faced *ikki*. "Mind your manners, peasant!"

"Hoh, what's this, old man? I don't see your topknot!"

The face of the man's wife screwed up tight. "Oh, leave him alone, he's not samurai, he's just crazy."

"I can't see through him or his damned ox cart."

"Get on! Yah!" Wataru turned away furiously, pushed two children off the high, latticed sides of the cart, and lashed the oxen. One groaned languorously, both moved forward. People parted before the pair as they stumped towards the cleared roadway. The big spoked wheels creaked and turned, plowed a furrow through the crowd. Necks craned forward to hear the latest sentence. Those he displaced looked on him with annoyance and offered insults, others tried to hush them.

"Where are you going?" the rock-faced sergeant demanded, flourishing his stick.

Anxiety swept through Wataru's belly. What if they stopped

him? Or held him up? Had he moved too soon or too late? His head bobbed and his manner became fawning. "I am ordered to the execution ground, Sergeant-*sama*. Ritual *sake* for the celebration."

"You can't go that way."

"How else can I get there?" He put a horrified expression on his face. "I have very big orders."

"I said, you can't go that way!"

"But I cannot disobey the orders of the lord!"

"What orders? By who's command?"

"A mighty captain," Wataru said.

"Which captain?"

He looked around and pointed across the square. "The one in the fine *kunari-kabuto* helmet, with the *yoroi* armor. Him. There, you see? His clan is Hasegawa, and he said that if I had any trouble with—"

"All right, old snake. Come with me."

The sergeant laid hold of the ring in the nearest animal's nose and tugged. Once again the beasts lumbered forward, into the lane down which fifty condemned *gaijin* had already been led to their reward.

* * *

Another orchestrated roar swelled out from the crowd, but this time it was louder. It echoed under the high arch of the disused guard tower at the corner of the Square of Perfect Harmony, and round the dark chamber within which Michie had hidden herself. The room was dark, but shafts of dusty sunlight speared the gaps in the tiled roof, piercing the gloom. The sounds of the vast show trial filled the space around her.

Oh, the gods must help me. Please, family gods of the Hasegawa clan, help me. Oh, the Seven Gods of Chance, the *shichi fukujin*, I beg you all, invisible *kami*, intervene and save him. Her heart hammered under her sweat-soaked peasant shirt. She tried to still the shaking in her fingers as she knotted the frayed end of a rope that ran up over the roof beam and down in a coil; she had tied it to the beam and knotted it at two-foot intervals, but it would be useless unless she could shift the heavy rice sacks and open the hatch which they covered. She sank down, braced her back against the wall, and kicked out at them, but she could not shift them.

"May the gods give me strength!"

The hatred of the people had blazed up each time sentence was passed, then each *gaijin* had been put ignominiously on a donkey and led beneath her to be pelted and abused by the crowd. Each time she saw it she had gone over the plan in her mind, growing more and more certain that it could never work, but knowing she had to try.

The sacks were of polished rice and milled rice flour. Each alone was too heavy for her to move, and the terrified kitchen servant who had let her into the store had fled, taking one of her nuggets in payment for aiding her so far. He had refused to help her further, no matter what else she offered him. The block and tackle hung above her head on its steel eye as if mocking her stupidity. She had unthreaded the rope from the pulleys and knotted it and there was no time to repair her mistake. She kicked out again at the sacks in frustration as the roar of the crowd rose to a new menace.

This time the *metsuke*'s denunciation attained a terrible pitch. His acid speech dwelled upon the treacherous robbery on Okinawa and the murdering pirates that swarmed in the Co-prosperity Sphere.

"*How shall you deal with these* gaijin *devils?*" he demanded of the crowd. "*Tell me!*"

The answering cry was poisonous with hatred: "*Crucify him! Crucify him!*"

Were they leading him down so soon? The thought filled her with panic. She stumbled in her haste to get to the window. Fell. Lifted herself up. Pressed her eye closer to the broken slat of the louver and stared out into the brightness.

There, standing upright and alone in the center of the great stage in his heavy collar, was her husband. She had no time to think. He would be under the arch in a matter of minutes.

"*This evil criminal was treated with all courtesy by the Emperor and his daimyo, and by the people of Sado, but how has he repaid you? Even now his evil brothers lie in wait to destroy all who venture into the void! How shall we deal with him?*"

"*Crucify him!*"

Michie cast around in desperation, then fed her trembling fingers through the shutter and broke away the dry, jagged wood, turning it over in her hand like a dagger. One of the *gaijin* was clattering below on a donkey. She could see his huge craggy face set in a frightful mask. Then she saw Wataru's oxen appear to the right, led by a sergeant of the guard.

It's too soon, she thought desperately. Go back. Go back! By all the gods, we're lost! Lost!

She watched Wataru's eyes stray up to the small shuttered window and then dart away. He nodded very slowly. As the cart rumbled twenty feet below her, she saw that its steep woven sides were bedded with hay and that it carried two great earthenware wine flasks, each big enough to contain a man. Between them was a long-handled weeding blade. She saw the old man reach for it, sun flashed on the newly honed curve of steel, and then the cart passed out of sight under the arch.

She looked at the sliver of wood in her hand and then at the sacks, cursed herself for a worthless idiot for not thinking of it sooner, uttered a silent prayer to Inari, the rice goddess, who had surely put the idea in her mind, and set to work ripping into the sacking.

Duval watched the storm of malevolence surge around him and abate. Silence suddenly filled the yawning space. Ten yards away Fukuda Ikku's head was a shining skull. His sunken face was turned skyward, his hands stretched out in a piteous gesture of appeal.

"Receive sentence now, you polluted and impure interloper whose sins are so grievous and whose crimes are too evil to be heard! The Emperor's most humble servants demand that you show humility."

Hishikari put his mouth to Duval's ear, whispering hideously. "Bow down and humble yourself in front of the cameras and you will receive clemency, even now!"

"Do as he says. Please!" his *komuso* begged him. "For your own sake!"

Terror swarmed in him again, but he shook his head. He would never kowtow before the *metsuke*, bowing down before the whole of Yamato in obsequious respect! Never!

"You may be spared the suffering," Hishikari told him, his features twisted imploringly. "Consider the punishment, Duval Straker! Think of the nails biting through your flesh, the pain inescapable as you hang there slowly to die! Show the people your obedience, your acceptance of the *metsuke*'s ruling, and the executioner will strangle you quickly! Bow down like a samurai! Or you'll be reborn a dung fly!"

"The *metsuke*'s been correct all along." He heard himself say it, coolly, defiantly. "I am not a samurai. I'm an Amerikan. A *gaijin*. And Amerikans do not bow down to anyone."

Then they were leading him from the stage and down the steps, his hands bound numbingly tight, and they put him on a small donkey so that his toes almost touched the ground. The animal trotted stiff-legged under his weight, stepping through the dung of the others that had come this way. His deadening fingers felt the roughness of its neck hair, bunched the bristled mane in his bound hands; his thighs felt the bulbous abdomen of the beast; the ridge of its spine knuckled his testicles as it walked, parading him before the shouting peasants. He looked straight ahead, unseeing, and as the street closed in he felt the dream falling from him. The killing ground beckoned.

Feculence rained down on him, strewed his way, spattered the street with stinking swill, spattered the dark blue kimono of the *komuso* that led him. The pungent smell of filth and corruption filled his nostrils. Suddenly he saw with great clarity. This was the circumstance of his own death march. It was real. Sharp. Actual.

I must ready myself for death, he thought, confronting the inevitability of it for the first time. He looked about him. The details of faces impressed themselves upon him. They were no longer a crowd. The sound of every throat was distinct. He saw each watcher—young and old; man and woman; samurai and *ikki*—as an individual vessel, each the receptacle of an individual human spirit. He saw that some wanted to see him nailed up, others to excuse him. He saw hate raw in the eyes of some, and in some there was horror. Souls dull, souls radiant, hysterical souls, souls pleasured by the prospect, others ashamed, how some were twisted with guilt, how some had pity and some mere curiosity and others yet a wonderful human compassion.

The crowd thinned as the lane narrowed. In the square the ranks of soldiers on each side had stood shoulder-to-shoulder with overlapped pikes held horizontally across their breastplates like a human fence against the press of the multitude; here they stood singly at attention, backs to the wall of the daimyo's residence. Several had left their stations, and as the shadow of the guard tower passed over him as cold as death, he saw why.

An ox cart blocked the street in the bright pool of light beyond. Soldiers struggled to unhitch the team and clear the way, but one of the oxen lay heavily in the middle of the road, lowing fearsomely. He saw oozing red on its hocks and hindquarters where it had been untidily hamstrung.

"Clear a way, there!"

Orders rang out. Troopers tugged helplessly at the deadweight, dragged on the horns, holding their wide-brimmed helmets back out of their eyes as they tried to unfasten the yoke. The cart shaft lifted, bucked suddenly upward, the cart tipped back throwing out its bed of straw, and a big *sake* jar was dashed to shards on the ground, splashing gallons of heady rice wine across the ground. Another rolled and tumbled, guttering its contents out also.

A sergeant jabbed the air with his sword. "Watch him!"

"You there! Get back to your prisoner! And you! Get that old idiot away from the cart!"

The cart driver scrabbled in the ruts bathing his hands in his lost wine and the straw that was scattered all around, bemoaning pitifully. Then Duval suddenly saw the man's face. It was Wataru Hoshino.

This can't be happening, he thought, his mind knocked sideways by the confusion. It can't be!

He almost shouted the name of his friend, but saw the intent in the old man's face. Wataru's eyes met his disbelieving gaze as a brawny soldier grabbed his waist.

"Get out of here!" he shouted directly at Duval, then he twisted away and began to wriggle out of the soldier's grip, raising as much noise as he could.

"Hold him!"

Duval heard a scraping sound above his head, then movement

drew his eye upward, but he looked away again instantly, certain that the tilt of his head would make others lift their eyes. White grains began to rain down from a hatch that was hinging open in the planking high above his head. It's a miracle, he thought. Either that, or I'm already dead. What's that falling? God's eyes, it's rice! Then a heavy coil of rope dropped on him from above and he grabbed for its knotted end instinctively, at the same time kicking out at the man who held his donkey, sending him sprawling and the beast skittering away.

"Zinan-san!"

The shout mortified him. "Michie-san!"

"Quickly!"

The square above his head filled with her hair and face and great gouts of rice. All around the arch, the hard grains showered down, spattering off the guards' armor like hail. He locked the rope under his wrist bindings. The rope jerked tight, wrenching his elbows half out of their sockets, and he was suddenly above everyone's head and climbing for his life, his bloodless hands as weak as a baby's. He lifted himself up to the next knot, clenched his thighs on the rope, got purchase with his feet, and thrust. Below, the soldiers came to their senses. A hand closed over his ankle but he stabbed furiously with his heel and shook it off. He pulled himself up another knot.

"Look out!"

A ripped sack toppled, pushed over the edge of the hatch, and fell past him to burst on the ground in a cloud of rice flour. Another knot. Then the sergeant was under him, thrusting up with his sword. The evil blade jabbed, lanced through the bindings of his leggings. He felt the back of the blade strake his shin as it ripped away. He was nearly halfway up but the strength was dying in his arms.

"Climb, Zinan-san! Climb!" Michie was screaming at him, showering the torn sacking and its load of rice flour into the eyes of those below. Her hand groped for his wildly and then his foot slipped off the knot and he almost fell back. He was blinded. Blinking. Rubbing his eyes on his shoulder. Coughing. Choking on the flour—each breath caught in his throat. The world was spinning sickeningly. And his hands! They were insensible to his commands, all feeling gone from them.

"Help me!"

"Get up after him! *Dekiru dake hayaku!*"

"*Ita-i!* He's falling!"

He felt the rope tighten under his instep. One of the troopers was climbing, but the man's weight only served to hold the rope straighter and stop its wild twisting. Then he felt Michie's fingernails graze his arm. Her grip closed over his elbow with manic strength. His head butted the lip of the hatch as he burst through, panting, rolling on the floor as she dragged him inside.

"The rope! Cut the rope!" His voice was hoarse.

She stared about her, looking for the slat of broken wood she had used to rip open the sacks in order to move them. It was buried under the flour or gone through the hole. There was no time to find it. And it would never cut through rope. The rope was creaking, twisting. A trooper's crested helmet appeared in the space.

Duval got to his feet as she swung the heavy trapdoor over on its hinges and slammed it down. It failed to close flush because of the rope, but the falling cry of the soldier told them he had dropped. Michie untied the slack rope and let it fall also, then they were out and running, through the maze-like corridors of the daimyo's residence.

THE DAITO SYSTEM, N.Z.

Ellis Straker's ship followed the nexus chain towards Yamato, her galactic longitude discretely decreasing as she receded from the Twenty Degree Worlds; her galactic latitude remained almost fixed, as near as possible in the equatorial plane.

This system was bad news. They were lying a dozen AU off the largest planet of the white A2-type subgiant Daito—a system primary known to the Earth ancients as Gamma Scuti. Unfortunately the inner planetary system had never accreted in respectable planets, and a vast Saturnian ring girdled the star in a rare and beautiful stellar debris belt. The time they would waste getting out of its way was irritating. They had to cross it, opting for a catenary trajectory arcing up and over the ring towards the Yod-Four-Six nexus. An easy transit to galactic south lay the aprons of Banaba where the *Constitution*'s sudden appearance a week ago had thrown the system into confusion, but she had cruised on, ignoring the bristling hubris of the enemy. Her engines creaked and her stabilisers squeaked drily now, making Ellis think of the many schemes of running maintenance he had been obliged to put in hand of late.

On the bridge, meson cutters fulminated violet, throwing up the characteristic full-bodied aroma of marzipan as the drones applied plex solution to the seams. The methodical chunking of a wheezee sounded as a bulkhead was reshaped. The drones bleated. Above, the bridge dome was leaden and opaque, the shields troubled by an unrelenting meteoritic peppering that was beginning to annoy everyone, a day of restless peace and short comfort for a captain and his crew who hated to cruise blind. It was a ship-day that seemed to presage violence and unlooked-for trouble.

He sat in his command seat on the bridge in the waning UT forenoon, riffle-edged hard copy spread across his knees. The quality of tabulated information was clearer on hard copy. He had noticed that. The same data was on sheet, screen, and visualiser, but somehow the mind latched into one easier than another, and it was important that his mind latch correctly. He was planning the last piece of daring of this campaign and needed to think over the matter, but the stuffy air would not clear his head. For a while he allowed his mind to steer where it wanted, but too frequently his thoughts returned to that fine Sado *han* constructed in his imagination where his brother enjoyed gains more ill gotten than his own. It was a picture on which his mind's eye often brooded, and one which distressed him greatly.

The chime of the talkback as it turned noon reminded him that they had precious little left out of the tons of logistic stores that had left Harrisburg with them. He stretched, called for a juice, downed it, and sent the steward down for one of the small, sweet real *mikan* oranges that ripened in his cabin. When he closed his eyes, there was a bright Liberty landscape, fresh with snow, glorious cold on his cheeks and frost numbing his toes. Oh, for a Lincoln winter, he thought. A wind that bites and blows through a man, skeleton trees, iced ponds, and those subtle grays that hold more hidden colors than any garish outworld scene. How I long to see the familiar constellations high in the night, and the Wild Goose overhead, ah, so much Duval has lost . . .

The talkback sounded and Ellis opened his eyes. The black ring-stone of reproof glinted at him from his finger, the eagle motif a reminder that according to the original boundaries fixed by Earth Central, Amerika stretched from pole to pole between galactic longitudes thirty degrees and sixty degrees, in the general direction of the Old Earth constellation Aquila—the Eagle.

The steward reappeared with the orange. He took it, thanked the steward, and began to peel the fruit. It was how Ayrton Rodrigo had first showed him the astrography of Known Space: an orange two hundred parsecs across, with the Sun and Old Earth at its center, and the Beyond out there, outside the peel.

He broke out an orange segment and looked at it. The Sectors of Known Space were ever expanding at close to the speed of light, the outer limits being pushed relentlessly outward by re-lativisitic robot exploration. Their longitudinal faces were the-oretically separated from one another rigidly by Earth Central treaty along galactic longitude lines, though the treaty had many times been violated and the boundaries redrawn: zero degrees to thirty, the Neutral Zone; thirty to sixty, Amerika with its asso-ciated semi-autonomous quadrants of Kanada and Kebeque and Izrael, occupying the orange segment between the Neutral Zone and Europa; then Latina, Slavia, Brasilia, and Afrika, each thirty degrees of galactic longitude. Between two-ten and two-forty degrees Izlam; neighboring them, Hindostan; then the two Sec-tors of China: the Indo-Chinese Confederation with its amalgam of small quadrants, and Han China or Xanadu, called by them "Chung Kuo"—the Middle Realm—ruled by the Dowager. Last, and pointing towards the galactic center, the power-hungry Empire of Yamato.

There it was in his hand: Known Space, a giant *mikan* orange with twelve Sectors, six hundred fifty light-years cusp to cusp.

Ellis ate Yamato and chewed it to juicy pulp, spitting out a pip into his hand. Though Duval was long since disowned, he was not forgotten. The shame of him could never be completely stamped out, nor could a man stop himself from wanting to see his brother again—if only to put unanswered questions to him directly. He flicked the pip at a drone, bouncing it off the curved casing with a *ting*.

This was the fourth day since they had come zipping from the nexus, and his meticulous collection of astrographical data in the last three systems they had visited were by now fully notated with readings and braking instructions and reminders of debris hot-spots and landing markers cunningly downloaded from the pilot computers of captured vessels. These were the real treasures he would bring back to Amerika because they would enable others to follow in his star-wake and significantly improve their chances of success. He looked on them with great pleasure, but there was a worm in his satisfactions, because there were just lately a whole stack of new problems to overcome, problems born not of failure, but of success.

Each month, the *Constitution* had plowed virgin systems, cruising eastward as far as the Solitaires, grazing the riches of Pandora and of Rotuma, before disappearing for a time to recuperate. In June, without warning, they had surfaced at Pine near the Ten Degree Worlds, taking some useful small game— two transiters and a bigger ship—among the Tonga planets. Then again at Bismarck, lighting up the *Constitution*'s hull with anti-Yamato slogans to terrorise and infuriate the new army of occupation just as Oujuku had done to give the slaves hope and ideas of rebellion. In October they had taken a great bucket of a ship in one of the Korean chains, a trunker full of tributary presents meant for the Emperor and sent by the Dowager of China, in which he found a casket of superb emerald jewelry belonging to the captain. He had leveled a Nambu blaster at Ellis's breast to protect them, but its power had been flat, or its mechanism faulty, and without doubt good psi had prevented the discharge.

Ellis had had the samurai ignominiously stripped naked and poked round the ship with his own electric slave prod to roars of laughter. Then he had "bought" the emeralds for a bottle of water and a *komuso*'s straw hat when the villain was about to be sent off in his shuttle fifty AU from the nearest inhabited planet—close enough to save himself, far enough away to give him a raging thirst and shivers from the radiation belts and to make him think again about his laughing persecutors.

"Tell your compatriots these little green gewgaws are presents for my President," he had told the man as he was put aboard his own shuttle. "Who, if you're still in any doubt, is Alia Kane of Amerika, and is real pissed with Yamato right now. So *domo arigato* and fare-you-well, you unpleasant little sonofabitch."

In the year that had followed, Ellis had cruised the *Constitution* into all the main systems that the enemy held in the Zone and found that no big ship could catch her. Those speedier craft that could overhaul his eighteenth-power-rated engines were too light to hit him, and he knew that while he kept his crew in good spirits he could afford not to worry about pursuit or ambush, because, thanks to Ganesh Ramakrishnan, in the matter of locating ships before they located him, he could certainly have no equal.

In December of last year they had harried the Ontong Java and Nukumanu systems from a temporary base in Choiseul, and in spring they had come upon the Honjara apron and took a guard frigate there, relieving it of four hundred pounds of argentium. Ellis's confidence had grown with each success, and he found his fame had spread among the nexus men on which he preyed so that now few dared to resist when he closed with them. In all the systems of the Zone no Yamato commander could explain Ellis's ability to find and assess enemy ships or how he was able to distinguish which were ripe and which to be avoided. He had not told Oujuku of his clever trick, and he never divulged his method to any other man, no matter how trusted.

Bowen was the worst for curiosity, and after him, Brophy. Feldman Sark, the gray-bearded software techie, thought it a hell of a thing but knew better than to ask silly questions. From the corner of his eye, Ellis had many times seen Bowen and Brophy standing together, trying too hard to be surreptitious during each spell he had taken himself into the astrogation chamber to use the Ramakrishnan jewel. They had even gone so far as to rig a microcamera in the chamber to spy on him. And after that he had mercilessly wound them up to breaking point.

"There's no big deal," he had told Bowen blankly when his best officer had brought the subject up for the fifth time. "Good ship-handling and a great crew. That's all. Competence. No more to it than that."

"Yeah," Bowen had replied, unhappily scrubbing at his head. "But how do you *know* when a ship's worth the taking when she's no bigger than a pixel on the highest scanner range?"

"Oh, I just play a hunch."

"But why do you go into the astrogation chamber by yourself? There's not another captain I know does that unless he's planning a transit."

"It's quiet there and I like to think before we engage the enemy. C'mon, gimme a break, will ya?"

"Ellis, won't you tell us what's that little box you pull out, and that necklace thingumee you kiss and put on your forehead each time we sight a ship?" Brophy had asked. "What are those *incantations* you whisper?"

He had stood up then, shocked at their intrusion on his privacy. Then he had been grave-faced. "You've been *spying* on me?"

They looked like kids caught with Choko round their mouths.

"All right, Mr. Bowen, Mr. Brophy, you got me cornered. I'll tell you."

"Yeah?"

"Okeh, Captain!"

"Well . . . it's black magic."

"Black magic?"

"Yep."

"Jeezus, Captain!"

After a while Bowen had said, as mournful as a bloodhound, "I guess you're not gonna tell us, are you?"

"Nope."

Bowen and Brophy had gone away unsatisfied, and Ellis had known that one or both of them would be back, a week later, two weeks, two months—whenever the next ship was found and his inexplicable feat repeated.

Smiling to himself, Ellis settled deeper in his command seat now and watched Bowen. The problem was worried ragged now, but still unsolved. He had told no lies. The secret of taking nexus ships was indeed mostly discipline and the correct keeping of his ship and crew. And there were other factors: his policy was always to promise his intended victims that they would be accorded clemency if they surrendered, but that on the first shedding of Amerikan blood no quarter would follow. And he had abided by that, landing prisoners within sight of habitation and playing host to their captains, generally with good grace, and by this means he was able to plant the seeds of rumor in his guests and in return learn news of the Zone and draw off intelligence and therefore come to some understanding of how intensely his operations pained the Emperor's officers and how those operations might be made more troublesome still.

Ellis eyed the leaden dome again with disapproval. It was more depressing than radio black, but necessary. Debris against the shields became incredibly annoying as it flashed the bridge intensely with random light. There would be no letup to the blindness today. Another day lost in the quest to correct his sectional charts for field variation, and in arriving at a better estimate for the differential time elapse rates—general relativistic time lag—in deep-grav-well worlds. Luckily big primary star mass meant a fierce burning star and therefore temperate settled worlds were a long way out, and since energy flux and gravitational field strength both fell away as the square of distance, there was never much correction to worry about. The man who has the most accurate pilot computer model is the man who lives longest out here, he thought.

So far, their blend of good information and good psi had held them above trouble. There were enough uncharted dim M-subdwarf primary systems in the Zone to plant a thousand bases, and enough slaves to free on Yamato-annexed worlds to provide each with a permanent garrison. They had discovered side chains for use in time of low Index or to elude enemies. Onplanet, the men made good use of their time and relieved themselves of the wants that starfield trash must endure. Bowen had gotten three women with child at least, and in three separate systems. He had sworn to each that she was his only wife, though none were that in any Christian sense, as Nowell, the Southern Methodist lay preacher, had scolded him. Despite Nowell's frowning disapproval many of the men had done likewise, and he himself had eventually yielded to the carnal temptations that psi delivered his way. As for the female part of the crew, they had been more responsible over pregnancy—just as was expected of them—but even more enthusiastic sexually. It was a well-known fact that a man reached his physical sexual peak during his late teens; for a woman, it was her late twenties. Most of his crew were in their late twenties . . .

A happy crew, then, he mused, and a contented captain. But there were times when he was alone and quiet when he was reminded that there was more to his life's quest than bandit enjoyment and the arresting of Emperor Mutsuhito's lesser traffic. The strange pseudo-nova star which had wiped out Nagoya had remained in his mind. Here it would be a another fifty more years before its radiation wavefronts lit up the blackness of the sky. It would be even longer before any other Amerikans discovered it, and he thought again how right he and Oujuku had been to put a moratorium on the information. Policy had changed at home before, and one day he might need to use it.

And like the waning of a nova, he had progressively forgotten the shape of Reba's face, the timbre of her voice. How was she faring? As a mother? As a woman? How was she faring as another man's wife? And there was that bottomless question he had had to ask himself in solitary and soulless moments: is she even alive?

Lately he had begun to think about the real aim of his labors—to return home with the means to take what was rightfully his. But that remained a ransom greater than any he had yet won. As season passed into season, and year into year, Ellis had seen the boldness of his crew increase in step with their competence. It gave him cause to consider, because he found that to keep his people sharp he had had to give them greater and greater challenges. They had begun to spurn the small trunkers that had once been their staple diet, looking instead solely to the bigger ships. Each arrested vessel had outstripped the last in bounty and the richness of its pillage, and he understood that soon they would meet their match when their power to intimidate by reputation alone would fail. It was the fate of many a privateer who had grown too greedy. Eventually a pitched battle would be joined on adverse terms, good people would be lost, they would not prevail. It was something Ellis knew they must avoid at all costs, because the people of his crew were no longer poor nexus rats with nothing much to lose. They were all of them wealthy with immense credit fortunes stacked up, and there were many who wanted to go home to spend it.

At first he had put them off easily, a joke here, a petty threat there, but their unrest had become cancerous. He had told Bob Butcher, the drone specialist who never could keep his mouth closed, that the aurium that had gone back to Liberty with Oujuku was in trust, and that Oujuku had agreed to deliver shares only if Ellis returned. The rumor had persuaded some to give up their agitation, but eventually a formal deputation had asked him straight: "When can we go home, Captain?"

He had roughly reminded them of their oath to him on Oujuku's departure when the choice had been put before them which captain they wanted to follow.

"You'd be traitors to our mission and to me! You gave your word to it, all of you! Gave your promises to me!"

Stubbs, their ringleader, had spoken up. "Captain, a person can live in only one house at a time and marry only one partner at a time. What more have we got to get to satisfy you? How many years and months more? We want to go home."

"We sail home when I decide. Not before. That was the agreement."

"Captain, our fortunes're made. We've lost our appetite."

He had shouted at them, brought to the boil by that. "I'll piss crystals before I'll have it said of me that I was defeated by my own crew! That my own people copped out as soon as their bellies were full! Goddamn you all if you don't feel you've got a duty to Amerika to live up to!"

So their opposition had subsided into muttering, and to teach them to count their blessings he had taken them up into Kiribati, to a frigid, Plutonic lump of space-rock, and planted the choicest of their booty in deep-dug pits and gone quite secretly about it in case some among his people entertained other ideas. Then he had ordered Xavier Dunstan to modify the *Constitution*'s strong-room so that the walls phased clear and everybody could see the empty space inside.

"How hungry are you now?" he had asked when they were ranked up before him on the following Sunday. "The President herself ordered me to take an Amerikan ship into this Yamato-controlled territory and do what I could to harass them. And so I have. *And we will not go home until I say so.* Got it? Good! And now, if it's excitement you want, I've got just the thing, boys and girls."

After that, there had been more digging, this time back on Okinawa, but the gun-loving *gurentai* whom they met with again told them that most of their stolen aurium had been got out by the authorities, but that a typhoonicane had hit shortly after, and the rains had washed away the spheres which they had sunk under the riverbed, so they had contented themselves with what little they could find and fled to the Cabezas, leaving three aurium mines in ruins and more than half of Yomitan stripped of its domes. He had seen that both Taito and Kin were bristling with new beam weapons and Ellis knew then that there was no alternative: he would have to find a big ship and take it, or go home unfulfilled.

The first likely ship they came upon got away under cover of radio black. The second scudded for a secure nexus and so also escaped. The third was no easier prey. They followed her for forty AU across two nexi and into the Hog Sty, and she was fast, almost taking them for fools in the maze of small worldlets, but when she saw she was cornered she made to fight, struck her Yamato ensign off her hull, and scintillated a black field set with a white skull, which enraged them because that was *Constitution*'s own private ID and it looked like mockery. Ellis had cursed aloud, though his profanity was shot through with disappointment because the joke was that the ID now made the other ship impossible to attack—she was a friendly vessel, and her captain a man know to Ellis.

"She's a captured hull," he told Bowen angrily. "That's Kim Gwon Chung's trick. He's a totally crazy man, and he's only got one thought in his head, and a whole lot of the independent Korean way about him. He'll steal anything, even a man's reputation!"

"Shall we put the frighteners on him, then?"

"Put the frighteners on Mad Kim? Hell, no! I want to know where he's been and where he's going and what he's doing here without my goddamned permission."

Bowen had grinned. "You speak like he's a trespasser across your own backyard."

"He is. Though a welcome one now he's declared himself."

Kim had come roaringly aboard and Ellis had received him with a fancy dinner, but that night the Korean had said much to unsettle them all.

He had taken out his knife and cut a paring from his thumbnail in the pause. Black hair stuck up from his head like iron filings on a magnet, a great tuft of it bound up at the crown into a stiff fountain. His black eyes were half lidded as he scraped the filth from under each of his fingers in turn. His English was heavily accented. "You ask why I come out here. Answer I give not please you. We Korean pee-po throw out from your Sector. You President she turn against us. Appease the Emperor of Yamato."

Alarm had run through Ellis, and he had stared hard at his officers to quell them. Another turnabout in Amerikan policy was precisely what he had most feared and he wanted to open

Kim Gwon Chung out. Doubts for Oujuku's safety and the safety of their profits seized him. "Go slowly, Kim, I've been away a long time."

"We Korean pee-po sent out of Amerikan system to do for ourselves, ey? Order was: no goods can be brought to Amerikan aprons for fleet serving Keun Whan Pai. That no way to treat allies, ey? And then what can we do? Just go back to Korean worlds? You remember idea we had long time ago about we take Pusan back from Yamato?"

Ellis had nodded. That plan had been to land a force on the planet and to resupply it from Amerika. "Yes. I remember."

"I make plan real, ey? Without ally we throw back on own resource. Still, we hold Pusan and one week more we take Taegu also."

"Desperation makes good fighters," Ellis said, seeing Kim Gwon Chung's resentment and fearing his news more than ever now. How far can I trust the Korean's account, he had asked himself, knowing that there was little chance he could now predict the reception he would find on his return to Amerika, or learn of the reception Oujuku had received? If Conroy Lubbock's counsel had held sway, the President would have been persuaded to open negotiations with Mutsuhito, perhaps even to offer to mediate between Yamato and the Korean independent leader, Keun Whan Pai, power-broking in order to get Amerikan rebels repatriated out of Yamato territory, and to set the seal on a partitioned Korea. A mantle of pleasantries would have descended over Amerikan-Yamato relations, and Oujuku's head, or his own, might have been an appropriate token for Lubbock to lay at Mutsuhito's feet. That, and the expulsion of the Korean privateering force from Amerikan space, might just have bought the conditions Alia Kane so wanted to secure.

"So the rifle of Korea has backfired on Mutsuhito?"

"Oh, shu. That very true," Kim Gwon Chung went on. "We find many way to stop them. When Baron Harumi came with big army to squash us, we blow nexus at Pyongyang. When Yamato attack Kangnung, they lose two hundred thousand troops, and at Samchok we send many skimmer across flood to relieve city." Kim's thick lips swallowed up another chicken leg, but his eyes were tempered by hard memories. His hand waved and banged extravagantly as he explained. "Because Harumi can't crush us, Emperor recall him like dog. Baron Makino go instead because Emperor think he better to talk, but we keep our base and shut the chain tight and starve him of everything until he terrify to death. No credit and no order, ey? When he die his scum go crazy, my friend, they riot through whole place. Burn and loot everything. Wonsan completely ruin and hundred thousand citizen dead. They delare Cho Sen of half quadrant. Very very double minus bad. But in independent Korea very different, ey? Keun president now. He take other half of quadrant and now too late talk because Yamato fury has unite everybody!''

''You say Baron Makino is dead?''

Kim bolted his mouthful and swilled beer after it with a gasp of satisfaction. ''Last year. Of assassin.''

''Who is his successor?''

''Who you think, ey? He's name as Prince Sekigahara, but I come here before he come there. My work in Korea finish, ey? I no have political fight now.'' Kim Gwon Chung nodded shortly. ''But I still try get rich. I kill Yamato, which I can't do now in Korea—or Amerika.''

Ellis had sucked in his cheeks. Prince Sekigahara, Yamato's new commander-general in Korea? Could it be true? They're calling their annexed part of the Korean quadrant ''Cho Sen,'' their old name for Japanese-dominated Korea. What could that mean? But if the terms of peace really included a free, partitioned Korean quadrant with Keun Whan Pai as president, just as Kim said, then Lubbock's policy had triumphed. The many factions in half of Korea united against Yamato tyranny? The army of occupation in that half to be disbanded? Mutsuhito still nominal Emperor in Cho Sen, but all liberties secured? No, he thought. It's more likely that Kim Gwon Chung's adventuring in the Zone has been prompted by another, more personal cause. I'll bet that you've been run off by the traders for some reason, Kim. You must have many enemies among the Korean merchant community after the way you gorged yourself indiscriminately on their cargoes during the blockade, and you're no diplomat. But what if you're telling me the truth? If Prince Sekigahara's really about to take over in Cho Sen, it can only mean that Mutsuhito wants to bring the quadrant totally under his control once more. Under the bastard prince's personal command, forces can be raised and gathered for a strike, and hadn't Cassabian always said that Prince Sekigahara's hawkish ambitions were the main danger to Amerika? The prince believes that Yamato can never consolidate power in Korea until Amerika is brought down to the status of the Emperor's vassal.

"I see by your ship that you've had success," he had said to Kim, switching the subject sharply.

"Some. You not first Amerikan we meet, ey? Many Amerikan beyond Ten Degree World. They say they suffered great loss. More ship destroy this three year than all time before."

"The Emperor's daimyos are under orders to reinforce their planets."

"That not reason."

"Then what?"

Kim's scowl had revealed an engrossing fear. "Don't know. But you be careful, something very bad cruising around, take men and ship wherever strike at Yamato. Maybe new gun Yamato have. Europan say too many their ship disappear off Palawan. They say monster loose in this space. I believe. That's why I take *Tenno* and destroy my own better hull, to go under Yamato ID."

"And then mine?"

"Oh, shu. That a joke, ey? Between two friend."

"You showed my hull patterning, Gwon. You stole it."

Kim Gwon Chung dropped the knuckle of meat into his plate, splattering himself with gravy. Slowly he said, "I hear Yamato hate your gut, Straker. They say you dog—can smell fear in victim. That good enough for me."

Ellis had grinned at that, knowing that his own ID channels seldom carried any recognition device until he judged good reason to allow interrogation. Only then did he show his death's head. He said, "I've never heard of a sheep in wolf's clothing. No more skulls, Gwon. Understand?"

"If you want, Ellis."

"I want."

He had bidden Kim good luck then, and given him a download of his data on Solomon and the fascinating system called Ball's Pyramid to help him in his prowling, then they had parted umbilici to trust to psi in their separate ways, knowing that once out of sight the Korean would continue to ID with the skull just as it pleased him.

That had been a month ago, and Ellis roused himself from his thoughts; the Index was rising and the noon chime had sounded, bringing up the starboard watch, so he went below to eat. He spooned down a fast meal, then he kicked off his boots and read a while, drowsing in his strap hammock until his mind was triggered by a commotion on the talkback. By the time Dannyl Peeters, his steward, had brought his boots back he was looking around, barefoot.

"Scanners pick up engine spectrum, Captain."

"Yep. Give me my belt."

Peeters's hands were red. He hovered anxiously. "You'll be wanting your flexi too?"

"I'll call for you if there's any likelihood of fighting."

"Thank you, sir."

Peeters took himself away sharply. His concern for his captain's safety was commendable, but Ellis wished he would restrain the urge to make him wear his flexiplex vest whenever the prospect of a little brawling came up.

As soon as Peeters was gone, he took the ion key from his neck, opened the safe, flung out his most precious belongings onto the floor, and unlocked the secret compartment in the back, sliding out the small box from inside. Then he took himself forward, clamped his secret cargo under his arm, and began to climb up to the astrogator's chamber. When he reached the vault door, he glanced down at Brophy, who was shouting something silently back down the corridor. He hooked Brophy towards him with an angry finger and sent him on a time-wasting errand to check out the port stabilisers before locking the vault and putting the jewel to his forehead. What he dreamed made his heart beat faster.

"Yes, by God! Look at that!"

Through Ganesh Ramakrishnan's wonderful device the alien ship became a babble of thoughts against a background of absolute three-degree black-body silence. The captain stood out among a rainbow of spurious colors that boiled like a summer's heat haze with that odd echoic feel the instrument gave to distant thoughts. She was a big ship: four-quad engines and a sense of security. Five thousand tons, if she's fifty, he told himself with unholy joy. His blood began to flame at the prospect. She's doing fifty gee, or I'm a Mexikan. What a beauty.

"Steer for her, Mr. Bowen!" he shouted. "Alert condition one!"

The answering cries barked up at him from the talkback.

This was what he had been hoping for. With luck, she would

be as mass-laden as she looked. In his third eye he watched her hull turn slowly above the stellar pattern, then, some minutes later, she began to shear off from the nexus.

He met Brophy on the bridge with his astounding conclusion. "She's a Yamato nexus ship, and she's seen us," he told him, unnerving the man hugely. "She's out of Seram, heading, I trust, for Dolak and the way home to Yamato, but it's my belief she'll try to hide in Tanimbar or Aru if she can. She's worth taking."

"If you say so, sir."

"Do you doubt it, Tom?" Ellis turned to Ridgeway, who was sitting at the helm console. "Follow her, keep alt green one-ten and to starboard and close as soon as you can."

As the seconds ticked away, the nexus ship grew, fulfilling the predictions Ellis had made. The asteroids and dust and un-accreted debris of the planetary system were strung out all around, slipping by as the UT afternoon wore on. The victim was making for the dense co-orbital plane of the belt like a rat bolting for its hole. It's her only chance of shaking us off, Ellis thought, as he watched the maneuver. In a straight chase she would be relentlessly overhauled by *Constitution*'s better speed, but the high mass of the transport was a powerful reason not to stray too far into the dangerous dust belt. The extra momentum made her vulnerable to collision with a lump of rock the shields could not deal with. Material objects could pass through a shield with an ease inversely proportional to their impact speed. Up to around a relative velocity of fifty miles per hour they would move as cleanly as a shark through water; after that the fields really started to bite, and even massive objects were slowed like a Ping-Pong ball trying to rise through a column of molasses. The energy shedding led to internal heating and usually burned the object up in a fierce flash of energy. If the object encountered was really massive, several times bigger than the ship itself, the burning would be explosive and would blast the ship with X-ray and gamma radiation. The only strategy then was FRM jinking—fast reflex maneuver. But in an environment like this, with thousands of potential collision objects, FRM would tax any ship to its limit.

I felt she had a desperate astrogator aboard, he thought. One who knows this system well. And a good pilot computer to take control as the ship threads her way. It's what I'd do, if I were in her captain's position. This one's got spirit and is willing to make a fight of it. The ship's a water buffalo, heavy, and crossing to Yamato. She has more than a hold full of freezees, but I couldn't tell what. Maybe she's rich. Maybe she'll be our last prize and our passport home. We dive through the ring plane in five hours. With good psi we'll catch her before then, and we'll find out.

20

Captain Arima Yoshisabura sweated as he waited for the pirate to close on him. He was a fleshy man, broad like Chiyonofuji, his sumo hero, and rolls of fat wreathed his neck. His good ship, the *Kawabata Yasunari*, belonged to Senpaku, a rich merchant corporation headquartered in Shikoku. Her holds were full of aurium, and her stern quarters carried twenty-five passengers, from the exalted brother of the daimyo of Oshima, who had embarked on the first day of the second month of this 29th year of the Kanei era, down to the *ronin* and his pregnant wife, who had come aboard three days ago at Chichi-jima and whose waters had broken the moment they had sighted the pirate.

"Why do the gods trouble me so?" he asked the screens. A shout of *mutsu*—six minutes—came from the helmsman. The ring was approaching as the ship bore along the steep trajectory. "I knew I should have denied that woman."

The cries of labor came from the passenger quarters, upsetting the crew and making them mutter about bad psi as they worked. *I knew there was something suspicious about them,* Arima decided, watching the *ronin* standing anxiously at the bridge rail. *And yet I allowed them to come aboard. The woman is beautiful, far too beautiful to be a wandering, lordless, half-witted, minor samurai's wife. And she has the bearing of nobility about her —I'd say a top samurai family, at least second rank. It was she* who had done all the talking, and the *ronin* has said little. He wore the two swords, but once he had thrust them into his sash cutting edge down, so they curved up like a monkey tail. That was something no real samurai would do. His accent's strangely unplaceable, that alone should have warned me. The men are right: nothing has gone right since they came aboard.

But there had been the aurium nugget which she had paid for passage. It had been too much for a man to resist. In Chichi-jima he had thought the nugget was stolen and she the thief wanting to escape to Yamato, but there had been no evidence of that, and since the ship was to light out on the next launch window with one corner of her accommodation yet to be filled, he had decided not to deny her. Even though the woman was perilously close to her confinement, and he had explained to her that the voyage would last at least five weeks, she had implored him.

"You understand that there are no special facilities aboard my ship for a woman who must give birth?" he had told her kindly on the Chichi-jima apron, turning the heavy nugget over so that it caught the light. "No freezee facility. No surgeon. Only par-amedic."

"So sorry, Captain-san. Do not trouble yourself. I have been on board a ship before, and so long as I may have privacy and cleanliness I shall be content."

"Your need to leave Chichi-jima must be urgent to put yourself in this position."

She had taken the nugget back angrily then. "With the *kempei* killing hundreds in Chichi-jima, Captain-san? My husband is *ronin,* and the *kempei* blame us for everything, as if having no lord were our fault. When the Old Man died without issue, his *han* was broken up and his less useful retainers scattered to the winds. My husband is not very quick in the head. Which course would you try? I must think of what is best for my baby."

So he had shrugged and allowed her to come aboard, even after she had produced her idiot husband—it was truly a very valuable lump of aurium—but he had begun to watch the man closely, and he had seen the way his apparent imbecility fell away from him when he thought himself unobserved.

Look at the way he regards my beam weapons to distract himself, Arima thought. Is that not an *examination*? He says nothing, but sits alone watching my men come to quarters, but is he not itching to tell them their errors when they run in and run out? And errors are not difficult to find, for this crew has been gleaned from every low terminal hole in Chichi-jima and Sado and is the scum of the entire Sphere. They are without even the basest elements of gun control. But, by the gods, there's no doubt—that's a look of appraisal if ever there was one! This man propped against the control console so innocently is no idiot *ronin*.

Arima looked out at the screen once more, eyeing the pirate solemnly. Because control of the ship was with his system software, he felt redundant and extraneous. This pirate was fast and would be upon them within the hour. He had gambled that they might shake her off among the dangers of the belt where no navigation system with special knowledge could help them. Without sufficient occupation, Arima's brain fretted for the safety of the Oshima daimyo's brother who was samurai of the first rank, samurai to the core, who would rather die than allow himself to be ignominiously ransomed. If the pirate was of a certain kind, he would think nothing of destroying them all for having dared to attempt escape. Pirate gun crews knew the business they lived by, but *Kawabata Yasunari* was a big ship and her guns were adequate and pirates feared the loss of their means of escape. A volley of well-placed beams might penetrate her shields and send her off after other carrion. And there was still a slim chance that she would vaporise on the treacherous asteroids of the debris belt.

He descended the bridge companionway, passed hurriedly by the nearest starboard side gun blister and by the *ronin*, who leaned against it, then he turned as if in sudden absence and commanded him to hand him the arming key.

The *ronin* bent to it immediately and his fingers closed over the handle of the ion mechanism used to actuate the arming of the gun. Then he froze, realising his mistake, and bowed his shaved head.

"So, *ronin*, you know something of beam weaponry and the firing of ship's guns."

"*Iiye*, Captain-san. No. *Gomen nasai*. So sorry—I don't know, sir."

"Don't lie to me! I'll order you frozen down when we get to Dolak."

Duval Straker stood under the captain's eye, thinking furiously and damning himself for his foolishness. The privateer, which was almost certainly Amerikan from the shape of her hull and the cut of her tail fin, would be upon them before the Hour of the Horse was up. That meant a running battle or surrender, and judging by Arima's actions so far and the stories he had heard of what lay in the vessel's cargo bay, there would be no surrender. He heard Michie cry out in pain from the baby in her belly, and icy sweat broke out over his face. The fear of battle or a stray beam that forced its way through the shield could easily affect the birth if they made a stand of it, but if he refused to aid Arima and the privateer overcame them, what then? How might a pregnant woman be used aboard a pirate, Amerikan or not? He itched to punch Arima's mouth for his rudeness, or to show him what he could do with a gun, but he maintained his humble stance.

A shout rang out from the bridge. "*Itsu-tsu!*"—five minutes!

"Please let me go to my wife. The birth is starting. Please, Captain-san, I only heard the technical words your crewmen speak."

"Liar! You are not samurai."

"Please, sir. I'm *ronin*, dispossesed of the *han* of Yamaguchi on Chichi-jima these past two years."

"I don't believe you."

"It's the truth, sir. I swear by my ancestors."

It was no lie. The escape from Sado had been miraculous. Almost the entire guard had been in attendance on the *kempei* show trial, and Michie had led him to the courtyard where a fast air-car waited. They went unchallenged as they fled, following totally deserted air lanes until they had run out onto the eastern flightway and the open country. There, Michie had proposed that they turn north and head away from Chiba to the place Katsumi had designated as a rendezvous, but he had overruled her on a powerful certainty that the escape had been too easy and that the daimyo's hand was deeply in the matter.

"Did you tell Nishima-sama that I alone possessed the formula that defined the shape of the compression chamber?" he had demanded of her.

"I had to, Zinan-san. To secure his help."

"Then we have to go east!"

"But Katsumi-san is waiting for us."

"Yes! He's waiting, all right! With a troop of soldiers and a

Probe. Don't you see? It's not me they want to preserve from the *kempei*'s crosses, but my secret. Katsumi would take it from me and send me back to Fukuda Ikku like a dog!''

''You must shave the top of your head.''

''What?''

''Shave your head. And get a change of clothes. It's the only way. If they think you are samurai, we may be able to bluff and bribe our way out.''

They had torn the engine out of the air-car, winging towards Niigata, where the *ya* would be packed with strangers, and then they had gone down to the apron and taken ship for Chichijima, where the *kempei* had not yet spread. They had transited to Chichi-jima and hidden themselves in a small town there. He had lived like a *ronin* so that their identities could remain hidden, and for two years he had drudged at bits of work, until Chichi-jima too began to come under the basilisk stare of the *kempei*. He was recognised by a soldier in the marketplace in the town where he had gone to sell hens, and immediately he had known they would have to leave, despite Michie's condition.

Arima's impatience flared up. ''I warn you, foolish man, don't try my patience. I give you a choice: If you are a gunner and agree to help us fight, then you may stay here. But if you insist you are *ronin*, you'll be a *ronin* below, in the brig. Now, answer me.''

''Captain-san, am I not a paying passenger?'' he wailed, feeling himself tighten inside. ''You cannot do this. Let me go to my wife!''

''*Yotsu!*'' Four minutes!

Arima let out a gasp of frustration. Four minutes! The belt was growing dangerously dense, but no matter how dense it became, the raider would always have the option to follow. ''Take him away!''

Two men seized him and pulled him below. Then the muffled boom of a contact sounded and a plume of orange light fountained off the shields overhead. It was the pirate's longest range beam—a range testing shot rather than a power shot. Arima wheeled and went to his command chair, forgetting about the *ronin*.

The pirate had come within range and it was time to make a decision.

Ahead the belt was beginning to widen menacingly. The probability computation gave him a result.

"*Chiku-sho!*" Damnation!

They would have a less than even chance of coming out the other side. Arima saw that now there would be no chance of shaking off the pursuit, and he determined to make his stand if the gods gave him the hint of a chance. He asked the helm to take a parabolic trajectory over the upper surface of the ring and then head for the open space where he might at least have unhindered time to bring his own weapons to bear. The pirate followed, understanding his decision and waiting for the moment menacingly. It began to dawn on Arima that there could be little hope of outthinking this predator. He ordered beams fired off from his forward blisters, for the purpose of exaggerating his report, then he gave orders for his ship to come to match velocity for tractoring. The words were as bitter as gall in his mouth.

The ID was full of interference across the intervening stretch of space—too much debris, and the words were indistinct and in strangely constructed and enunciated Japanese.

"Please to speak with us, for we are Amerikanmen and therefore well disposed to all if there be no cause to the contrary. Those who will not, or those that run from us, then his be the blame! Know also that if there be cause for warfare, we will be demons rather than men!"

Arima's fleshy frame quivered with frustration. Then he shot a glance at his first officer and said, "Tell them we'll comply."

21

As he was guided below through the fusty darkness, Duval could hear the soft moans of his wife's efforts. He was banned from attendance at the birth by custom. But a real samurai would have belonged to a *han* and that *han* would have had maternity facilities and equipment and midwives to assist instead of one terrified maid who knew nothing.

"Please do not imprison me, I beg you," he implored the hand. "My wife is helpless."

"Captain's orders," the man said woodenly, then he relented. "I have children of my own. Go to her and help her if you can."

"I promise I will not leave my wife's side," he said gratefully.

"See you keep your promise, or I will lose face, and the captain will punish me."

A makeshift delivery bed filled the narrow test-room chamber that was their accommodation. The narrow hole was crammed between the hot starboard stabilisers, just under the mid-hull airlocks, and was ablaze with small screens showing the output of every conceivable monitor or scanner aboard the ship. The plex spacers that supported the deck above thrust out across the cabin only a couple of feet above Michie's head, and she had braced her hands against them to fight the contractions. At her side a horrified young girl, the servant of a Senpaku corporate *bucho*'s wife, who were the only other women on board, dabbed sweat from her face with a rag.

"You can't come in," she cried when he appeared. "The baby's coming."

"Calm yourself," Duval said, wishing he could do the same. "I'll help."

The stifling heat was almost unendurable, the bed was soaked. Michie looked up at him and her exhausted eyes broke his heart. I wish I could help you, he thought, but how can I? He held her hand then, squeezing, willing his strength into her. Her pains ebbed and she breathed pantingly, so tired and waiting for the next surge. When the forward beam weapons fired, the maid jumped, but Michie merely rolled her big eyes up, oblivious to anything beyond the confines of the room, then the sweat began to stand out on her face again and she gathered herself to fight a fresh wave of agony.

Duval looked up at the dozens of monitor and scanner screens and glanced at those that showed the privateer. Through the light-haze of dust particles that glowed as the shields were peppered, he saw the two ship fields coalesce. A shuttle was approaching, probably packed with armed men. He could see from the markings that they were Amerikan. That's something at least, he thought. At least if they come here I can bargain with them. Or maybe not. Was it just propaganda that Amerikan pirates killed everyone. Was it? And what would they make of his samurai hairdo? With luck they'll loot us and leave and there'll be no firing, he thought. God forbid that there's any firing.

Michie's hand tightened and he held her as she grunted. The young maid knelt between her splayed legs. She looked up over the great swollen belly with a look of awe on her face. "I can see the baby's head. Push. Push harder!"

The wonder of the moment possessed him as he looked on. He heard the sounds of a boarding party entering the mid-hull airlock, of heavy feet on the deck above, then the oaths and gruff shouts in Amerikan of a body of raiders systematically combing through the ship for loot. But Duval Straker had only ears for his wife's grunts, and eyes only for the wrinkled head that was emerging from her. He stared, mesmerised by it. Wisps of dark hair and, incredibly, a small bloodstained face screwed tight against the shock of the living world, then a narrow shoulder, slick inside its mucous coat, and a perfect tiny hand. He reached out to deliver the arm and the torso and the purple trail of cord which he cut with his sword as soon as the legs came free.

Michie lifted her head to see.

"It's a boy, Michie. A son!"

He wiped the face and saw the toothless gums as the mouth opened, and some instinct told him to clear the slime from it with the tip of his finger to allow the first intake of breath. And there was a shuddering angry wail, like that of a small animal. Michie received the baby in her arms immediately and cradled him, and Duval saw the joy and adoration shining from her and he knew that he had witnessed the mystery of a profound miracle.

Slowly he became aware of a deathly silence pervading the ship. The Amerikans had gutted the *Kawabata Yasunari*'s cargo bays and gone, and he pictured Arima's men dourly watching the shuttle struggle away with their wealth. Then a torrent of cries rang out from somewhere, and he turned and looked up at the miniature monitor screens again.

There, sliding out into scanner range from the concealment of the ring plane, was a big warship. And her ID was Yamato.

22

On his bridge Ellis Straker watched the boarding party returning, and he took a reported assessment of the value of the haul they had brought off. It looked good. Very good. Bowen was on the screen, elatedly waving his arms from the copilot's seat of a shuttle that was loaded to its non-tare limit by the mass of four aurium flasks. He had told Bowen particularly: "No greedy diversions, no time-wasting. You'll take only what's in the cargo bay and the strongroom and we'll be away again. Don't even bother to disable her guns, she'll never catch us."

The *Constitution*'s own fearsome singularity weaponry was conspicuous in its obvious blisters, trained on the enemy's bridge dome, guaranteeing there would be no rash change of heart by her captain, but as Ellis watched he saw that there was activity on the other's decks, more than there should have been. When on previous occasions under similar circumstances they had lifted spoils from their victims and let them proceed, Ellis had almost been able to taste the burning humiliation of the ships' samurai masters. It had manifested itself as a sullen paralysis. No shouted insults, no bravado, just the shame of defeat and a skulking resentment. But this was different.

"Look, Captain! She's moving!" Brophy warned.

She can't be, Ellis told himself incredulously as he too saw the victim pulling away very slowly. The shields decoalesced, snapping into discrete ovoids, still ringing with a faint pink light of dust impacts. Because of the Hakon Effect, nexus ship shields repelled one another, but would coalesce like soap bubbles if a sufficient force carried the ships together. The fact that the repulsion force remained between the two ships when both were enveloped in the joint shield meant that pirates usually preferred to order their victim's shields shut down—unless they were very good at close-quarters steering. Unlike soap bubbles, however, the shields did not add algebraically: two coalesced shields were actually stronger than the sum of two individual ones—a classic case of the parts summing to a greater whole. A certain force had to be overcome in making the shields separate, and it was that kick that had alerted Brophy.

Ellis saw the *Kawabata Yasunari*'s gun blisters springing to life as the shields separated. Can't her captain see this is no bluff? he thought. We've position and enough firepower to tear her to pieces. And she's already lost her cargo. Jeezus, what's he doing? Okeh, at this range she'd cripple us if she could hit our shields for long enough, but we'd blow her to hell before she processed a byte.

"Keep us matched on her quarter, Feldman!" he shouted forward.

"Okeh, sir!"

A vision of horror came into Ellis's brain. They're unpredictable, these samurai, hotheaded, yeah, and as proud as cats. What if he's weighed his losses and decided he can't take responsibility for it? What if we've brought so much off him that he can't show his face again? Ever? He'd risk plenty to counter that, but he must be aware there's nothing he can do. He's raging! That's it. The mad sonofabitch's slicing his own belly open!

Ellis swept up the device that hung inside his shirt, licked it, and pressed the jewel to the node of his forehead and searched the other ship. He registered two men at the beam weapon on her dorsal blister, lining up on the shuttle as it drifted through the enemy shield towards *Constitution*. But there was something else, something undefined that rippled his psi-sense with instinctive alarm. Then he saw the scene dissolve in bright light, and the sound of the discharge reached him a split second later and the beam slammed into the shields. It was closely aimed, virtually stripping the tiny halo shield off Bowen's shuttle and throwing the craft into a violent spin. Had it been a destructor, it would have blipped the shuttle to atoms, but it was not.

"Get our own tractor on her! Now!"

Then pandemonium broke free on the talkback.

"Unknown vessel approaching! Azimuth red three-zero-decimal-two!"

"Captain!"

Ellis turned, taken totally by surprise. The screens showed the hull of a trader ship cutting into scanner range. The ship was thundering up from the mass of objects that made up the ring. He saw at a glance that she was a big, old trading vessel, with few guns and what there were probably old and weak, but she was accelerating towards them very fast, and her radio black must have been very good to deceive the discriminators so long. He located a commanding personality, a samurai who knew himself as Arima. Despite his thoughts being in Japanese, Ellis saw that he felt the fierce emotions that were associated with shame and the desire to avenge himself, and now unexpected hope directed towards the second vessel. Ellis realised immediately that the *Kawabata Yasunari*'s captain had registered her approach and it had fired his courage—and stimulated his fear.

"We can take them both without trouble," he told Brophy, holding the jewel to his forehead. "Starboard beam blisters, train on ship."

"Guns locked on," Nowell, the gun captain, shouted back.

"Teach them a lesson they won't forget, Jake!"

"Sir."

A second beam tautened from the *Kawabata Yasunari*, locking dangerously onto the shuttle. It was a powerful tractor, and the two beams wrestled for the craft, jerking it under huge stress forces in the space between the ships. *Constitution*'s tractors responded massively. Ellis reflected on the acuteness of their situation. Bowen's shouts of "Puuull! Puuull!" were anxious. They had a mile or so to drag the shuttle, but it was a tug-of-war they could not win.

"She's out of singularity range and taking the shuttle with her, by God!"

"Fire!" Nowell's brassy voice bellowed. *Constitution*'s full complement of beam weapons seared out, flinging lines of luminous energy at the *Kawabata Yasunari*. Tongues of raging fire were spattered up from her shields, shuddering her. Ellis turned to the new ship, something eating at him about the speed she was making. She'd be in range in seconds. He lifted his jewel once more and studied her echoing mind images. At once the unease grew within him. Nothing squared. She was closing with all speed, maneuvering as if to come deliberately alongside his guns. But there was total silence on her bridge.

Not even deep-sleeping minds were that silent. Not even freshly dead corpses. Something was wrong. Was it possible that some quirk of the ship's design was acting as a shield to the amplification powers of the jewel? Ellis studied the ship's trajectory carefully.

Either her captain's a fool or he's the bravest man alive, he thought. She can't fence beams with *Constitution*. Surely he can see that? Surely he can see what we're doing to the other ship! He can't be trying to bracket us. Then his third eye ran along the smoothness of her sheer. She was handsome in profile, and under the beakhead the lateral lines were neatly tapered into the stern engine pods. He followed their line back across the bridge and dorsal line, searching for an echo image. He found nothing except a curious rippling, and as she rolled into a banking turn he clearly felt it: *the entire length of her main deck and bridge were empty.*

"It can't be!" he roared. There were certainly minds aboard, but where? He just couldn't locate them.

He squeezed the jewel in his fist in exasperation, polished its big flat facet on his shirt, looking to Bowen's shuttle and willing the tractors to somehow prise the craft from the other's grip. He lifted the jewel, fitting the clean facet once again to his node. The strange rippling image was still there, and there were defocused voices coming from behind it too! Almost as if the decks were . . . *hidden behind holo animations?*

It was crazy. Tri-vee holos, got up to look like deck activity! But why? To conceal what? *My God!* Look behind! Jeezus H. . . . Look at the firepower she's mounting!

The *Kawabata Yasunari's* reply roared out. One after another, three energy beams stabbed toward the *Constitution*. One crashed into the shields and was deflected in a monstrous red plume, another slashed through the space between them and began to force their shield inward with intense pressure, but the third was tightly aimed at the place where the tractor beam emerged, and a snaking bolt of energy discharged inside the shield above the bridge, blasting the dome with intense radiation. The ultra-optical shutters sheared closed over the dome, but the ship was jolted. The deck bucked, a partially stowed meson cutter overturned and was flukishly activated by the static field. By the time the drone had caught it, it had sliced a hole two feet long by ten inches wide in the millimeter-thick plex base of the dome. The one atmosphere of standard air in the bridge began to blast out of the slit like a steam jet. A gale ripped through the bridge.

The A-section near Ellis was carried away and he was thrown sprawling. When he regained his feet, he was momentarily dazed.

Brophy ran to him. "Captain, you're hurt!"

"Get back to your station, goddamn you!" His ears were popping and he was swallowing like fury to ease the pain.

He searched the deck for his jewel. It was gone. When he reached the slit, he saw that it had been plugged by a raft of loose objects torn away in the sudden hurricane, including Sherl Martini, and that a drone had already creted over her lower half with some pink tacky gloop to seal the depressurisation. A sickly marzipan smell filled the air. Through the dome he saw the mask of her face, surrounded by a halo of long, straight blond hair, each strand standing out stiff as if with fear, but actually because of the intense static charge on her body. Her eyes were open and her mouth flapped horrifically. She would be dead in moments. There was no way to do anything for her, and everyone who saw her hammering soundlessly on the dome knew that it could easily have been them.

The *Constitution*'s second broadside charged the air with ozone, punishing the enemy's shield.

"Give fire to the other ship!" Ellis shouted, marshaling his people to get the *Constitution* under way. "The fight we came here for has sure as hell started. Whatever happens, we've come to our last battle. Show them Old Glory!"

Colors broke out along the entire hull. Down in the blisters and across the lateral line his gun crews struggled to line up on their new quarry. A running fight the newcomer wanted, and a running fight he would have. He looked at the efficiency and commitment of his crew and knew there was no force in God's universe that could match them when their spirit was in full flow. Suddenly his oppressive fears left his shoulders. His lungs filled with hi-ox air and his soul flamed. All the injustices of Niigata were ranged before him, and he felt the omnipotent power of the Great Satan of the Court of Kyoto falter and fade. Nobody could face down the sons and daughters of Amerika's ideal when they were free and fighting. Nobody. This was the beginning of the end for Mutsuhito's foul, slaver Empire, and the warriors of freedom would not be denied.

Bowen watched with slitted eyes as the mother ship's maneuver engines fired. The space between his shuttle and the

Constitution's bay that his own engines had valiantly fought to narrow began to widen—a quarter mile, a half mile, three quarters, as the engines glowed brighter. No matter how hard their own engines labored, they could not catch the *Constitution* now, but that would not stop him trying to the limit of his ability. His crew were terrified. They looked over their shoulders at the Yamato ship and he saw their agony. A couple more newtons per square meter from the *Kawabata Yasunari*'s tractors and they would be taken.

"We're losing," Zpinskoye cried.

"Yhare! Puuuull, you sonofabitch!"

He saw Stubb's face on the screen. "We're gonna have to let them have the shuttle, Bowen."

Bowen's fist crashed into the console. "I'll rig the destruct. Die clean and take a few of those bastards with me!"

"No, man! Bale out! We'll take you by tightening the tractor!"

"Can you make three one-ton flasks?"

"Let's experiment!"

They suited up and slammed up the overrides. The big doors sheared open and, one by one, three aurium flasks ejected, to be accelerated away by the tractor. Zpinskoye's red-suited body tripped out and dived away under the tight-beam force, followed by the rest of the boarding party. Meanwhile Bowen worked fast on the destruct panel, twisting in the two big ion arming keys and estimating the time.

The Yamato ship's tractor dragged at the shuttle inexorably, and it was accelerating faster as the balance of forces was upset. Bowen threw himself out, coiling in space and lashing out with his arms and legs. The *Constitution*'s beam picked him up and began to spin him back towards the shuttle bay. A dozen suited hands fell on him, hauling greedily, and as the *Constitution*'s bay doors sealed and the area pressurised, a dozen helmets came off.

Meanwhile, a new beam volley had blasted out from Nowell's weapon banks, shattering against the shields of the false trader that had stolen up on them. Ellis knew that the seven high-energy guns that were jammed along her lateral line would be lethal, that her captain knew she only had to close until they were virtually shield-to-shield and then a prolonged power blast with the big guns would cave the smaller Amerikan vessel's shields in. All pretenses had been dropped, and he thanked psi that he should have had the ability to see the threat soon enough to escape it.

"That's the bastard Kim Gwon Chung spoke about," he told Brophy.

"Yeah! I'll bet she's worked that trick on many a ship. She nearly worked it on us—and she might have a few other tricks."

"Not as good as the trick we've got for her!"

"Closing to singularity range, sir!"

"Fire at will!"

Nowell's guns blasted through the decoy ship's shields. His singularities cut through her raked-back hull just below the bridge dome. The devastating mass-eating saucers propagated through her, ripping her systems to ribbons.

"We'll see her bleed her atmos before we leave!"

Without her engines balanced, the enemy ship's tail juddered, spilling energy from her shields, and her captain was forced to crash off all power. The compensators failed. The hull bled gas at her stern, a cloud of evaporating solvents breaking from the neat holes in her. Amerikan fists punched the air. Cheers rang out. Lockjaw Smith flung Nowell's hat on the decking and stomped on it.

As the strange particle ring of Daito sped by beneath them, the *Constitution*'s singularity guns slowly reduced the Yamato vessel to a hulk. Unstoppable shots set her bridge alight, and searing explosions inside the now crazily transparent hull blew out of the pierced holes like volcanic vents. Ellis watched the *Kawabata Yasunari* flee away at a hundred gees, to save herself, away from the maze of asteroids, and he allowed her to go, seeing her shuttle bay smashed to a ragged pulp by the exploding shuttle. In that condition she would not make the Yamato Sector, and he was not surprised to see her captain take advantage of a shift in the Index to make a run for the inner system nexus, towards Chichi-jima once more, back the way she had come.

The rejoicing that night was prodigious. Bowen had succeeded in bringing aboard three flasks of aurium, and after the accounting, Ellis told them all on his life that he was satisfied, that they were done with roving the Zone, and that they would return home by way of their buried hoard for lack of any more space to fill in *Constitution*'s cargo hold.

There was a gawping silence, followed by a trickle of cheers.

"Have we really got to go back right away?" one woman somewhat crestfallen at the news asked him.

He left them, shaking his head, and found his own quarters then, to muse on the mighty awkward nature of crews and what they professed to want.

23

LIBERTY

Marsh mists hung low over the Potomac. The tide was flowing, but the skimmer sliced over the gray waters like a knife cutting silk, bringing the President's guest to the White House. The orange disc of Liberty's primary was scarcely above the eastern horizon at his back. It was half past seven by local reckoning, a week short of Liberty's northern winter solstice: he had been away for exactly two thousand days UT.

The velvet waters glittered with embroidered silver like the dew that gathers on autumn spider webs as the red-bladed propellors pushed them steadily upriver, forcing the sharp-prowed vehicle forward and shattering the peace. At the stem the gilded eagle of Amerika stood erect, the flag of the President fluttered at the sternpost. Amidships the engines and abaft them the canopied seat in which Ellis Straker sat like the President himself. His muscular calves were knotted inside his trousers, an old dress uniform jacket hung tight around his shoulders, making them massive; in his lap lay a casket of huge Yamato emeralds, the report of which he had sent on ahead to security.

At the pier the engines sputtered; Squaddies used their batons to keep back the curious and the idle who were gathering at the yellow barriers. Despite the earliness of the hour, an honor guard had been got out. A blaze of guns announced him as he stepped on Lincoln's shore.

"Well met, Ellis."

"Mr. Cassabian, it's good to see you."

"You will remember Otis le Grande?"

"How are you, sir?" Ellis nodded abruptly and crushed le Grande's hand. The strains of political life had marked his sallow face, but his wit was intact.

"I see you've forgotten your lessons on Lincoln etiquette."

"Captain Straker has had little occasion to show respect for anyone these past five years," Cassabian said pointedly, and Ellis felt the turn of his words like a razor slash. He had forgotten the keen edge that politics and the daily pursuit of power put on a man's tongue in Lincoln, and felt momentarily disadvantaged. Perhaps there was some battle going on between them at present. He decided to tread with care until he had learned more, thinking fondly of the judicious preparations he had made against things falling out badly on his return. He said jocularly, "Too few I've met with just lately have been Amerikans, and those that weren't generally had a hard time of it."

"Indeed!"

"And you, Mr. Cassabian? I hear that you've become secretary of state, the office Conroy Lubbock once occupied."

Le Grande jumped into the explanation: "He's our whip in an unruly administration."

"Aren't you Congressman Cassabian or Senator Cassabian?"

The spymaster avoided a direct answer. "I don't care for titles. You know that, Ellis."

"Jeezus!" Le Grande grunted and gestured undiplomatically. "The President's policy has always been hinged on recognition. You understand that Alia Kane makes a man work for his honors. The rarer she makes them, the more prized they become. But don't worry, Pharis's star is in the ascendant."

"He deserves it."

"Thank you, Captain, but it's not a good idea to praise a bridge until you're over it. We've got work to do."

"Events aren't going to your liking?"

"Could be better."

Ellis glanced around and stopped. He had expected Hawken to be here, and his absence had put him further on his guard. "Tell me: how was John Oujuku's return taken?"

There was silence, then Cassabian pulled on the tab of hair under his lip and walked on. He said evasively, "Well, you've got to realise that his return was somewhat—inopportune."

"Oh, yeah?"

"We were obliged to act on his behalf."

A shock of concern speared Ellis's belly. "Where is he now?"

"You expected him to be here to greet you?"

"Yes."

"John's not around. But don't worry about your unfinished business. I have your credit safe and I'll give you the details presently."

Ellis's frown deepened to anger. "Stuff the credit, Pharis! What about John? He's okeh, isn't he?"

"He's alive," le Grande said gently. "But we don't speak about him out loud these days."

"Will you people stop talking in circles!"

"Calm yourself, Captain. Otis only means that Oujuku is not with us here on Liberty. Ask in Norfolk and Harrisburg and you'll hear that he's trading to Europa. Ask the Free Korean merchants in the Exchange and you'll find talk of an expedition to Chung Kuo."

"But you know better," Ellis said, his fears multiplying.

"What if I tell you that his most important voyages recently have been to the other side of Lincoln?"

"I swear, Pharis, if you don't explain yourself, I'll—"

Cassabian whispered genially, "To the ashram of delights up the river."

"Okeh! I understand." Ellis grinned and punched Cassabian's shoulder with unseemly enthusiasm. If Oujuku had been to Ramakrishnan's ashram, it must mean there was some expedition approved by government under way. Doubtless some grandiose undertaking. "Where? The Zone? Slavia? Izlam? Afrika? They say there's a fortune in rare earths comes out of there each year. This is your doing, Mr. Cassabian!"

"Partly."

"Cassabian's credit backs the voyage," le Grande said. "Secretary Belkov is the principal investor."

"Nikolai Belkov, eh? He's rich and getting richer. Must be about the biggest fortune in Amerika by now."

Le Grande ignored the remark. "I'm also part of the venture. My nephew too. None of us have any particular quarrel with the Free Koreans."

Ellis racked his brains thinking of the charts he had seen in Ramakrishnan's ashram and visualising the parties that must have assembled there during the long, light evenings of the Lincoln summer: men of daring and men of imagination. What destination would they have chosen? What would they attempt?

The Beyond! Ramakrishnan's dreams lay out there. To find a way of pushing the boundaries of Known Space out faster than 0.99 cee. But Cassabian and le Grande would certainly have been more interested in a project in which Oujuku spent his time actively damaging Yamato . . .

"Yamato!"

That was it! Whether Cassabian had said it or not. Oujuku had gone across the Zero Degree Plane, into Yamato itself!

The extravagance of the plan captivated him.

Once inside the boundary nexi of the Zero Degree galactic longitude plane, Yamato's nexus lanes would be wide open to attack. All of Yamato was an exclusive preserve. Only Yamato ships were permitted through the heavily defended guard nexi, only they were allowed in the five-thousand-transit network of the Sector. A whole slice of ten million cubic light-years was lying there for the taking. Yamato transports plied those routes, filled to their bridges with all kinds of valuables, utterly fearless of attack because no foreigner had ever dared to come inside Yamato. Unarmed ships carrying the Emperor's wealth would be at Oujuku's mercy—if he could find a way there.

Reluctantly he laid aside his speculations. There was immediate business to put in hand. It was important to learn where he stood and what changes had overtaken Amerika in his long absence. He probed le Grande on the main elements, saying nothing of his chance meeting with Kim Gwon Chung.

So, Ellis thought as he listened, Cassabian has got his promotion. He's been principal secretary since Christmas of '26, and Lubbock has so far resisted the pressures of le Grande and Cassabian to intervene in force in the freeing of Cho Sen. The President has kept her hand on the controls of Free Korea by spending vast credit there and sending "military advisors." So—Kim Gwon Chung had broadly spoken the truth about affairs across the Boundary.

As le Grande's fountain of information ran dry, Cassabian briefed him with further details, warning him that he had to understand a good deal before he met with Lubbock. It was no easy task to appreciate the intricate web that had been spun by the President's ministers, but in essence it was simple: the disquiet in Korea remained Amerika's great guarantee. The expulsion of Free Koreans from Amerika had been a masterstroke conceived by Cassabian's fertile mind; the notion had been transplanted whole into the mind of Lubbock, where it had taken root and begun to flourish.

Cassabian watched Ellis's easy muscular movements as he walked beside him through the sprawling White House grounds. The years had changed the big man, coarsened his manner and filled him with a confidence fit to break empires. He had thrived on his crusade and put behind him the consuming distraction that had once driven him, that of his captive brother. It was just as well. For in coming time Amerika would have need of all her heroes.

Cassabian recalled the day he had advanced the idea.

"Convince the President to throw out the Free Koreans?" Timo Farren had asked from his deathbed, mystified by the suggestion. And at supper that night Ursula had looked at him questioningly. "You bend credulity to its limit, Pharis. Beware. One day soon your policies will snap in two and you'll slide back down the way you came. If that happens I won't complain. It'll be a blessing."

But he had comforted her, understanding that his continual business with spies and extra-Sectoral correspondents had tried their marriage. Most of the finance behind his initial rise to prominence had come from Ursula's father's will, and she had aided her husband's ambitions. But now she was sorry that the same fire still drove him so fiercely.

"You'll see that there are great rewards hidden at the rainbow's end," he had told her.

"You talk of rainbows, Pharis, but it no longer holds any luster for me. You've been saying it for too many years."

When they lay in bed that night, he had offered her a lucid observation. "I'll be principal secretary within the year, and you'll have the fine house on the river. The one I've been promising you."

"By throwing honest Free Koreans to their doom?"

"I think so."

"You'll be the Emperor of Yamato before Alia will do that. I hope I'm pricking your conceit, Pharis. And your conscience."

"C'mon, Ursula!"

"I will not c'mon."

"See, Lubbock wants a settlement with Yamato over the Zone. He's talking to Baron Harumi through the Trade Commission. He'll see the idea as an appropriate overture."

And so the President had ordered the Korean raiders out of the Kalifornias and Hawaii, just as Mutsuhito had wanted. But the Koreans that departed Amerika's aprons were not the pathetic refugees that had landed ten years before. They, like Kim Gwon Chung, had grown strong and dangerous, nourished as they were by the killings they had made in the Neutral Zone.

"Yes, Ellis, they were well-armed and equipped, desperate people. I thought that if Mutsuhito wanted these privateers expelled from Amerika, he might as well be obliged, eh?"

"You think Conroy Lubbock saw your design for what it was?"

Cassabian smiled. "Well . . . he certainly thought that Harumi—and the Emperor himself—would be very pleased by the President's new accommodating attitude."

They came to a courtyard containing a modern junk-revival sculpture, a fountain filled by rainwater channeled from the roofs and raised up on stilts in the form of angels. Under it, four naked-man holos faced in the cardinal directions, attending a bizarre machine of rods and levers and toothed wheels. An urn filled patiently from a slow dripfeed and tripped the mechanism as they watched. The holos' muscles glittered like real bronze as they pirouetted in a graceful dance and came to rest again, showing the time.

Cassabian told Ellis elaborately of how a presidential decision had expelled Keun Whan Pai's ships from their safe Amerikan havens, sending him into the Zone. "Lubbock sent Jos Hawken to do the dirty work. They went straightaway—all of them, Kim Gwon Chung's maniacs too." Cassabian examined the back of his hand. "As sweet as you like and without complaint. Then they took Pusan a week later."

Ellis gave a broad smile that recognised the genesis of the plan. "To take up old business."

"Keun and I thought that Pusan might be a good idea: a fair system, not much of a garrison, a serviceable apron. The inhabitants welcomed the privateers like liberators. We sent supplies of weapons and equipment and so on. And I seem to recall that there were a few Korean Amerikans who responded to the call for volunteers. A call that was somehow posted in every military base in Amerika.''

"Korean Amerikans or Amerikan Koreans?''

"What's the difference? But they must have been some kind of Korean because they found their way around the quadrant pretty quickly. They landed at Wonsan and Samchok—and took both.''

Ellis laughed, seeing how the tactic had been to strangle the quadrant and seize the greater part of it.

"There was a happy coincidence,'' Cassabian went on innocently. "Keun's brother, secretly in Cheju Do with twenty-five ships, and General Kwang with more marshaling in Taiwan.''

"A three-pronged attack.''

"Mutsuhito called it 'an unfortunate coincidence.' ''

Cassabian had known that it was more than enough to keep any thoughts of offense out of Harumi's mind. Attack was just a superior form of defense, but the impecunious Kwang had been held up on the Boundary and Lubbock had gotten wind of the extent of the plan, and his meddling had turned the plan into a standoff between Free Korea and Yamato, with Amerikan aid to the privateers regulated tightly to keep the pot simmering.

"Lubbock was convinced that once Harumi was destroyed, the Free Koreans would pour into Cho Sen and seize it, with all the consequences which that must bring for Yamato policy against Amerika.''

"There can never be victory without a decisive blow,'' Ellis said, watching the water clock's artful operation with interest.

"If only I'd succeeded in marrying Alia to the Dowager's son.'' Cassabian shrugged his shoulders in regret. "Then we might have joined forces in obliterating Harumi. But the President was turned. She became opposed to a policy that would completely evict Harumi from Free Korea. We were commanded to engineer the most level balance we could achieve in that quadrant, Yamato counterpoise to the Chinese—that was her ideal. But I didn't believe that our promise to aid Harumi against the Chinese would guarantee the ancient freedoms of the Korean people, or free them from Harumi's tyranny, or expel the *kempei* from the Zone. But—'' Cassabian threw up his hands in a gesture of loss. "The Peking massacre changed everything. With the

Cho Sen puppet leader dead, Kwang's brave gamble failed. He retreated to his stronghold systems.''

"Which must have affected the shogunate," Ellis said.

Cassabian remembered the way that the President's looked-for balance had almost been achieved through Lubbock's patient diplomacy. Cassabian told Ellis, "As a gesture of amity, Baron Harumi was taken out of his post and replaced by the less martial Baron Makino. But in March last year he was poisoned, and Mutsuhito's *bakufu* council chose to send Prince Sekigahara instead. It was a costly decision.''

Ellis nodded as if the information was news to him. "The victor of Hainan? But his repuation is that of an extreme hawk.''

Le Grande said, "He's had a setback. Before he could reimpose control on his army, they mutinied and sacked Wonsan, which did not please the Free Koreans at all. The demands made of Prince Sekigahara were uncompromising: they wanted the samurai soldiery sent out of their quadrant altogether.''

Ellis listened unmoved as le Grande explained, then said skeptically, "Do you suppose Free Korea can remain free from Yamato domination? A self-governing quadrant, with guaranteed liberties?''

"No. Even if Cho Sen continues to recognise nominal sovereignty, Yamato will not allow that.''

Cassabian redoubled his efforts, seeing from the gestures of the water clock sculpture that there was little time. "Listen! I know much better than Lubbock does that all balances are unstable; without constant care they're easily disturbed. Lubbock is an intelligent man, but he's a bureaucrat to the bone marrow. He thinks Sektorpolitik can be managed by quiet tinkerings and fine tunings and in his scheme there's no place for men of fire and imagination. What he doesn't comprehend is that without them any power must slowly slide into complacent decline. The worst of it is that because Lubbock himself lacks imagination, he supposes that that applies to everyone else. I tell you, Ellis, that is a big mistake. Prince Sekigahara is no weakling; he'll never concede to Free Korea their demands. The Korean president knows that and will never accept the prince's demands. Deadlock, so far. But I cannot believe Prince Sekigahara will crawl away with his tail between his legs.''

Cassabian knew that although the prince's outward design was to pacify both Koreas, he held another, less ostensible ambition.

Now he had his proof: Prince Sekigahara had fostered strong links with pro-Yamato Amerikans exiled abroad, with the renegades' seminary on Juno, and with the arch-traitor General Waters. Through his spies there, he found that Prince Sekigahara planned to embark his troops for Yamato, *but land them in Amerika*. He had boasted that he would marry Alia Kane himself and then order her to commit *seppuku*, as would be his right.

"That's where the President's credit will go, Ellis. Of the vast riches that lie in your ship in Harrisburg, one hundred billion is already earmarked as a loan to Keun; fifty ships and three divisions of first-line infantry and a thousand assault vehicles are to go out under Colonel Northridge's command. We'll make Free Korea accept Keun's brother as their leader, and insist that Sekigahara's troops are sent off to the Zero Degree nexi, by a ten-transit backwater chain that keeps them off our Boundary. If the President will only listen to reason."

"Do we go to the President now?"

"No, to Lubbock. He has news you'll not want to hear. In your absence you've been outmaneuvered by a consummate businessman, as he'll no doubt tell you himself."

24

"That's our contract, Captain. You understand the terms as well as I do. One half of the total belongs to Amerika."

"As it has done since it was taken from Yamato's ships."

"A further quarter of the—cargo—is to be divided among the following investors." Lubbock read out their names— twenty-five of the richest and most powerful men in the Sector —along with the percentages they would receive. Lubbock's own name was not among them. "That leaves you the remainder."

Ellis tried to appear outwardly gracious, but saw that the VP was feeling for his true opinions. "The remainder for myself *and* my crew. My own personal share is a little less than a half of what you're showing there. Also, you can exclude the most exquisite item. I intend to make that a personal gift to Alia— let's say a Christmas gift—a quantity of emeralds, a debt of thanks to her faith in me. So that's twelve and a half percent for the crew, who bought the stuff with their blood and their sweat, or for their bereaved kin, and ten percent for their captain, who figured it out in the first place."

"Do you wish it was more?"

Ellis shrugged. "If I'd thought that, I'd have gotten more."

"A pity you didn't, then." Lubbock's eyes narrowed in a shrewd look. He rose from his seat and touched his hand to the real fireplace. "Because the investors I just named all sold their shares to me. Two years ago, when news came back that you were dead."

"Remind me to thank you for your faith in me," Ellis said sourly, concealing his shock and anger as best he could. "I hope the shares didn't cost you too much?"

"On the contrary. The price was cheap. They cost me half what I would have paid on your departure, plus the going rate for a believable rumor. I wish to build a house in Northrop, and my mansion here in Lincoln is a costly enough place to run as it stands. However—I can afford to make some of my gains over to you and your crew. Enough to make them all blissfully wealthy men, and yourself a Liberty magnate, with enough credit to buy half a dozen ships."

Ellis's voice betrayed him. "Oh, yeah? I can be a Liberty magnate, can I? With what's mine already? I must be witnessing a goddamned miracle!"

"I can make you a man of means."

"Is that a fact?"

"Yes. It's a fact."

Ellis's voice sank low, but his eyes never faltered as he stared at Lubbock's own. "Strange to think that you believe I can be transformed into a man of means. I kind of thought that you were of a different set of mind: that a man's quality lies in his possession of Halide corporate stock."

Lubbock's confidence was undented. He said mildly, "Men have been given position for serving their Sector's interests be-fore."

"Government sinecures are not yours to give."

"Nevertheless, I can confidently promise you one."

"Your promises are other men's burdens, Conroy."

Lubbock delighted in the danger into which the exchange was plunging. "Let's turn our minds instead to—"

"No, Conroy! Let's think of what gives a man self-respect and what does not. It seems to me a matter of achievement and reward, as in your own case."

"What do you want?"

Ellis's gaze remained steady. "You know fine well what I want."

Lubbock sighed and put up his hands. "My daughter is a married woman."

"In name."

"In *fact,* sir!"

"Not according to my understanding."

"Damn your understanding. And damn your eyes! You forget yourself!"

"I forget nothing, Mr. Vice-president. I've refreshed my mind daily with the thought of my Reba and of a son I've never seen yet. I will see her, and you will not interfere with that!"

Lubbock felt anger prickle him, whipped by the coarse tongue of a man who had no proper humility, who had issued only commands to others for five long years. He turned, tight-lipped and furious, and began to stalk away, then he halted, and he knew precisely why he had done so.

Lie to whomever you want, Conroy, his conscience told him. But never lie to yourself. It had to be admitted. The last five years had been years of continual torment to his daughter. No sooner had Ellis gone to the Zone than Kurt had begged the President for permission to give him a passport also, so that he could go into the Zone in a big nexus yacht he was fitting out. She had, of course, refused him, liking his presence at her White House soirees for the sake of his dancing and his manners and perhaps for his quarreling spirit, which she admired in young men and enjoyed watching.

Reiner had thought the prohibition was Lubbock's doing, and there had been some truth in that, because he had given the President honest opinions on the matter. "The spoiled brat'll kill himself," Lubbock had predicted balefully, part of him wishing as much could be arranged. "A yacht allowed into the Zone with Kurt as its captain will be loaded with three kinds of bad psi.''

Oh, yes, he had thought, a triple helping of the worst psi: one, in that Kurt would surely have caught pinkeye, or got atomised in a psi-storm, or had himself blown to fragments in an engagement with a *rikugun* patrol ship; two, in that he would bring the President to grief over this—and she hardly to be in a position to need bad press; and three, in that he would probably provoke Yamato sooner or later, if he didn't die, and in so inexpert a way as to result in his capture and expensive ransom, or, conceivably, the rupturing of that delicate membrane that kept Amerika and Yamato out of war with one another.

Reiner had sworn to revenge himself on Reba.

''I'll see her cry her eyes out,'' he had warned poisonously. ''I'll damage her. See if I don't!''

Lubbock had humbled himself to plead: ''You know the President herself says that you can't take your yacht beyond the Boundary, Kurt. You want to disobey Alia?''

''*Disobey?* I don't take orders from anyone! If she doesn't let me go, I'll go fight in Korea as a mercenary, and find honor there!''

And he had gone, without the President's consent, relieving Reba, who had grown to detest the tread of his foot across the threshold. ''May he be shot through the head,'' he heard her pray one night. ''Swift and clean, but final. Sweet Jeezus, I want him away from me and my child.''

It was then that Lubbock had known the depth of his daughter's anger and despair and the enormity of the error he had made, and how right Vara had been in the matter of her daughter's wedding. But he had set his face and, like everyone else, part of him had assumed Ellis Straker dead. A year and a half without word had been a long time, but still he had traded those shares in Straker's adventuring mission, just in case, swapping them one-for-one for shares in Oujuku. Then Oujuku had come back with his booty and his wild tales, and many had sniggered in private because he had sold out on a winner and bought in on a dead man.

But they were not laughing now. Not now. And Lubbock felt no pleasure, nor even gratification, only a cold dread at Ellis Straker's return that outweighed the credit. *Why?* And in any case, what was done was done. And though Reba might wilt as a flower wilts in a climate that does not suit it, she had married and her vows had been made at the altar, before God—and more important, before the President. But that was not accounting for her willfulness.

After the Korean episode, in '27, Lubbock had had Reiner smuggled home by the mercenaries who were glad to be rid of him. He had induced him to apologise to the President, which he did genuinely. Having seen a little of war—in the flesh, so to speak—Reiner had renounced it as disgusting and unworthy. His pretentions to an adventurer's life had already been reduced, diverted from this to that by the news of Okinawa and Oujuku's fabulous reception. A marvel how the publicity over that had turned every other young man in Liberty into one ardent mass ready to cruise into the Boundary, but Reiner had shunned the celebrations, calling the whole privateering thing an adolescent fad of which he had wearied. And so he had returned instead to his youthful posture as a poet of genius, because in that pursuit there was no hard standard to be set against him, only opinions and critiques which might be easily twisted to his self-satisfaction.

Lubbock cringed inwardly as he thought of the burbling hexameters that Reiner had offered up for praise, and—God save us all—the tight band of dissolute hangers-on whose whole game was to wait upon Reiner as if he was a new Messiah. The following year Lubbock had disbursed him a sum sufficient to take him off on a tour of Europa, to Milan and to London, but he had returned home within a year, crammed with new poses, totally conceited, overspent, and sporting a new Bristol air-car and perfumed clothes and canvas after canvas of fine art. He had presented a Freud painting to the President, but there had been nothing for his wife, and thereafter he had been a stranger to her, and she almost banished to the mansion of Xanadu.

Cassabian had been disgusted, and le Grande delighted, until he was brought to the brink of choking. "What does Kurt imagine he looks like?" he had said, laughing scornfully, but out of Reiner's earshot. "Jeezus H.! A Goochie hat, like an oyster. And all those French cambric shirts! Ha! I've seen better-dressed men on Dakota II!"

It was Simon Belkov who had caught the bile that should have been vomited over le Grande, for poet or not, fashion-maker or not, Reiner's violent temper was intact, and he had made war on le Grande's nephew with offers to duel and even an extravagant contract on his life.

Lubbock looked at the iron-hard man who stood in front of him. Tempered in real war and toughened by genuine adversity. Here was a man who knew exactly what he was, exactly what he wanted, and would brook no opposition to that. Small wonder Reba contrasted him so readily against the man to whom she had been matched in wedlock.

Lubbock faced Ellis stubbornly, sure in the state power at his disposal. The time had come to employ it. "You swore never to speak of my daughter again."

"That oath was made under duress. It is *revoked*." Ellis's fingers snapped, recalling the day the soldiers had taken him blood-drained and amazed from Ramakrishnan's ashram.

"You're a shameless sonofabitch!"

"No, Conroy! It's *you* who's shameless. Didn't you force your firstborn daughter into a bad marriage against her wishes for your own ambition? Didn't you deny your grandchild his birthright? *Didn't you do that?* Eh, Mr. Vee-Pee?"

"I warn you, Straker—"

"And I warn you! Not a Cho Sen *jeon* of the aurium I've brought out of the Zone will reach you, or the Treasury, until you oblige me."

Lubbock straightened, weasel sly. "It is unwise to threaten me, Ellis. I have your ship on the Harrisburg apron—under armed escort. This time, you can't get away. Guards!"

Six servicemen sprang into the room, their blasters leveled on him. Ellis fell quiet, stared at his feet, inwardly delighting that his foresight had put him in this position. Even so, he remained carefully self-possessed.

"I had no intention of trying to get away, Conroy. I guess the whole planet'll be wanting to talk to me tomorrow."

"Your arrival is still secret."

"It can't remain secret for long."

Lubbock, recollected now to his cool and reasonable self, called his private secretary, who brought the papers. "The people want to see you on tri-vee, and I don't want to interfere with that, because the people's wants are my wants and my responsibility. But hear me well, Captain, if you want to cause me trouble, I'll just as soon take the people's hero away from them and put him in Camp Worth."

"You did that once before, I remember," Ellis said.

"You dare to smile at me?"

"I'm not smiling at you, Conroy. Simply at your bribery. I think that you're about to make a new offer."

Lubbock's anger showed but he locked it away. "All right: keep your word and you'll be a world-state governor. You'll have the federal warrant for Utah. What do you say to that?"

Ellis's thoughts leapt again to John Oujuku, to how Amerika had gratefully received his billions of credit from the Okinawa adventure, and paid him off with little thanks and a sinecure as deputy assistant gewgaw of Nebraska.

As the conflict with Yamato had cooled, Oujuku's embarrassing presence in Amerika had had to be dealt with; he was sent to Nebraska to make laws on moonshine mash and grizzly bears.

Oujuku had hated it. "A fair fight at best, something to get my teeth into, that's what I like," Ellis had heard him roar after Okinawa, though to tell the truth, Captain John Winston Oujuku preferred huge odds against, believing like an ardent Amerikan must do that he was a free man and could only prove as much to the satisfaction of all by overthrowing a burden of oppression somewhere. That he had gone off on his extravagant expedition now was a mark that he had lost none of that firmness of belief. A man *complete*, sure, full of his own self. A *man*.

An image of John single-handedly attacking a grizzly with a rolled-up hard copy of a bear-control statute leapt to mind and made him smile. Ellis felt suddenly careless of the circle of servicemen who surrounded him. He brushed one blaster aside, ignoring the way the remainder made at him threateningly. Seeing the intimidation fail, Lubbock signaled them impatiently to put up their arms.

So Lubbock thought it convenient to let Oujuku leave, Ellis told himself. He could have vetoed Cassabian and le Grande and all the rest of them had he wanted to. Yet Cassabian said that Yamato's irritation with Amerika was boiling up once more. Ellis felt the change in the Index and steered accordingly. For what reason did Lubbock want a valuable privateer commander to kick the butts of klansmen in barbarous Utah? It's a diversion—shelve me, keep me from the Zone, keep me from Reba also. Stick me in a backwater, neither at home nor away.

"What do you say?"

"I say no."

"The offer's good."

"Utah? To be governor of a piss-pit like that? No chance."

"You *will* oblige me in this."

"No."

Lubbock shook his head and looked down at the contract, striping a line through it matter-of-factly. "In that case your ship is confiscated, and all it contains. And you, you sonofabitch, are under arrest."

"A real shame."

"You'll soon think so, you respectless devil!"

As the guards closed in around him once more, Ellis thrust up his hands as if addressing the heavens. "Lord God, take me from this stupid old bastard before I split my sides!"

And the peals of his laughter rang out as Jiro Ito escorted him away.

25

Ellis got down from his air-car, thoughts of Christmas turkey and Kansas klaret far from his mind now as he parked. The ground was white with snow and deeply covered; the east wind had blown everything dry and hoary and crisp. He was alone and strung so tight inside that he felt he was about to snap.

The house of Xanadu seemed to him dreary and quiet under its steep roofs. There were flakes in the air, and no echoes because of the white blanket. The white walls were made creamy against the virgin burden of the roof. A snowman stood on the lawn; pebble eyes, twig nose, and a huge grin to welcome him. It wore a cloak and wide-brimmed hat and held a broom, but it might have been a *katana* for all that it struck him with shivers.

His mouth was dry. At his back the air-car engines ticked and cooled.

The day Lubbock had imprisoned him he had marked the afternoon with a nap and the tuneless whistling that often accompanied his most strategic thoughts. He had counted the hours until enough had passed for a Revenue car to get to Harrisburg and back, then he had listened out for returning footsteps. Ito appeared within the hour to fetch him before Lubbock, who was white-faced with rage. He had shaken his fist in Ellis's face and demanded, *"Where is it?"*

"Where you can't get it."

"I swear I'll give you the Probe, Straker."

Ellis said nothing.

"I'll Probe your crew!"

"A-a. They don't know anything."

"That won't stop me."

"How will the President take it when she hears that you're victimising her privateers?" He had sucked in a breath and shook his head like an air-car mechanic looking at a lemon. "Her mood'll deepen if she can no longer execute her policies in Korea for lack of finance."

Lubbock spat at him, enraged. "Amerika has enough credit for that."

"Oh, yeah? Does Congress know about that? And what about the credit she needs to rebuild the Navy?"

He pushed open the gate, sweeping a sector of snow up behind it, trying to savor the moment he had imagined so differently so often.

As he did so, he grinned, thanking psi that he had remembered the rumors that had surrounded his and Hawken's return so long ago, rumors of how they had buried their profits to avoid the Revenue.

All that had happened since planetfall proved the wisdom of his prudence: he had told Lubbock that the aurium was buried in Kalifornia.

"Kalifornia?"

"On a desolate little asteroid. Five hundred feet down a bore hole where nobody can spend it until I'm real satisfied."

In actuality, he had had it committed to a Yamato store hulk taken in one of the Aleutian systems and brought right into Norfolk. The whole treasure lay there now, a few miles away, packed into containers and guarded by Bowen with a singularity gun rigged ready to swallow the lot showing all the jealousy of a dragon on top of a hoard.

Ellis took off his driving gloves and walked slowly up the path, his boots crushing the snow with a sound like grinding teeth. He was suddenly hot and he loosened his collar and threw open his jacket. A small brown bird fled from him, shaking down fine snow from a twig and putting a nursery rhyme about robins into his head.

Then he caught a flash of fair hair and a twitch of curtain at the window. The light, high voice pierced him and he steeled himself to lift the heavy knock-ring, but as he reached for it the barking of big dogs began within, and the sound of them rushing to the door made him step back.

When the chained door cracked open, it revealed their dripping muzzles and their anxiety to be at him, but a female "servant" shouted for aid to restrain them, and Ellis was roughly asked his name and his business.

"I am Captain Ellis Straker, and I'd like Mrs. . . . I'd like Reba to know I'm here."

"The mistress does not receive callers."

A small voice squealed. The blond-haired boy he had glimpsed at the window galloped into the hallway. He wore a tidy little one-piece and straddled a hovering plex toy made like a shuttle. He stopped when he saw Ellis looking at him and twisted about with incredible coyness. Then he slapped the nearest dog's eye and told it to hush, which it did resentfully.

"Is this Mrs. Reiner's only child?"

The servant nodded. "He is, sir. But you can't—"

"How old is he?"

"Five years UT, but I must ask—"

Ellis knelt to the boy, "What's your name, son?"

"Hayden."

"Hayden," he echoed back tenderly, taking his hand. Then he drew a large, brown love bear from his jacket and gave it to him. "Hold him tight and he'll hear your heart beating and go to sleep."

And as he turned he saw the woman in somber green standing at the head of the stair. It was his Reba.

B O O K 2

29TH YEAR OF KANEI/A.D. 2431

Summer grasses,
All that remains,
Of warrior dreams.

Matsuo Basho
1644–94

Material excerpted from "A Manuscript Found in
Space,"
by A. Hacker:

Material excerpted from the Ozma Vault
Transmission Package KVFG #2975,
Copyright Synthetic Educator Corp, Orenburg, VIR.,
By Permission of the Central Authority,
Old Earth. A.D. 2420

[Ref. Module MMVII-124.288762]

[Cross-references to other SEC modules in CAPS.]

KNOWN SPACE

Definition: at any one time that sphere of interstellar
space centered on the SUN and lying within the exploration boundary surface. Presently approximately six
hundred LIGHT-YEARS in diameter.

Following the first statements of the GRAND UNIFI-
CATION THEORY and the FUNDAMENTAL HYPOTH-
ESIS OF PHYSICS [Ref. Module MDCDXVII-
507.873523], the way had been opened for interstellar
exploration. By the twenty-second century A.D. technical control of the GRAVITATIONAL INTERACTION
[Ref. Module LCXI-000.976432] had become relatively
sophisticated, by A.D. 2100 comparable with command
of electromagnetic forces achieved two centuries before. GRAVOMETRICS [Ref. Module LCXXI-002-

495271], useful techniques connected with gravitation and the manipulation of space-time geometry, were employed in the creation of the NEXUS [Ref. Module MDCXVIII-115.2936] network of KNOWN SPACE [Ref. Mod. *ibidem*].#

. . . HACK INTERRUPTED . . .

#two key technological developments allowed colonisation of space: the discovery of a means of faster-than-light travel, utilising nexus [Ref. Mod. *ibidem*] points, small space-time singularities which could be detonated anywhere in EUCLIDEAN SPACE [Ref. Module MCXXIV-024.240354]; and the technology of TER-RAFORMING [Ref. Module DCCIX-929.220922]—the fast transforming of suitable seed-planets from chemically hostile environments into quasi-Earth-like environments with atmospheres, oceans, imported ecologie#

. . . HACK INTERRUPTED . . .

#tomatic ramjet spacecraft, a VON NEUMANN MA-CHINE, traveling at near-CEE has arrived at a nearby star system, it "detonates" the nexus, a semi-stable torus quasi-singularity, rotating in the imaginary time-domain. The PIONEER DRONE then replicates and the daughter craft move on to the next closest systems. It is then possible for near-instantaneous communication to be effected from other systems which also contain a nexus point. (At a constant acceleration of one hundred GEE, it takes the pioneer drones approximately three to four days, UT, to reach 0.9 cee, and about the same time to decelerate at their destination. Typically a four-to-five-year journey lies in between, during which its computers are closed down, hibernat#

. . . HACK INTERRUPTED . . .

#sts giant TF ships can be sent to each new system to start the work of terraforming. Any system based on a single (nonbinary) Main Sequence star with a spectral type in the range A to K can be searched for planets, and if suitable bodies exist in TEMPERATE ORBITS, then virtually any orbiting body from a mass as small as Mars to one as great as Uranus can be modified using gravometric techniques to create a planet close to a one-gee gravity. Chemical reconfiguration and planetary architec#

. . . HACK INTERRUPTED . . .

#ultant exploration and terraforming has happened. At present a geocentric globe of space has expanded until it is some six hundred light-years in diameter. This volume is referred to as Known Space; it is 113 million cubic light-years. The star density in our vicinity of the SPIRAL ARM is approximately twenty-five stars for every ten thousand cubic light-years. So Known Space contains some quarter million stars, of which half are uninhabitable multiples, whilst three quarters of the remainder are dim M-type primaries. Only half of those that still remain contain easily terraformable planets. Nevertheless, that still amounts to more than 15,600 systems, all linked together by the nexus netw#

. . . HACK INTERRUPTED . . .

#is why nexi have been described as "smoke rings in space." They are rotating quasi-singularities with a toroidal event horizon through which ships are able to navigate, so long as they have a PSI-ASTROGATOR aboard. The semi-stable nature of these nexi means that they are prone to almost unpredictable PSI-STORMS. They must be approached at speeds ranging from 0.1 cee to 0.9 cee, at the correct injection angle and ship attitude. The choice of these parameters is an intuitive rather than a mechanical process. The psi-astrogator is a talent, a rare individual who has PSI-abilities to "feel" his or her way through these holes in the fabric of spacetime.#

. . . HACK INTERRUPTED . . .

#esponse to the crushing overpopulation of EARTH and the oppressive forces of uniformity that developed, the EDICT made provisions such that each SECTOR could develop its own ways of living, and live according to its own laws, unmolested. The intention was to re-create the cultural diversity that was an enriching feature of Classical Eart#

. . . HACK INTERRUPTED . . .

#e Edict allowed Izlamic, Han Chinese, Hindu, Anglo-Saxon-Skandinavian, Afrikan, Brasilian, Slavic, Latin, an#

. . . HACK INTERRUPTED . . .

#Izrael occupying part of the Amerikan-Europan boundary along the sixty-degree plane. The twelfth Sector, pointing in the direction of the galactic center, is the NEUTRAL ZONE.

Over the centuries the boundaries have shifted and distorted, and discoveries at the expanding outer shell of each Sector have been a source of territorial dispute as new nexi were detonated in the BEYOND. What was not foreseen was that the most zea#

. . . HACK INTERRUPTED . . .

#in Euclidean space, the distances between planetary systems is vast. Even with nexus technology a trip from a given star system to its neighbor takes several days. Ships have to "run at" the nexus, approaching the gravitational SINGULARITY with a certain minimum kinetic energy that necessitates accelerating to a significant percentage of light speed. Transit-capable ships must also approach at precisely the correct injection angle to prevent tidal forces ripping the ships to pieces. Only psi-astrogators are able to accomplish this relia#

. . . HACK INTERRUPTED . . .

#. To travel from one side of Known Space to the other is difficult and expensive. It requires more than a hundred nexus transits and approximately two years' journeying. Since only matter may penetrate a nexus (light, radio waves, etc., are stopped by the QUANTUM SKEW EFFECT), there is no way to create a practical network of intersystem broadcasting that would link the Sectors tog#

. . . *HACK ABORTED.*

26

SEOUL

To Choi Ki Won the knowledge of the president's death was like a knife constantly twisting in a wound.

He dismounted heavily, swabbed the sweat from his face, and riffled the mare's hogged mane affectionately with a broad hand. "We're in a big hurry now. Still, a horse must drink, eh? You see how I take care of you?"

The low morning sun played on his horse's dusty quarters as she lowered her head delicately to the trough. Then, as she finished, he remounted and scanned the road that he had traveled a hundred times before with his pigeons, knowing that never in his life had he felt such urgency and damned the technology ban that existed beyond the Seoul City limits.

He had ridden hard for almost an hour and was midway on the journey, coming from his house in Seoul City, going to Pangojin, the village near Kunyang where the rumor had originated. He had known that, given the faintest hope that the story was true, he must go himself, and quickly. As the mare pulled around he brushed his heels across its sides, sending it cantering down the rocky decline towards the village, and towards the "ghost ship" of which the fisherman had spoken.

A crashed ship, blackened and deserted, that's what they'd said, so he had left, immediately and as unobtrusively as possible. Like so much valuable news to come out of the low-tech preserve, it had reached him first. Starting with the sardine fisherman, he'd always taken pains to maintain a cordial relationship with the people who lived between Kunyang and the Cape of Pangojin on the coast. It was important—after all, they were his eyes and ears, and had he not grown rich keeping his eyes open and his ear to the ground in what was, in effect, a telecommunications and transport shadow zone? The low-tech zone included almost half the single Borneo-sized continent of Seoul; the rest of the world was a shallow ocean, except for the uninhabited polar landmass.

What business was better than selling information? he thought. You've got a commodity. You sell it. You've still got it. What could be better than that? Unlike Amerikan wine, however, information rarely improved in value in the keeping, and the information Choi Ki Won dealt in was volatile and, now that President Keun was dead, immensely dangerous.

Choi Ki Won geed his horse again and slapped its withers. He was well liked by the people of the merchants and farmer classes with whom he dealt, famed for his garrulous good nature and as the father of five grown sons. His family made a good living from all the settlements on the main continent of Seoul, buying from foreign traders, sending bonded technology inland as far as the mountains, and handling luxury foodstuffs for what remained of the Amerikan trade. He could afford to be a generous man, a man who kept a big open household, mostly out of choice, but also to show everyone that he had nothing at all to hide and that no one need fear anything from him.

But difficult times were coming, and in difficult times a man needed a staff on which to lean.

"Yes," he told the horse, "that's the Choi Ki Won everyone knows: a man who spends his time listening to local gossips and quietly building his prosperity. The townspeople, my fellow traders, Captain Yim at the garrison—even the filthy pro-Yamato politicians—they all know that I'm a good and generous man who'll help anyone and harm nobody."

And yet I'm sure there are those who wonder at my luck, and there are certainly some who draw their livings from the seaports of the Seoul City hinterland who're jealous of the inexplicable way I've grown richer than they have. They're the dangerous ones.

He saw the ship the moment he arrived at the quiet line of gray and white fishermen's houses that made up the village of

Pangojin. She was lying in ocean a quarter of a mile down the inlet. Many times he had seen damaged nexus ships limping into Seoul's massive apron after being caught in psi-storms, but this ship was exceptional; she was almost a hulk. She was seriously damaged: her plex hull was blackened in parts and both her cargo bay doors had been taken off by what must have been a huge explosion. What remained of her radio black had been upset by the seawater, and her hull patterning tried feebly to keep pace with the sparkling sea. A gantry of sensor aerials had been jury-rigged at her bows and left to melt away to stumps on atmospheric reentry. But she was right way up and seemed to have soft-landed.

She might have been in the sea for days—or months—blown in like flotsam from the deep ocean by fresh east winds; she sat low in the water as if she was sinking, but he saw that her bottom was grounded on rocks as the waves lapped about her; water swilled into the cargo bay, but there were no signs of life aboard.

By her lines she might easily be a Yamato ship, he thought, but what made Choi Ki Won view the battered hull with greater interest was that she had been in a firefight—and she had been severely beaten.

Choi Ki Won's spirits rose. So! Old Tian had been right! There *was* a "ghost ship"—and she had come into his arms. There was good credit to be made in salvage. This was not an opportunity to pass up lightly. Already there were too many villagers on the beach, scratching their chins and wondering how the ship had come to be in the middle of the estuary. But the women were chiding their children and sending them indoors and the men had pulled their fishing boats high up on the beach. No other outsiders had yet come to the village, and Choi Ki Won realised that time was critical.

Tian Meng, his young local agent, hitched his bridle and helped him down. Tian's grandfather, Old Tian, a man twenty years Choi Ki Won's senior, white-haired and leathery, was by his side.

"I don't like it," Old Tian said, mistrust flashing from under his rambling eyebrows. "I don't remember anything like this ever happening before. It's because the president died—"

The young man shifted uncomfortably. "You must excuse my grandfather, Mr. Choi, he is a very poor businessman."

The elder drew himself up. "What of it? Our family have been here on Seoul for more than a hundred years. I am a fisherman, from a long line of fishermen, and proud of that."

"A noble calling, Mr. Tian, if I may say so," Choi Ki Won said, knowing Tian's great-grandfather had been one of the ten Chinese refugees to have come here after the Shenyang disaster. The whole community still clung dutifully to the Chinese tradition, unabsorbed, unintegrated, despite their long history on Seoul. Only Tian Meng was a black sheep.

"Is not the August Personage of Jade's wife herself, goddess of the sea?" Choi added indulgently.

"Of course. And the Empress of Heaven, T'ien Hou, also."

"Then I am in good company."

Young Tian put his hands on his hips and jutted his chin towards the ship. "That could mean a lot of credit. For *us*, Grandfather, don't you see?"

"She's a ghost ship, I tell you. You won't persuade anyone from here to row near her—no matter what you offer. She's bewitched."

"But she's not a ship, she's a spacecraft!"

"It doesn't matter, you young good-for-nothing! We're simple people here. It would be better for you if you had fewer of your big ideas."

"These superstitions!"

"When did she come in?" Choi Ki Won asked.

Tian Meng began to answer but the older man raised his voice stubbornly. "In the dead of night, Mr. Choi. She came in on the early morning tide all lit up by the moonlight. I saw it myself. I was out in the bay in my boat, with my lamps, casting for shrimps, when she rose up out of the ocean like a—"

"Like a gossamer ship blown here on a moonbeam! Ha! Therefore she must be a ghost ship. Isn't that right?" Young Tian's sarcasm was incisive and very disrespectful. Choi Ki Won hushed him and gestured for the old man to go on.

"Well, I rowed home as fast as I could. I am not as young as I used to be, Mr. Choi"—Choi Ki Won nodded indulgently—"so I said to myself, 'Tian,' I said, 'this is the very work of the Supreme Lord of the Dark Heaven, who is also the Regent of Water.' And what does a man do with news of supernatural events? Of course, if he is a pious and dutiful man, he takes his report to the proper authorities."

"You informed the authorities?" Choi Ki Won asked with ill-concealed dismay.

The old man cackled, regarding his grandson's expensive silk shirt. "No, no, Mr. Choi. I thought immediately of my son's son. Where the gods are concerned he is the one to consult! Fine feathers make a fine bird, but fine clothes do not make a fine man!"

Young Tian stifled his irritation, muttering under his breath.

"Time is short," Choi Ki Won told him quietly. "By now news must have reached the Hill. Plenty of army people will be here soon. They take every opportunity to inquire into 'celestial events' and this ship will be no exception."

"Yes, sir."

"Venerable Mr. Tian, may I beg a favor of you?" he asked, extending his hand to touch the old man's arm. "May I borrow your shrimp boat for just a little while?"

"I'll not go out there, Mr. Choi. Not for any credit you might offer me."

"Grandfather!"

"That's not necessary. I'm sure that Meng is willing to row me to the ghost ship."

The old man shuffled uncertainly. "You say there may be credit out there? *Mard* credit?" he asked. A flicker of interest lit his dim eyes.

With a show of conspiratorial secrecy Choi Ki Won unhooked the purse from his belt and loosened the drawstrings. "Here, one golden *won* slottee. For you to hold."

"Eh?"

"It's a new Amerikan idea. Anonymous credit in discs of silver and gold."

"They're not plex," Tian said suspiciously. "Are they really credit?"

"Of course, of course!" He bent the fisherman's horny fingers over the heavy coin with its square central hole. "And a promise that if we do not return with your boat, you may go to my son, Il, and ask him for a quarter the coin's value. That's twenty-five *jeon!*"

"I don't know about this. It's not the same as a plex smart card. You always know where you are with plex!"

"Try it, Mr. Tian. The old-time Chinese had great respect for gold metal."

Old Tian chewed on the gold and spat. He said something in the old language followed by a shrug of acceptance, then he dug a finger at his grandson. "Be careful with my property, you young viper. Master Choi is a worthy man. I can trust him—but it's more than anyone can say for you."

Choi Ki Won took the old man's arm and nodded towards the other fishermen. "I want you to persuade them to keep back. Tell them I have a best-lacquer idol blessed by the great god Ts'ai Chen against sea misfortunes. Ask them if they have any such protection."

Old Tian cackled, screwing his face into a grin. "Oh, master, you are a wise man."

Tian Meng watched his kinsman wander away with an exasperated stare. "That was too much, Mr. Choi. Twenty-five *jeon* for the ransom of his waterlogged shrimp boat. He is a villain to take your credit."

Choi Ki Won laughed. "Don't worry, I intend to return with his boat intact. Which is it?"

"There, the blue and green one. Please."

They crunched down a gravel beach that smelled of crusted salt and sun-bleached fish heads. Tian laid his hands on the stem and slid the boat out clear of the pebbles so that it rocked in the water, then Choi Ki Won waded knee-deep and heaved himself in, steadying the oars.

It was a pull of five minutes. Choi Ki Won put his back against the sternpost and studied the ship carefully as they approached. When they came to within thirty yards, he told Tian to row them no closer. He cupped his hands and shouted. The greeting echoed back eerily, but there was no answer.

At a word from the merchant, Tian sculled slowly in, meeting the ship on the beam. The plex hull rose up thirty feet above them and Choi Ki Won could see beards of deep green weed pulsing on the rocks below the waterline. Could she have been abandoned? he wondered, his fingers tingling with hope. He had heard tales of nexus ships being caught in psi-storms or orbital emergencies, of them being grounded and then left by their crews. Perhaps a privateer attacked them. Perhaps the crew are all dead and it homed down on autopilot. But why would she be using chameleon-skin stealth if not to deliberately avoid detection? It's a mystery!

"Ai-ee!"

He shouted again. Still no reply. The young man was searching the empty gun blisters, fear contending visibly with avarice on his face. "Ai-ee! Anyone there?"

"Maybe there really is no one on board."

"If that's true, then she's ours. We found her, didn't we?"

Choi Ki Won swallowed, wishing despite himself that he had the fictional best-lacquer idol to brandish. "Free Korea is not a signatory of the Inter-Sector Salvage Treaty. According to the law we have only to board her to claim her."

Tian licked his lips. "Maybe we should go back for weapons—for the others?"

Choi Ki Won turned towards the beach. Three upright figures in red robes and black three-tongued hats had arrived there in a six-wheeled rough-terrain vehicle; they sent a shiver through him—Harmonious Apron Police.

"Go back? And share the prize with the Revenue? Are you mad as well as frightened?"

They sculled inside the echoing cavern of the flooded cargo bay. Impulsively the younger man stood up and leapt for the rail. He heaved himself up onto the platform and froze there, listening and looking into the airlock.

The emergency release mechanism cycled faultlessly. Inside, the gun deck was empty, there was no sign of life. Choi Ki Won watched the youth's caution as he surveyed the empty corridors. Truly it was as if the crew had been lured away by T'ien Hou herself.

According to the legendary Chinese story, the Empress of Heaven had once been a girl on the planet of Mei-chou, which was a celebrated place of piety. She had four *tao* astrogator brothers who plied the space lanes in the same convoy. One day she fell in a swoon and was only brought back to life by powerful drugs, but as soon as she regained consciousness she complained that she had been brought back prematurely. Later, three of her brothers returned and told of the psi-storm that had assailed them, of how she had appeared to them and saved them. The fourth brother's ship was lost.

The girl of Mei-chou died soon afterwards, but it was said that her spirit frequently intervened, helping astrogators in peril or ships attacked by pirates. After that she became Princess of Supernatural Favor, then a Celestial Queen, and finally she was rewarded by the title of Empress of Heaven.

Tian looked back over his shoulder momentarily, and Choi felt the hairs lifting on his own spine. A Yamato ship, he thought. This was a big craft, no warship but a trading vessel, lightly armed to allow bigger mass cargoes, like most of the ships that plied the Neutral Zone routes. Tian went as far as the assembly area and looked down the companionway into the darkness.

"There's no one here at all," he shouted, and returned to help Choi Ki Won up into the vacant lock.

With fervent hopes that the derelict was filled with valuable cargo, the merchant went first to the container lift and found it inoperative. Then he went aft. It smelled foul and dense, like fermenting brewers' soy mash. The captain's cabin would be the place to start if he wanted to unravel the mystery. Oh, most certainly she's Yamato, he decided, glancing up at the squiggly *hiragana* and *katakana* script that was embossed here and there on the plex walls. He knew the script and the hateful language very well from the days of his youth when it had been his mother tongue. Yes, Yamato-built, and Yamato-worked, he thought, feeling the old panic rise in his guts. He had seen many different ship hulls in his time and had learned to distinguish the external signs that showed origin, but with Yamato ships it was often difficult—they were rarely distinctive, but owed their lines to Amerikan or Europan or Chinese designs. This dogfish was certainly made in Yamato, and the shipyard's maker plate in the bridge confirmed that the frame of the ship had been constructed in 2416, at the Nissan Yards on Kure, specifically to be operated in the *kin kaigun* fleet. Could it be? Had she really once been one of the Yamato *aurium* transports? Choi Ki Won's hope soared, but he steadied himself. But she was now owned by Senpaku, and Yamato crews did not simply abandon fortunes in aurium, even at the cost of their own lives. What horror had evacuated the ship?

He went further aft, passing out of the harsh bluish light. The smell of fermentation gave way to a cloying stuffiness. The hum of power looms and microscopic switching as fans and pumps deep within the ship ducted and recycled the air and conditioned the shipboard environment. The ship's nose lifted and settled on each gentle motion of the tide, sending unearthly groaning noises through her. How much simpler if she had been Korean or Amerikan, or even Cho Sen, he thought. But the August Personage has seen fit to send a Yamato ship, and that could only mean officials and bureaucratic investigations and endless delay. Ultimately it must mean confiscation, for this was Korea, and Korea's independence was still a poor and threadbare thing.

If only our President Keun had seen sense, he thought. Why in God's name did he go in that car-cade? What stupidity! What madness to jeopardise the free Republic! Aiee! An official visit to the Front Line Worlds was an expensive and ludicrous exercise, no doubt an idea put there by an advisor whose pockets were a-jangle with Yamato aurium. That Keun should be killed without any credible minister to succeed him! There's only Vice-president Park now, Keun's aged uncle, and beyond him Mutsuhito the Accursed, who waits like a crocodile to devour our quadrant. It's their design to destroy our cherished independence. They know the vice-president cannot hold this fledgling state together for long. There is no one except Park, with whom Mutsuhito must contest ownership of Free Korea. Oh, how the work of a single vile assassin, the death of a single peerless leader, casts all of future history onto an unhappy track!

A more uneven contest was difficult to imagine. The vision of Free Korea subdued like Cho Sen and the so-called Neutral Zone by Yamato's military-industrial machine burgeoned garishly in Choi Ki Won's imagination. Already Mutsuhito had armies stationed along the Boundary. He could now lean so heavily on Free Korea that her state policies, both internal and external, would be distorted out of recognition, whoever ruled. Mutsuhito itched to absorb his independent neighbor and snuff out the ancient identity of the Korean people. The strategic and material benefits of a bloodless conquest of all Korea would be overpowering when set beside Mutsuhito's greed. And Keun has given him the perfect excuse! Two years, maybe three, as the senile Park loses his grip on the coalition—then what? Butchery and terror—or the meek acceptance of Yamato domination. And then it will be the death of all good things.

Choi Ki Won damned the watching fishermen on the beach. They had brought him the news, but they had also propagated the rumors that had brought the officials. He damned Mutsuhito to hell. To the deepest, hottest, and cruelest of hells. Then he damned all things out of Yamato.

Yamato embargoes on Amerikan ships and Amerikan goods, the *kempei*'s terror in Cho Sen, Yamato's meddling in Free Korea—these things have slashed my profits by half, Choi Ki

Won thought, staring into the gloomy depths of the ship. But, by all the gods, they'll repay me!

Is it not an invariable rule that the horse of a warlord tramples the poor merchant underfoot? There's no justice in the cosmos, only the eight Great Immortals who enjoy irony. Still, they comfort the suffering people in times of great loss, and I know they stand by those who seek to stand up for themselves.

Choi Ki Won gritted his teeth at his secret thoughts. He detested Yamato fulsomely, hated the idea that it could seize Free Korea. Yes, a Yamato ship! Maybe she became detached from the annual *kin kaigun* in a psi-storm. It often happens that ships get lost. Perhaps pirates have not attacked and stripped her. Or maybe she's a lone private milk-cow that attempted the crossing in secret so that Senpaku could avoid Mutsuhito's shit-eating taxes! Now, that would be justice!

The way the mill wheel has come full circle! Aiee! If I lose credit this year I'll have only myself to blame. My monthly accounts will certainly show small returns on hardware, but the sale of information is much more lucrative. The facts concerning the scheduling of ships into the vast and complex Korean nexi must be worth more than all the hardware in Seoul City, though the payment I receive is comparatively meager. Think positive, Choi!—as those Amerikans always say. Yes, I will think positive. Perhaps this ghost ship is sent by the gods as a reward!

He pushed open the door that led to the captain's cabin and entered it, filled with a growing confidence. Then the confidence left him as he felt the touch of a muzzle between his shoulders and whirled to see a ghastly face and two Nambu blasters set to "burn" and pointing at his belly.

The apparition was fierce: yellow eyes with pinpoint pupils, a clenched jaw, menace in every fiber of him. The man was shaking as if from a terrible fury, raving as if in fever, and his voice was like a demon's.

"Put your hands up, dog!"

The order was sudden and savage, but Choi Ki Won understood the Japanese. Involuntarily he took a step back and raised his palms above his ears. Then he watched with incredulity as the man's unearthly eyes rolled up, one of his blasters almost trembled from his grip, and his knees gave way under him so that he crashed to the deck.

Then Choi Ki Won's shock was penetrated by a familiar noise.

It took him a moment to identify it because it was the last sound he could possibly have expected to hear in this place. It was the wailing of a baby.

*   *   *

Duval Straker staggered, overcome by another wave of agony. Desperately his mind clung to the sounds he was hearing, and he fought back to consciousness and tried to muster his faculties once more. He got to his knees, and his blaster wavered in an opaque blur. Stand up! Find your feet, or you're a dead man. This is Yamato! Yamato, don't you see? Lord God, how could you betray me like this? We've landed while Arima Yoshisa-bura's still alive. Didn't I promise you I'd believe in you again, if only you'd smother that worthless bag of rotting shit before we reached Yamato? Wasn't that the bargain? How many times did I tell you that the captain's going to betray us to the *kempei?* Michie and the baby, who I've fought so hard for—*they're going to die!* Don't you understand? The bad guys will have won. Who's more important: Arima, who lies stewing in his own black vomit, or your innocent little baby? Shall I murder Arima now we're safely down? Shall I cut his throat with his own sword as he lies there writhing? Come on, God answer me! Wouldn't that just be a mercy to him as he suffers now?

Duval's eyes popped. The sound of screams in the dim distance, the music of rage ringing peals of bells in his head. It was as if a giant hand had slapped him. Listen to your son cry, Duval! Listen to him cry! You must stop gawping and seize the initiative now! Do what's right!

He saw, penetrating through veils of mist, as the frightened man raised his hands. The man was well dressed, an expensive robe and boots, his girth supported by a wide, sagging belt, a strange pinch collar, and above it a forty-year-old's face, nut brown, high forehead, badger-streaked beard, and eyes full of surprise. He did not have the shaved pate and topknot of a samurai. Why don't you rush me? Why don't you try to burn me with my own gun? Can't you see I'm next to helpless?

"Please don't—"

"Get back!" Duval growled, fighting back the dizziness that threatened to engulf him. "Try me and I'll burn your throat out!"

"Don't shoot, sir. I mean you no harm. I am not armed." The intruder's Japanese was oddly accented.

"I told you to put your hands up! Up! Higher!"

"Are you the captain? What ship is this? I only want to help you."

"Back, now! Move yourself! In there!"

The man fell back before him into the cabin, Duval keeping him on the end of his Nambu; he did not take his eyes off him until they were safely inside.

Arima groaned from his bed. Suddenly Duval's mind became lucid as the wave of nausea passed from him. He forced himself to remember how he had come to be locked into this dangerous strategy. However he looked at it, there had seemed no other way. Didn't Arima try to have me locked up? Didn't he swear to me he'd tell the *kempei* at the apron terminal as soon as we came in sight of the Home Worlds? But in the attack he lost so much equipment and so many crew sealed in blast-proof compartments he could hardly run his ship. The Dovers were smashed, many of the systems disrupted including the freezees and the med units, but luckily the maintenance nerve center of the ship where Michie and the baby and I were stuck had gone into an emergency lock-out spasm that could not be overridden from outside. The software was convinced that the ship was still under attack. Without food the situation grew desperate, and when I finally got out, I was turned on as a competitor. I was forced to systematically stalk those of the crew who remained, just as they stalked me. They used meson cutters to try to get into Michie. I evacuated the atmosphere from the compartments they were working in. Those who survived suited up and continued. I found a way to remotely shut off the power to their cutters. They used egress cell packs. I dummied round behind and sniped at them. They gave up, and I burned their cutters, hoping there were no more, and resealed the bulkheads with a noninterruptible mask to keep them bottled up.

Finally I got to Arima, knowing that I needed the astrogator alive, and I hit him and burned him badly. I brought him an emergency medikit and it was then he swore he would keep our true identities to himself after we landed. He saw us through three nexi, but I still don't trust him. He's a pragmatic man, who cuts his promises to suit his situation. And he's in need of credit and dignity now, and the awe of the *kempei* has too powerful a grip on his mind. He must hate me for what I did to him and his ship. He'll recant his promise for a few *yen* and he'll blame us for everything, and they'll arrest us and deliver us to torture and the Probe and the hideous crosses all over again. I should have burned Arima's brains out last night. But I couldn't then, and I can't now. Not a pitiful starving wretch with the stink of death coming off him. Not in cold blood. Even when Michie's life and my son's life and my own life all depend on it. Maybe he'll die yet. Maybe. Maybe . . .

The shaking was starting again inside him.

"You'll be my hostage," he told the man through chattering teeth, grimly hanging on to his blaster butt. "That's a fair bargain. A rich merchant like you, in exchange for passage to Amerika. I want nothing more than that. The means to get my wife and son off of this planet. A bargain. Just like the one at Niigata. Only this time there'll be no payment, no trusting to treaty, and no mistakes."

"How many are you?" the intruder asked. Despite the order to keep his hands up, he bunched the broad sleeve in his hand and clamped it over his nose and mouth, then he leaned over Arima. "This man is close to death."

"Yesterday there were ten alive. All dying just like him. All bottled up in the nose section. Today I don't know. The thirst . . ."

"Please, sir, put up your gun. I want only to help you."

"Get back from me!"

Duval felt the crest of the feverish tremor pass over him. Each day the lassitude of starvation had made it more and more difficult to concentrate his mind, to climb from deck to deck, to roll from his strap hammock, but he had hunted down meat, and Michie kept producing milk for the baby, and he was still well enough now to pull a trigger. He looked at the hostage, then down at the unconscious Arima. Die, you sonofawhore! he told the man silently. Die and let my secret die with you!

"You must let me help these men, sir. If they are dying. Where are they?"

Arima opened his eyes. He would not give up his life easily. He was a fighter, and though his struggles had brought himself and his crew to the gates of hell, he had done as he had sworn to do. He had brought his ship home. After the pirate had disabled the *Kawabata Yasunari* he had tried to make Chichi-jima, but the Index had been low and the nexus had tossed them towards the side chain where contrary psi had seized them. For two days and two nights they had fought on, but the power of the nexus had left Arima unconscious and they had drifted helplessly until they had identified the destination system as a branchless dead end, and they had had to go back the way they had come.

Arima had sent out all but one of the ship's distress beacons, hoping to get a message to Chichi-jima, or the Twenty Degree systems, but not one had returned, and for weeks they had languished in the miserable system of Delta Scuti, 6.6 parsecs away from Daito, running short of everything, stuck like flies in amber, until in desperation he had realised that they must attempt another transit or they would all perish.

"Can you hear me? My name is Choi Ki Won. Where are the others?"

"I hear you," Arima said weakly but coherently. "My crew are dead, or dying like me. I am the captain of this ship—"

"Hold your mouth, samurai!"

Choi Ki Won's eyes narrowed at Duval. "You are not samurai yourself? Then what are you?"

As Duval's feral alertness returned, he jabbed the blaster forward. "I'm Amerikan. I want food and water and passage aboard an Amerikan nexus ship," he told the man, his voice rasping now. "I demand—"

Choi Ki Won stroked his chin warily. "You're in no position to make demands, sir."

"I'll shoot you before I'll rot in any Yamato prison. Do you hear?"

Then, incredibly, the tenor of the man's voice came back at him in puzzled amusement.

"But, sir, you are not in *Yamato.*"

"Not Yamato? Then where?"

"This is Seoul. *You are in Free Korea.*"

Duval felt the resolve drain from him. If this was Free Korea, there was no need to hide. If this was truly Seoul, they were safe . . .

Then a young man's arms came around him from behind, seizing him in a plex-like grip, and the blaster was wrested from him.

27

SEOUL—TWO YEARS LATER

Michie was sitting in the adjoining room with Choi Ki Won's wife, and the sound of their laughing came to him. The tuna fish dinner had been exquisite, and after the fine red wines, as rich and heady as Kansas klaret, he felt relaxed and receptive.

The ocean was dappled with starlight in the narrows that sheltered Seoul City's harbor. From the window Duval could see the water chopping up as it became the open sea, the Western Ocean that stretched around the planet, twenty thousand miles along an unobstructed parallel of latitude to the far side of this same continent.

"Look at the fishing junks, Kenichi. See that one with the red lights?"

He stroked his two-year-old's hair gently, but failed to capture his attention. Kenichi began to cry. Choi Ki Won swept the infant up and stood him on the sill, careless of the precipitous drop below.

"Be obedient to your father, Kenichi," he said, pointing up at the night sky. "That's where you were born. Out there in space. Someday you'll cruise the space lanes as your father did and win glory for Free Korea."

The sight of the sea and the velvet sky soothed the child. Duval too felt the restless draw of it. Memories of past rigors no longer had the power to hurt him. He was healed. How different was this pleasant house and the soft comforts it afforded to the horrors of the *Kawabata Yasunari;* how delightful the hospitality of his good and generous friend, Choi Ki Won.

"You know," he told him wistfully, "when I first set out to cross space, my shipmates used to call me a Yambo, owing to my looks—as a joke, you see. And I would laugh with them. Then when the *kempei* came, they told me I was half racial

Japanese. Now I'm in Korea it's hard for me to know where I belong.''

Choi Ki Won smiled. "You are at home here! You are a Seoul dweller. Seoul Immigration says so!"

He remembered the official confirmation that had arrived two days ago; it was nominally the reason for the celebratory dinner they had just eaten. "I thank you for that. And it is true, you have made us very welcome.''

"But something tells me you yearn for your own world still.''

"I have no home world now." Duval drew a lingering breath. "At one time I was Amerikan but was called a Yambo, next I was a stateless slave, and then an honorary samurai. After that I was told that my genotype was not derived from the people I had thought were my parents. Now I am in Korea—but only as an officially accepted foreigner. In truth, I don't know what I am.''

"You might go into Amerika when the next convoy comes in. Many ships that come here are out of Liberty, as you know, and I have the friendship of many an Amerikan shipowner.''

Duval shook his head soberly at his friend's probings. "I can't have a Japanese wife in Amerika, Ki Won. Race as such is disregarded there, but she would be obliged to adapt her behavior. It would hurt her to think she was losing her cultural heritage. And if there was ever open war—I would fear for the safety of my family.''

"Is there more tolerance for you here?''

"Thanks to you." He smiled. "I have a living. And I have friends, and harmony at last.''

"But for how much longer? Go to Amerika, my friend.''

"Why should you say that?''

Choi Ki Won lowered his voice, and as he spoke his words grew bitter. "The peace is crumbling. Though Park is Korea's choice, Mutsuhito has a dynastic marriage link with the old Korean Emperor's line of Yi. According to the old ways, his blood claim is undeniable, and he has massed his legions on our Boundary so he can impose his will. Each week, more and more Yamato traders are flooding into Cho Sen and all the Open Ports. They are the shock troops, sent in advance with their bribery and casuistry." He checked himself, remembering that he must keep his loathing for Yamato partially concealed. For all that he hated them, he had to admire their efficiency. The way they had persuaded the Seoul authorities to send Harmonious Apron Police to impound the *Kawabata Yasunari* within hours of its discovery, and afterwards, how their tireless diplomacy had arranged her repair and speedy dispatch to Yamato, robbing him of his windfall.

But he had robbed them of a far greater thing. He had struck a blow that had been waiting to be thrown for twenty-five years.

The Harmonious Apron Police had seen Tian Meng waving at intervals from the bridge, beckoning them, and so it was that half an hour later they had come out in a second fisherman's boat, three of them, with three constables and Captain Yim in the bows. Poor Yim, with the imperiousness of the minor nobility, impractical and hot-tempered, and utterly under the sway of his own ego.

Yim was a tall, thin man in his early forties wearing the immaculate scarlet robe that was part of his superintendent's uniform, with that look of complete, single-minded self-possession that only those schooled in Seoul's Academy of Harmonious Corrections could attain. Choi Ki Won had winced at the sight of him.

Old Tian's empty shrimp boat had been drifting aimlessly fifty yards away and so he had waved his arms and shouted out of the airlock to them. "Thank the gods you've come at last, Captain Yim! And you too, brave policemen!"

Yim had ignored him, cupping a microphone to his mouth and hailing the ship with a distorted blast. But one of the constables had peered into the flooded cargo bay inquiringly. "What are you doing here?"

"Our boat drifted. That good-for-nothing Tian Meng can't even tie his father's boat up properly. We were stranded here, Captain. If you hadn't come I can't imagine what would have happened to us."

Then he had clamped his sleeve tightly over his nose and mouth again while Tian Meng had stood beside him, mutely under orders.

When the frightened fisherman in the police boat had shipped his paddle and brought his fishing boat alongside, Yim had asked, "Is there no one else aboard? We thought you must have been attacked."

Then Yim had tasted the air suspiciously. "Why do you hold your sleeve to your face, Mr. Choi?"

He had given a hacking cough. "Can't you smell the stink? This ship is full of corpses, Captain. And others alive still, but covered in red sores."

"Red sores? How many crew?"

"Yes, ten, I think. Maybe a dozen. It's so hard to tell. I've seen nothing like it in all my life. It's horrible. Here, help me down into your boat."

"Get back!"

The captain had seized the oar and pushed the boat back from the lock. His face graven now with fear and anger.

"Please, Captain Yim! What are you doing?"

"It's a disease!"

The Apron Police had looked from one to another in panic.

"No, no—please. Don't think that. Come now. You must let me off this stinking wreck."

"Row for the shore!" Yim had ordered. "It's one of those terrible plague diseases!"

Instantly the stern oar had been unshipped and the wobbly little boat set in motion.

"But Captain Yim!" His helpless plea had rung out and he had begun to run from side to side in the airlock, secretly delighted at the success of his ploy.

"You must stay there, Choi Ki Won. With the hatch shut. I command it! This ship and all its disgusting microbes is quarantined. For forty days, do you hear me?"

"*Forty days?* But there's no food aboard. I shall starve! And these poor men—"

"Food will be sent."

"But they need a medical unit!"

"Do what you can for them."

"No! Captain Yim, I beg you! Come back!"

The boat had stroked rapidly away, and under cover of night Tian Meng had swum to his father's boat and recovered it and they had crept to shore with the Amerikan and his wife and the baby.

But there had been a good deal of substance to the ruse. Choi Ki Won recalled the scene that he had witnessed in the nose section, men wasted with starvation, ragged and feverish, dead or dying. None except Arima able to stand and he a yellow skeleton. He had had a samurai's tenacity that drove him on when other men gave up. Perhaps he had survived, for the Yamato ambassador's people had found the courage to board the ship the following day. In any case, they had found him gone, and because of the delicacy of the negotiations surrounding the *Kawabata Yasunari*'s release, and because the imposition of a quarantine order would have hampered them, his name had appeared in no official reports, and within a week the entire ship had been sealed in a vast flexiplex bag and the lot air-lifted back into orbit, doubtless to be taken off to Kyoto for examination.

"Do you think there will be much resistance?" Duval asked him, bringing him back to the present. "If Yamato invades, I mean?"

Choi Ki Won put his hands together thoughtfully. "It's said that Mutsuhito's appointed Baron Harumi to head his invasion. If he's opposed, Yamato troops will destroy our pitiful army and then they will trample Seoul City. They could raze all of Korea as they choose. We are already in their power. That is why my advice to you is to get out now, while you can."

Duval glanced at his friend, reminding himself that Choi Ki Won knew only that he had escaped the *kempei*'s cross. He had never told him his true profession, nor the reason Arima had valued his discovery. So far as Choi Ki Won was concerned he was nothing more than an academic who had been victimized by the *kempei*, and in that, somewhere, had been the bond between them.

"You're a wise man, Mr. Choi."

"If you permit me to write a letter to my son, he will arrange passage on an Amerikan nexus ship."

"No."

"But you don't know if Captain Arima survived. If he did, and spoke of you to the *kempei*, you will already be marked. Once the invasion is complete—"

"I ran once, I cannot run again. I'll trust that Arima died, or that he chose to forget me."

"Reconsider, please."

"Thank you, but no."

Choi Ki Won put out his hands in appeal. "I beg you. For Kenichi's sake. For Michie's. Listen to me."

His son began to cry again, wanting to get down from the sill, and Duval lifted him to the floor. Ki Won's words are wise, he thought, beginning to feel the weight of his friend's persuasion.

In a Korea ruled by Yamato a single indiscretion could uncover us and unleash the terror again. But there's no place in the cosmos that's any safer for us than here. At least in Seoul City we're among friends. Living here in the low-tech zone suits us. It's almost like home to Michie. In Amerika we know no one, we have nothing. Twelve years is a long time to be away, and they say that in an Amerika at war there would be no peace for any racial Japanese.

"We'll stay here."

Choi Ki Won sighed, his tact failing. "President Park has support in New Wonsan. Perhaps that will remain truly Korean. Perhaps if you—"

"No. I said I'm tired of running, Ki Won. We'll take our chances in Seoul City. For good or ill we'll make our stand here."

"Is that to be your final decision?"

Below, a delivery car rumbled by loaded with crates of chickens and fresh vegetables, gutted fish, great stoppered jugs of wine, water, pails of shellfish, and big hocks of meat for tomorrow's markets. He remembered the first day of his deliverance in Korea in this same house. He had wanted to eat ravenously but had known that the shock of food on a starving body was like swallowing red-hot coals. He had drunk a little and he had fed Michie very sparingly and tried to make sure she did not gorge herself. Then doubts had speared him. His mind had tried to unknot the problem. Choi Ki Won was a rich merchant. Surely he only wanted to ransom them to the authorities—yet he had insisted that he did not. All along, Choi Ki Won had been at pains to comfort him and to provide for his family. He had jeopardised himself to become the willing helper of an Amerikan. That doesn't make sense, he had reasoned. No one in Choi Ki Won's position would want to clash with the authorities. I can't understand why he's working so hard to preserve us. Would either of the Hawken brothers have reacted that way if they'd come aboard a Yamato ship downed and half wrecked in the Rappahannock Estuary on Liberty? No! Then what was it that had made a serene man like Choi Ki Won hate Yamato with such a personal animosity? And what was it that made him hate samurai most particularly?

"Why are you doing this for us?" he had asked him directly.

Choi Ki Won had given his patient smile and pointed to Amerikan ads on the terminal building of the Seoul apron. "I told
you. The owners of some Amerikan ships are my friends. Before
the troubles Amerika and Korea traded for years as allies and
our friendship has prospered both Sectors."

Duval had been unconvinced by Choi Ki Won's superficial
reply. "You're asking me to believe that you'd risk your life to
save us. Why?"

"In Korea as in Yamato, Mr. Straker, the merchant has little
status. Big men make promises and the small man keeps them.
We must protect our own interests. For the merchant, taking
risks is our way of life."

Duval had felt deep guilt at the way he had doubted Choi.
Then he had looked into the man's dark eyes and he had thought
he recognised the mark of an honest man.

"I ask you again: is that your final decision?"

"Yes. I will not leave here of my own free will."

The broad, kindly face of Choi Ki Won clouded then. He
became grave and stern. "Well, then, come with me to the cool
of the garden. We must talk, you and I. For all is not what it
seems here in my house, and if you will stay in Seoul City, you
must know the truth."

They went down past banks of tamarisk and gorse under which
night lizards darted. Among the green blades and purple dragon-
headed blooms of flowers-de-Luce they walked side by side,
Choi Ki Won speaking and Duval Straker listening, until the
Korean had told of the other trade in which he dealt, the trade
in secrets and sealed reports, and the place where he sent them.

The Amerikan felt himself sober up, despite the twice-fer-
mented rice wine that ran in his veins. He judged himself fully
admitted to his friend's confidence now, and so he likewise
unburdened himself, telling of the skills he possessed, to which
Choi Ki Won nodded sagely as a man does who receives a great
responsibility.

In trust he listened to Choi Ki Won then, and heard him speak
with difficulty of the first family he had had, the one of his youth,
a quarter century ago, when he had been a samurai and the *kempei*
had discovered him wanting. And as he listened he discovered
the answer to a question that no one else knew enough even to
ask—what a man born a Yamato samurai was really doing living
in so grand a house in Seoul City.

28

LIBERTY

"Mr. Straker, there's a gentleman to see you!"

Ellis Straker looked up impatiently. Reba, sitting quietly in the boat's prow, scrolled the page of her book. The servant was breathless; his shoes, thick with mud, thumped the dirt bank, sending rings rippling over the glassy surface. Vibration at the lakeside always disturbed the fish, and this would ruin them for the rest of the afternoon.

"You can see I'm fishing, Matthew," he called back gruffly as he picked another roach out of his pail. It was four inches long, and its gills heaved as he threaded the barbed hook into its back. When it touched the lake it fled, red fins blurring as it towed the float on a line of micron-thin plex.

"He says it's urgent, sir."

"Damn you, you foolish object. Can anything be more urgent than a twenty-five-pound pike?"

"I didn't think to ask him that, sir."

"Did you think to ask his name?"

"Oh, yes, sir, but he won't tell it. He's a fine gentleman, though."

Ellis roused himself from his study of the reeds, exasperated by the synth servant that Reba could not be persuaded to get rid of. "Then, tell the fine gentleman for me to take his ass off of my property."

He had been brooding over the neo-Puritans of the town who had recently somehow conceived the idea that the owner of Xanadu mansion was living in sin with another man's wife. If one of them had had the balls to come here—

The boat swayed as Reba laid aside her book and sat up. Ellis spread his legs to steady the boat.

"Perhaps you ought to attend to it, Ellis."

"If he hasn't got the manners to give his name, he can't expect civility."

"I'd like to think that any visitor to our home might expect that. And I wish you'd treat Matthew as a creature entitled to a little dignity."

Ellis looked at her calm determination and knew he had been justly corrected. Of course she was right. It was unnecessary to be so sharp towards the synth, who was always so amiable and polite. But for all her composure Reba must have had some small suspicion, as he did. Was this nameless visitor the one that they both knew must eventually come to disturb their quiet life together?

In the time they had lived here, Reba had borne him a second child, a daughter, Kat, and another, Deb. And there had been inevitable unvoiced questions among all kinds of people, seeing as how the Halide heir *never* came to his wife's house, and it was odd how the nexus ship captain appeared to have taken his place. But Ellis was no longer a nexus ship captain. For the sake of his family he had forsworn space travel and all it had once meant to him. Except for business visits to Lincoln and frequent trips to the various aprons of Liberty, he had renounced nexus ships forever, telling himself that he had fulfilled all promises and realised all potentialities. This little lake was his cruising ground now, and the twenty-five-pound pike his only adversary.

It seemed only yesterday that he had pushed open the garden gate and come inside to reclaim his Reba, but it had been almost seven years. That first Liberty spring he had secretly acquired Xanadu through an intermediary, relishing the power of his outright ownership. He had demolished the Yamato-style tea house in the garden to make way for stone brought from a local quarry, and then he had built two new wings so the house had the form of an "E," to literally stamp himself on the place, but perhaps more to erase all trace of the previous owner.

The house now contained no plex and no curves, a strange choice for a man who had lived so long in a nexus ship. It was built from the bones of the planet; his home, rooted in the stuff of Liberty, this quake-free planet, whose architecture was characteristically solid and strong and aspiring, and therefore, he thought, inspiring. So he had chosen it: a foundation of stone, walls of Liberty redwood, a roof of Algonquin slate covering all, solid and stately. And though there was an antique stone fireplace, that had once graced a big house on Earth, that was his one concession. He had had no doubts that the swell of Liberty's green hills was his proper surroundings, or that the best occupation of a wealthy man was philanthropy and the management of credit and materials through signature. For seven years he had played the mercantile game and consigned his privateering past to a locked chest somewhere in the back of his memory. But it was undeniable that the spirit of the times was altering, and that Yamato's martial spirit had been undimmed by the distractions of Korea. Events were moving swiftly towards the day when he must open that dusty chest and look in upon its treasure once more.

He regarded Reba with love and with respect. Her power to surprise him had never waned, and her intellect was an awesome thing that made her advice indispensable, especially when he retreated into the smoldering angers that once might have been doused by a little action. They would ride their Palominos together when he needed space, racing across the green hills to the fringes of the forest. Or he would hew timber with an ax until his muscles were sweat-oiled, and the fresh summer light of Liberty's primary turned him to bronze.

"The weather's changing," he said stiffly.

"Yes."

"I don't suppose we'll see any more of the pike."

"If you say so."

"Yep."

Cloud blighted the sky above the slate planes of the house. A rain of golden leaves shimmered from the aspen trees beside it. He closed his eyes. Yep, there was more than just the weather changing. More than the season too. He could feel it in the air, just as he had felt it back in '25. Throughout the uneasy peace, Amerika had steadily built up her defenses and her economy, finding new trade in Germani and the United Baltic States for her manufactures, sending raw materials and know-how to Muscovi, and pushing boldly into the markets of Brasilia and Afrika to do trade with the new republics. Ellis had made astute investments, growing richer still, putting his credit into the Eastlands Corporation and helping to set up a new venture to trade into Hindostan/Pyxis/Puppis. But the weeping sore of Korea had continued to fester, and Mutsuhito's annexation of Free Korea had added to Yamato a much greater power to strangle and control any who dared oppose the Empire. The worlds just beyond the Boundary had grown as perilous for Amerikan shipping as the Twenty Degree Worlds had once been for Yamato shipping, and the immense riches of the Zone, Outer as well as Inner, were as much a Yamato preserve as ever. In Lincoln, too, many things were in need of setting to rights. Too many conversations there had verged on treason and brought him to overturn tables that he no longer gained any pleasure from the city. The President's party itself seethed with factions that wanted to see a détente with Yamato bought on any terms, and too many of those that remained were cowards who could not see the inevitable.

He grunted. ''Who would come here and refuse to give his name?''

She sighed. ''Go and see!''

''Yes. Okeh. I will.''

He wound the line back and stowed his pole, giving the last captive roach in his pail its freedom. As he propelled the punt deftly forward, a cloud passed over the sun-star, there was a sudden chill, and the water's surface lost its silver. The Liberty summer, a maid of fickle mood, had grown capricious, and before they had reached the house a heavy, dousing rain had begun to fall.

Ellis's muddied Texas boots crunched across the path, skittering gravel. He strode around the corner of the house trailing the pink-faced androgyne, Matthew, in his wake. Anger lay like a coiled diamondback in his chest and he wished he had his firewood ax in his hand. Then he saw the Bristol air-car.

I'm gonna beat on Kurt Reiner's man until he's black and blue, and send him away to think again, he told himself. It was not a course open to a respectable businessman. Okeh, then, what if I treat his boy real polite and get a meeting with that drunken sonofabitch, and then break his head?

He turned the buttressed corner of his entranceway and sensed a figure step out through the rain behind him.

''Git yo' hands up, ya lazy bear!''

He whirled.

''John!''

''*Senator* Oujuku—let's have some respect, now, brother.''

He advanced on Oujuku and they gripped forearms, hugely pleased to meet each other again. Rain dripped from the brim of Oujuku's hat, spangled his black beard with diamonds. The scar that had been put between nose and eye by a misadventure during his voyage into Yamato wrinkled as he smiled broadly.

"Ah, let me look at you, now!"

"Man, you look like Lord Shit!"

"And you his butler."

"Is that any way to address a senator?"

"On my patch of ground, yes. But this senator is very welcome. What brings you here?"

Oujuku's voice went dark brown. "Y'know . . . just passing through."

"Come inside. Will you smoke a stogie with me?"

"Gladly. And you can tell me all about your retirement."

"Retirement? I don't think of it as such."

They passed under the arch side by side. It was good to see Oujuku buoyant again, buoyant enough to rib his friend over his quiet style of life.

Their last meeting had been unhappy; the one before that, glorious. That had been the triumph of Oujuku's return, when he had landed the *Arizona* back on Harrisburg apron after three years laden with fifty billion in Yamato aurium. Then Oujuku had received the highest accolade the Sector could bestow. The President had thrown off all objections and come herself to Harrisburg, to the very cargo bay of his ship, to meet him. And how Ellis had basked in the glory of it, knowing, as his President gave her best profile to the foreign cameras recording it, that by her act the diplomatic snub to Yamato had been made immense. Drinking with Ellis afterwards, Oujuku had said delightedly that the simulcast was bound to reach Mutsuhito's own tri-vee screen and would cause the sonofabitch to spit bile, and both had pledged themselves to firing up their wild pasts at some future time when the Sector's need arose.

They had been great days. This Amerikan had fought his way into the newly constructed nexi amid the Blue Beacon supergiants of Ara and Scorpius. He had thrown himself against the might of Yamato and had put such heart into Amerika for his pains. But last year Oujuku's wife, Marie, had died and he had grieved her deeply. They had spoken together again then, and Ellis had aided his friend as he had once himself been aided, and both had been uplifted. Still, as if by mutual consent, neither had renewed their ideas of going out again into the Zone.

This year the Index had risen again for Oujuku. According to his occasional calls, he had found employment working on the Navy Commission. He had been elevated from governor to senator and he had found the love of an heiress in Justice Secretary George Packer's daughter. It seemed to Ellis that the prospects of making a good marriage had brought Oujuku to fine condition.

They sat down in armchairs, surrounded by mounted ship models—*Constitution* and *Lexington* and *Valley Forge*—and indulgently reminisced, Ellis speaking of his investments and Oujuku telling tales of Court, both sucking on tobako stogies until the room filled with a noncarcinogenic blue haze.

Oujuku regarded the polished wood and tall windows with approval. "So you're enjoying your leisure?"

"Certainly am." Ellis nodded. "And you? How're you doing with the Navy Commission?"

He watched for Oujuku's reaction. In the time since Hawken had been appointed Navy treasurer, Oujuku had mentioned his Navy work only once, and that dismissively.

"You know, I been doing a lot of thinking about our little secret. I don't know how much longer we can rely on the people who saw that nova—or whatever it was—keeping quiet. There were nine of them who knew something was amiss, the amnesia drugs only worked on five, two're dead now, the other two're on a helluva pension each. Kort, she's okeh, but Keever—I think he wants to split the secret. And he drinks more than he ought."

"And?"

"Well, I don't know. I wonder if we shouldn't split it first?"

Oujuku said it so lightly that Ellis tuned immediately to the bass chords of his guest's manner, to his gestures. Yes, he thought, there's definitely something amiss with him, and it's not connected with the quasi-nova. He fenced in his curiosity and, equally lightly, said, "I might think it over."

"Okeh. But I tell you, I feel kind of spooked."

"You think Yamato's discovered the ultimate weapon, don't you?"

Oujuku's eyes searched his face. "Yeah, Ellis. I do."

"You think they figured out how to destabilise a stellar interior and wipe out a whole system."

"Ellis, what if they have?"

True, it wasn't any ordinary nova. But it had been in an inhabited system. An experiment gone wrong? Maybe. But the shock and panic that would escape across Amerika was unthinkable if it was suspected that Yamato had a weapon capable of destroying a whole system in one go.

"The way I see it, there's two alternatives," Ellis said. "If we sit tight, we got plenty of time. I don't see anybody else getting near the Zero Degree Boundary, not the way Yamato's fortified since your little holiday. If nobody's going in or out of Yamato, that's it—in regular space it's axiomatic that light only travels at one light-year per annum, John."

"It's been more than ten years."

"Okeh, but at the Earth radial distance we're talking, it'll take decades before the waveshell breaks past the Twenty Degree Worlds. Listen, if what we saw could be demonstrated to be a natural phenomenon, then we got nothing to worry about. We could talk about it, tell the defense chiefs, et cetera, et cetera. If we could show that it couldn't possibly be a usable weapon, we'd be okeh."

"But we can't show that."

"Right! Mention it and we have an instant panic that no crisis management team could damp down. That leaves us with two critical courses. Either the thing is a weapon or it's not. If it's not, we won't have served any purpose in talking about it, nor protected much in keeping it secret. That's a low-payoff strategy eitherhow."

"But if it *is* a weapon, what then?"

"Then we'd be in deep shit. And so would the rest of Known Space. But then that would be true whether anybody knew about it or not, so it may as well stay our little secret."

"But if we talk now, we can develop a similar weapon! Threaten them when they threaten us!"

"It's not the weapon—*if* it exists—that's the problem. It's delivering it to its target. While we've got a strong Navy we're safe. We go where we please inside Amerika, and no one comes here from Yamato unless we give them the say-so."

"That's what's bugging me, Ellis. The Navy—"

"Oh, I'm content to leave Navy matters to Navy men." Ellis deflected him, probing subtly with his maddening disregard for what Oujuku was trying to tell him. He knew that if he got involved, it would be up to the scalp, and he had made his promises to Reba.

Oujuku reacted, changing the subject abruptly. "Did you

know that when President Park came to Amerika for aid, I spoke to him?''

Ellis cocked his head. "Oh?"

"It was at a White House dinner. Everybody in their parrot suits. 'Give me that knife,' Conroy Lubbock says. 'Would you look at that! If that hybrid vegetable don't remind me of Ping-Pong,'—meaning the Dowager's youngest son. And Alia says from right down the table, 'Conroy, wasn't that the Chinese prince Pharis wanted me to marry?' "

Ellis grinned at Oujuku's gesticulations.

"Yeah, and there's the Chinese ambassador sitting not ten feet away, and he don't know where to look. And, later, that sonofabitch Belkov, who's richer than hell just lately, he comes up beside Otis le Grande and tells him about the latest terraformed system up against the edge of the Beyond. You know, the one that's just coming up to completion. 'Of course, Otis, I'll call it "Virginia," in honor of Alia.' But Otis is full of booze, and running off at the mouth, and he tells him back: 'Hey, now—"Virginia"? That's a misnomer and I know what I'm talking about, boh.' "

Ellis laughed, then he shook his head and sucked in a sharp breath. "Le Grande and Belkov both get pretty crazy when they've been drinking."

"They'll go far."

"Or *too* far."

"Yeah."

"Yeah. Though sometimes Amerika needs men with spirit. Like now."

There was a space pregnant with silence, then Ellis said, "So, John, you been enjoying yourself up in Town. You've a taste for gossip you never had."

"I've a taste for getting what I want. And I came to see that my old straight-talking way was too blunt for Lincoln. Your advice in that regard was better than any I got from you about cruising space."

"Well, a senator's got to be amusing, and an ambitious senator something of an intriguer. Now suppose you tell me, what really brings you here?"

Oujuku's face shed its smile, growing suddenly serious and intense. "Dirty stuff."

"Yeah? Well, I guess it's too dirty for a man of leisure like me. One who's—*retired*."

"I need your help, Ellis."

A curl of smoke spiraled up from the tip of Oujuku's stogie. The other end of it was clamped in his teeth, and his eye was steady on Ellis's face.

"Do you, now?"

"Yeah—call it ambition and intriguing if you want, but do you remember in 'thirty-four how I planned to get up a fleet and take it into Korea? How the President agreed and then changed her mind?"

"Uh-huh."

"I'd like to put it to her again—if you'd come."

"Oh, my cruising days're over, John. There's no call for the likes of me while the peace holds."

"You're wrong." Oujuku leaned forward, fired now with his old passion. His eyes smoldered; his hands gripped the arms of his chair. "Since Yamato took Free Korea everything's up in the air. Amerika has got to prepare for war. Now. Quickly. Before it's too late."

Reba stood in the doorway, a posy of garden flowers in her hand. Her face had lost its warmth.

"It's always been the policy of Yamato to extend their power across their boundaries," she told Oujuku coldly. "But they annex by marriage now, rather than war. When Yamato arms overran Free Korea, the Presidium on Seoul recognised Mutsuhito as Emperor through his wife's bloodline."

"That's true, Reba, but they also exiled President Park, who has the democratic claim. He's the man the Korean people want."

"Then we should be glad he found little help here. When he and his loyalists went after Cheju Do with a Chinese fleet, he was smashed to atoms by Baron Harumi. Had it not been for the President's change of heart, they might have been Amerikan ships, Senator."

"I beg your pardon, Reba, but Baron Harumi's victory was a beam weapon action. In that game Yamato has no peer. But would I, would Ellis, have allowed the baron's ships to come to grips with ours like the Chinese did?"

Ellis's dismay mounted as he heard Oujuku out, fearing his

infectious words and the way they wounded Reba. "C'mon, we're not gonna talk politics all—"

But Reba was insistent. "Please, let Senator Oujuku have his say."

Oujuku's fist balled. "We must fight. Because I've been. And I've seen. And I tell you, the whole Zone beyond the Kalifornia Boundary is a Yamato preserve. To their Empire they've added a thousand low-population worlds: the Remnant, a great aurium extraction plant on Sado and another on Okinawa, fabulous wealth. Yeah, and now Korea, with the most strategic of nexus chains in Known Space. But the biggest prize of all is Seoul. You're blind if you fail to see the purpose of that. They're set on overwhelming us, Ellis. They want to sweep us away in one massive blow. Don't lie to yourself that it's peace. It's just a temporary halt."

Reba dropped her flowers down onto a table and left the room. Ellis checked himself from following or calling to her. She was only thinking of him, of the children. But Oujuku was right, and right to speak. After the battle of Hainan, Yamato fears over the Chinese threat had been obliterated. The Three-Thirty Degree Boundary was secured, and when Free Korea fell under Mutsuhito's claim, two space-spanning nexus chains were put under his sole direction. The moment Imperial troops had landed on Seoul, Yamato had become a power with an easy chain stretching unbroken for two hundred light-years, and in the center of it, the greatest multiplex nexus junction in Known Space: Seoul's Yod-Seven-Seven. Overnight, Yamato had taken possession of Korea's nexus fleet—a dozen huge transports and their armaments, their naval fabrication yards, their arsenals and stockpiles. Then there were the extensive private trading fleets that plied the Twenty Degree routes, that Mutsuhito, as Emperor of Korea, could commandeer at any time. The title had given him mastery over the Zone in the same way that his destruction of the Chinese fleet had given him mastery over the Three-Thirty Boundary. The focus of his attention was shifting and his fascinated stare was now falling on the *gaijin* of Amerika without distraction.

As if from a great distance Oujuku's voice urged him. "We've got to speak with Secretary Cassabian, Ellis. Will you come now to back me?"

Ellis said nothing, only turned away.

"Not even to hear me speak to him of the crimes of Jos Hawken?"

"Hawken?" he heard himself say.

As Oujuku spoke Ellis looked beyond the great windows of the house, watching the rain slash down across his lawns, watching the ragged line of hills and the dark dappled forest. This was his peace. His home. His haven. Two of his children were next door in the library with their tutor, the third lay upstairs sleeping. At the back of the house Reba would be pacing in a fury, knowing what was happening here. Must he go to her and ask her to take it calmly and tell Matthew to ready his air-car?

He bowed his head, put his face in his hand, plowing the fingers through his hair. Oujuku, his closest friend, had brought him a bigger impediment to his life's tranquillity than any sniveling Halide creature sent by Kurt Reiner. There *was* change in the air, and he knew that what Oujuku had told him was true.

Goddamn this man, he thought, this brother who's filled the gap in my heart left by the brother I lost so long ago. Must I leave everything? Must I give up my peace?

Then he thought of the proverb that said that blood was thicker than water, and he had his answer.

29

Ramakrishnan's ashram on the river had lain deserted for a long time, sealed by the President's personal order. The contemplative garden that was walled and locked was full of dead things, its meditation niches poisoned, its grass bleached or burned. At the fringes all was overgrown with brambles, its high wall a multicolored masterpiece of graffiti, but, in the center, the garden was only brown: desiccated wood, fungi and molds, and the filthy suppurations of decay. Rain beat against the broken statuary beside a pool of green and slimy water. Once Zen carp had swum here, and the devotees of the astrogation school had learned to concentrate and cultivate their psi-talents under a strange and moody genius, but no longer. It was a sobering place to talk of treason.

Cassabian pulled the chain from the gates and pushed against complaining hinges. Ellis shut one eye against the shafting rain, following Cassabian and Oujuku out of the air-car. The secretary's men, he noted, made no move to follow from their vehicle but looked to one another superstitiously, which pleased Ellis because he wanted secrecy.

He regarded Cassabian closely. Trust your first impression of him as you stepped off the skimmer, he told himself. Sharp-tongued? Yes. A man full of political ambition and subterfuges? Again yes. An underhand dealer? It couldn't be denied. Oh, but you're a less righteous man than I once thought. And you're not a friend, because I know you keep me only as an ally. You have weak faith, because you once sold your stake in me to Conroy Lubbock. And you're hard in the soul, because your business is knowing secrets and weaknesses through the buying and twisting of other men's greed. All these things damn you, Mr. Secretary, but, by God, there's one side of you that saves you. You're not a traitor and so I can trust you.

"Tell me what you hope to find here, Ellis."

"In good time, Mr. Secretary."

Ellis looked about him at the devastation, eerily appalled. "This is a terrible place. Did it die when Ramakrishnan departed on his Europan wanderings?"

"Before. It was ruined by psi experiments. Even the life of the soil has been destroyed."

"It's clear to me why Ramakrishnan has been called a Satanist and a black magician by most of the Adventer churches, and why he's gone."

"You can't hold a man like that," Oujuku said. "So, Mr. Secretary, where's he gone?"

"It seems the great man knew enough to prophesy the arrival of his enemies on Prague three weeks ago. I can report that he escaped beyond the grasp of the Europan authorities, who would surely have expelled him had they caught him. But he's not infallible. He made a grave miscalculation going to Paris and the Rosenberg seminary."

"Miscalculation, you say?" Ellis said.

Cassabian rattled the ion keys. "Yes. So completely did Ramakrishnan convince the French of his greatness that their hospitality was extended to him indefinitely. He's to stay on Paris until he's turned all Rosenberg's psi-talents into astrogators."

Oujuku grunted and took the ion key from Cassabian. "If the Rosenberg seminary wants astrogators, they'd be better off doing it themselves."

"An altogether more difficult prospect," Cassabian disagreed drily, adding, "Ramakrishnan can't be coerced."

Oujuku unlocked the door and went inside. Ellis, following, pulled out his torch and struck a beam of light into the interior. All was musty and dank: rain had got in, birds had found their way through the eaves, liming the furniture; insects had wintered and summered in the rooms and vermin had made nests in the laps of the Buddhas. As they moved throughout the sprawling warren, Ellis realised how little prospect there was of finding what he had come for.

"Genius, I've heard it said," Cassabian said portentously, examining a carved idol face-to-face, "is in inverse proportion to orderliness."

Oujuku eyed him coolly. "This place stinks like cat piss."

"You were wrong to let Ramakrishnan leave Amerika, Mr. Cassabian," Ellis said. "Why did you?"

Cassabian took the accusation smoothly. "He was growing meddlesome in government and getting too close to the President. I was happy to have him travel elsewhere."

"A mistake. Men like Ramakrishnan are rare. A resource more precious than aurium. I thought you, better than anyone, understood that." He pulled a plex box from under a stack of moldering hardcopy, opened it, and looked inside, then he discarded it carelessly into a gloomy corner.

"What're you looking for, Ellis?"

"A copy, or a plan."

"Of what?"

"The jewel. It was an incredible device, and it might save our astrogators a great deal of trouble if we find its secret—and then someone who can make another one."

"You've brought me here so that you could look around?" Cassabian's impatience erupted. He stiffened angrily. "Our people have been through it with a fine-toothed comb."

Ellis ceased his ransacking and leveled a finger at Cassabian's eye. "I brought you here to talk. There's no better place in all Amerika, and no more important matter to disturb the silence with. This is one place you can be certain nobody is going to overhear us."

Cassabian's shoulders sagged and he acquiesced. Oujuku planted three chairs around the table and they sat down in the gloom as Ellis began.

"Mr. Secretary, the Sector's heading for war. And when war comes we have to be ready. Say what you will, our Navy is still all that stands between us and the snuffing out of our liberties, but there's a traitor in it." He thrust a document onto the table. "I have it here."

Cassabian examined it, listening simultaneously to Oujuku's catalog of teachery. Ellis already knew about it: Hawken had profited greatly from the dealings they had had with Okubo. The success of that had brought Hawken position and power. He had first succeeded to the post of treasurer of the Navy, inherited with Conroy Lubbock's connivance, from his own father-in-law, Ben de Zharian. Later, he had been promoted once more, this time to a post that gave him ultimate say over the hull-building facilities. Since then, his avarice had been unbounded.

Ellis boiled with anger as he listened to the corruption that Oujuku was reporting. Hawken had gone into partnership with the plex-manufacturing corporations of his friends, with suppliers and engine designers, and now with the procurement people. Between them they had defrauded the Navy, building their own hulls in private hangars and getting lucrative contracts.

"It makes me burn to think that this man can send Amerikans offworld in ships less well equipped than they should be because of his greed. And in such a time of crisis."

Cassabian stared back at Oujuku. The two men were so utterly different. They had never liked one another, which was why Oujuku had asked for Ellis's intercession. He said softly, "Leave the matter with me."

"Act!" Oujuku's fist slammed the table, knocking over the torch. "Make it known! Tomorrow! Unseat Hawken! And unseat Conroy Lubbock!"

"No! There's a better way!" Rain drummed in the silence, then Cassabian smiled for the first time. "On the nexus lanes, it may be your method to fight fire with fire. Here on Liberty we have another way. We fight fire with a pail of water.''

Oujuku's anger stalled, his forehead furrowed, and then he too smiled.

30

In the secretary's house the three men met again. Cassabian paced anxiously, seeing no way out. Amerika's peril ran far deeper than either of his guests could know. The spies of the Empire were secretly pouring into the Sector. Ninja, infiltrating Liberty under cover. Refugees, the vast majority bona fide Koreans, were arriving, and Amerika's liberal laws did not allow them to be detained. But there were those among them intent on paving the way for invasion, striking at the heart, sapping strength by their subversion, and reporting everything faithfully to Yamato.

It required a huge investment in time and credit to track such people, and Cassabian's resolve faltered as he considered his task. Admittedly there had been successes. Hadn't he infiltrated a swarming nest of traitors in Philadelphia? Hadn't he penetrated the Yamato network through Jiro Ito? Hadn't he arrested the seditious pro-Yamato radical leader Ali Akhbar and disposed of him? As he had lain bleeding from the ears under the Probe, Akhbar had talked, but too late to get hold of the Black Orchid Cell or Akhbar's controller. Even now, that monster was running back and forth between Kyoto and Seoul, Guam and the Ten Degree Worlds, designing revolution and the President's assassination. Hadn't that been specifically ordered by the *kempei*? And hadn't Earth Central received a deputation of rebel Amerikans, an unparalleled intervention? Why, if not as precursor to an invasion? To rally waverers and deep-run cowards and those who chose to stay quiet? But what else?

Cassabian saw it clearly now, shuddering at the force of the idea. After news of Keun's assassination and the overrunning of Free Korea had reached him, his spies had said that Baron Harumi, Yamato's foremost warlord, had wanted to assemble a two-million-strong force in Wonsan and Guam and then ferry them into Kalifornia II in two hundred hulls. With Amerika's Navy on the Boundary that idea was as doomed as it had ever been, but then Harumi had returned from his victories against the Chinese bursting with confidence and laid before his Emperor another, more ambitious enterprise.

Yes, he thought despairingly, it was the only answer! Mutsuhito must have sanctioned the massive invasion that his shogun wanted launched from Seoul: five hundred ships, fully one hundred fifty of which were gigantic purpose-built warships. Thirty thousand crew. Three million troops. The greatest single battle fleet ever assembled. An unopposable, invincible force.

This time, there would be no expensive-but-limited irritations like the rebellions of Dakota, which had been shut down almost before it had started, no abortive attempt like the one Prince Sekigahara had almost mounted before he was replaced as Mutsuhito's commander in Cho Sen by Harumi. No, this time, the entire might of Yamato would be focused on Amerika. Directly. Like a magnifying lens on dry straw. And *still* Conroy Lubbock imagined that war could be avoided!

A tremendous weight of responsibility pressed down on Cassabian as he thought of the terrifying news he had received from Yamato. Months ago, plans for an attack via Florida II had been thwarted. Under the Probe, the double-dealing Milton Klingsor had confessed to his complicity. He had run a conspiracy between the Yamato ambassador, Kamakura, and the still-imprisoned Lucia Henry. He had succeeded in sending Kamakura the same way as Okubo had gone, but what of the arch-conspirator herself? What of Lucia? To have the least hope of warding off the threat, Lucia must die. And the President must be persuaded to sign her execution.

Cassabian closed his eyes, feeling the stares of the two men at his back and the sweat beading the peak of his hairline. He wiped it away and examined his hand, imagining blood.

His spies had picked up a thousand terrifying clues, all pointing in the same direction. The darkest days of '24 were a pale shadow compared to the evil gloom that presently mounted against Amer-

ika. She was besieged on every side. Now, Yamato was twice
as rich, her navy twice as powerful. All over the Zone, in Cho
Sen, in the other Korea, in the Solomon League and the systems
over which Yamato arms held sway, a ground swell was beginning. And the hub of it all was the family shrine in the fortress-
monastery-palace of Chiyoda-Ku. Yamato's foremost daimyos
were being recalled to Kyoto, assembling in ranks to the beat
of war drums, bringing with them arms and levies and the implacable martial spirit that had conquered the only unassigned
part of Known Space, all gathering for a decisive blow.

Now Oujuku's and Straker's revelations about Hawken had
shaken to the foundations the one pillar on which Amerika's
survival depended. And Hawken was Conroy Lubbock's man.

He tried to drag his thoughts back to the present. Straker was
right, Amerika needed her able men now, more than ever before.
The old Amerikan worlds close to the Earth Exclusion Zone were
drawing together, divisions were being mobilised, but it was
being done with painful sloth. Under Conroy Lubbock and his
chiefs of staff, the newly organised planetary defenses were
inadequate, and certainly no match for Harumi's war-hardened
veterans. The Navy was Amerika's only defense, her only hope
of survival.

Ellis told him: "We must have nexus-going ships to guard the
Boundary, fast vessels capable of outrunning any ship sent
against us, to free our war wagons for work other than system
defense. And those big ships must be of the new kind, like the
Iowa, well armed with singularity guns that outshoot the Yamato
ships at close range. This must be our strategy."

Oujuku nodded his assent. "Yeah, and we have to cut out the
parasites in charge of the Navy, the ones who're sucking the
lifeblood out of our defenses."

Cassabian protested. "But the size of our fleet—"

"If numbers were the crux," Ellis told him, "we'd already
be dead men. Numbers are not critical. Quality is the key. Two
dozen ships—that's all I ask. But two dozen like the *Iowa!*"

The meticulous designs that Ellis had worked on spilled across
the table. They dated back to his confinement in Camp Worth
and had been augmented by a thousand incredible ideas patiently
collected by Ramakrishnan and the self-destructive mathematician, Timo Farren. Years of careful thought, refinements drawn
from experience, details teased from Oujuku and from the other

privateering astrogators. It was the essence of change, designs that would make an unparalleled fighting force of the Amerikan Navy.

"Though Amerika depends on it, I can't get these measures being accepted while Hawken is at Navy and while Conroy Lubbock keeps him there."

Every nerve in Cassabian's body itched to tell them that the improvements would be put in hand, but he knew that he could never present the President with such an expense. Free Korea had been a bottomless pit. The government had given Park thirty billion in inter-Sector credit units to finance the retaking of Wonsan, and sent him away with a further ten billion, and then sent a division to him with the promise of fifty billion more, all to convince Mutsuhito of Amerikan-Chinese solidarity. And still Harumi had triumphed. On the day before Keun's death, the President had sent a message to him that in war and peace three things alone mattered: credit, credit, and once again credit.

He explained haltingly, all the while searching for a way out of the problem, but as he finished, Ellis gave Oujuku a significant look. Incredibly both men seemed oddly satisfied to hear the objections wrung painfully from him.

"What I offer you, sir," Ellis said slowly, "is no expense. But a saving."

The airless room closed in around them.

"A saving?" Cassabian said with incredulity, sure only that if any argument could sway the President, the one least likely to drain her budget must win the day. "You say a *saving*?"

Ellis planted his elbow on the table. "Implement these plans and the cost of the Navy will be cut from ten billion in credit annually to half that. See, there's not a captain offplanet who wouldn't prefer two hundred and fifty good crew to three hundred incompetents—if the ships can be crewed that way."

Oujuku backed him, leaning in on Cassabian fiercely. "It's not skill we lack, but the *will* to organise."

Ellis nodded tautly. "Credit makes the galaxy revolve, as they say. If we're wise we'll plow back the seedcorn. Reinvest the saving. And pitch our prices at the right level. If we don't we're dead."

"Take our people," Oujuku insisted. "Ships are hulks without good crews to staff them. To make them good we must pay them well. Look at this: the *Missouri*. The charge of wages and supplementary sums for three hundred crew at twenty-three personal credit units per crew member is point-six-nine fiscal. The same ship with a complement of two hundred fifty but costed at twenty-seven-point-two units per hand is point-six-nine fiscal. Make no mistake, you can't expect the best people unless you pay for them. Show them their Sector values them and they'll know who they're fighting for.''

Cassabian wiped at his brow once more, utterly weary, but feeling the grim capability of the men beside him. "Yes," he said. "Yes! We'll try Conroy Lubbock. He may be persuaded. If he's not, I'll go to the President herself!''

31

Conroy Lubbock received them in his office in the river precinct on Pennsylvania. He was courteous and listened to Cassabian with thoughtful silence. At last he raised his head and said pleasantly, "Let me take your spreadsheet, gentlemen. I promise I'll give it my attention. And I thank you for your concern.''

"I want your signature on a warrant of arrest for Jos Hawken,'' Cassabian demanded less than respectfully.

"Oh?'' Lubbock nodded slowly and looked Cassabian up and down. "I'll have to consider that at length.''

"If you don't reach a decision by noon tomorrow, we'll be forced to approach the President directly.''

"The President is still involved in fiscal matters. By her own request she cannot be disturbed.''

"I *will* see her. That is my right.''

"As you wish.''

"And when I do, Jos Hawken *will* answer these charges.''

Conroy Lubbock sighed inwardly and thought again of the

tremendous economies his patient work had brought. A tight rein had been held for twenty-five years, despite the credit spent in Korea. Though rebellions had swallowed up all the extra taxes imposed in that time, still Amerika's foreign debts were paid, and the obligations left by Lucia Henry also, making Amerika's interest rate half of what Yamato was forced to pay. For twenty-five years Amerika had prospered, a quarter century nurtured by his careful guidance, which had brought with it a payoff that other, more impulsive men might have squandered on needless war.

In those years, Conroy Lubbock calculated, there had been a tripling of wealth in the Sector, but it had come only by hard work and diligent effort. The aurium that Ellis and Oujuku and the rest of the privateers had waylaid were as nothing beside that.

He smiled inwardly. It had been a wise policy. Wise to keep at arm's length high taxation that would raise credit, but at the same time buy the privilege of tinkering in affairs of state for sticky-fingered congressmen. Although he had first conceived the policy as a way of avoiding political control, it had paid immense and unlooked-for dividends in another way. Low rates of interest and low taxes had fostered commerce and the manufacturers. Successful trade and successful commerce were the key. For the first time all the wants of civilised life could be supplied by Amerikan hands at Amerikan factories, in Amerikan yards and from Amerikan fabricators. No longer did the Sector depend on expensive imports. Nor did it need Seoul. Exports went out through Europa, trade flourished with Muscovi and the Slavians. Brasilia was taking raw material and terraforming equipment. Even distant Izlam had been among the new customers.

Oh, Pharis, can't you understand that subtlety? Little by little. In military matters half the battle's concerned with hiding true weaknesses from the enemy. The other half's concerned with hiding true strengths.

"Hawken will answer these charges before the President. Confirm that to me, Conroy."

Conroy Lubbock turned on them admonishingly. "I warn you, Pharis. I warn you all. These matters are best left to me."

"In all sincerity I doubt that, Conroy. Our Sector's plunging into a war *and you will not see it,*" Cassabian insisted.

"Seems to me that some people would have us plunge in all the faster."

"Hawken is a traitor!" Oujuku burst out. "And you, Lubbock, are his protector!"

"C'mon," Conroy Lubbock told him mildly, shaking his head. Cassabian's bellicose table thumping is still dangerous, he thought. He's never learned flexibility. I was right to clip his wings in '31. That's the reason I sent him on a diplomatic mission of pacification to Peking, a mission contrary to his own stance and doomed to failure, and in the Wilderness, politically speaking. I wasted three months, but I prised him away from the management of the Sector at a vital time. That's also why I let him waste his energies on attempting to arrange the Chinese marriage. I let him embroil himself in a hell of a mess. And now he's realised the backwater he inhabits, and he understands his own impotence, his temper's got worse. He's going to have to bear the brunt of the President's vacillations, but that frustration has done nothing to break him of his readiness to meddle in affairs best left to me. If it wasn't for the growing menace on the Boundary and his sources of information there, I would have side-footed Pharis Cassabian into the gutter long ago. But I have my own sources, sources he knows nothing about, and I'm not as ill informed as he believes.

He approached Ellis, who had remained silent throughout the interview. The man's magnificent, but he's a continual embarrassment to me, a real thorn in my side. Why do I tolerate him? Because Reba loves him? Because while he's with her Reiner dare not go near her? Because while he's at Xanadu he's not offplanet? Perhaps. But perhaps because he's the devil's own trident. It's not yet time to use him, but the moment's arrived when he must be handled. He's precipitated it before I thought he would, but what does it matter now? He'll strike the blow that breaks the fleet that Mutsuhito is building . . .

He stood in front of Ellis smilingly. "Can you really believe that I'm a traitor, Captain?"

Ellis drew himself up straight. "Sir, I believe you're mistaken in your attitude towards Yamato. I believe you're reluctant to admit that war with Yamato is inevitable, though the evidence for it is clear enough."

"You astonish me. Do you really imagine you know more about the Emperor of Yamato's intentions than I do?"

"Pharis Cassabian knows more than either of us, and his opinion is the same as mine. As far as these complaints we've laid out before you today are concerned, I can't think other than that you've been deceived."

"By whom?"

"By Jos Hawken, amongst others."

"So you believe Jos Hawken is a traitor?"

"What else can I call it? There are two edges to his sword, he cuts two ways. Here's hard evidence that he's been dealing with Yamato agents. That's more than stupidity, more than plain greed. It threatens the security of Amerika."

Conroy Lubbock sighed, went to his desk, and pulled out a closely printed sheet of hardcopy. "This came into my possession some time ago. You may be interested to read it, Captain. It was dictated by a man, one Cadet Philips, who knew your brother in Sado, and who subsequently found his way back into Amerika."

Ellis was thrown for a moment, then he took the sheet and read it. As he scanned the lines his eyes clouded but the rest of his face betrayed nothing. The paper was an affidavit describing the fate of Duval, how he had been imprisoned, sentenced, and then crucified by the *kempei*.

"Your brother was making singularity guns for the Sado daimyo. Guns whose only purpose was to smash Amerikan ships. Guns that might even have been used against you yourself!"

"Yes."

"In that case you already know he's a traitor. To you, and to his Sector."

Ellis's jaw clenched. The blood had drained from his face and he found difficulty in speaking. "Yes."

"And you still accuse *me* of harboring traitors? Of shielding traitors? Of *using* traitors?"

The silence that enveloped them was punctuated by the sounds of the city that drifted up through the open window. Vigorous sounds of air traffic and crowds and daily business. To judge from the way Ellis's stiffness left him, they must have seemed deafening to him.

"I disowned my brother long ago, Conroy. It's a relief that he's dead. I would have killed him myself if I could have done so."

Conroy Lubbock's demand was suddenly as sharp as a samurai sword. "You swear that's the truth?"

"Yes."

"You swear?"

"Yes, I swear, damn you!"

"Good. Good. There may come a time when I'll ask you to remember that." Lubbock recovered the sheet and put it back into the drawer. Yes, he thought. A devil's trident. Handled, but not yet thrown.

He took up his pen. "Captain Oujuku, here's a warrant ordering your presence at the meeting of the Security Council in three weeks' time. There we'll discuss your plans to embark preemptively and in force against Yamato forces in the Neutral Zone." He turned to Cassabian. "Give me thirty days. In return I'll immediately put Captain Straker's suggestions before the Navy Commission and I'll personally insist they're discussed. I'll even require that some of them are adopted."

Cassabian considered. "And when the thirty days are up? What about Hawken?"

"When the thirty days are up, you can come to Camp Worth and put Jos Hawken against the wall and shoot him if you still want to."

32

SEOUL

Michie met her husband near the Seoul terminal as she did every seventh day at this time. It was early evening, before dusk, and the sky was full of golden streamers behind a black haze of military transport fumes. The Emperor's enterprise was gathering for the final blow.

Huge nexus ships lined the herringbone service structures, sometimes hooked up six deep. More sat out on the apron and on the auxiliary stacks: vessels of all sizes, from the small supply ships and orbital shuttles to the lumbering, round-bodied transports and the high-built sleekness of Korea's warships.

Along the terminal a great quantity of ships' stores had been stockpiled and all kinds of technicians and subcontractors had erected temporary workshops among the chaos. Thoughout the day, a vast array of human endeavor had come together, but this was the peaceful hour when the toils of the day paused and the builders of the battle fleet looked to their rice bowls instead of their work.

Michie took her husband's hand and sensed again the unbearable tension in him. He had put his own work away after a busy week; with Choi Ki Won away across continent and extra statistical analysis work coming in every day from the Seoul Port Authorities, he was ready to rest, but it was not simple tiredness she felt in him. There was something else, something worrying him and destroying his inner harmony. She squeezed his hand and asked, "Do you know why Ki Won-san left Seoul City?"

He did not look at her. "Why does Choi Ki Won do anything?"

"To trade or to talk—sometimes to see and remember what he sees."

"Then you know already what Ki Won is doing. Why ask me?"

"Zinan-san, why does he take with him his sons?"

"His sons?"

"Oh, yes. And those cages of pigeons."

"I don't know. And I don't care."

He volunteered no more, and she chose not to pursue it, seeing his nerves were raw. Perhaps he was regretting his decision to stay on Seoul, realising that the tide of events could no longer be turned, that the Yamato invasion juggernaut was now unstoppable. It seemed capable of tearing down anything that stood in its way.

I know you understand that truth, my husband, she told him silently, feeling nothing but devotion towards him. You watch the soldiers coming and the ships arriving and the invasion fleet growing stronger every week, and you feel helpless and Choi Ki Won feels helpless and, though you yearn to act, there's nothing you can do.

They walked together in silence along the broad service roads that edged the terminal, threading their way past many-colored, varishaped containers and flasks and hi-tech cabins that were being unloaded from vast multi-wheeled ground transporters and air-lifters, and transferred by great waldos into the ships that were attached to the numbered quays by looms of umbilicals so that they resembled the severely ill inside their medivacs. And all the time as they strolled they secretly noted and memorised as many details of the preparations as they could, to be recalled later verbatim to Choi Ki Won.

It had been like this for at least a year now. From the ship-building yards and hangars of the vast Seoul apron and from all the aprons in Yamato great ship after great ship had come here to be rigged and outfitted. Hundreds of technicians and freezee installation engineers labored at their work, putting down an average of one soldier every ten seconds, day and night, round the clock, for over a year. Ships' quartermasters and provosts supervised round the clock, overseeing the lading of supplies and the payrolling of crews. Each ship had been designated its own assembly point, transports to their main terminal stations, big globe ships to their special anchorages. Between them, a thousand craft of all sizes plied the twenty-five-mile by fifteen-mile extent of the Seoul apron, weaving back and forth endlessly with men and materials under the glare of B-type-blue arclights.

Michie saw the helplessness in his face as he watched the preparations and asked him gently, "What is it, Zinan-san? Please tell me what it is that especially troubles you."

He stirred. "What?"

"You seem so full of cares tonight."

"No more than usual. I'm just thinking."

"If you want to, you can tell me what it is that weighs on your mind."

He squeezed her hand briefly, stifled a sigh, and looked out again across the vast plain of crete and plex. "The fleet seems much bigger than it did only a week ago."

"Do you think the time approaches? That it will take off for the Flying Horse nexus soon?"

"No," he said. "I think this is only the start. It's much bigger than I imagined. The Emperor is bending every resource to this single end. It's staggering."

To Duval, the Emperor's minions seemed prepared to spend

all, apply all, risk all, on their government's fanatical desire. For months Seoul had been drinking in men: samurai soldiers brought across the Zone, *ashigaru* from every world of every prefecture of every quadrant of the entire Sector: from the biggest of the four quadrants, the main Honshu prefectures of Mino, Hida, Echizen and Ise, Shinano and Harima, and all of the forty-three others; from the six Shikoku prefectures of Tosa, Iyo, Awa, Sanuki, Awaii, and Izumi; from the twelve Kyushu prefectures and the eighteen of Hokkaido; from every Mutsu world not required to stand in defense against the Chinese; and from all *han* of the Empire samurai of every rank. Oh, yes, the fleet was far from completed. Choi Ki Won had said that it was so far only a third, a quarter, of what it must eventually become. Yet already it was an awesome sight, the greatest assembly of nexus ships ever undertaken.

Not all the contributions had been willingly given. Duval's eyes flickered over the place where the huge *Toyotomi Hideyoshi* squatted, her vast and powerful black bulk frowning down over the ships and tiny human figures that surrounded her. The massive warship had arrived in Seoul weeks ago. The idea was that she was to be sold and sent on to the Chinese. She had been called the *San Francisco* then and had belonged to the España quadrant of Latina, but Baron Harumi had taken a liking to her. He had commandeered her to be refitted as flagship of his Yamashiro Squadron, and put his soldiery aboard to make sure his plans were not overthrown.

As they continued to stroll, the outer walls of the main ultra-security terminal loomed nearby, opaque plex without color of any kind, "point four nines" absorbent black, like velvet, huge-domed and impregnable. The gates were guarded by a dozen men, and only Yamato soldiers and specially summoned persons able to show the correct ID were permitted inside. Duval thought again of the great ammunition store and beam weapons arsenal that lay within and his palms began to itch. Since Choi Ki Won told him of the armory he had been unable to put it out of his mind. Inside these walls were the high-intensity weapons that would be used to subdue Amerika's Navy. But to gain entry was like trying to get inside Camp Worth. It was impossible.

They began to return the way they had come when a voice called to them fiercely in Japanese.

"You!"

They stopped and Duval noticed for the first time a soldier ten paces away leaning heavily against a huge ship anchoring flange among the shadows. He pointed an evil-looking ID gun at them, but he seemed like a man who hadn't slept for seventy-two hours.

"Yes, you! Come here!"

Duval complied, Michie following a pace behind, with tiny steps, as was required of her. Duval's blood was rushing to his stomach, flooding his belly with fear. Their ID was not good, but they had always risked it before, knowing that security could not possibly cope with the hundreds of thousands of individuals that had every right to be here.

"I saw you looking at the gates." The soldier's voice dropped to a growl. "What business do you have here?"

Duval considered, almost denied it, then decided to gamble. "I must fill an order for statistical analysis work," he lied.

"Let me see your ID smart."

Wordlessly Duval took the card from his pouch and handed it over. It was a Korean credit smart, from the days of Free Korea; it was unmarked.

The soldier appeared to check it in his type-two reader, then he hit the device with the heel of his hand. He broke wind noisily. He stank, was stubbled, and his eyes were shot pink, rolling up as he blinked, as if he was coping with an impossible strain. He was just going through the motions. "So—you're a Korean mathematician?"

"A chaos theorist. As the ID says." He leaned forward, but the soldier pulled the reader back broodily.

"So what's your business here, chaos theorist?"

"I have a contract to do analysis work," Duval repeated. "As it says on the smart. Is there a problem? Do I have to get confirmation? I'd be happy to. My hardcopy work's a bit involved because of my specialisation, but if you want to read it, I can bring it along now."

The soldier held the reader up once more, inclining it to the light. It was obviously faulty.

"The smart's all in order. But you can't come this way. A restricted area." He handed the smart back grudgingly and gestured over his shoulder at sixty or seventy refrigerated flasks stacked inside a garish lime-green-and-black-striped container that drones were in the process of unloading. "You speak good

Japanese, so you should know what those signs say: 'Danger, Argentium' and 'No Unauthorised Access.' It's my responsibility to check everyone who comes around here. You had no visual on your ID when I scanned you, see? I thought you were a spy.''

Duval nodded at the man, mirroring his grim humor. ''Supervisors! They always want you to do things but they don't give you the right hardcopy work, eh? I haven't known one of my corporation IDs to interrogate properly on Seoul. Maybe it's the gravity here. I'm still not used to it. Everything feels so heavy, not like Wonsan. Where's the argentium going to?''

The soldier vaguely indicated the apron; he leered crookedly at Michie, wiping the reader on his sleeve. ''Who's she?''

''My—assistant.''

''Korean as well?''

''Er, yes.''

''It's a shame you're in a reserved occupation. I could've spent a lot of credit on you, eh, Rose Petal?''

''Is your regiment short of men?'' she asked, forcing herself to smile back at him. ''You seem like a man who has worked very hard.''

''Short of *real* men.'' He reached out and grasped her arm. ''You want to make a date?''

Duval broke in. ''Maybe I could find you some Seoul City bad boys who'd like to come up here. Maybe we could split the credit. How many do you need? What's your name?''

The soldier's grin died slowly, then a sickly anger overcame him and he brushed at Duval, letting go of Michie. ''Get on your way, Korean shit-eater! You ask too many questions!''

They retreated, the soldier still calling after them. Duval carefully stored away his thoughts on the drunken guard as he and Michie merged with the crowd. Here, along the South Boundary Road, a temporary shopping mall had been set up under transparent flexiplex, selling z-suits, tools, power packs, and a hundred thousand assorted luxuries. A knot of well-dressed samurai stood back as their representatives haggled on their behalf over the price of a tri-vee, another loitered as his twin white-faced whores looked over a garish display of Europan commodities. Next to them blue smoke drifted up where barbecued meats basted and spat on a makeshift hibachi, filling the air with a mouth-watering aroma. Lights began to come on in the gathering dusk. A hundred little stalls had been set up to do brisk business:

Korean sausage and cured chicken and piglet, mummified duck heads clustered hanging on a hook, their bills pierced, their eyes black pits, the bones of their long necks visible under the taut, crispy yellow skin. Noodle sellers and sushi bars, giant melon sellers, and tubs of big, live, spidery crabs, bubbling, all locked together and struggling weakly.

Duval steered Michie through the press of customers, amazed at the increase in trade that had occurred in only a single week. It was as if every samurai in the Empire had suddenly descended on Seoul in a vast deluge to seek honor in arms on the great crusade. Every day religious orders and private corporations of troops arrived, landing in great phalanxes of shuttles and marching across the city in processions, sometimes in forced marches lasting all day and all night. Every last guesting house and spare room had been turned over to accommodate samurai officers, and acres on the outskirts of the city were now under flexiplex tentage, as hundreds of thousands more *ashigaru* made their bivouac under Seoul's bright stars.

Nunki shone down on them now, the brightest star in the Seoul summer firmament. It was a blue giant, five light-years away in what was once the Old Earth constellation of Sagittarius, blazing clear in the twilight at a magnitude of minus two, its system huge and populous with three terraformed planets and a smallish gas giant about which there had once been a sensational xeno-life rumor. Of course, it had all come to nothing—it seemed almost certain now that no life existed in the galaxy, except that which had originated on Earth and had been dispersed across Known Space by man's titanic terraforming machines. Why? When there were so many star systems with planets? So many planets within the temperate zones around their primaries? And so many planets with atmospheres and oceans and all the chemical wherewithal to allow the complex process of evolution to get started? It was now the biggest, most mysterious question facing science: are we alone? And if so, *why?* So far, the answer was a resounding yes to the first question. Not so much as a single provably xeno-biological RNA analog had been detected in a virgin system. The answer to the second question—why? —was far from being answered.

The stray thought made him shiver. What a bleak aseptic universe it will be, he thought, if we don't find anything out in the Beyond. It'll take us a thousand years more to extend Known

Space across the Carina-Cygnus arm of this big type-Sb spiral galaxy we live in; thirty thousand years to colonise half the Milky Way; another fifty thousand to consume the rest. Maybe "infect" is the word. When all we do is fight among ourselves . . .

He glanced at Michie and felt the warmth of her concern for him. Fighting isn't the whole story, but sometimes it's hard to see the good for the forests of evil that seem to hem us in. What an incredible, futile, insane expense, he thought, looking around the immense enterprise on the apron, trying to calculate the scale of it. How can the Emperor continue to bear it all? There's almost too many men here for the Seoul City area to support, and even with the troops freezeed down inside their vessels, each passing month is a month's fouling of the ships, a month's refrigerant and catalyst consumed, and a month's wages owing to the crews and technical support people. The Emperor's exchequer is not bottomless; he must be mortgaged to every bank in Yamato. God alone knows what rate of interest he must be forced to pay.

As they reached the far side of the terminal the last rays of sunset deserted the sky across the darkening west. These were the drilling grounds, and all around them, exercising troops dressed off in columns to be marched to camp behind z-suited officers, their places quickly filled by more lines of men. Others burdened with full assault kit formed queues to receive bowls of Dover noodles, then wandered away to sit in groups and drink down the steaming stock water noisily.

But the lethargy of the hour was stirring, pierced by shouted orders and sergeants striding among their platoons. Duval saw the multitude of men begin to rise to their feet. Rumors passed through them like a breeze rippling a cornfield, and they were alert and craning to see, suddenly expectant, as if a saint had appeared above the Mordor towers of Seoul City downtown.

Michie gripped his arm and pointed to the sky. "Look, Zinan-san!"

He saw it in magnificent silhouette: a great ornate air-car, low and slender, triple-tailed with tilted-back wings folded tight to a sweeping, open gondola, the engines stroking her swiftly in a banking turn. She was an *ika*, one of the special ceremonial shuttles built for VIPs who had the rank to bridge the gap between hi-tech and traditional forms. She knifed through the still, calm air above the apron, her sharp snout seeming certain to punch into the ground as she swooped. Then the drumbeats sounded from her gondola and the rhythmic shouts of her Imperial guard rang out as she maneuvered like a scorpion to confront the landing space.

Black *kempei* uniforms glittered inside. Duval remembered the sentences served on his shipmates many years ago when Fukuda had ordered them onto the crosses. He had to stop himself from searching the rows of *kempei* faces for Fukuda and his fellow interrogators. *What if he recognises you?* he asked himself with sudden alarm. Then he realised that recognition was impossible: these were not *kempei* at all, but black-toothed body-guards of the Imperial household.

The drumming beat changed and changed again, and the long shallow craft began to turn with impressive smoothness in her own length and to back, stern-first, into the landing slot.

Her stern was stepped high and pavilioned in red and yellow stripes, and a great brass arc threw its beams onto the embroidered threads of a snow-white ensign emblazoned with a centipede *mon*. It was the family device of Baron Harumi, supreme commander of the Imperial Navy.

Duval caught his breath, his heart pounding now. This was the man in whom the Emperor had vested his total trust. The invasion was his responsibility alone, all matters were in his charge, everything was under his personal control. Duval felt the anguish rise in him unstoppably. Soon he would glimpse the man who had begged to be permitted to destroy Liberty.

An undercarriage was flung down, the craft's weight settled on the runners pneumatically, and a banistered gangway was run out to one side of the scrolled sternpost. To left and right of it an honor guard in five-piece *go-mai* armor and grotesque black helmets assembled, arms clashing, flaming *sashimono* back flags raised high.

Duval was awed by the cold anger that welled up inside him. *If I had a knife, I'd kill him,* he thought. *I'd kill him! No! That's madness! Think of Michie, of little Kenichi.* But look, an opportunity to do something at last! To burst forward and kill Yamato's greatest warlord! *They would inflict terrible torment on you before you died!* But their shogun would be dead, and all the strategies in his head would be gone forever.

His hatred possessed him as he and Michie were swept up in the rush of men. It was made starker by the waves of respect and awe emanating from the thousand men who now rallied to the baron's arrival. Baron Harumi's standard-bearers came down, upholding his banner, and a line of robed and hatted dignitaries followed them. Then a knot of men appeared in the shuttle's gondola, tall, long-faced, and solemn. A short, solid figure suddenly emerged from among them in a hard black *eboshi* cap. He was sixty years of age, with a white handlebar moustache, and wearing magnificently corded black and red *yoroi* armor. Duval saw that below his fine silk *hitatare* his legs were armored in *suneate* to the knee. From beneath his neck guard a pair of thick cord protectors hung, his *mon* incised on each in crimson. As he advanced, they clattered against the laminae of the baron's breast with a noise like mah-jongg tiles being played, emphasising the bulk of the man. His nose was very flat and his face mask-like, deeply lined as if he was in constant pain—not at all the figure Duval had imagined.

As he mounted the head of the gangway, ranked troops punched the air shouting their terse regimental huzzahs in unison and knelt on one knee with bowed heads. He walked down, then paused, nodding his approval of the martial reception, standing no more than five paces from Duval. *Five paces*. He held Michie tightly. A knife, a *sepukku* dagger, any blade at all—a sudden thrust at the jugular and it could have been over in a moment. But he had nothing. Only his bare hands. And then the baron's officers came close about him again, and the moment had passed.

Michie's hand closed tightly on Duval's arm and pulled him down.

She turned, jostling, and turned him also, forcing him to creep slowly away through the press of awe-struck soldiers, and as they broke free of the crowding men, she guided him across the crete roadway and away from the glare of the landing lights. For a moment Duval resisted. He turned her, then he saw the fear in her eyes as she tried to hide her face.

"What is it?" he asked, dumbfounded, after fifty paces. "As your husband I order you to tell me, Michie-san, what's the matter with you?"

"Didn't you see him?" she whispered with astonishing urgency. "Didn't you see who that was?"

"The shogun?"

She shook her head wildly. "No! The one following!"

"Who? Tell me who?"

"*I swear it was Katsumi-san.*"

"*What?*" He stared at her in disbelief, a spasm of panic clutching at his bowels. "Are you certain?"

"It was his armor, and the Hasegawa *mon* was on his breast. I swear by the family gods it was my brother—he looked straight at me."

He glanced involuntarily back towards the baron's party, but was unable to distinguish anyone in the pool of brilliant light. Then he held Michie tight to him and pushed her out at arm's length once more. "Did he see you?"

"I don't know."

"Michie-san! Did he recognise you? Did he? Think!"

"I don't know!"

33

Hasegawa Katsumi looked towards the citadel, following a single pace behind Nishima Jun. His mind was in turmoil, and anger gripped him. The pride of all Yamato had been wounded, and an answer had to be found.

The news from Ise was incredible. The Amerikan corsair, Oujuku, had actually dared to land a pirate rabble on the sacred soil of one of Yamato's outlying Home Worlds. His filth had looted the city of Tsu and desecrated the Jingu shrines. Now he had taken off again and was cruising back towards the Korean Boundary. If only he could know what a force of nexus ships lies waiting for him here, Katsumi thought savagely. The baron will soon turn you into dog meat!

Katsumi followed Nishima Jun dutifully. They had built a traditional battlement on a ridge half a mile high and overlooking the apron, so that the baron could stroll here and look down, God-like, across the entire mass of preparations. It was a practice he was known to enjoy. The climb to the great citadel was long and twisting, as tortuous as the strange path that had brought him here to the brink of this most ambitious of enterprises.

It had begun years ago, in the middle of an airless and sultry night in the daimyo's residence in Kanazawa. Nishima Jun had summoned him late to his private apartment and there he had spoken strangely, with an odd light in his eye, as if testing him, as if about to single him out for some immensely dangerous task. At last, sweating and dressed in nothing but a thin cotton *yukata*, Nishima Jun had delivered the stunning news: "The Emperor's brother is dead."

Prince Sekigahara? Dead? The governor of the two Koreas, dead? Calamity!

Katsumi had pitched onto his knees and bowed respectfully, but he had felt immediately foolish under the daimyo's harsh laugh. "Get up, Katsumi-san, unless you would mourn the death of a syphilitic blackmailer."

He had stared back at his superior, utterly stunned, certain that his ears had deceived him in the thick air.

"I beg your pardon, Excellency?"

"I have placed Prince Sekigahara's death at the head of my prayers every day and every night for ten years, and now at last the gods have seen fit to answer me."

"Excellency?—but I don't understand."

Nishima had turned to his window then, regarding the visible token of his domain with total abhorrence. "Momentous changes are emanating from the Imperial Palace of Chiyoda-Ku, and this wretched, insect-ridden planet is to have a new daimyo."

That had stunned him, but he had thought quickly. "May I conclude that His Imperial Majesty has recognised your magnificent work here in the Co-prosperity Sphere, Excellency?"

He had said it with trembling voice, hoping and praying that this was some kind of reward the Emperor had offered in recognition of the fortification of the main aurium source planet. By all the mansions of heaven, please promise me this is not a mark of the Emperor's displeasure, he had begged the gods silently in the streaming humidity of that Sado night. Grant me that this doesn't mean a posting to Eniwetok. Anything but Eniwetok! I couldn't stand being sent there!

Nishima Jun's deep-set eyes had locked on him, as black and expressionless as pitted olives. The dark stubble of his chin had underlined his weariness, but his voice had cut suddenly formal. "Captain Hasegawa, I ask you now: wherever I am sent, will you follow me as my principal staff officer?"

His hesitation had betrayed him. "Follow you? But *where*, Lord?"

And Nishima Jun's heartless olive eyes had fallen, and his voice had become a whisper. "What a terrible thing it is for a man to be truly alone in this life. My dear Katsumi-san . . . I see that not even you can bring yourself to trust me. If I tell you it's not Kwajalein or Eniwetok, then will you pledge your service to me?"

He had showed eagerness then. "Where? Nishima-sama, please tell me. I would be honored to serve you wherever you were, ah, appointed daimyo."

The strangeness in the daimyo's face had been made clear to him then. It was the face of rapture. *Could it be that the Emperor was to entrust Nishima Jun with Korea?*

"Where?"

"Oh, how I've waited for this, Katsumi-san. I thank the gods of good fortune the assassins took Prince Sekigahara before it was too late."

"Where, Excellency?"

"Ah, I feel magnificent. Magnificent!"

"*Where?*"

Nishima Jun had smiled then, as if answering from within a state of *satori*. "Oh, unless I'm quite mistaken, Katsumi, we're going to Chiyoda-Ku."

"Chiyoda-Ku?"

Of all the *go* stones Nishima Jun might have played, this was the killing play, the most incisive, the most devastating. Chiyoda-Ku was the location of the Imperial Palace on Kyoto, the fulcrum of power. Kyoto was a dream come true.

It had taken a year for the Imperial summons to appear, and the best part of another to hand Sado over to the Emperor's new nominee, but Nishima Jun had reached Kyoto in time to see Free Korea fall and in time to be appointed to the military council specially convened to assist the Emperor in an examination of the ways and means of subjugating that lazy and immoral monolith, Amerika.

Katsumi swelled his plex-plated breast and checked that he was in step with his superior as they mounted higher towards the tower. Apart from the apron, the power of this foreign city to impress him was slight. Proudly he could say that the tatamis of the Imperial Palace itself—the Emperor's own pavilions—had been warmed by his shins. He had worked there for five magnificent years, helping Nishima Jun to advise the Emperor. Five years inside the very heart of the Chrysanthemum.

In truth, the vast palace complex had been no decorative flower. It was like a temple raised up on a massive recurved plinth of shaped stone. A vast, perfect precinct of magnificent traditional buildings, with square white and steel-gray castle keeps at each corner, rising to pagoda roofs. Each wall was pierced by hundreds of tiny, slitted windows that watched all who approached. Within were miles of passages, thousands of rooms stuffed with Imperial treasures, a Confucian monastery, the Imperial mausoleum, and in the inner sanctum, the hermit-like water pavilion where the Emperor lived and worked in ear-shot of the multicolored human-faced carp that rose up and snapped at flies or lurked in the shadows around the pavilion's pilings. It was said that His Imperial Majesty had sworn to build the immense red-beamed Heian shrine to the memory of Emperor Hirohito—whose memory he revered and glorified—and that the ancient Emperor's bones were contained in Mutsuhito's personal reliquary. It was said also that he possessed in his most private and sequestered retreat the head of another saint, a skull crowned by an iron tiara, which he consulted over the most important matters of state—the *gaijin* shogun Dugurasu Mukata.

Whatever the truth of it, the counsel the Emperor had taken had led him, in these latter years, to the greatest triumphs mankind had ever known. Year by year His Imperial Majesty had increased his prestige. The two Cho Sen prefectures and all their retinue were taken. Baron Harumi, president of the Council of Government, and Yamato's most able general, had almost completed his reconquest of the rest of the Korean quadrant; his patient diplomacy had set Korean and Korean to tearing at one another's throats once more. Harumi had dissolved the unity of the rebels, and his military skills had begun to push back the last fastnesses of the quadrant. Keun was dead, Seoul recaptured. Yes, the Emperor had chosen Prince Sekigahara's successor well. The laurels had mounted higher and higher. Even Chung Kuo had been humbled. Baron Harumi, the greatest warlord alive, had destroyed their fleet of sixty ships, and Prince Pi Wu had finally been isolated and brought to sign a secret accord with Yamato. One objective remained. One alone. How could they fail now to bring the woman President to her knees? Soon it would be time to mount the assault on the ultimate bastion of impurity, Amerika.

"What are we going to do about Oujuku?" Baron Harumi asked suddenly. He stopped, and his officers stopped also.

"The latest reports are that he's coming this way, lord," Nishima Jun said.

"Yes, I know. I asked what we should do about him."

"When did he depart, Captain Hasegawa?"

"Two days ago, Excellency," Katsumi supplied respectfully. "He's heading along the chain of Hoganji, towards the nexus the Amerikans call Yod-Two-Two."

Baron Harumi grunted. "Of course he's heading along Hoganji."

"Oh, but that's bad psi. Very bad!" Nishima Jun said. "We must take steps."

"Steps!" Baron Harumi snorted, and resumed his climb towards the donjon.

The news had been consistently bad for weeks, Katsumi reflected, disliking Baron Harumi's manners greatly. Pirate Oujuku's fleet had appeared in force, swooping in at minus eighty gee from one of the most vicious nexi known, in the Ryukyu Worlds along the Yamato-Korea Boundary at Zero Degrees. He had such incredible good fortune: the terrifying nexus in the Nansei system that normally spat ships out with vast kinetic energy had given no ship of his fleet more than a half cee. He had injected into Nansei orbit in what must have been record time. There, with diabolical perfidy, he had demanded all the aurium on the planet from the local daimyo while setting his nexus ships to prey on defenseless interplanetary craft. Then, when he had got what he wanted, he had dropped all pretenses and allowed his pirate bands to ransack the entire capital city, doing damage worth three hundred million in credit, stripping and desecrating the Kinkaku Temple and breaking venal slaves out of their *han* all over the continent.

"How does this despicable pirate imagine he can get away with it?" Kinoshita Heisuke, one of Baron Harumi's most experienced warriors, asked.

"Because he's got a fast fleet and exceptional psi and two

thousand crew aboard, and because he knows we can't move our own troops fast enough to catch him," Baron Harumi said, adding drily, "He's not brave or foolish enough to attempt a pitched battle against a samurai army, and quite right."

"Perhaps we should put some effort into catching him and punishing his insolence," Nishima Jun suggested.

"I can't agree!" Aoki Zengo, tall and thin, Baron Harumi's elderly second-in-command, waved him to silence. "That's just what the Black Dragon wants. To draw us out of the Seoul chain, unprepared and with our swords only half drawn, so he can eat us up! The Black Dragon is—"

"Ei! I'm tired of hearing that nickname!" Baron Harumi growled, stopping and turning. He was short of breath from the climb, and equally short of temper. Here the stepped way opened out into a punishment area where several gibbets had been erected. An assortment of chained samurai prisoners awaited flogging for insubordination or execution for dereliction of duty. Their jailor barked an order and they got down on their knees and pushed their faces hard into the dust as the party approached.

"Get up off the ground!" Baron Harumi shouted. They struggled to obey. "Until your topknots are cut off you're still samurai, not animals! Remember that!" he said, and marched on.

"I agree with Nishima-sama," another general said, hardly noticing the line of wretches. "We should confront the Amerikan. Show him he can't insult us. I long for the day when I shall see his head set on one of our spikes."

Aoki shrugged his bony shoulders. "But why interrupt our preparations just to oblige him? Why else is he heading for the Seoul system if not to tempt us out?"

Baron Harumi's low growl cut across the argument. "He's not heading here."

"*Gomen nasai, wakarimasen, Harumi-sama!* I don't understand, Lord! Not heading here?"

"Seoul's impregnable. With our new heavy beam weapon batteries and orbital defenses he'll never get in, and he knows it. He's cruising this way because he wants the *kin kaigun.*"

No one but Baron Harumi had dared voice that possibility.

"Obviously he'll try for the *kin kaigun.* Oujuku's no fool— and it's what I'd do in his place. He certainly has strength enough for an interception. That's why I've already taken steps, Nishima-san.'' Baron Harumi braced his back, his eyes flickering now over his subordinates, clearly enjoying this demonstration of his strategic prowess. ''Think about this: imagine what would happen to our preparations here if Oujuku were to succeed. His Imperial Majesty's tied down with loans that all hang on the arrival of the aurium in Kyoto. Without it we'd all be as bankrupt as *sangokujin* beggars.''

''Then he could halt our endeavor whether we leave Seoul or not?'' Minami Yoriyasu said, appalled.

Baron Harumi resumed his climb. Behind the party the flogging was taken up again.

''Cheer yourself, Minami-san. We cannot ignore any possibility, but Admiral Kurita and Admiral Kofuji are both experienced men. Both know what they're doing, and they have explicit orders to keep to as difficult a course as the Index will allow. I have faith they'll make the Home Worlds unmolested, but I'll say this: it's a mistake to underestimate Oujuku and his like.''

As they came to the doors of the pavilion, Katsumi tried to digest what he had heard. He was greatly disturbed at the way Yamato's foremost generalissimo was prepared to accord a filthy corsair such respect. Though his blood was indisputably linked to the Imperial line, Baron Harumi sometimes exhibited the bluntness of a peasant and the manners of the gutter. Such a pity that Nishima Jun was not appointed commander in chief, he thought. But perhaps I have only myself to blame? Myself and Michie-san. Nishima Jun still blames me for allowing my sister to spirit the Amerikan out of his grasp. And I was a fool to think she could be trusted. Yes, such a pity. Katsumi rued it for the thousandth time. Especially now, when the Emperor is preoccupied with the success of his invasion fleet. The Amerikan weapons are a lost secret that might have made Nishima Jun shogun.

34

"Go indoors and play, Kenichi."

"But, Father, I only wanted you to mend my kite—"

"I said, go indoors!"

Duval felt the warmth of Seoul's primary star on his back, but inside he was as cold as ice. He watched his son leave him, and his stomach tightened. Above him a dozen or so plump pigeons, puffed up and strutting, displayed on the conical green-tiled roof of the dovecote. Overhead, the sky was a deep and featureless purple. He watched Choi search it once more, unable to rid himself of the bottomless fear that had opened up inside him.

An hour ago, he had told Choi of his suspicions regarding Katsumi. He knew the merchant well enough to understand that they had come out to the yard for a definite purpose. As yet, however, Choi had made no explanation, and his unhurried manner was grating on Duval's nerves.

Choi held the bird expertly in his hand, its red claws clamped between his fingers, the light fully iridescent on its neck feathers as he stroked it.

"There, my little chick. Isn't she beautiful, Duval?"

Duval was distracted with worry, his voice barely controlled. "How can you remain so calm when they're closing in on us?"

Choi's face creased with a secret satisfaction. "Maybe they are, and maybe they're not. But I'm prepared to bet that they're not as clever as these pretty little birds, my friend."

Duval looked up at the familiar high walls of Choi's house. The walls of a fort or a prison, they seemed to him now. He had brought Michie and Kenichi here, seeking refuge, and for a week they had lain low, praying for Choi's speedy return. All that time he had slept hardly two hours together, worry stretching his nerves tauter and tauter until his head ached and his hands shook.

He had sent a message to the office that he would be away on business, and for his assistants to take over. They were capable men. Trustworthy Korean academics. They could easily be left to work on the contracts, but what if they had been visited? What if there was already a search being conducted throughout Seoul City for them?

A maid slipped quietly from the kitchen door and cut across the yard, carrying a big woven basket of laundry. Duval felt the old anxious dread eat at him, dread in case Kenichi stole away to fly his kite, dread that their clothes were recognised by a passerby, dread that there would be a knock at Choi's door.

None of the servants in the Choi household were party to their master's secrets, none knew of his past identity, and none were aware that the master's friend was in hiding. Choi's wife had said it was the only way. The nature of his business life was very open and the house was frequently visited, so they could not hope to stay here in secret very long. Duval thought of Michie and the boy and felt a punishment collar tighten around his throat.

"Do people keep birds as pets in Amerika?"

He tried to rouse himself to Choi's words. "I'm sorry, what did you say?"

Choi repeated his question. "Pigeons. In Amerika. Do you know if they're kept?"

Choi's calm inconsequentialities maddened him and he shrugged. "I—think so; people like pet birds. But they prefer small, singing birds like canaries."

"For no other reason than decoration and singing?"

Duval sought Choi's eye. "I suppose not. Some people race pigeons for a hobby—and there's pigeon pie." He broke off suddenly. Today, finally, Choi had returned to Seoul City with the incredible news of John Oujuku's attack on Tsu and Nansei, and yet here they were talking about *pigeons!* "Listen, Ki Won, do you think there'll be an attack here too? A landing?"

"On Seoul?"

Duval nodded.

"I fear for my adopted home world," Choi said. He set the bird down on a plex ledge mortared into the wall of the dovecote and shielded his eyes, scanning the skies once more. "The whole of Yamato has been sunk in mortal dread of John Oujuku. He's teaching them a lesson they don't like. But no, I don't fear for Seoul because of any attack John Oujuku might launch. The place is being ruined without him. I don't know how much longer it can go on.''

"Until the baron is ready to leave."

"May the gods grant that that's soon." Choi reached into a sack and broadcast a handful of corn over the yard, bringing a dozen more pigeons down. "Oh, my poor Seoul! In all quarters trade is booming but it's sick trade. Unreal commerce. The influx of so many offworlders is draining the whole place dry. Food, technical equipment—everything. Demand for commodities of all kinds has outstripped our capacity to supply it. Prices are rising every day, doubling and trebling. The poor are going hungry. It's no trouble to Yamato. More meat for their slaving gangs.''

Duval shook his head. "No, they already have more men standing idle than they can use or occupy. It's an impossible job keeping their army all fed and processed into the freezees. Trouble is setting in. Desertions have begun. They've started confining whole crews and entire companies of nonsamurai troops aboard their ships. The whole fleet's like a time bomb. *They'll have to lift off soon.''*

Choi knelt among the birds that had fluttered down around them and picked one up. "The invasion fleet is too big. It will never be ready to lift off."

"Is that what you're telling them in Amerika?"

"That's just my opinion. In my reports I confine myself to the facts."

Duval watched Choi's face closely; he saw anxiety there, buried and suppressed, but it was massive. And there was surely an inconsistency too in what Choi had said.

"Ki Won, where did you go to last week?" he asked.

"I told you. To see my brother on Wonsan."

"That can't be."

Choi flashed a glance at him. "It's the truth. I have a contact there."

"Then how can you know so much about Yamato when it's in the other direction?"

Choi gestured towards the birds. "They're the reason I went to Wonsan. And also the reason I can know so much about what happens in Seoul. The authorities try to keep people under control by designating low-tech zones. Sometimes it backfires. Like this.''

Duval was mystified. "Pigeons?"

"Yes, pigeons."

"But—I don't understand."

"They have a wonderful instinct to return to their home. It doesn't matter where you want them to go, so long as the apron's not more than a couple of hundred miles from their home. It's something discovered by the ancients and long forgotten."

"But how—"

Choi turned the pigeon over and began to unscrew its leg. He carefully removed the false claw. "Pigeons are by far the best messengers on an occupied world, better than one of Yamato's comms ships. Very, very secret. I ship them to other worlds, labeled as breeding stock, and my contacts there ship them straight back again. If you release them from the cargo bay of a newly landed nexus ship, they will circle once, twice, then away they go to the place where they first broke from the egg. No entry controls on them. No searches. No communication signals, however weak or scrambled or coded, to be intercepted. They would never be guessed at!"

"That's incredible!"

Choi nodded smugly. "Oh, yes, incredible. But true. And very useful. Of course they don't fly at night and they're brought down by rain, and sometimes by hawks, but even so . . . There's a network of watchers across the entire quadrant. I cannot tell you their names or which worlds they live on, but I'm their paymaster, and whenever anything happens it's relayed to me by sending a consignment of my own pigeons to Seoul apron. That's how I heard about the arrival of the *Kawabata Yasunari* before the authorities did. Old Tian contacted me from the low-tech zone and I got a head start. It's also how I know about John Oujuku.''

Duval was amazed. "Who will you report the success at Nansei to?"

"An Amerikan. In Japanese, they pronounce his name Josu Oken.'' Choi fell silent, then he said, "Perhaps it's time I told you. Almost twenty years ago, when I first came to Korea, I lived on Cheju Do. I began working at the shipping terminal. There I made the mistake of giving succor to an Amerikan ship. She was trying to find her way back from the Zone, and I didn't know she had been in battle against Yamato ships. Like the *Kawabata Yasunari* I found her insides had been heavily damaged and she was full of starvation and I offered my help as any man would.''

''What ship was she?'' Duval asked, a nameless unease stirring inside him again. The astonishing workings of psi and the acausal principle had meshed!

''Her name was *Richard M. Nixon*. And her owner was Jos Hawken.''

''*Hawken?*'' Duval cried, numbed with shock. He stared at Choi sightlessly. The years fell away, and his mind swam back almost two decades to the apron at Sado and the way he had fought to hoist his brother's blood-sodden body aboard the *Richard M*.

''I remember he was in a high fever,'' Choi was saying. ''Most of his crew had died. They were in a terrible condition and needed help, and so I helped. I arranged for water and food to be brought, and I alerted another Amerikan ship in the port. But then the authorities discovered what I had done. They accused me of breaking apron rules, and I was arrested and routinely genotyped. When they discovered I was racial Japanese, they made me leave.'' He gently cast the pigeon up so that it clattered free into the air. ''Afterwards I escaped to Seoul. I made contact with Hawken again through Amerikan shippers in the Days of Freedom and he sent credit to me. All this''—Choi waved a hand towards his house—''comes from him. In exchange for information.''

''Jos Hawken,'' Duval said again, his voice breathy with shock. ''But I went with his expedition to the Zone.''

Choi smiled infinitely sadly. ''I know. And I also know that your real name is Duval Straker and that your brother is Ellis Straker, the famous privateer. Two years after you came to me, when it became clear Yamato would destroy Free Korea, I sent a message to Hawken about you. He said I should persuade you to go aboard an Amerikan ship, but you would not go.''

''You should have told me about Hawken.''

Choi spread his hands. ''How could I? I didn't dare expose him as my contact. He's twisted himself in many double deals with Yamato on your vice-president's behalf. Yamato is convinced he's working for them, so much so that the Emperor has awarded him a secret dispensation for after the invasion. I couldn't risk it. If you had been taken and Probed so that you revealed him, his plans would collapse and even in Amerika he would be in danger of arrest for treason.''

Duval felt an intense blade of fear slash at him as Choi's words echoed over and again in his mind: ''if you were to be taken by the *kempei* and Probed . . .'' Suddenly he was back inside his deepest terror, vividly, seeing the snouts of the Probe ripping into his mind and the crosses of the crucifixion grounds, and he knew that he could not face that a second time. It was not the fear of death, but the fear of mental pain. Terrible agony, piously justified, repeatedly applied, deliberately inflicted, to his mind and to the minds of his wife and son. He felt the punishment collar tighten on him further, choking him, and the panic began to rise up inside him more intensely than he had ever known. The sweat on his face turned icy. *How can I get out?* his brain screamed. *What can I do?* But no answer came, and he saw that he was trapped beyond hope, and falling, and falling . . .

Then Choi was shaking him, looking in his eyes with fatherly understanding. ''What is it? Tell me.''

''The Probe,'' he babbled. ''I was dying. My legs—their strength was gone. The Void opened under me and I was falling. You must help get Michie and my boy away from here . . .''

''Calm yourself. I know what it's like. I know what you're feeling exactly. Please believe that. But we *must* be strong. We must go on, no matter what.''

Shame crashed over him like an ocean wave, humbling him as he realised that Choi must be seeing him as a craven coward. ''It's not that, Ki Won,'' he said shakily. ''It's not cowardice. I promise you. I saw the future clearly. I *saw* it, I tell you.''

''Of course. Of course. After the Probe a man's mind sometimes plays tricks on him.''

Choi helped him inside. Maids and kitchen servants gathered, concerned to see his pale face and his distress. He sank down onto a stool, swaying.

''Give him some air!''

''Fetch water!''

''Is it an offworld fever?'' a young maid asked, round-eyed.

''It's nothing at all, now,'' Choi told them, clapping his hands sharply. ''Quickly, now! About your tasks, before I send for the mistress!''

He helped Duval into his private business room, the windowless place where he kept accounts and locked away his profits. It was cool and quiet and smelled of incense and candle grease.

As soon as they were alone, Choi brought out his microscope and opened the tiny capsule he had knocked from the hollow in the pigeon's claw. He found a minute sliver of plex, placing it delicately on the stage of the machine. He read it, then touched it into a phial of solvent and shook it until its message was completely consumed.

"Where was it from?" Duval asked, feeling the warmth returning to his limbs. He wiped his forehead and looked at his fingers. They were trembling.

"The Yamato Boundary. Bad news, I'm afraid."

"What did it say?"

Choi tried to put it aside, but Duval pressed him. The blow had been a hard one. "This year's *kin kaigun* has reached the Home Worlds in safety. John Oujuku has failed to intercept it."

* * *

Later, they sat together on the balcony that overlooked the city, trying desperately to fathom a solution. Duval felt a clarity of mind he had not known for weeks. The blackout had settled him like a psi-storm settles a nexus. In its passing the black fear that had engulfed him paled and ebbed, and in its ghastly currents he had seen the way. He knew now what he must do, and the decision was all that remained.

"What did you mean about Michie earlier?" Choi asked him quietly.

Duval shifted himself, leaning his elbows on the broad sill. The night was silent and windless. "Is it possible for you to get her to Amerika?"

"To Amerika? Why?"

"Is it *possible*, Ki Won?"

Choi shrugged. "Perhaps. I don't know. But tell me why."

"I know I'm trapped," Duval said, not knowing how else to put it. "I know I'm a dead man, and I feel relieved. I've made a decision."

"Have patience, my friend." Choi's face was that of a Zen teacher. He touched the streaks of his moustache, the whites of his eyes glistening, the stars, like a halo around his high forehead, shimmering. "It's hard to bear, I know, but nothing worthwhile is ever easy. There is a reward: there's the knowledge that you're helping to oppose a great evil. Dwell upon that and—''

"No!" he hissed, his mind absolutely made up. "Listen to me. A week ago, on the apron I saw refrigerated container loads of argentium in stockpile, and a voice inside me spoke: 'Destroy it! Do it now! Destabilise it! You can strike openly! Here's your chance for real thunder and lightning!' Do you see what I'm trying to say, Choi Ki Won?''

Choi shrugged helplessly. "But that's ludicrous. They'd replace it inside a week, and you'd have achieved nothing.''

"Exactly!" Duval stepped across the balcony, his fists clenching, his voice rising. "But you don't understand. Your way there's never any tangible result. I watch and I watch and the invasion fleet grows and grows. Unstoppably. Swallowing up everything on the planet like a great mouth. I'm full of rage and I must act. But I'm just one man. I'm impotent. And I know there's nothing I can do that'll have the slightest effect on the invasion. Nothing. Nothing at all—*except one thing*.''

"What's that? To make a big fireworks show?" Choi said, trying to keep his words soft despite his dismay at the eerie change that had overtaken his friend.

"No. Not fireworks. That's just how I began to see what I must do. The same night I happened to see the baron arrive. Baron Harumi himself! He stepped down onto Seoul amid a thousand troops. He was as far from me as you are now. And I knew that if I'd had a knife I would have used it. I would have plunged it into him, Choi Ki Won. Do you see now?''

Choi looked at him, aghast. "You can't be thinking that. Oh, no! That's madness!''

"I could have killed him a week ago.''

"But it was just sheerest chance that his shuttle landed beside you. And you said yourself he had a thousand fanatics around him. May the gods bring you to your senses, he's inside a high-security fortress. *High security*. You can't get in there.''

"I know how I can get inside.''

"But even if you did, you'd never get near him. He's guarded everywhere he goes. It would be suicide!''

"I'm a dead man already.''

"But you're *not* dead!''

"So sorry, Choi Ki Won, I've seen the future and I know what I must do.''

35

LIBERTY

The Potomac's muscular waters were restless under an equally troubled gray sky.

"The river's up higher than I've ever seen it, Ellis," Hawken said. They stood five paces apart in a narrow sloping street that ran down to the bank, Ellis loathing him utterly. "The rain god's in a mighty rage today, wouldn't you say?"

He faced Hawken as a man might face his mortal enemy, having no stomach for small talk. Hawken had twice asked for this meeting, and he had twice turned him down, believing that nothing Hawken said could possibly assuage the despicable crimes he had committed, nothing he did would restore the respect Ellis had once had for him.

"It's just a wet month and the spring tide."

"No, it's a rage," Hawken insisted, his eyes hard on Ellis. "I can smell it in the air. Can't you?"

"The only smell hereabouts is the stink of treason."

He had agreed to meet after Hawken's third time of asking, but only after Reba had whispered that he must. But he had not gone alone. Dressed down like a stevie, wearing his thick belt and a cap set back on his head, he had a Wesson sitting on his hip, but even so, the first sight of Hawken had raked up a mix of powerful resentments that put him immediately on guard.

"Say what you have to say," he told Hawken abruptly, planting his feet. "And we'll have done."

"Not here on a street corner, Ellis. I've plenty to say to you, all of it personal."

"This is as anonymous a place as any."

"Criminals seek anonymity. I want security. I have words that can only be said in confidence. I'll only speak them aboard the *Chesapeake*."

Alarms rang in him. "Oh, no."

"It would benefit you. And I'll not speak freely except aboard my ship."

"I'd be a fool to follow you there."

"Why do you think that?" Hawken's smile showed narrowly. "What're you afraid of? That I'll murder you? Has your trust fallen that far? In any case, I can see that Wesson on your belt's no ornament."

Ellis put his fingers to his lips and blew a shrill blast. Hawken stepped back suspiciously, his hand straying inside his jacket. "What's this?" he demanded.

"Who should talk about trust now?"

Instantly two men appeared from nowhere and ran to present themselves to Ellis. He turned his back on Hawken and whispered to the taller, then dismissed them.

"Who are they? What did you say to them?"

"They're my insurance. I told them that if I'm not on the Memorial steps by seven o'clock, they're to complete the contract on you. Now, where's your air-car?"

"I have no air-car here."

Ellis knew his surprise at that must have showed. He remembered pretty well the incident years ago when Hawken had been viciously gunned down by one of his enemies whilst riding in a ground-car along Pennsylvania. The attack had been in broad daylight, in Lincoln's widest, most prestigious thoroughfare, and Hawken had almost died of his wounds. Since then he had maintained discreet precautions at every level. To trust himself alone in an air-car with an armed man who was now all but sworn against him was almost unthinkable.

"You've no transport here?"

"How can I expect your trust if I don't show that I trust you?"

"*Trust?*" Ellis's laugh was short and bitter. "Your stocks are bankrupt there, Hawken."

Hawken turned away, tight-faced. "I'll call a cab. Unless you want to."

Perhaps it is a trap, Ellis thought, but some of the tension fell from him as the skinny young driver who had won the haggle steered them away from the waterfront.

"Norfolk apron."

"Yessir!"

All the while the lad chattered at them in high spirits, spinning a tale and offering fifty services for sale, until Hawken told him roughly to hold his tongue.

No, the lad's no killer, Ellis thought, nor in anyone's pay but his own. And Hawken seems to want me aboard *Chesapeake* badly. If it's not a plan to detain me or kill me, what is it? What can he be wanting to say? He faced his old employer warily as they pushed out from the cluster of small craft waiting beside the tall, round-towered, weather-stained building known as North's Tomb. The tide of vehicles was now reaching its peak, taking the air routes out of town and blackening the sky with rush-hour shadows. Watch Jos Hawken, he's as slippery as a sumo wrestler, still massively involved in intrigues, deeply scheming on all fronts. He's slid out of the belt hold that Cassabian threatened to hoist him with well before Conroy Lubbock's thirty days expired. And it was done with such smooth grace and skill that a man just has to respect it—but not necessarily admire it.

Of course, it's Conroy Lubbock who's protecting you, he said silently as he watched Hawken's eyes scanning the shore. He's paid off Oujuku and Cassabian handsomely to maintain you. A miraculous pretext arises for privateering, one that in less crucial times would have been quietly suppressed in the corridors of the White House, but which instead you made sound important. A carrot to dangle in front of John. Yes, a chance of going into Yamato again: the only credit that could have bought John Oujuku for you, and you knew that, didn't you? And Conroy Lubbock's style of management is written all over it: the inconsequential arrest of some small Amerikan nexus ships that tried heading into the Earth Exclusion Zone and were stopped. Suddenly it's mushrooming into a patriotic cause. How? Like this: credit spent; the word put about; the broadcasters getting out lurid programming and tri-vee catalogs of Yamato atrocities; public opinion lit up and the flames of indignation fanned; then plex-hard political pundits demanding retribution—that's how Oujuku had got his mission.

Yes, Ellis reflected sourly. Oujuku had dutifully lit out to punish Yamato and then off to the Zone with a fleet of twenty ships to give the Remnant hell and havoc as he really wanted.

Cassabian also had fallen silent. Some deal had been struck there, but it had been too deep and too secret in all its convolutions for even Reba to have fathomed it out. The most obvious bribe was that Cassabian's stepson, Carlyle Balaban, had been given a Navy commission and made Oujuku's second-in-command in the Sado operation, but there were other ingredients that were as yet hardly rumors.

So Oujuku got out of the Sector and Cassabian appeased; it was obvious that Ellis too must have his price. Paid off. Bought off. Put off. But they'll never buy me like that. The moment Hawken suggests it I'll burn his guts out.

"Was this meeting Conroy Lubbock's idea?"

Hawken shook his head. "No."

"I don't believe that."

"I'd like to shake the pride out of you, Ellis," Hawken said in the tones of a man who firmly occupied the moral ground. "I'd do that for the VP willingly. I'd have done it years ago, but he would not permit me."

Ellis watched Lincoln slide by below slowly as traffic piled up in the lanes. Air-cars impatiently breaking from the designated zones suffered a mandatory tractoring. At Borobridge the quays with their barges and heavy lifting waldos were shaded by the skyway blizzard. Behind, the soaring, spireless towers of the financial district, a buttressed stump dominating an endless clutter of buildings that tumbled down to the waterfront: Squad Central. Ahead a hundred traffic tractor towers held up the sky above the mass of the city: St. Martin's, Walbrook, Burlington, the spire of the Hill. On the south bank the Palace of Pleasures and Paris Garden and the riverside walk where lovers came to stroll, and the oval arenas for open-air *tai chi*—all were congested with traffic.

"You gotta pay the toll," the cabman reminded Hawken.

Hawken nodded his assent. "Let's see you ride this thing, boy."

"Wanna get there fast, huh?"

"Correct."

"Okeh—if you want the backways."

Ellis settled himself against the seat, his hands unconsciously poised to grip his blaster as they spun down out of the lane. A sharp fetid riverine tang lay on the wind that streamed past the polycarb dome, and the sound of rushing air from the fins. Up ahead Ben Thompson Market spanned the river, plex and very modern, with buildings precariously erected on twenty narrow arches seeming about to topple into either Faneuil Park or the

Potomac. It had been a very wet week and the ebb was at its height; the great boat-shaped piers on which the Market stood forced the river into a series of narrow gorges on this side, and the press of water churned and foamed in each tunnel-like gap.

Ellis felt the tractor grip the youthful cabman's vehicle as he steered the nose of his cab for the nearest span. Clearly he lacked experience and did not want to risk his livelihood shooting the narrow channels at full ebb, but he had got the fare against stiff competition only by agreeing to take them direct to Philadelphia apron and the *Chesapeake*. The only way to do it was to somehow break the inexorable grip of the tractor before it spiraled them down to a waiting traffic violation drone.

As the Market loomed up he aligned the cab as best he could in spite of his fears. The river was up too high. There was no clearance. It was insanity! Ellis felt the suction leave them abruptly and the cab spurted suddenly forward. Where the sharp piers cut into the river, swirling vortices of churning brown water were shed, roaring water breaking up and echoing under the arches. Then everything went black and it was as if the bottom of the cab had fallen out. The front end pitched down and a gout of water sluiced up over the dome and through the window and over Hawken's knees. Then the roar was behind them and they were out in the light again and only the marbling foam of water beneath the cab spoke of the danger they had faced.

The cabbie piled on the power; the tractor had been broken and the run to Norfolk took them just five minutes. He looked at the *Chesapeake* visible now up ahead on the Norfolk apron and, as he turned, his sharp-featured face was smiling.

"Wanna stop off at a rest room and clean up?"

Hawken grimaced at him, his best cut of clothes drenched. "That ain't funny, boy! But you won't be laughing soon. You've lost your fare!"

Ellis cut him. "C'mon! Leave him be. It was you told him to ride out of the traffic lane."

"Yeah, and he took the job on! The asshole."

The youngster's eyes slitted and his mouth set. "You'll pay me in full, or you'll walk from here, even if it is three hundred feet up."

"You young runt! I'll knock your teeth out!"

"You wanna try it?"

The lad coiled like wire in his seat ready to spring should

Hawken try for his neck. In the lad's hand an ugly stunner had appeared. For a moment, Ellis considered pulling his blaster, but decided against it. Instead he asked mildly and with raised eyebrows, "Do you know that you're threatening a real famous nexus captain? One that's cruised into the Zone and back more times than you've eaten burgerettes?"

The youth was plainly unimpressed. He remained bunched up against the door. "It's him that's threatening *me*. And I don't give a sack of shit who he is. This is Amerika, not Yamato. I'll tell you something, my name's Jimi Derby, cab guildsman, and I'm the captain of *this* ship, so what I say goes, else I'll land and whistle up a few of my good buddies to you."

Hawken continued to look darkly at him, but Ellis grinned and held out a credit smart forward. "Here's your fare, fellah. C'mon, take it."

The young cabman made no move. "Jeezus, that's authorised for ten thousand. You real?"

"Take a credit tip—for your spirit. You shot that hole like an astrogator."

Hesitantly the cabman reached back, his stunner still gripped in his left hand and a feral light in his eye as he tried to see the trick. Then he quickly took the smart and striped it through his slot, watching both his passengers mistrustfully as he recovered his seat and steered them past Sears and the Reformed Synagogue and the half-built Murdoch Tri-Vee headquarters

"Thank you, sir," he said grudgingly a moment later. "And anyway, how do you know I ain't a psi-talent?"

Ellis winked at him. "You might say I was in the business, once over. Next time, take the widest span and relax your mind from the stomach."

"Relax my mind from the stomach? What the hell you mean?"

"Here, see, from the diaphragm. Loosen up. And take this card to the address marked on the back, if you want to develop your psi. I'll tell you now, it's dormant there."

The lad looked at the card and his eyes lit. "Hey, thanks, Captain Straker."

The *Chesapeake* was set down on the very end of the apron, beyond Wright Terminal. Ellis went aboard her after Hawken, admiring the sleek lines of the ship despite himself. The caretaker crew seemed orderly and well disciplined. Their first officer welcomed Hawken with due dignity and answered the owner's questions promptly until he was dismissed. Then they went aft to the captain's cabin, Ellis expecting some surprise every step of the way but there was none.

"Will you share a bottle of mash with me?"

"I wouldn't crack a bottle with you if it was the last bottle in Known Space."

"Ellis, Ellis. Sometimes you're a difficult man to deal with."

"We're on your vessel. I'm ready to hear you. Say what you want to say quickly. Then I'll be away before your corruption makes me spew."

Hawken drew himself up then. "You've got me wrong, Ellis. And I hate to see a man whispering behind my back."

"You're a swindler and a thief, Jos Hawken. Yeah, and a traitor. How's it sound to your face?"

Hawken showed no anger at the insult. He dashed amber liquid into two small ceramic *choko* and set them down, pushed one towards Ellis, and lifted the other.

"Ellis, you're a stiff-necked bastard. And blind. But unless you're stupid too, you'll listen to me. There have been developments since you took your slanders to Conroy Lubbock's office." He held up his hand and ticked off the fingers. "Firstly, John Oujuku raids Yamato and the Zone. Secondly, Ramakrishnan makes a breakthrough regarding the Beyond. Thirdly, Bernardo Spitz destroys five Yamato ships on an apron in the Zone. Fourthly, your crazy pal Kim sets up a base at Marshall IV from which to harry the Remnant. Fifthly, your improvements go to the Navy Council for consideration. Sixthly, there's a plan up before the President to send ships to intercept the Yamato aurium fleet before it reaches Yamato. Now, do you think all that's coincidence?"

Ellis's stare was as heavy as lead. Everything Hawken had said was true but irrelevant. "Have you finished?" he said levelly.

Hawken's anger exploded. "No! I have not finished! It's Conroy Lubbock's work, Ellis. All of it. Everything's happening with Conroy Lubbock's knowledge and consent. Jeezus! You're not the sole prophet of Yamato's intentions, you know."

"I never said—"

Hawken cut him down. "You have embarrassed me, Ellis! You've *accused* me unjustly! And when I could make no public denial. Had it not been for Conroy Lubbock's patient handiwork,

I might have been shot by a Daughter of Freedom, or arraigned for—'' Hawken pressed his thin lips together, stemming the outburst. His face was pale with anger, but still he seemed able to find the resources to control himself as he stood up and paced. ''I'm a broad-minded man, Ellis, and I can understand why you did what you did, but I'll never forgive you for swallowing John Oujuku's allegations whole and setting yourself so hard against me. Couldn't you see that most of this has come from Kastner and Belkov and the Lucia Henry people? I *made* you, Ellis. I grew you from a seed! And yet you turned on me. I credited you with more intelligence. Yeah, and more loyalty.''

''Loyalty?'' Ellis struck back angrily. He knew that the expense of keeping nexus-going warships in commission was great, and although the Navy was controlled by Hawken as joint chief, the posts of surveyor of ships, surveyor of weapons systems, officer of supply, and clerk of ships were all occupied by his main political enemy, a man whom Hawken had himself accused of obtaining a vast income from corrupt practices. Now he was trying to shift blame to Nikolai Belkov again.

''It won't work. John Oujuku brought me evidence. Written evidence. What should I have done? Ignored it because you were once my employer? No, Jos Hawken. You got the wrong man here. I won't put any one individual before Amerika.''

''Oujuku is a great astrogator, better psi than I ever had. He's full of courage and he's an admirably honest man, but more than that, he's a hothead. He always has been. All fire and fury. And because his honesty is so complete he has no skill whatsoever at secret maneuverings. He doesn't understand them. But you, Ellis—you should have seen through all of that chickenshit.''

The scorn in Ellis's voice was bitter. ''You're not fit to stand on the same planet as John Oujuku, you fucking snake!''

''*Don't you understand?*'' Hawken's face was contorted as he struggled to change Ellis's mind. ''My God, and after all I've taught you. It was *me* who showed you how to give a juicy rumor to a young cadet and see where it ended up *so's to test him*. Are you forgetting that? This rumor went to John and then to you. And although Conroy Lubbock warned you, you wouldn't leave it alone. Like a goddamned *T. rex* at an illegal circus, the pair of you! Jaws snapping. Slavering for blood. And Cassabian whipcracking like a meddling ringmaster . . .'' Hawken's hooded eyes dropped, then fixed on him like shards of sapphire. "When I first took to running the Navy's affairs, they were in a pretty fine state of disarray. In the first deal I struck with the President I promised to clear out the corruption and end the decline that had dragged Amerika's defenses so low. And so I did! But I made enemies, Ellis, enemies of the self-same men whose bubble I'd burst, and as soon as they could they came back at me, saying that I'd framed them and defamed them and abolished their posts expressly to benefit myself. I had to have those parasites out."

Ellis shook his head slowly, mockingly. "So it was lies, then? All those accusations and suits served against you by half the administration?"

"Yes, lies! Secret, premeditated opposition. A campaign against me. Deliberate. Willful. They wanted to tear me down! Nikolai Belkov wanted to push me out. Lucia Henry wanted to see me thrown off Liberty. Do you see, Ellis? Do you see now?"

"And that's the truth?"

"I swear."

Ellis's face remained immobile. His eyes met Hawken's own, staring him down. "You're a goddamned liar. When you first got hold of the Navy's affairs as a joint chief, in 'thirty-two, Amerika's Navy had two hundred and twenty nexus cruisers. Now, after six years of your misrule, we've got two hundred and thirty. Do you call that preparation for war? I saw signed orders. Requisitions that had come from your office. Hardcopy transferring the Sector's aurium and argentium stocks and the Sector's dockyards and the Sector's credit to your corporate business cronies as 'surplus to requirements.' Government facilities hived off to become yards to build merchant ships for your own profit! Yes, you sonofabitch, ships like this one! To line your own pockets and to sell out to Baron-goddamned-Harumi the moment his samurai come pouring out of the Kalifornia nexus."

Hawken's fist pounded out his words. "What you saw was false accounting."

Ellis stood up, suddenly enraged by Hawken's barefacedness. His seat scraped back across the luxury flooring with an ugly sound. "*False accounting?* Do you think I don't know a scam when I see one? Can you really take me for so complete a fool?"

"There were hundreds of requisitions! I dreamed them up! I wrote them all! Every last one!"

"Then you *admit* it! You sonofabitch!"

"No!" Hawken stood up also. He too was angry and stabbing with his finger, Ellis's muscular bulk totally disregarded. "I admit nothing. You're so goddamned quick to accuse, ain't ya? You're so goddamned sure of yourself. Well, let me tell you this, Mister-fucking-Clean, you don't know the first thing about politics on Liberty. You're as blind as a newborn babe. And John Oujuku, who collected the evidence against me so patiently, he's blind too. Together you were the danger! Unwitting—yes! From the highest motives—surely! But you were more dangerous to Amerika's Navy than any Yamato flotilla." Hawken broke away, leaned heavily on the psi-screen console. "Of course, war is coming. I've known that since the day we dined with that rat, Iwakura, back on Sado, and you saved my skin by your action. Oh, I haven't forgotten that: I remember it when I chose to sell you *Constitution;* I remembered it again when you were locked up at Camp Worth and I walked the White House corridors, wondering how I could get you out; and I remembered it again when I argued on your behalf before the President that she ought to maneuver Kurt Reiner into selling Xanadu mansion to you."

"*You did that?*" Ellis hissed, astonished at the discovery. He could not find the words. His amazement was so complete that he sank back into his seat. "You interfered even in *that?*"

"Sure, I did. And more," Hawken said, aggrieved bitterness building in his voice. "Many things have passed between us. Most of them were unknown to you, and all of them were kept from the public. But because they were done in secret, does that make them any the less constructive? Hush-hush. That's always been my way in business. It's the foundation of my fortunes. What kind of conceit is it that would make my dealings common knowledge from the Senate to the bars on Sunset Avenue? No, sir! I don't allow it! Secrecy. Stealth. Discretion. These are my watchwords. They're what beats an enemy in the end. *And so it's got to be with the Navy.*"

"But . . ." Ellis felt his anger draining away as Hawken's words bit into him, then he sagged inside. Suddenly everything was starting to become clear and the enormity of his error was dawning.

"But *what?*" Hawken saw that he had taken the initiative and his voice turned scornful. "Are we so witless a people that we've got to tell every goddamned individual in creation our private business? Only a fool tells the opposition what weapons he's got. The stock market swarms with two-faced Chinese financiers, the Yamato embassy here on Liberty is full of sophisticated listening gear, all our ports and aprons are covered by *kempei* spies; each day they report the strength and disposition of our fleet and the readiness of our vessels to repel an invasion. So are we going to advertise the exact measure of our ships into the bargain? 'Sure, Mr. Emperor, we got four ships here, five there, over thataway a half dozen more?' That would be real clever, Ellis!''

It was as if Ellis Straker had been hit by a sumo wrestler. He shook his head slowly.

"This ship," Hawken said, jerking his thumb up at the third-deck blisters. "Is she a warship, or is she a merchantman?"

Ellis said nothing, understanding perfectly what Hawken was saying, letting him run on and spend his anger and accepting the humiliation as he knew he must.

"You don't know, do you? Because you can't tell by looking at her! If she's laden with cargo, then she's a merchantman; if she's tooled up with guns, then she's a fighter. Her purpose is not implicit in her design. You can't tell what she is. And if you can't tell, neither can Baron Harumi's spies!"

Ellis bowed his head. The lessons being read back to him were the same he himself had first set down at Camp Worth thirteen years ago for Ramakrishnan.

"You . . . you were taking the guru's counsel, even then?"

"I was taking *your* counsel. I intercepted your every letter. It made good sense. 'Versatile cruisers mounting singularity guns, not fixed-function ships equipped with beam weapons, that's what Amerika needs.' You wrote that. And you were right. Yamato's admirals are living in the past. They still believe space warfare can be a matter of emerging from a nexus and blasting their way into a system with a sledgehammer. Baron Harumi proved as much against the Koreans. Without constant thought, war strategies become obsolete faster than any other work of man. The Emperor's spies will count the two hundred thirty battleships of our fleet and he'll think they're the same outdated hulks that Lucia Henry left us with. But they're not the same. Internally they're totally rebuilt. Baron Harumi and his advisors will hear reports of small, weak engine clusters and he'll think they're freight carriers. But he sure won't have reckoned with the guns those babies'll be carrying!''

Chow time chimed throughout the ship. Ellis felt a tremor pass through him hollowly, as if his guts had been torn out by a singularity. He had made a cardinal mistake, one for which he would have pulled up any cadet: he had allowed his personal dislike of a man to interfere with his judgement. Shame for the way he had hounded and insulted Hawken rushed through him, followed by intense relief that his accusations were unfounded.

''I owe you my apologies,'' he said throatily. ''I was wrong. Very wrong. Completely wrong.''

Hawken's pale eyebrow lifted, then his expression softened almost imperceptibly. ''Yes. You were. But I'll tell you this: I'd have done exactly the same in your place, which is perhaps a testament to how similar we are under the skin.''

''Then you'll accept my apology?''

''I'll accept. But there are three conditions. First, should I ever ask you, you must put your seven ships freely at my disposal. Your crews too.''

Ellis nodded, deeply chastened. ''Agreed.''

''Second, when John Oujuku returns from across the Boundary, I want you to help me build this Navy into something that can stop anything Yamato sends against us.''

''Agreed. And the third condition?''

''That you drink this *choko* of Jim Beam with me now.''

''Agreed!''

Ellis stood up and lifted the ceramic cup, thinking ashamedly of the time and how he had set a limit on his return. He despised himself for his motivations of two hours ago. ''Sure, I'll drink with you, Jos Hawken. I'll drink a toast to the man who grew me from a seed.''

''And I'll drink to a faithless sonofabitch who became an oak tree.''

36

Within a week of Oujuku's return from beyond the Boundary, Ellis met him in Hawken's company on Fort Bush, the main orbiting station of Liberty's planetside defense chain. The fort occupied a stationary orbit, standing guard over the atmosphere of Liberty and the freight dockyards at Port Wilson where the silver bulk carriers appeared with their vast loads of mineral wealth from the moons of the outer system gas giants. Fort Bush was a vast spinning top, peppered by a million tiny fosfors that shone like starlight. Oujuku had been away ten months, and during that time Ellis had labored ceaselessly to put Amerika's nexus cruisers into good fighting order. An ominous pall was hanging over all of the Sector with new rumors every week increasing the nervousness of Liberty. In the White House, it was said, the President was like a mad thing, half crazed by anxiety. Her aides avoided her—servants fled, secretaries curbed their tongues and their manners, no one dared ask for either favor or reward. Conroy Lubbock himself had twice been sent out of the Oval Office, his ears on fire, cursed at and screamed out. Although Oujuku's return had muted some of the more doom-faced oracles at Long Island and Harrisburg, Alia's mood continued to feed off the unease of her presidential staff, and the mood of Amerika took its key from her.

But above the planet's surface the talking was straight.

Oujuku, on his way up to orbit, had already received Hawken's full account of the current state of naval preparation and had been told of Ellis's work. In return, he had given a report of his actions in the Zone, a report he was most reluctant to repeat.

Oujuku counted his voyage a failure; it had achieved nothing in terms of creditary return or strategic dividend and, though he had done much to lift Amerikan morale, he was accustomed to far greater achievements. Ellis quickly learned that Otis Le Grande, the Hawken brothers, and the President had been chief among the syndicate which had backed the voyage. Unfettered enterprise had grown up in the Sector and everyone was benefiting, but this deal was crucial. Other prominent shipping parties had been involved also, and Ellis began to wonder if he had been deliberately excluded from the syndicate.

He watched Hawken's dog, a big, gangling, foolish hound with a liver and velvet coat, brown nose and eyes and whip tail, zigzagging restlessly around the station, sniffing at everything and marking territory on every corner. Hawken had given it a studded collar on which was written, ''My name is Tojo: 1400 Pennsylvania Avenue.'' Ellis wondered again what the real reason was for the truth being kept from him concerning the allegations he had made against Hawken. There had never been anything tangible, but he had sensed that Hawken was keeping a whole lot from him still. It had played on his mind for several months now, ever since the day he had stepped out from the shadow of the *Chesapeake*, chastened and humiliated and feeling like an idiot.

''The President blew hot and cold over my departure,'' Oujuku was explaining unhappily. ''She's still swayed by the peace lobby, from meek and deluded souls who believe it's possible to avoid war with Yamato. I told her that ninety percent of wars were ultimately about trade, that that was the lesson of history, but she wouldn't have it. She was convinced that Amerika's ships should stay in the Amerikan Sector.''

''What did you do, John?''

''Just looked for some alteration in her that would prohibit my going. Then there was some trouble with a pack of the President's aides who wanted to come on what they called a 'fact-finding mission'—as if it was some kind of pleasure excursion I had in mind. I eventually left, September fourteenth, in *Ticonderoga* with twenty other ships and eight shuttles, most only half prepared and half staffed, again through fear that the President's countermanding order would turn up at the last minute. We cruised about in the Zone long enough to prove to the Emperor that Amerikans don't care nothing for his ass. Even so, if we'd been quicker getting away, we might've had something less abstract to celebrate. As it is, the rest of my account's pretty dismal.''

Ellis listened as Oujuku related how he had missed the '38 aurium fleet by a single day, and how he had cruised instead to Sakishima Gunto to antagonise the Emperor's subjects further. There his crews had picked up a virulent fever and it had killed some of them before the medics had been able to get a program on it. He had sighted Ishigaki Shima a week before Christmas and set about a systematic unpicking of Yamato's illegal possessions. He had stormed and taken Shika; at Iriomote Shima he had done the same, but he had missed the '39 aurium fleet, and too many astrogators had died of the fever by then to mount the intended attacks on Hateruma and Yonagumi. As he returned he had attacked the Yamato presense in Taiwan and touched down to bring away prisoners captured off the ill-fated *Potomac*, but there was little joy in Oujuku's mind about any of it.

"What do you think?" Ellis asked him directly.

"Too little. Too late. After last time, a lot was expected of me. I made some pretty rash promises, but I brought back only seventy-five ticks on the credit to my investors, which makes it hard to call what I was doing trade. I missed the fleet, Ellis. Both times. And it's my fault. It's gonna cost us."

"Shit," Hawken said stiffly, his eyes searching for his errant dog. "But you're right about the cost. Two years' aurium is enough to pay off all Yamato's outstanding loans, and their success in refining it'll make their bankers the braver when it comes to advancing more. Also, the damage is doubled because the aurium might have been ours. Without it, we're gonna be hard-pressed."

"About Lucia Henry and Nikolai Belkov—have you had any more trouble from them?" Oujuku asked, determined not to dwell on his failure. "It was a wise move to sign Belkov's son aboard my expedition. Lucia Henry is a creature I heartily dislike." He turned to Ellis, his ebony face brightening. "By the way, your brother-in-law acquitted himself like a man in the fighting."

"Thanks."

"I've already commended your son's handling of the *Roanoke* in dispatches, Jos."

"Yeah." Hawken took the compliment condescendingly. "My son knows what he's about. He'll go beyond Known Space one day, exploring the Beyond, John. If Ramakrishnan's right, he'll make it to the Galactic Center someday. God grant that he

gets the chance. As for Lucia Henry and Belkov, they've almost
given up. They're beaten and they know it. But the truth is I
wish I was rid of the pair of them. They're old, with old minds,
and neither has it in them to adjust their views. The President
did the right thing appointing me above gray old bureaucrats like
Belkov. It's a good policy to make a businessman the head of
any undertaking.''

They walked on, Ellis feeling the tension in the men around
him who manned the fort's plex corridors. It was as if each one
of them saw the war approaching—a war against an enemy that
would expect and give no quarter. He told Oujuku, ''For every
nexus ship officially on the Navy lists there's a private vessel of
equal maneuverability and firepower in the hands of a commercial shipping operator. That means we maintain crews and operational ships at nil cost to the taxpayer.'' He pointed through
the observation blister with pride. ''Al Vega's *Nebraska* is a
good example, a fine ship of six thousand tons mass, available
for Navy charter with minimal notice. It's expensive to keep
ships in commission, as the Emperor must have discovered. And
with the credit we've saved and funds Congress has allotted we'll
build eight nexus-going cruisers, two good warships like the
Kentucky, and one nexus plotting ship . . .''

They debated for more than an hour, Oujuku still moodily
ashamed at his half-failure, Hawken lecturingly, striding along
the curving concourse of Fort Bush, throwing Doggi Choos from
his pocket for his idiot animal to catch, all the while saying that
time was short and that they must look to the future instead of
the past.

To revive John Oujuku's spirits, Ellis showed him the real
strengths that lay beneath the superficial appearance of neglect.
He went through the foremost points with enthusiasm, detailing
especially the proposed change of manning, and all the while,
Ellis was thinking of the question he had wanted to ask Hawken.
He had perhaps been waiting for Oujuku's return before putting
it. He felt bound to Hawken now by promise, oath, and duty,
obliged to atone in full for his past misjudgements of the man.
He was working hard for him, trying to make it up.

It's an unnatural state for me, he thought, knowing that Hawken alone in Amerika had the trick of manipulating him. Christ,
how I wish I was back aboard the *Constitution,* shooting through
on a nexus, cruising free, making my own decisions where to

go and when to fight. On Hawken's staff I'm like a dog on a lead. And I want to be off it!

Secretly he thought of the mess John Oujuku had made of his chance to upset Yamato's plans. I'd have done the job properly, he thought with some shame for his arrogance. But it's a fact! God knows it's not right to damn John for his one failure, and I don't know enough about the circumstances, but we sure needed to stop that aurium fleet. Hasn't John demonstrated his capabilities? He's a great astrogator. A great captain. He took his ship through uncharted nexi and home again with a hold full of Yamato's aurium, but still . . .

Ellis sighed. Still the uncharitable thought would not leave him. Jeezus, I'd never have set down on Sakishima Gunto, it's famous for designer diseases. And I'd have taken the aurium fleet instead of hanging about on Ishigaki Shima. Next time it'll be my chance. My chance.

Apropos of nothing, he suddenly asked Hawken, "Why weren't John and I told the truth when we first put our accusations on Conroy Lubbock's desk?"

"Maybe because a secret is best kept by fewest people," Hawken answered carefully, stepping from between them. "Conroy Lubbock wanted the scandal to break out long enough for Yamato to get wind of it so they knew pretty well the deficiencies of Amerikan defensive strength."

"We could have played our cards close to our chests well enough," Ellis said.

"There's no play realer than real life, Ellis."

Oujuku held his tongue, watching as Ellis pressed the point. "We were deliberately kept in the dark, and for an unnecessary period. Why didn't you deal straight with us? It's as if you didn't trust either of us."

Hawken laughed. "Hardly so. John was trusted with twenty ships and a mission against the Yamato aurium fleet."

"Some might see that as John being deliberately got offplanet and out of the way. I remained on Liberty, but still I wasn't taken into your confidence."

The smile fell away from Hawken's mouth. "I asked to see you twice and was turned down."

"Oh, sure. You could have gotten to me."

"I never deal against the play." Hawken grew jovial once

more, his dog bounding up to him with a chewed piece of cable insulation. "Ellis, what is it you're saying to me?"

Ellis let it go, knowing that this was not the time to pursue the matter, then Oujuku asked Hawken about the thrust of current policy, leaving him to ponder on the soundness of the answer he had received.

"I know you want to put up a blockade around Yamato. But the President won't countenance any direct and unprovoked act of war. I told her, and Conroy Lubbock told her, that we must prevent Yamato from equipping their fleet at all costs."

"An expedition might be the answer," Oujuku said, warming to the idea. "Refugee Koreans might be got together under their exiled ex-President's leadership. It could be a big deal if we brought in the Chinese and—"

"I've thought of that," Hawken told him. "And I've put as much to Congress, but that too was vetoed as aggressive. What they don't realize is that Yamato ships cost three times as much as ours to get into space. Already Baron Harumi has assembled a fleet of four hundred ships and a hundred thousand shock troops on Seoul and there's a second force almost as large concentrating in the Hokkaido quadrant. He sure as hell isn't gonna want to wait long."

Ellis rubbed at his chin as he listened to Hawken relating the precise strength of the Yamato fleet. He stared through the plex blister at the bright points of light that were the other orbiting defense forts, wondering suddenly how Hawken could have such detailed information at his fingertips. He said, "I'll allow that a blockade of the key trans-Yamato nexi is untried, but it's worth the attempt. Our biggest ships can stand off the nexi for a couple of months at a time before needing to return to Amerika to refit. If the most crucial months are chosen, we might hamper them enough to make them cancel their plans. At least we could delay them until they're forced to rethink, and every day we succeed is a day costing Yamato three times what it costs Amerika."

"Even so, the President won't allow it. Too many voices close to her doubt whether a blockade of Yamato can work," Hawken said cautiously. "The argument used against us in the Security Council meetings is that of a Yamato fleet getting through despite the blockade. If they broke out and our ships were evaded, Amerika would be dangerously exposed."

"So we're just gonna sit here and wait to be attacked?" Ellis asked, aware that his disappointment was showing.

"You heard John's view of the President's attitude. It took all Conroy Lubbock's persuasion to make her agree to the reprisals on Sakishima Gunto, and even then she was only finally swayed by an outcry of public opinion and the survey of voting intentions."

"We're gonna wait like lambs in the slaughterman's yard," Oujuku said grimly, walking away along the fort's main access corridor.

Hawken looked to him sharply, shouting after him, "Nobody wants to be at the sonsabitches more than I do. It might've been possible if you'd come back with a bit more aurium." He turned to Ellis. "The truth is, his failure's crapped it up for us all."

Ellis's fist balled with sudden fierceness and his eyes met Hawken's own. "It's by decisive action that wars are won. Give me a strike force of fifty nexus ships and I'll do the work. A massive preemptive blow. I'll blast into the Seoul system and smash Baron Harumi's invasion force to ions."

"I've told you," Hawken hissed back with unexpected violence. He looked around as if checking that they were not being overheard. "Don't even think that way."

"Sanction it, Jos! Imagine! Let's hit them just as the whole goddamned hive is stirring—"

"Quietly." Hawken's voice sank to a whisper. "As I said, I don't have the power to sanction that."

A series of yelping barks rang out. Hawken's dog had found a maintenance drone and was trying to turn it over, but the drone was unimpressed and at every turn the dog flinched back, blue sparks from the drone's meson tool crackling at its nose.

"Get away from it, then, you stupid synth animal!" Hawken roared at the dog, striding across to slap its flanks with the lead.

Ellis followed and grabbed Hawken's arm. "Try Conroy Lubbock, then. Make him see sense!"

Hawken looked slowly down at Ellis's hand until he was released. "Not even Conroy Lubbock. The President is dead set against stripping Amerika's defenses for the sake of any damned fool adventures." He paused. "Besides, the Seoul system is sealed up tighter than a silex reactor. You'd never get in past the beam weapons, and if you did you'd never get out again."

The fire in Ellis's belly burned up higher. "What does that

matter so long as I got amongst them? And I know I can. I can get into any system, and I've thought long and hard about Seoul and its so-called impregnability. See Conroy Lubbock. Persuade him.''

Hawken shook his head. ''Conroy Lubbock is busy with Cassabian.''

''What do you mean?''

''Just that. Lubbock is involved in difficult matters. Matters of the utmost importance.''

''What the hell can be more important than this?''

Hawken watched him a moment, considering. Then he said, ''It's confidential. My duty to him prevents me from speaking of it. Even to you, Ellis.''

''But you know what it is?''

Hawken nodded slowly.

''Tell me.''

''I can't.''

Ellis watched after Hawken, watched the dog bound after him as he followed Oujuku. Inside his head alarm bells were ringing loud now. From his tone Hawken was certainly hiding something, but what was it? And what was it that had made him rile up at the mention of an attack on Seoul? Whatever was being stitched together by Lubbock and Cassabian, he wanted to be a part of it.

37

''Please sit down, gentlemen.''

Ellis placed himself in one of the wooden armchairs in the VP's study. Apart from Ellis, only Hawken, Cassabian, and Oujuku had been called in here. The meeting had been convened at Conroy Lubbock's house, in camera, and under conditions of great secrecy. Guards had been stationed at both ends of the corridor to prevent eavesdroppers, and the cold courtyard below the electroscreened window was empty except for a pair of women standing at attention by the gatehouse. A roaring real fire blazed in the grate, filling the room with radiant heat.

Conroy Lubbock had grown gray in the guardianship of the Sector. His long face was as pale and mournful as the high winter moon of Liberty, accentuated by his white beard and the velvet cap which was set askew and back from his high forehead. He put out his power in measured words. "I have called you here to tell you how it's going to be. A conspiracy of circumstances stands against us and I've chosen to undo them, with your help, by the means I'll set before you. Tomorrow we'll begin the first moves in a chain of events that will save our President's neck, yes, save it for her—*despite her own best judgements.*"

Every man in the room stiffened at that. Ellis thought of the time he had brought the *Richard M.* home, the time in the Cheju Do system when he had been obliged to put down a mutiny. Then he thought of the other time, just before burying the *Constitution*'s aurium hoard in the bore holes, when he had seen signs enough to prevent a rising. Conroy Lubbock's words sounded unwholesomely close to mutineers' talk. Only this time it was not the overthrow of a ship's captain that was at issue but the captain of the Sector—and that crime was not called mutiny, it was called high treason.

"I can see what you're thinking," Conroy Lubbock went on. "And you're right to think it. But hear Pharis Cassabian out and you'll understand the reasons. I hope we can reach accord, because if we cannot we're all of us dead men, and Amerika is lost."

Cassabian sat on Conroy Lubbock's right, strained, tired, swathed in fawn and tan except for a neat collar of white Afrikan cotton that enclosed his throat. Grave-faced, he said, "An invasion of Amerika must always be built on three columns: an army to threaten us, a navy to convey that army to us, and a rising of Amerikan sympathisers to aid and applaud it as it makes planetfall. This last pillar has as its pedestal Lucia Henry. For above a year, since the last attempt on Alia's life, Lucia Henry has been kept incommunicado by order of the Council. It was hoped by some that this measure might pinch off the diplomatic intercourse that passes between her and the Boundary, enough at least to disable any pro-Yamato faction betrayals of Amerika.

However, some time since, by my own initiative, I deliberately opened up a channel by which coded hardcopy might reach her. In June, four months ago local time, this deception paid me back in full. I intercepted a message from a certain Tony Bola, a young lawyer enrolled at Armstrong College and known to me to be onetime associate of the traitors Lewis de Campion and Robert Jansen. He is the instrument of a conspiracy to bring spies into Amerika. Bola's message was looking for Lucia's approval for a rebellion, her full compliance in a Yamato invasion, and her explicit agreement to the assassination of the President. In her reply, Lucia Henry put her name to all of these plots.''

Ellis sucked in his breath at that. Oujuku was half out of his seat. Both looked to Hawken, who nodded grimly as Cassabian continued. ''I had Lucia's message copied and then I allowed the original to reach its destination so that others party to its intentions could be apprehended. I need not belabor the point that by these free actions the ex-President has transgressed the New Statutes of last year in that she did as an Amerikan citizen willfully involve herself with a plot against the President's life. In consequence Lucia has laid herself open to the death penalty.''

''But she's an ex-President,'' Ellis said, astonished at Cassabian's intentions. ''How can she be executed?''

''Oh, she'll be tried. Before a commission of judges, security councilors, and congressmen. And once she's found guilty she'll be speedily dispatched to Camp Worth and the bore hole. Once she's brought to trial no power in the cosmos can save her, except Alia herself, who might still refuse to sign the death warrant.''

As Cassabian flashed a glance at the VP, Ellis's mind thundered with the revelation. Now he saw the reasons for the incredible storms that had swept the White House, for Alia's refusal to sanction a foray against Yamato, and why when Hawken had personally put the idea to her she had spat bile at him and allowed him only to take the fleet to its Boundary stations. With Lucia Henry dead everything would be plunged into turmoil.

''Lucia is a foremost ally of Yamato,'' Ellis said, putting his view direct to Conroy Lubbock. ''If she's executed, surely the storm in Yamato will be so great that the Emperor will be driven to back the efforts of Harumi all the more, multiplying the danger to us.''

"No!" Cassabian cut in. "Naturally, when Lucia is executed there will be howls of indignation from Yamato, but the Emperor will find himself without a recognised ally to lead any insurgency."

"But you have a point, Captain," Conroy Lubbock said, nodding towards Ellis so that his fine white beard shook among the dazzling threads of his jacket. "The President fears that the execution will so tarnish the ideals of Amerikan justice that we will lose every last stitch of credibility among the other Sectors. It's my belief that unless we're able to armor her against accusations of murdering a political opponent, and an ex-President, Alia will not permit Lucia's death."

Ellis shrugged tautly. "So how can your plan proceed?"

"That's no concern of yours at this stage," Conroy Lubbock told him sharply. "Understand that this matter is disclosed to you on pain of death, Captain. It is disclosed only that you can be properly briefed in another matter. Jos?"

Hawken leaned forward, propping one fist on his hip, the other on his knee. The gravity of the matter clearly pained him. "As soon as Lucia is dead, the last hope of the appeasers is smashed. She is the compromise solution, and without her, Alia's unseating means their accepting as a puppet president some other figure from their own diversified ranks, a leader none of them will be able to agree on, because without Lucia they're split. The alternative is to accept the direct Emperorship of Mutsuhito himself. That will not appeal to appeasers of any persuasion, so Harumi's armies will find no enthusiastic reception on any Amerikan world."

Oujuku spoke up, seeing a flaw. "But conversely, wouldn't Lucia's death remove the last obstacle between Mutsuhito and the absorption of Amerika into the Greater Yamato Co-prosperity Sphere? It'll become full absorption or nothing."

"Yes," Hawken agreed impatiently. "Which is why we'll then be forced to take direct steps against Yamato."

Ellis stirred in his seat. He had noted the oblique way Hawken was approaching the kernel of his argument, and his heart had jumped to his throat at the implications: by forcing the issue Conroy Lubbock and Cassabian were making a preemptive strike against Baron Harumi's forces not only permissible but *essential*. Suddenly the undertaking he had been perfecting and pressing on Hawken and pleading for over the months was more than a possibility, it had become a likelihood.

"The assault on Seoul!" he said as if suddenly filled with light from a supernova.

"Yes," Conroy Lubbock said. "Assault, if you will. I'd prefer to call it a naval action, carefully designed and planned." He turned to Oujuku. "I'll inform the Security Council, who are apprised and firmly with us in all points, that you, Congressman Oujuku, will command the expedition. I shall further inform them that you'll appoint Nikolai Belkov as your vice-admiral—as protocol demands."

Ellis felt a cold hand seize him inside, utter disappointment descended on him, then his jealous suspicions ballooned. He saw clearly that in Conroy Lubbock's mind he was unrecognised. He had always been placed and rooted in Reba's father's consciousness as a scheming pirate, a psi-happy astrogator, a criminal system-robber to be despised and ignored. The distinctions conferred by a role in the political pyramid had never been his, had never lifted him above the rank of citizen as they had with Oujuku, who was presently a congressman. That he had crossed Conroy Lubbock had deepened the resentment, excluding him completely from any commanding role in the very expedition that he had studied and planned for.

Ellis's flesh crawled and his nostrils filled with the stink of Conroy Lubbock's hypocrisy. He saw starkly etched on the VP's face the admiration for false values that only a politician could believe in so totally. I'm the architect of this undertaking! he raged at Conroy Lubbock silently. And what part am I being given in my own mission? None! You know how deeply this cuts me, you bile-pissing bastard. You understand that I ought to be appointed to lead it, and though you know how much this operation means to Amerika, still you humiliate me! Still you try to keep me from my right and due! Still you try to pay me in your counterfeit credit!

Icily he said, "Am I to have *any* part in the operation, Conroy?"

Lubbock ignored him. "The precise form of the mission will be in your care, Congressman Oujuku, but if it all goes as I hope, you'll have a number of Navy ships at your disposal. It will be your last chance to intercept the invasion fleet before

Baron Harumi's preparations are complete. Now, go and think it over. Amerika and the future of Known Space are in your hands.''

Conroy Lubbock looked hard at Ellis before signaling that Oujuku should leave and that Cassabian should accompany him. Oujuku laid a consoling hand briefly on Ellis's shoulder as he passed. Then he fingered his compac and within seconds one of the guards was at his side. He gave quiet instructions, his fingers playing about his lips, and the guard departed.

"I ask you again, Mr. Vice-president. Am I to have any part in this mission?"

Conroy Lubbock regarded him for a long moment, then he said, "Do you remember when we met last time, how different the circumstances were then?"

"I have apologised to Jos Hawken, and he's accepted my apology," Ellis said, his spine rigid now.

"Good. It was about time. But relax, I've no wish to carry on any part of that unfortunate and *unnecessary* debate." Conroy Lubbock adjusted the sleeve of his garment fractionally. "You may also recall swearing to me an oath on that occasion? One concerning your brother?"

"Yes . . . but I don't see . . ."

Lubbock moved on, deliberately switching away from the source of Ellis's unease. "This meeting was called for your benefit, Captain. You're a cunning man and I think you must have understood that the intentions expressed in the last few minutes are a complete volte-face of the policy I've always promoted. Also, you must have guessed that I was driven to agree to it." Conroy Lubbock paused again as Ellis nodded. "I regret the solution we've proposed, but I believe that Pharis Cassabian and I have arrived at the only accommodation that'll give us any hope at all of preventing total disaster. You see, it's become apparent to us that if our Navy were to wait for the invasion to arrive in Amerika, we would be totally overwhelmed."

That's not true, Ellis wanted to say. Even in the last resort, we stand a better than even chance. We have the ships and the guns to assault them, to herd them out of their formation, then to run them down and pour fire and brimstone into them one at a time with our singularity guns, blasting at close range until they're destroyed or sent running. But something stopped him;

Conroy Lubbock had closed his eyes as if shutting out a terrifying vision of the future. Hawken began to speak, his own eyes never once meeting Ellis's.

"I had hoped to avoid this, Ellis, but events have caught up with us. Your brother is alive—"

The room closed in around him.

"—Duval's on Seoul. He's making singularity guns for Baron Harumi."

"No! God, no!" Ellis was paralysed by shock. He felt his face drain, and he buried it in his hands, the throes of anguish rushing through him. Despite the cool currents drawn across the room by the aircon, the atmosphere was suddenly too cloying to breathe. His mind filled with a hundred knotted questions, but none became clear enough to ask.

"I didn't know the whole truth before." Hawken's words were hurried, as he fell over himself to get them out. "I knew that Duval was alive. That he had escaped the *kempei*. That he had somehow got to Seoul. He married, has a son. He's been working for my Seoul contact, the man who was the center of our intelligence network in Korea. You remember Choi Ki Won, Ellis? The same man who helped us when we put down on Cheju Do aboard the *Richard M*? He was fired and went to Seoul. He became my business contact in the days of Free Korea, and when Yamato began to threaten he became an admirable spy and crucial to our efforts there. He was such a key man that I didn't dare risk his life. Duval's life depended on that. You understand me, Ellis? I didn't dare risk him. Not even to you."

Ellis's mind swam in the welter of words as he struggled to comprehend. "Then Duval's no traitor . . . If he's working for you, he's no traitor. Yet . . . yet you say he's making singularity guns for Yamato? I don't understand."

"Duval was caught. Or gave himself up. Choi's dead and we have only a hazy report of events, but at least we know he's in Baron Harumi's possession and that Yamato's using him."

Ellis gasped. Then Conroy Lubbock was right! With singularity guns the invasion would be impossible to stop at the Boundary. Suddenly the sight of Hawken's synthetic dog snapping at the maintenance drone came to him. The electrostatic sparks had made it yelp . . .

He heard the sound of footsteps in the corridor. Conroy Lubbock told the Marine guard to enter; he led two oriental women in. One was of middle age and graying, shrewd-eyed but puffy-faced with crying. She was dressed in a long, dark cloak that completely enclosed her. The other who followed was taller and some fifteen years younger. A woman in her prime, beautiful with high cheeks and olive skin, and samurai pride shining in her face.

Ellis swallowed involuntarily as he rose from his seat to greet her.

"Ellis, this is your brother's wife."

38

They walked like trespassers through the banqueting hall, where the walls were covered in rich oil paintings in bright, gorgeous colors of gold and crimson and verdant green. The paintings were seven in number, each six feet tall and ten or fifteen yards long, big enough to clothe the entire room. They were from the Old Earth White House, from the days when Old Earth had been consumed by the fad for the enigmatic Symbolist school. They had been hung here to show visiting ambassadors that people who performed Amerikan high politics could match any of the courtly convolutions of Yamato or Chung Kuo when it came to metaphorical double-talking.

"Wait here, Captain," Cassabian told him. Ellis thought of the complex web that had brought him back here to the White House, and the irony of his position. Since Lucia Henry's execution, Conroy Lubbock had been banished from the President's apartments. Alia's public fury had been like hell's furnaces. So totally had she dissociated herself from those who had "maneuvered" her into signing Lucia's death warrant that she would see neither Conroy Lubbock nor her principal advisors. At least Cassabian had had the presence of mind to temporarily install the eminently expandable Jolen Davison as secretary in his place, and a diplomatic ailment had meant that it was Davison and not he who had brought the death warrant from the President. Davison had become the scapegoat and had gone to Camp Worth.

"She's coming," Cassabian whispered, seizing his arm and turning his back to the Marine guards. "Remember, she's read the letter, but your meeting is not arranged; it must seem coincidental. Now I've got to leave you to it."

He hurried away, leaving Ellis bare seconds to compose himself. This is the crux, Ellis told himself, steeling his nerve. That the future could depend so completely on this carefully arranged chance meeting appalled him.

"Why me?" he had asked Cassabian.

"Why? Because it's your plan. You'll have to plead for it, and as eloquently as you can."

"But what about Hawken? Oujuku? The Navy admirals?"

Cassabian had shook his head. "The Navy is too closely tied in with Conroy Lubbock, Hawken likewise. And John's brusque charm has little appeal to her after his financial failure, even less to the ambassadors who know his reputation."

"But I'm no statesman," he had said. "She won't talk to me."

"Oh, you underestimate her, Ellis. She certainly remembers you. You never once failed her and—she likes you."

The approaching commotion in the corridor grew louder, then all at once the hairs stood up on Ellis's neck as Marine guards snapped to attention and aides began spilling into the hall.

The President appeared. Her incredible presence seemed to fill the entire place. Then she paused, and her retinue stepped back, parting so as not to crowd her.

She had seen him.

Immediately he took off his cap and nodded, sweat trickling down his back, staring fixedly at the floor until she came over to him.

"Who're you?"

He looked up but he was unable to meet her eye.

"I asked you who you are?"

"I . . ." he stammered. "I'm . . . my name's Ellis Straker."

"Ellis Straker?" She aimed a long finger at him. "I remember you. Aren't you the privateer who took a brotherly interest in Conroy's daughter?"

A ripple of laughter passed through the assembly.

"All right, then, Ellis Straker, what are you doing in here? What do you want?" Her voice was a stiletto.

His heart raced, hating the jokes she was making at his expense. He looked to the wall and back, knowing he was lost. "I was . . . I was inspecting—admiring—the fineness of your Old Earth paintings, Miz President."

"Yes?" Then she asked him sharply, "And how do you like them, Captain Straker?"

"Oh, they're real pretty, Miz President."

She turned suddenly, her eyes searching his face for embarrassment. Her aides were at her elbow, mischievously watching him. "Oh? And which one's your favorite?"

Ellis cleared his throat and looked quickly at the two that hung closest, entitled "Music" and "Dancing," subjects dear to the President's heart. He rejected them. You must have permission to embark, a voice told him. Impress her now and the presidential warrant to cruise beyond the Boundary could be in your fist by tonight. But take care! She's a difficult one to steer. A wrong move could cost you the chance you've been aching to take.

"Let me see . . ."

"Stand back! Give the captain a little room!" one of the aides said.

Alia noticed his eyes dwell briefly on the hanging of "The Deadly Sins." He seemed not to approve of it, still less of "The Triumph of Time over Fame." "The Triumph of Fame over Death" and "Hannibal" were quickly glanced over.

"Don't you think this is the finest one, Captain?"

She opened her hand at "The Triumph of Death over Chastity." The significance of it, as of them all, was clear to him. Alia Kane would never marry Prince Pi Wu, nor anyone: she would die a spinster. She watched his forehead furrow, his shaggy blond brows knit over the choice.

"To my mind, Miz President, the subject hasn't got much appeal."

"Is it the same mind that imagines the shape of our Navy? And fantasies the future of Amerika on my behalf?"

She noticed his hands flex as Conroy Lubbock's did when he was in combat with any problem. He was simmering now under the eyes of the dozen aides, men and women experienced in the ways and word games of high politics. They knew how suddenly a pleasant stroll through the White House in the company of their President could turn into a penetrating cross-examination of political motive and loyalty. Ellis was obliged to answer.

"If you mean that our fighting ships are now the envy of Known Space, I guess you're right. I've worked to improve them. As for the fine arts, well, I don't understand too much about that, but I would say that there are two paintings here that I like."

She heard an aide whisper to her; the man's piercing blue eyes glittered and she took his suggestion.

"Let me guess your choice."

Ellis watched stricken with paralysis as the President walked the length of the room, her heels echoing on the hard polished floor, filling the high ceiling with their sound. She paused and paused again, then returned, facing him with ice-green eyes that stabbed through to his soul. The russet fire of her hair blazed in tight curls around her head and her slim hand fingered a great emerald pendant that hung from her neck on a chain of worked platinium. He saw that it was the finest of those he had given to Cassabian to present to her as a Christmas gift so long ago. Then it had seemed he and his crew might be shoveled into the diplomatic fires that burned between Amerika and Yamato, and the gift had been a symbolic monument. He had made a pact with a she-devil. The cold fire in the massive jewel exactly matched the meson flame in her eyes.

"No," she said. "I can't guess."

The aides were frozen like statuary. They saw the way she looked at him and recognised the ominous tone in the President's suddenly coy perplexity.

"Captain Straker, I can't see at all what you have in mind. That worries me greatly. Tell me, do you like *this* one best?"

She stretched a bony finger at the painting entitled "Dancing."

Holding himself tall he said politely, "No, Miz President. I don't."

She drew back her hand, suddenly irritable. "Then which?"

Ellis took a pace back and turned. He strode boldly to stand before "The Triumph of Fame over Death." Deliberately he turned his back on it, then pointed across the hall to the painting depicting Hannibal bringing the spoils of Cannae to Carthage.

"With your permission, Miz President, I'll tell you straight. That's my favorite."

The aides drew breath as one, then there was silence. The

canvas depicted the legendary general of far antiquity in the glory of his victory over the Roman legions. Everyone present knew that at Cannae Hannibal had destroyed the power of the greatest empire of the classical world, annihilating an army of fifty thousand men and laying bare the defenseless heart of Rome. The meaning was clear.

The President, standing back by her stony retinue, threw wide her arms and tossed her head. The stridor of her laugh tore through the hall.

"Captain Straker! That's good. Very good. You'll have my blessing for it—and your ships."

The presidential party swept on, following Alia Kane from the hall, leaving Ellis to stand alone, watched balefully by a pair of rod-straight Marine guards. They held their blasters stiffly at quarters.

As soon as the great doors banged shut he punched the air and whooped like a Texan.

39

SEOUL

As he watched the elite of Yamato's military hierarchy enter the citadel and make their way up the steep steps toward the council chamber, Katsumi thought of the singularity gun maker and felt a powerful thrill of anticipation run through him. Tonight a glorious war would be made in the blaze of a thousand torches. Here, inside the closed and heavily guarded fortress that dominated Korea's capital, a heavenly rage would be formally launched at the impure heart of Amerika. It was good to be alive now that the pact was sealed. He felt the strength that only warriors know, the intoxicating taste of best-quality White Heron *sake*, and he knew that his own future, Nishima-sama's future, all of Known Space's future, depended upon a decision as intricately complex as the placing down of a *go* stone.

Whichever way the stone was placed, he knew, the killing play would be Duval Straker, coupled with the solemn and murderous agreement he had made with Lord Nishima only twenty-four hours ago. War was opportunity and war was glory, that's what Nishima-sama had said. In war ambitious men were noticed—especially those fortunate enough to be distinguished within sight of their commanders. And those so distinguished became, in time, commanders themselves. That was the Way; the Way as it had always been. The Way of the Warrior.

That's why tonight is the real beginning, he thought. Tonight the armies of white stones and black stones will clash, and I, Urawa no Hasegawa Katsumi, will be privileged to see the confrontation. I am no longer a young man. This is my last chance for true recognition. And if the groups Nishima constructs do not turn out well, then I shall, as agreed, overturn the board and scatter the stones in the six cardinal directions!

Katsumi followed as they took their appointed places along the giant, low map visualiser table. Baron Harumi knelt cross-legged at the head, his commanders, accompanied by their *hatamoto*, ranked to right and left. On the tatami around this board was gathered the greatest concentration of samurai chivalry since Hainan: Aoki Zengo, Baron Harumi's second-in-command, was paired with Admiral Kurita Imari. The two Yamaguchi admirals, Kofuji and Matsumoto, cousins who hated each other, were discreetly placed at opposite ends of the position plan, separated by General Cho and General Sumita. Minami Yoriyasu and General Yonai faced them. Nishima Jun knelt in the middle, facing General Uehara, his electric-blue formal attire provocatively woven with the ring-dragonfly symbol of Yamato.

All were distinguished men, men of proud accomplishment and prouder bearing. All wore the badges of their rank and the honors of past victories about them, and the sign of their high station burned as much in their faces as on their armor. These were the custodians of armies and navies that had fought victoriously for the Emperor for a hundred years and who now ruled, at the command of the gods, virtually the whole of the Two Sectors.

The hall echoed into silence as they settled to business. The admiral astonished them by drawing out his sword, an incredibly fine blade made by the Old Earth smith Munechika. It was said that the gods allowed the swordsmiths to make only one sword in a thousand years as perfect as this, a sword that never lost its suppleness or its cut and never rusted. The intricate *nioi* patterning that covered the blade testified that this was Mutsuhito's priceless personal gift to his shogun.

"This meeting is long overdue," Baron Harumi told them, his voice a low growl. "His Imperial Majesty is growing tired of delay. He will bear no more excuses. And now there is another reason why we must decide finally on the battle order of the *kaigun*. It has been communicated to me tonight that His Imperial Majesty's agents in Lincoln have reported a great crime. The Amerikan usurper has executed the rightful leader, Lucia Henry."

The whole assembly knelt in stunned silence while Baron Harumi went on. "Therefore, before I close proceedings tonight you shall know my decision regarding the ordering of the fleet. First, though, hear me out on the generalities of the matter."

Despite his shock at the news of Lucia Henry's death, Nishima smiled inwardly, knowing that his appointment as generalissimo of the planetary invasion troops was virtually assured. The order was as good as signed by the Emperor himself. *The Henry woman's death changes nothing*, he thought. *Alia Kane has merely set a useful precedent for her own execution.*

"Each of you will have the opportunity to contribute your thoughts in due course." Baron Harumi looked from face to face as he spoke, his pained eyes and the way his fingers gripped his leg tightly just above the knee the only evidence of his unremitting physical discomfort. He bent over the visualiser campaign maps, touching the images with the tip of his sword.

"My intention is to assemble all nine squadrons of ships here at Seoul. As soon as conditions permit we shall venture along the Seoul chain, keeping at all times within formation, until we enter Hawaii. Then we shall strike out across the Amerikan Boundary, taking advantage of the excellent Index, on a course that will take us to the nexus of the Floating World, here, ten light-years from the Amerikan system of Kalifornia II. This means we will enter the Sector as far along the radius as possible and then track along that chain. The purpose, of course, is to terrorise the Sector. Every planet, every city, every apron, and every orbital station along the entire flank of Amerika shall see what a mass of arms is thrown against them. Every man, woman, and child will know intimately the strength of Yamato resolve, and how useless it would be to contemplate opposition."

The assembly began to nod, relishing Baron Harumi's plan. All without exception were absorbed by the baron's words and felt privileged to hear so accomplished a master strategist expound his thoughts. "It is my intention to catch the western squadron of the Amerikan fleet in its bolt hole of Carolina. If it is there, we shall enter and destroy it. Then we shall cruise immediately to the nexus of the Lone Pine, here, midway along Amerika's main internal chain. There, at Massachusetts, I shall land a force of six hundred thousand troops to establish a beachhead, occupy the system, and obliterate all resistance. With the eastern aprons in our hands the main landing will be made. Our main army will be able to disembark with little opposition and begin their thrust across the Red Plains chain towards Liberty." He paused, looking around the table appraisingly. "As soon as this force is landed the fleet will light out again and continue to the Marshalls, where a second force under the command of General Yamaguchi will be embarked. There our task will be to screen his transports as they cross the Boundary, and run escort from Korea to the three Kalifornias. Thus, by the time Yamaguchi lands in the Liberty system, we will have their capital world between hammer and anvil, ready for the crushing. Then and only then will our fleet engage the remains of the Amerikan Navy."

Baron Harumi watched their enthusiasm rise. He quieted them, then added, "I call upon General Uehara to explain in detail how his army will approach Lincoln and lure the Amerikan planetary forces into direct confrontation."

Nishima stared, totally unable to believe what he had just heard. Uehara's army? Uehara, that oily-haired upstart? But *I'm* to command the landing force on Liberty. The Emperor himself has said so! Beside him Katsumi paled. The stone had been played. And the group had proved to be one-eyed—as dead as if they had been played by an amateur. Never mind, he told himself. We still have *sente*. We still have the initiative—Duval Straker.

General Uehara, grizzled and meticulously formal and supremely self-confident, rose to his feet and bowed. His voice was steely. "Honorable Lords, we would do well to remember that the Amerikans have suffered no real external threat since the creation of Known Space over four hundred years ago. And whereas our troops have yearly hardened themselves against the Korean rebels, there has been little action to exercise the Amerikans for better than half a century. Even now they possess no satisfactory army; just a rabble of untrained levies who hardly know one end of a blaster from the other. Our samurai infantry will easily push them aside as I approach Lincoln from the southwest of the main continent.'' He called a detailed map of northern Liberty in front of them. ''My first objectives will be to seize and destroy the fleet aprons of Harrisburg, Philadelphia, and Baltimore, and to raze the cities in the region between. As you can see, all these targets are conveniently north of the equator and should pose no problem to a force approaching from a high polar orbit. At the same time our transports will cross the Liberty nexus here and descend directly upon the impure heart of Lincoln itself. By the time that city's buildings are burning, our main infantry force will have straddled the western continent. If it is found that the usurper has fled to Detroit, this will have driven a wedge between her and Lincoln; if not, she will be prevented from finding refuge there. Simultaneously a second force will strike east to cut off the northern paths of retreat from the city before turning south to close on it. It is said that much of Lincoln has overflowed its old defenses, and the manner in which our troops acquit themselves among the hovels and Christian temples there will continue the baron's example in Harrisburg. Alia Kane must be pinned down in the southeast, for then all resistance will collapse. At all costs, she must be prevented from getting offplanet.''

Minami Yoriasu, a highly experienced commander who had served in the Hainan campaign, had been listening coolly. He now offered his objection. ''What if the Amerikan fleet is blocking the Lone Pine when we come upon it?''

''What of it?'' Baron Harumi asked.

''Shouldn't we bring them to battle as soon as possible, Baron-sama?''

''No. In that case we shall cruise immediately for the Red Plains.''

''Surely we would have better strength to overwhelm them if we engaged them *before* disembarking our troops?''

Suddenly everyone was speaking and Baron Harumi waved

his sword flat across the visualiser image to halt the discussion. "You forget that this is a joint operation with General Yamaguchi's army. If we are able to land a single force of five hundred thousand men on Liberty, Amerika will be ours. Nothing there can withstand one Yamato army of that strength, let alone two. The disembarkation *must* remain our priority."

Aoki Zengo nodded in agreement. "It makes sense. Why attack the Amerikan fleet when we can bypass it? They will not dare approach us so long as we maintain order and keep together. I say we follow Uehara-san's plan to the letter."

The young General Cho spoke up cautiously. "We must not underestimate the power of Amerikan naval weaponry, Baron. It was my father who brought His Imperial Majesty to Amerika thirty or more years ago, and he was impressed by their fleet even then."

General Sumita, in his sixties but as dashing as Uehara—it was he who had captured the Chinese flagship at Hainan—spoke next, his tone scathing, dismissive. "Their fleet has long since moldered away. And the present one has been wasted by the miserly policies of the woman they call President—it's only half the strength it was then! They're all pirates with pirate minds and no understanding of organisation. What do they know about the proper maintenance of a fleet?"

More nods of agreement were exchanged, then General Cho put in keenly, "I agree. A landing along the Red Plains is repeating history. That's the chain our Emperor traveled when he went into Amerika. Our troops will think that a good omen for success. Not that we need to depend on omens."

"May we consider what happens if the Amerikan fleet launches an all-out assault on us?" Aoki asked Baron Harumi.

Baron Harumi smiled, pleased to deal with the question. He understood the apprehension that frothed just beneath the surface in all of them. It was the unspoken horror of the Black Dragon and his fellow privateers that now permeated the whole of Yamato. Baron Harumi knew that their terrifying reputation was justly deserved. The damage they had inflicted on Yamato pride during their assaults had been out of all proportion to the actual physical destruction they had wrought. The baron saw his chance to allay his subordinates' fears; he had conceived a strategy that would cope with any attacker.

"If that happens," he said, his hands moving up and apart in a sweeping circle, "we shall adopt this formation. It's a shape we've all seen on the Imperial standards at Hainan—the radiant sun. When held tight, the Hakon Effect works to add the shield defenses of our ships. With hundreds of ships, an impregnable defensive formation will be formed! Our globe ships and transports in the middle, protected by an impenetrable wall of warships at the outside.''

Nishima boiled as he watched Baron Harumi explain the tactics. The flush of pride he had felt at the prospect of being appointed Mutsuhito's generalissimo had been obliterated at a word from the baron. Over the months he had come to understand that Baron Harumi's position was absolutely central. *The baron dares to overrule the Emperor himself on strategic matters and to direct the* kaigun *as his own,* he thought angrily. *All major decisions are being taken by him alone, and how these naval men defer to him! Uehara too—doubtless because he knows he's going to get his own way. But that's going to change. Oh, yes, that's certainly going to change.*

His eyes strayed to Katsumi, suspecting his aide could almost read his mind.

"I sympathise, of course, sir," Katsumi had said the night the singularity gun maker had fallen into their hands. "But surely it's Baron Harumi's prerogative to shape the enterprise as he sees fit.''

"Unfortunately, yes. But with Duval Straker in our possession once more we can arm the *kaigun* as it should be armed. Think about it. You've seen how tired and drawn Baron Harumi looks. It's clear he overexerts himself. He's starting to make bad decisions. Naturally I've mentioned it to the Emperor in my dispatches.''

Katsumi's reply had lacked conviction. "But the Emperor will not tolerate any postponement. I understand he's writing to Baron Harumi daily urging him to launch the invasion.''

"I have heard that the sex disease that afflicts Harumi-sama is going to kill him within the year," Fumiko had said balefully. She hated Seoul as she had hated Sado, and Baron Harumi had become for her the living reason for her forced removal from Kyoto and for all her discomfitures. "Perhaps the baron can be persuaded to exert himself even more. After all, he's not long for this life. The Emperor has never liked stubborn men, men who oppose his will. Once you remove him, you can use the

Amerikan to your own benefit at last—like you always wanted to.''

"He's unimportant," Nishima had lied. "And Harumi-sama is strong enough to see the invasion out. The Emperor thinks he needs him.''

"Well, you can always help his decline a little," she had jibed. "That's one thing I know you can do.''

He had given her a daggering look then and tried to gloss over her words, but they had obviously registered with Katsumi, so he had switched his plan, daringly laying out his most secret thoughts in a last bid.

"Suppose Baron Harumi does die before the attack can be launched," he had said slyly. "Have you considered that?''

Katsumi had pondered. "The Emperor will have to appoint someone else. Someone in favor and in full health, someone capable of becoming commander in chief, of becoming shogun.''

Nishima had smiled then. "So who do you imagine he'll promote?''

"Obviously, Aoki-sama. He's second-in-command.''

"No, no. That won't happen, Katsumi. He's old, and he's too much Baron Harumi's man. With the baron dead he'd be like a geisha without a mama-san. And I know that the Emperor doesn't approve of him.''

"Then the choice will be between Admiral Kurita and Admiral Kofuji—and, of course, yourself, Lord.''

"Quite so. *Quite so.* Therefore we must take care to foster the Emperor's goodwill. We must demonstrate our loyalty and our capability. What do you suggest, Katsumi-san? You have an organizer's mind. What case can we make for ourselves?''

Katsumi had grimaced. "Lord, at the moment it's a case of great haste and small speed. The operation is a logistic shambles. Some ships are half manned while others have twice what they need. Some crews are incompetent, others have experienced men in superabundance. And the apportioning of weaponry is ludicrous! There's simply not enough heavy beam weapons to go around, and even at this rate we'll have no more than thirty tubes per gun. Of course, we still have the Amerikan. Perhaps it's time to use him.''

"Yes. How many singularity guns can he make for us between now and our departure?''

As Katsumi made his calculations Nishima's thoughts had

dwelt on Kurita. What of Kurita? What Katsumi said is true. The man's a formidable nexus fleet commander, renowned for his service to the Emperor. He's from much the same mold as Baron Harumi himself. I don't fully know how the Emperor regards him, but whatever his standing I can undermine him. Mutsuhito won't want his invasion commanded by a man whose adherence to the Way is in doubt, a man who once stooped to blackmailing a *metsuke*. He accused Fukuda Ikku of possession by demons, isn't that what his enemies always maintained and were prepared to swear to? No, Kurita should be no obstacle at all to me.

"At least fifty, Excellency. Though that will mean purchasing more argentium to energise them."

"Then I'll ask for a hundred. Prepare a budget for that. The expense of the invasion has already amounted to four years' contributions of Sado argentium. A little more won't hurt the Emperor. He's resolved on his great undertaking whatever the cost."

"Couldn't you write to him and beg him to come to Seoul himself?"

"Why should I do that?" Nishima had asked, surprised at Katsumi's naiveté. While the Emperor remained on Kyoto, writing despatches to his nephew in Korea, to his ambassadors everywhere and to Baron Harumi, all was safe. "No, Katsumi, that the Emperor never leaves the Imperial Court is our greatest strength. He's a virtual recluse, and that's good, because the last thing we want is his meddling here. This way, I describe everything that happens in Seoul and he has no choice but to believe what I say. That's power." He had sipped at his *choko* of *sake* then, pleased at the way events were leading. "You may be right about our weapon-maker. Perhaps now the time is right to use him against Baron Harumi. But one thing still puzzles me. Why did he give himself to you, Katsumi?"

He had asked himself the same question daily since Duval Straker was first taken, and the answer Katsumi had given then had stayed with him.

"I don't know, Lord. He seemed to think we were bound to find him sooner or later. Of course, I had him Probed—"

"You had him Probed?"

"I wanted to discover what he had done with my sister, Excellency."

"I hope you didn't damage him."

Katsumi had picked off his sandal, pulling at his toes one at a time in his maddening way. "Duval Straker was temporarily rendered half conscious, and it was then that he spoke of Michie-san. He seemed to be worried about her. Perhaps he thought we had taken her. I wanted to discover where she was."

"And did you?"

"Not yet, Lord."

"No more Probings. That's an order. I'm only interested in his skills. He's a very rare commodity. Don't jeopardise him because of some whim about your sister."

"Yes, Lord."

That had been months ago, and since then, Duval had been confined in secret until the right time to produce him arrived. To have produced him sooner would have given him to Baron Harumi. He was sure of that.

"I still can't explain why he came to us, Lord," Katsumi said. "Perhaps he's telling the truth, that he just wants a sum of credit. Who can say how the minds of barbarians work?"

Nishima had grinned then, pleased at the miraculous gift. "Haven't I always forgiven you your sins, Katsumi-san? I didn't punish you as some might have done after you mislaid him on Sado. You see how the gods reward the virtuous?"

Katsumi's silence had made him think of the night they had put the old man to death. There had always been a cruel streak in Katsumi. Though Wataru Hoshino had been the mainstay of his plan to allow Duval Straker to escape crucifixion, he had turned viciously on the old man when the plan went wrong. He had taken him to the rendezvous outside Kanazawa, but when the wait had turned out to be fruitless Katsumi had stroked his sword through the old man's neck, thereby satisfying, he had said later, Hoshino's wish to die as a soldier. After that, despite intense searches by both the secular authorities and the *kempei*, they had never discovered any trace of Katsumi-san's bitch of a sister, or of the Amerikan. Of course, reports had been many: Guam, the Marshalls, Korea, even tales of a nexus wreck and one of escape to Amerika, but there had never been any hard evidence. Until his reappearance. It was amazing. Perhaps too amazing. Curious that he should offer himself like that at such a time. What can he want? Still, he's too precious a resource to have Katsumi snuff out in a rage.

"Yes, you must treat Duval Straker with care," Nishima had said, leaning back against his cushions. "Are you still loyal to me, Katsumi-san?"

Unhesitatingly, "Yes, Lord."

"And to the Emperor?"

This time Katsumi had paused, evaluating the trap. "Without reservation, Lord."

"I wonder." Nishima had stood up, recklessly abandoning himself to the idea in his mind. "Yes, I wonder. What would you do if I told you the Emperor's patience with Baron Harumi is at an end? That he wants the shogun dead? And that I had offered your name as a mark of your fealty to him?"

What indeed, he thought, relishing again the way Katsumi's jaw had fallen at that. He rubbed his palms together unobtrusively, his mind suddenly alerted to Baron Harumi and to the present by the striking of the nearby shrine's great bell.

Nishima looked around the assembled Council of War, then studied the Baron closely. Yes, I'm still not sure about you. They say your blood's poisoned by the sex disease and you'll be a dead man soon, but will you be a dead man soon enough? On the other hand I've always been able to rely on Katsumi. He won't take my word alone, but he's stupid enough to have no qualms about disposing of you once I show him the correspondence I've received from the Imperial Court.

Mutsuhito's last dispatch was the most urgent yet, complaining of Baron Harumi's sloth. In it the Emperor had asked to be advised minutely of the state of readiness of the invasion fleet, to have a detailed evaluation of the baron's intentions and a list of proposals for how Baron Harumi's difficulties might be eliminated. The tone of the letter had been characteristically ambiguous, and Mutsuhito's dispatches had always been capable of two or more quite separate readings.

Yes, he thought, stirring from his smoldering reverie, just as I was used by Prince Sekigahara to murder Mutsuhito's lunatic son, so I will use Katsumi to murder Baron Harumi.

The invasion of his thoughts was sudden and unexpected. "What have you to say, Nishima-san?"

"Lord Harumi?"

Harumi fixed him with the stare for which he was famed. "You seem to be anxious to say something."

Languidly Nishima knelt up straighter and made his bow. "I

should like to underline the need for proper armament. It is my belief that we should wait until we are able to ship singularity guns. Half the research establishments of the Two Sectors have donated their best minds. It would be an insult to the Emperor to depart before we had the means to—''

Baron Harumi's eyes sheered away arrogantly. "Yes, I was forgetting. You're an expert on how ships may be properly armed to oppose the Amerikans."

General Uehara saw his opportunity and spoke. "Surely more important than that is a quick and decisive infantry campaign. Naturally that will depend on quick departure. What date can we now expect to light out from Seoul?"

"Patience, Uehara-san, you'll be at them soon enough," Baron Harumi assured him, still ruffled by Nishima's obstructive attitude. "Your men will fight soon. We shall depart in the fifth month, the sixth at the latest. Six weeks after we cross the Boundary you'll be standing on the ramparts of Lincoln's fortifications and the next day drinking green tea in the ruins of the White House. I can promise you that."

"Excuse me, but is that possible?" Kurita asked, knowing also that Mutsuhito was growing increasingly irate at the delay. "Are we really able to ready the fleet by then? That's only eight weeks away."

The baron drew himself up. "We could leave now if I chose to order it." Kurita bit his tongue, and Baron Harumi continued. "I'm only waiting for the squadron now assembling at Chongjin. As soon as that arrives we'll get under way."

"But we're still short of heavy beam weapons," General Cho said bluntly. "Nishima-san's quite right. It's something which needs to be rectified."

Baron Harumi's voice rose, something of the pent-up anger that had made him a living legend at the Imperial Court showing itself. "I can't agree. So long as we have sufficient firepower to keep the Amerikans at a distance we'll prevail."

"Excuse me, but does that mean you are prepared to gamble the whole invasion?" Nishima pressed. Immediately all eyes locked on him and he cloaked his following question in a mantle of lukewarm indifference. "Of course, I mean no disrespect, Baron-sama, but aren't you in your anxiety to light out jeopardising the entire operation? In my opinion it would be better to wait another month. We could still take Lincoln in the way you have planned, but our ships would contain armament lethal enough at shield range to destroy any ship they sent against us.''

Kurita said, ''Yes, most honorable Baron, what difference will another month make? Why must we light out by the sixth month?''

''Because the Emperor says we must!'' Baron Harumi rapped out furiously. ''And if we lose a few ships, so what? That's to be expected. We are samurai! Samurai with pride! Soldiers! Warriors! We know war means risk, but we are not cowards, we glory in it! Isn't that so?''

Some showed their approval, others bowed their heads wordlessly.

Baron Harumi looked hard at Nishima, imposing his will. ''Isn't that so, Lord Nishima?''

''Of course, most honorable Baron, it's just that—''

''That's right! There *are* no objections! And who says otherwise? We are Yamato's sons! We follow the Way. We know our duty! No man may tell us our business! No man may beat us down! No man. If the Emperor says we shall invade Amerika—*then we shall invade Amerika!*''

No one moved to Nishima's defense. Baron Harumi's eyes bulged with anger and the vein in his forehead stood out. His gaze dwelled upon them all in turn, finally falling on the man to his left. ''Admiral Kurita?''

Kurita hesitated, then said with cool courage, ''There may be some wisdom in what Nishima-san says, Baron. Several times the Yamato Guard has experienced the effect of these unstoppable Amerikan guns. At short range they can be devastating. However, I agree there's little to be gained by waiting. We may supply the whole fleet with singularity guns in three months' time, but by then the Index will probably have turned against us and we might be forced to wait another year—''

''That's not necessarily true,'' Nishima interrupted, racking Baron Harumi with yet another reason to delay. ''No one can predict the way the Index will move with certainty. I tell you that the weapons facility houses here on Seoul can be producing these incredible new guns, as good as Amerikan ones, in little more than a month from now.''

''Impossible!'' General Yonai retorted.

''*Sumi masen ga . . .* Is this true?''

''What are you talking about, Nishima-san?''

"Silence!" Baron Harumi's order stilled them. "In little more than a month from now we shall be cruising the nexus lanes, moving against Amerika. His Imperial Majesty has ordered it, and so it shall be. Now, Kurita, I want the battle order announced."

"Yes, Baron." Kurita bowed and began reading from Baron Harumi's notes. "The most honorable baron shall personally command the Yamashiro Squadron of fifteen nexus ships, ten of which shall be assault cruisers, supported by five transports. The flagship shall be the admiral's own *Ieyasu Tokugawa*, of twelve thousand tons, presently at Chongjin.

"The Kuzuke flotilla shall be commanded by General Cho: ten transports and four assault battlecraft, including the *Ieshige*.

"The Squadron of Shinano: General Sumita. Fourteen transports, two battle cruisers.

"The Bizen Squadron, ten transports and one globe ship, to be commanded by Lord Kinoshita.

"The Settsu Squadron of eleven transports, two battle cruisers: General Cho.

"And finally in the first battle line, the Shimofusa attack column, the ten globe ships of Admiral Matsumoto, who shall be aboard *Iemitsu*. Nishima-sama will travel aboard the *Takeda Shingen* with Aoki-sama."

There was a stirring and Baron Harumi examined each man for his reaction. Some had yet to be named, others would not be named at all. But the compromise had been the best he could work out, and though no one seemed to be fully satisfied, still none were resentful to the point of a public demonstration, not even that loathsome practitioner of dumb insolence, Nishima Jun.

"Are there any questions?"

"Do I have your permission to go ahead with my efforts to equip your ships with the new guns in case there should be any delay?" Nishima asked humbly, inwardly delighting at the way he was tearing Baron Harumi away from his best instincts and forcing him to publicly announce his intention to light out within the Emperor's ludicrously tight schedule.

"Nishima-san, as fifth in command, you must try to restrain yourself from tinkering with matters that do not concern you. Your task is to make certain General Uehara's troops are properly equipped and embarked on the appropriate transports at the right time. Nothing more.'' Baron Harumi regarded him briefly, as if drinking in his stony response, then he turned to Kurita. ''Read out the rest.''

''*Hai!* The second battle line is to be as follows . . .''

As Kurita spoke again, Nishima's eyes glowed like coals. He watched Baron Harumi's imperious gaze ripple across his subordinates.

''Does anyone have anything more to say? No? Good. I have one thing and one only.'' Baron Harumi paused for breath. ''I have commanded many expeditions and fought in numberless campaigns, and each battle has taught me that success in warfare is absolutely dependent on the correct functioning of the chain of command. Those beneath must take orders from those above. Immediately. Willingly. Without question. I have chosen you all after careful consideration. Some of you may not be happy with the gifts of duty I have bestowed, but whether you are or whether you are not, I solemnly ask each one of you to put your personal feelings aside and to pledge loyalty to me and to your Emperor.''

Admiral Matsumoto offered himself first. Then each in turn showed his humility and Baron Harumi went from man to man, to bow formally and receive his promise, face-to-face. Finally Nishima gave his word, seeing that the moving little ceremony was giving the admiral considerable satisfaction. ''You'll have all the support I can give you,'' he promised as they locked eyes, ''so long as you shall live.''

Baron Harumi took in Nishima's bow and nodded back to him stiffly. ''That is well. Now I call upon the priests to bless our enterprise.''

They knelt before the Shinto priest to dedicate their mission to the glory of the Emperor, the Son of Heaven, each man wearing a string of beads on his hands as he pressed them together in supplication. The priest's voice began to intone a droning chant, but he had been mouthing only moments when he was drowned out by shouting beyond the door. The remonstrations with the guard grew louder. Heads turned from the priest. Then the baron leapt to his feet.

''What's this?'' he raged, appalled at the intolerable intrusion. ''Who dares to disturb our prayers?''

The door burst in and a messenger, quaking with fear and white-faced from his tussle with the guards, ran to the baron.

He crashed down before him, offering up his communiqué in both hands.

"What is it?" Baron Harumi demanded.

"A terrible calamity, Lord!"

"Calamity?"

"It's the Black Dragon! His flagship and a great fleet of other ships! He's been sighted in the Chain of Heavenly Peace! He's tracking here, to Seoul, to destroy us!"

40

A SECRET RENDEZVOUS POINT IN THE NEUTRAL ZONE

In his old cabin aboard the *Constitution,* Ellis turned his ears to the familiar sounds of his ship. She was just like she had always been, kept trim by Johnson Curtis, her quartermaster, and Gedi Bolton, her captain. It would be magnificent to feel the command chair under his butt again, the ship's engines putting out two hundred gee, and her nose diving towards nexus Resh-Four-Nine. The promise he had sworn to Reba was suspended. Never more will I ride the nexi, he'd told her, but this was no recantation. She had released him from his vow. This once. As she'd known she must for the sake of his self-respect and his sanity.

He lay back, drifting as he tried to unravel the reasons why Hawken had kept Duval's existence in Seoul secret from him for so long, only to reveal it once the mission to shatter the Emperor's shipping in the Korean aprons looked certain.

With foreboding he called up the file of sealed orders from his chart organiser and peered into the screen at the locked pages as if trying to divine their significance. Today was the day that the files would lose their classified seal. The day they came into the Chain of Heavenly Peace, the main nexus route to Seoul. He saw the seals blip off the documents, but he did not open them. Opening sealed orders was an admiral's duty. And John was the admiral.

He looked down at the data the Yamato woman had given to Lubbock. She had said it was computed by Duval's own efforts, that he had made this detailed survey of the Seoul astromechanical approaches and defenses himself. Could this really have been compiled by Duval?

There were two injects, the main transport orbits that ran over the poles, and the high equatorial zone stacking-lane, crammed with standing satellites and way stations, which was treacherous and monstrously protected. The Seoul City apron itself was patrolled by a squadron of fast, armed air-cars, and across the whole stretch there were fortresses and beam weapon batteries that made entry impossible to any enemy. But what was the plan? And what about the promise he had made to Lubbock? The news that Duval was thought to be arming the Yamato fleet troubled him. He knew that with singularity technology an invasion of Amerika must surely succeed.

It was five seconds to one UT. He counted them down and —*thunk!*—the engines cut out and whined down and the compensators switched into free-fall mode, maintaining one gee smoothly. With his peace unsettled he scrolled the data and went up to the bridge, where his ensign waited. They went to the shuttle deck. The new craft was fast, his pilots happy to show him what they could do, and within the hour he was walking along the umbilicus of Oujuku's *Kalifornia*.

Oujuku had been appointed admiral with Nikolai Belkov his vice-admiral, just as Lubbock had wanted. Hawken had explained that Belkov was there to conveniently remove him from Liberty and so part him from the mischief he was planning. He had said that the sealed orders would explain the rest.

"So you persuaded the President that Rome was there for the taking?" Oujuku had roared gleefully on Ellis's arrival at Harrisburg after gaining the presidential warrant to mount the preemptive strike. "I hope you didn't tell her we'd do it with elephants!"

Ellis had grinned back. "I promised her we'd stomp on his shipping."

"Okeh!"

The Harrisburg terminal was heaving with crew who had

waited for this day. Since getting down from his air-car Ellis had met countless ghosts from his past: Cornelius the Irishman had come down with Captain Glass and Tom Brophy the Texan, whose own ship was renamed the *Kiss My Ass*. Nowell the gunner was there, and he saw an oriental face grinning from the mass, Cao, a silex merchant and shipowner for the last ten years; he'd come from Phildelphia in his trader-warship to see what he could offer. There had been other people who had suffered with him on the Niigata apron, and many more who had shared the riches of the happy homecoming ten years on from it. Oujuku too had attracted his old adherents. There had been no shortage of experienced nexus rats to set against Yamato.

Then Oujuku had taken the warrant and read from it to the assembled crowd: "Whereas it has pleased the President of Amerika to grant to John Oujuku her commission as admiral, dated March fifteen, A.D. 2441, for an action to be carried out with a privateering force and four assault ships and two attack frigates of the Amerikan Navy . . ." And they had cheered.

The promise of the Navy's four ships had triggered the cautious stock market. Alia's presidential seal on the commission had been enough to demonstrate her approval. He had pointed out where it had been signed by a crew of financiers, investors, fund managers, bulls, and wolves—Cordell, Watts, Banning, the Boreman Corporation, Hugh Lee, Robert Flick Inc—all Ellis's mercantile acquaintances willing to venture a fiscal credit or two in hope of a profit. They had fitted up a fleet at the Newport News Hull Corporation hangars: on hardcopy, ten "armed merchantmen." In reality they were battle cruisers.

There was no point in keeping their intentions secret any longer. To loud acclaim he had offered a flourish to the broadcast cameras: "We're ordered to 'impeach the territories illegally claimed by Yamato, to distress His Imperial Majesty's nexus ships wherever we find them.' Now, what do you think of that, people?"

And during the cheers, privately, Oujuku had listened as Ellis had told him, "It's a free hand, John. A free hand at last. Much more than Lubbock would have gotten us."

"It's precisely what we needed."

"Cassabian warns that there's a snag to it."

"What?"

"Within the week Alia will tell Lubbock that she has changed her mind, and he'll send Jiro Ito here with a message to stop us."

Oujuku had turned at that. "*What?*"

"If we provoke a war, Amerika will get the blame. She must try to prevent us—*officially*. You see?"

The fullness of the plan dawned on Oujuku and he cackled, then he thundered. "We need two days more to light out, then two under acceleration before the comms are lagged a day late and the security frequencies are redshifted into twenty-one cm hydrogen background. We can always have a malfunction at ground base. I'll send Abee Harris and Joni Fenner's cousin up to Fort Bush. They're incompetent enough to detain anyone."

Ellis had nodded approvingly. "And there's this: the comms vessel that delivers presidential dispatches, the one that'll be sent with the orders to recall us if a message fails, is the *Birmingham*."

"Yeah? So?"

"So her pilot is Jos Hawken's son."

"Oh, you're a clever man, Ellis! A real clever man!"

So they had left Harrisburg on April Fool's Day, streaming exhaust and blue fire across the waters, bristling with arms and crew, sixteen assault ships and seven frigates, all raring to show Yamato who they were.

Oujuku met them as they came aboard the *Kalifornia*. Though all of them thought Seoul was their target, none except Ellis knew their actual destination.

Nikolai Belkov, corpulent, unhappy at the indignity of having a privateer seven years his junior to command him, coming from the *Arizona*; Kent Fenner, Oujuku's man, a good astrogator and one who had been there during the last attack on the Home Worlds; Hal Bel, discreet, honest, and efficient; and Ellis Straker himself.

As usual, Oujuku let them have their way, listening quietly, then Belkov gave his reasons why Seoul was an impossible objective.

At length Oujuku broke his silence. "I agree," he said simply. "Which is why we're not going to try it."

"Not try it?" Hamilton said, shocked to his boots. "But I thought you said that . . ."

"You heard me well enough. I said we'd hunt down Baron Harumi's flagship, the *Ieyasu Tokugawa*. It's equipping right now with the second force at Chongjin."

THE CHONGJIN SYSTEM

At three hours, relativistically corrected UT, just after local noon, on Wednesday, the nineteenth day of Universal April, they came upon the apron that basked in the fierce light of a blue giant midway between the Twenty Degree Worlds and the Korean border. The metropolis of Chongjin itself stood on a rocky island connected by a bridge to a long spit sweeping out from the mainland into a lime desert. The city overlooked the northern Outer Apron, but there was a second, Inner Apron, almost completely surrounded by terminal outworks, containing the military pads and the more secure zones within. It was from here that a vessel of Colonel Koizumi's ground defense squadron advanced to meet the leading ship of this unknown and unexpected flotilla.

That ship was the *Constitution* and Ellis sat in her command seat, exultant that he had had psi good enough to give them so high an Index on the last transit. As he watched the intercept aircraft come on, he tried to put out of his mind the terrifying instructions that had been contained in the sealed orders. At the breaking up of the captains' conference aboard the *Kalifornia*, Oujuku had punched up hardcopy and let him read it for himself. There were no orders, just a personal letter from Hawken, reminding him of his oath aboard the *Chesapeake* and of his promise to Lubbock. It had explained that Duval's work on the singularity guns at Seoul was now confirmed and that he must be stopped. Hawken had had the communication sealed for two reasons: firstly its secret nature, and secondly because he had wanted Ellis to consider it only when he was standing off the Seoul system. The request was that he bring Duval out, or if he could not, to honor his promise in full.

"What will you do?" Oujuku had asked him when they were alone.

"What can I do?"

"Hawken's right. Duval must be stopped."

He had groped for the answers. "But why me? Why his brother?"

"Because Hawken would rather you brought him away. And if any man can do that, you can."

"And if I can't?"

"You will."

But he had chosen to disregard the request. He had sensed some adroitness in Hawken's style, but he had known that he could not decide in a matter like this without deep meditation. So, for the first time in his life, he had thrown the burden up to psi, uncolored by his own desire. This time, the pure currents of chance would choose for him, and Ellis knew he would receive his answer as they passed into the system of Chongjin.

"Fire a warning over her," he told his gunner as the aircraft's spike drew dangerously close on the ranger. Two beams plumed the air on either side of her and he watched the sleek atmospheric craft sheer off. It looked like she had been expecting to challenge some harmless Korean merchantman; he imagined the panic that would ensue when ground control recovered from their surprise. As in the past, panic and John's fearsome reputation would be their best allies.

Behind, the Amerikan ships cruised on, passing through the dangerous high meson-flux levels of the lower atmosphere and closing on the planetary surface, and Ellis knew that the tactic of surprise must now give way to boldness. Almost as one the red-on-white stripes of the Navy ships broke out across the hulls, and as Ellis turned his eye once more on the apron he saw with disbelief that the squadron of ten defense craft was scrambling to meet them.

Their commander's mad to force an attack here, he thought, unable to understand what was going through Colonel Koizumi's mind. Doesn't he realize that his only advantage is speed? He can't prevent us from landing and we've beaten him once we set down. Ellis knew that had he been in charge of the interceptors, he would have sent them back to base and imposed heavy shielding to keep the Inner Apron secure, but the colonel seemed determined to prove his worth.

As Ellis watched through the panoramic bridge blisters, the interceptors appeared on visual and began to maneuver into attack formation, the classic low-level wedge that protected the flanks of the aircraft and made as small a target as possible for the beam weapon armament of the intruders as they swept into the attack. At near-ground level they could be lethal to ponderous merchantmen; their swift skimming made them a match for any nexus trade ship when it was below five thousand feet altitude, but here their show of strength was about to be wasted.

"Signal from the *Kalifornia*, sir!"

It was terse. The four Navy ships, having greatest armament, were to engage the interceptors, and Ellis was to penetrate the apron and lead the other ships in among the grounded Yamato fleet.

Ellis silently thanked the interceptor commander for his chance to lead the charge and thundered down onto the Outer Apron, under the batteries of the Chongjin terminal, steering his followers between two air-car lanes. Then his eyes lit at the sight that greeted them. Standing on the crete stackways were thirty-two ships of over ten thousand tons mass. These were the ones intended to be sent against Amerika, but there were thirty other ships, either tied down among a Medusa's head of umbilicus tubes or in various states of strip-down. Some were without engine cowls, others were in the middle of embarking ordnance or having alterations carried out on their internal structure.

"They're cutting their cables, trying to get them into the hangars," Hal Bel, his co-astrogator, shouted. "What'll we do?"

"What do you want to do?"

"*Hit them*," twenty voices told him.

"So who's stopping you?"

"*Aye, aye, sir!*"

At their backs Oujuku had engaged the interceptors, downing one and chasing the others away. Then the warships bent their noses south, overflying the panicking technicians who scattered like a nest of ants below. There, naked to their assault, stood rank upon rank of new ships, hooked up and helpless, without power or crews to work them, without shields to protect them or guns to return fire.

For the next three hours the entire Outer Apron was ransacked. Shuttles loaded with implacable prize-hungry Amerikans scoured the entire area, going from vessel to vessel in search of booty. Deserted by their crews, the Yamato ships were systematically looted and detonated until two hundred thousand tons mass of nexus shipping had been ruined. Only one ship defied them, a huge eighteen-thousand-ton merchantman, and they closed in on her like wolves, their singularities tearing her to pieces while the gunners who hacked her into Swiss cheese bemoaned the loss of her as a prize.

When night fell they congregated in the middle of the Outer Apron, out of danger from the heavy batteries who dared not fire on the circle of intact invasion ships that had been carefully left all around.

For some hours yet they would be safe from the massed land forces that were being defreezed, pouring to the defense of Chongjin. The apron was lit by the burning hulks that now littered the taxiways, and sporadic beamfire crackled from the batteries and towers that dotted the terminal. Oujuku called his captains to conference to consult them and get their opinions. Many of them had just doubled their personal fortunes and were willing to follow Oujuku into hell itself. But there was one dissenter.

"We've done enough here, and I say we get out while we still can," Belkov insisted.

Ellis, who disliked Belkov's manner, said nothing.

Oujuku's eyes narrowed, smelling fear and mutiny in Belkov's words. He said, "Our job here's only half finished."

"If the Index drops, we'll be trapped. Then the interceptors can come back and we'll be standing targets," Belkov said, speaking now in worried tones.

Oujuku's considered words cut at him. "There's a beginning to every enterprise, but it's the continuing of it to the end, until it's thoroughly finished, that really matters."

"You don't understand my objection."

Quietly: "Oh? Don't I?"

Belkov stirred himself. "Captain Oujuku, so far we've had good psi. We've bloodied Yamato's nose. We can't ask for more."

Ellis saw the dangerous light in Oujuku's eye, knowing very well his unwavering rule never to brook opposition from people he did not respect. Harvis Dowty had mutinied during the harassing of Yamato, and Oujuku had had Harvis Dowty put down.

"Let's forget about today. It's over, isn't it?" Oujuku asked with deceptive calm. "Let's think out our plans for tomorrow instead. Psi has no memory, as any dicer will tell you."

Belkov blustered, deceived by Oujuku's calm. "Do you intend to dice with all of us, then? I'd rather get offplanet. Quickly. Now. To retire victorious while we can. It's the only sane—"

"Shut your mouth!" Oujuku shouted. No one dared say a word. "You'll keep your mouth shut until I say you can speak. Okeh?"

"I protest!"

"Protest? *Protest?*"

Belkov's mouth tightened. "You're flouting my right to voice an opinion, and I'll report your disregard for naval procedures —"

"This is not a Navy operation, Mr. Belkov. This is a private quarrel between myself and the Emperor of Yamato, and you'd better tread carefully if you want to come away from it alive."

Belkov puffed and blew at that. The exchange had enraged him, but he backed away.

As they left the vicinity of the *Kalifornia*, Ellis warned Belkov against his course coldly.

"That was foolish, Mr. Belkov."

"But we've got to get out of here. All the treatises of naval warfare say—"

"Hang the treatises. You shouldn't upset John Oujuku, or he'll hang your ass on a meat hook—for a coward and a mutineer. He's the boss here, and you ought to remember that."

The rumors of the summary way Oujuku had dealt with the quarrelsome Harvis Dowty must have run through Belkov's mind.

"Captain Straker, I'm only here as an official observer. The VP sent me as a representative from the Navy. Some of those are our ships. I'm thinking of the good of the mission. If the Index drops—"

"Just do as you're told."

"You forget that I'm not just a mission investor. I hold a Navy rank of admiral and I'm second-in-command here!"

"Just do as you're told," Ellis repeated, his words hard as iron now. "You're scum, Belkov. John'll have no opposition from a man who misled us, *and who turned us against Jos Hawken as you did with your lies*. It was you and your cronies who were bleeding the Commission dry, putting crews at risk. We believe the punishment should fit the crime, is all."

"What do you mean?"

"Just that you can bet your life that wherever the fighting's thickest on this trip *you're* gonna be in the middle of it. Maybe that'll teach your fat ass some respect for the dirty end of policy."

At that, Belkov settled into silence until they regained his ship. Ellis saw the fear dance on his face. Sure, and piss blood, you fat-assed sonofabitch, he cursed silently. It's justice that you've been brought to book. You deserve the freezeeing John would give you if he could. Your government career is over. But it's a shame that you're completely right about what we should do. I agree that the Inner Apron is a dangerous trap and no place for us to hang around. In his desire to punish you, John has lost touch with his inner feelings, yep, and with his reason.

Ellis knew that the lure had been irresistible. Baron Harumi's own flagship, the *Ieyasu Tokugawa*, a great twelve-thousand-tonner, was parked at the end of the taxiway. He knew how the reports must have inflamed Oujuku's imagination, and now the argument with Belkov had driven him to a poor decision. As he climbed once more aboard the *Constitution* Ellis wondered if that was the answer he had been waiting for.

When the next day dawned, they went in against Baron Harumi's ship. A swarm of shuttles approached her, blasting their way aboard, storming the hapless vessel until she was taken. They overran her, stripped her, and burned her out, then they did the same to six other ships carrying holds packed with thousands of tons of refrigerant. His own eager crews lifted a quantity of plantinium from the last of their victims, and as they landed four big strange-looking security containers on the crete beside the *Constitution*, they asked him if they could use a singularity gun to shoot off the top of them.

He agreed and they blipped out the first two locks to fragments, but as the first lid was thrown back they found nothing but neatly folded *komuso* monks' kimonos and woven baskets.

"What the . . . that's no prize!"

"It's all basket-head trappings!"

"Worth nothing! Torch it!"

"Naw! Leave it to rot!"

Their disappointment was acute. Some tried the other containers with the same result and some went off to find other booty and a few started tearing the garments for the sake of it, but Ellis stayed them. An idea had germinated, and he began to imagine its multiple possibilities. This was pure psi, he saw that. As strange an answer to his question to have received as any, but an unmistakable answer nevertheless.

The Index began to die at local noon, as they finished their work, and the raiders on Amerika's warships looked up to find themselves suddenly prey to another attack by aircraft interceptors. The terminal batteries they had scorned for a day and a night began to open up, despite the fact that their own parked ships were taking most of the hits. The vessel Belkov was aboard had sullenly swung up off the apron and had got into difficulties with the aircraft. A shuttle was sliced in two and Oujuku grudgingly ordered them to light out.

"We'll leave them something to remember us by as we go," Ellis told his crew as they struggled into orbit. The exodus was close run, the big beam weapons of the equatorial girdle targeted them, but the shields held and they made escape velocity without further loss. Behind them, the pearl of Cho Sen had been left in total ruin. Twenty-four of the thirty ships they had found were smashed beyond repair. Baron Harumi's own vessel was smashed beyond recognition.

They met together after the deceleration phase coming out of Gimel-Eight-Oh-One someway along the Seoul chain, and there Ellis announced his intention to try for Duval. Oujuku departed for the Boundary, dragging Belkov behind him to an uncertain future. He said he would see his ass freezeed down in Camp Worth for cowardice and that until then Belkov would do as he was told, as a lowly vice-admiral must.

42

SEOUL

Dawn came in bloody rags over the vast apron of Seoul City. Duval wiped the sleep from his eyes and looked down over the command citadel walls to see what the disturbance was. He had watched the comings and goings of messengers and high-ranking officers all yesterday. Something enormous, something unexpected and immensely important had happened. The reports were being beamed straight to the command citadel without interference from the apron. Tremendous activity was suddenly necessary. What had happened? It smelled like a disaster.

Duval brought his gaze back within the compass of the walls. He had been imprisoned here since his insane approach to Katsumi. Michie had screamed at him that he was killing himself, growing hysterical as she realised he could not be persuaded away from this obsession.

Choi Ki Won had finally acquiesced and had gotten Michie and Kenichi aboard a United Baltic States nexus ship that would touch Amerika enroute for her home port of Riga. He knew the captain well and could trust him. Duval felt the void inside him shift as he remembered the parting. Michie's last words to him had been that she loved him and would always love him, but that she knew in her soul she would never see him again.

That had broken his heart, and he had had enough time to dwell on it. He had been confined under Nishima's orders instead of being sent inside the command citadel as he had hoped. Choi Ki Won had sent his own wife and three youngest sons away on the same nexus ship. And within a month of Duval's surrender, he also had been arrested. It had been Katsumi's doing. After it was ordered that the Probings must stop, Katsumi had looked for another way to discover where his sister had gone. Choi Ki Won had been an easy target. Many people knew that the mathematician and the merchant were close friends. Katsumi had had him crucified on the castle walls. It had taken him three days to die.

Why doesn't Nishima use me? Duval had asked himself, unable to understand. Then, suddenly, when it was almost too late to hope, Nishima had produced him and set him to work.

During his close captivity Duval's hatred had solidified into a hard mass. He knew now he could afford to mark time and await his chance. Though the command citadel laboratories were working night and day to arm the invasion ships, their efforts would not now affect the fundamental strength of the fleet. The invasion was within three weeks of lighting out, and they had made only twenty singularity guns after the new pattern. In a fleet of two hundred battle cruisers, that was negligible—enough to arm only two big ships properly. The months wasted by Nishima had cost the Emperor dear. If the gods granted the opportunity, Duval had vowed to make him pay an even greater price.

Only one thing mattered now. To kill Baron Harumi. Without him the invasion would lose its impetus and its guiding intelligence. Without him, it would not be half as effective. *If only the opportunity would arise.*

Duval looked down across the curving plex roofs again and into the street to identify the disturbance. This time it was not a bannerman or messenger, but a religious parade. The monks approached, walking solemnly. Their heads contained in *tengai*, voluminous reed baskets, their hands thrust inside loose blue gowns that hung down to their *geta*-clad feet. At each shoulder a cloth bag swung, held by two cords representing the *yin* and *yang;* inside, he knew, would be a sword and a *shakuhachi* flute. They were *komuso*, the same order as the monk who had attended him during the darkest days of his interrogation by the *kempei*, and the sight of them awakened feelings of terror within him. The narrow road cleared respectfully before them, early morning ground traffic moving to a halt, people bowing and pressing back against the terminal walls so that the procession could continue on without breaking formation.

At the head a monk waved a fuming thurible so that perfumed smoke billowed out to left and right as he walked. Beside him another held aloft the staff and pennant of the order, a white triangle on which was set the *mon* of the Kunesoki clan. Behind came a cadre of twenty-four monks, four abreast, and behind them eight pallbearers carrying the red lacquer coffin over which was spread a white mantle. The bearers were flanked on each side by a single column of eight, and a second block of twenty-four brought up the rear.

One of the monks was chanting, a sad tremulous wail that the others took up in answer.

"Wheyeeee-ee-ee-ee . . . Whoaoh-oh-oh-oh . . ."

The sound made Duval stare. He had never heard any religious chant like it before, but the rhythmic power of it sounded strangely familiar. They must be Cho Sen Koreans, he thought. Koreans or men from the peculiar quadrant of Hokkaido. Then he saw the hands of the coffin bearers raised high in the flare of a torch, and he saw a sleeve fall away to reveal a tattooed forearm.

Suddenly he knew what the chant was: an old rhythm, often sung aboard Amerikan ships during the long deceleration periods. *Jeezus, it can't be,* he thought. *It can't be!*

He watched wildly as they came on, passing the citadel guard, who admitted the entire procession, respectfully and without question, then they passed out of sight behind the tall plex walls. He ran to follow them and found they were coming straight towards the research block.

Instinct pressed him back against a wall. Then he saw the huge coffin drop down and the monks begin to tear off their baskets and *geta*. Loaded arms were broken out: hidden blasters, cutter guns, and blocks of meson explosive appeared as if from nowhere. One of the command citadel guards stumbled round a corner, unprepared, and was hacked down, a hand over his mouth. Then several assailants lit up their weapons. Almost silently and with great discipline the force split into four separate units and dispersed.

Duval mouthed a prayer. Whoever they were they knew the plan of the citadel well enough to find what they wanted. Already the lead unit was among the research buildings, laying fire on the security systems. Someone began to yell. Weapons crackled out and three of the research workers turned and ran back inside, pursued by attackers. A violet meson flux began to lick up the outside of the annex. Then a huge explosion took off the roof and threw it into the still dark sky, throwing him to the ground.

Dazed, he saw a great orange pall mushroom up over him, felt the heat sear his face.

Debris rained all around. When his vision cleared, he saw the gates of the inner command citadel slamming shut high above. Armored troops began pouring from the guardhouse below, their leaders falling as a volley of electric-blue fire ripped into them. Duval watched, shock draining him as the assailants converged on the armory. They were coming this way. *What about Baron Harumi?* his brain screamed, then something snapped inside his mind. *You can't get at him now the inner citadel's locked tight! But he must die! He must die!*

He bolted out from his cover, his obsession possessing him completely now. A hail of sniper fire was slicing down among the chaos from the citadel walls, lightning zinging off the plex walls and crete roadways. The research block had become a roaring furnace, throwing running forms into silhouette against it, and casting huge, distorted shadows across the smoke-filled yard. Then one of the destroyers saw him and charged after him, a broad-beam weapon in his hand. He saw he was trapped.

"No!" he raged at them in his native tongue. "Stop! You're ruining everything! It's Baron Harumi who must die! Baron Harumi. Don't you see?"

The attacker crashed to a halt, paces from him, his face grimed black and full of fury, his plex breastplate glittering under the tatters of the midnight-blue priest's robe. The boss on the breastplate was phased to chrome, reflecting the inferno from his chest like a burning heart.

Duval tensed for the laser slash, but there was none. Instead the blaster rang to the ground and he felt his arms seized in a demonic grip.

"Duval! Duval! Don't you know me!"

He was paralysed. This was a terrifying nightmare. *"Ellis?"*

"I've come for you, Duval!"

"No!" He shrank back from the apparition, loathsomely, struggling with every fiber of his being as he had against the *kempei*'s Probe.

"Listen to me!"

"Get away!"

"I'm taking you, Duval! Back to Amerika! To your wife and son! To your home!"

"You can't! I must stay! You're not real!"

He fought against the nightmare *kami*, fearing madness, holding to the only certainty there was. He could not leave Seoul while Baron Harumi still lived.

Again the impossible apparition raised its hand, this time to strike, but again the blow failed to come. Instead the demon with Ellis's face was blasted back from him, a sniper's beam dead in his heart.

He tore his eyes away from the body and fled to hide himself, looking back only once to see the hell wraiths descend on the body and carry it, fleeing away to where a big blunt-nosed shuttle had dropped down like magic over the walls, absorbed them into its gaping mouth, and burst away at incredible speed.

43

LIBERTY

Ellis pushed through the rain-soaked crowd and scraped the filth from his boots before following the secretary's man into the pillared splendor of the White House. He was glad that the freezing weather had abated, but the rain had blackened his mood and made his chest twinge where his ribs had been cracked last June in the Seoul assault.

The sniper's beam had caught him above the heart, but the hit had struck him square on the boss of his plex breastplate and the intense heat had spread unevenly, snap-warping the ceramic backing, breaking ribs, and knocking the wind from his lungs. His boys had carried him back to the apron where two captured orbital shuttles had fought their way up under the walls of the fortress. It had been a superbly orderly escape with only three troopers killed, and he knew he should feel grateful to be alive, but he had not taken Duval, nor had he killed him, and at that he felt only shame and huge apprehension.

The Liberty spring was upon them now and all the red-bud

trees in the city had come alive. All the signs were for a hot summer, but the meteorologists had so far gotten it all wrong: Liberty had never seen rain like it, and the impending invasion had turned the once-serene avenues into slushy barricaded tangles of crete and plex and steel ready to take on the invaders in hand-to-hand fighting.

"You had a pleasant journey, Captain?" the immaculately uniformed Marine lieutenant guard inquired politely.

"Thanks, but the truth is I had a foul journey. This whole planet's awash with antipersonnel defenses and heavy transport and rain. At the gates, I came through a bunch of new draftees gawping at the building—hell, Sergeant, they're just boys."

"Ah, that'll be the Kansas volunteers. They've just hit planetside today from the Cornbowl. Organic agrics mostly. Not many of them have seen a city before, let alone the White House."

"Most of them haven't seen a goddammed house at all, to look at them. What the hell's Deke Copeland thinking of, bringing in farm boys like that?"

"Amerika must do as Amerika can." The guard shrugged. "They volunteered, Captain. And we don't turn away willing hands."

"Well, I guess not."

Ellis wiped away the last of the mud from his boots and followed the other up the steps. He had come at Cassabian's urgent request, hoping for news to equal the reports which had greeted him on his return from Seoul in July. At that time he had visited Cassabian to be told how triumphant the rest of Oujuku's mission had been, and that had gladdened him. Although the rumors of it had been rapturous, the truth had not fallen far short either. According to Cassabian, Oujuku had come back four days after Liberty's summer solstice to an ecstatic reception. It had been in celebration of his handiwork at Chonjin, because after their parting Oujuku had cruised back towards the Inchon chain where Korea's second most strategic nexi were clustered, and there he had led his forces planetside to capture the fortified stations of Andong and Wanju. These commanded the nexus chains from Chonjin to Seoul and he had waited there a month for Admiral Matsumoto's Okinawa battle cruisers, eager to take them on, until the politically motivated Del Hamilton had panicked and ordered them home. Half had gone before Oujuku could stop them, and, left with a depleted fleet, he had had no choice but to think of following.

But even as John Oujuku had swung back along the Inchon chain with home in mind, he had pulled them out of the critical path to wait up a day or so for no apparent reason. Miraculously they had happened on a great prize: the transporter *Hizen Maru* returning from Chiang Rai with her hull phased to radio black for maximum secrecy, and laden with *refined* aurium.

To anyone but a psientist it would have been called inexplicable, beyond all reason, beyond naming even, except to call it pure chance. But it had not been pure chance. John's sure psi-sense, he knew, had felt the currents of psi-energy shivering and detected the passage of the big ship into the nexus. He had *known* there was aurium and argentium on board by their sheer mass: four thousand tons of each, plus twenty thousand tons of hypon, and added to that, four hundred and ten crew captured, twenty Neutrals who had been in transit released, and even an Amerikan prisoner got out . . .

As he was conducted to the secretary's Pennsylvania Avenue–facing office, Ellis shook his head in wonder, reflecting again on the many ways their covert operations had profited their cause. Those eighty-seven days had saved the Sector— Yamato's preparations had been thrown into confusion for three months; all Amerika had taken heart at the news that a fifth of the invasion fleet had been destroyed at Chongjin; and because of the *Hizen Maru*, the spoils had been enough to repay the effort handsomely *and* to swell the Treasury's coffers by forty billion inter-Sector spot credit. Even so, the year's grace they had bought had been more precious than all the rest heaped together. Though they had obliterated twenty percent, still eighty percent of the monstrous invasion fleet remained, and, like a wounded Nebraskan tiger, it was now all the more dangerous for its injuries.

Ellis's mood deepened further as he considered again his brother's struggles against the rescue they had attempted. Duval had not *wanted* to leave. It was as though a Zen straitjacket had been put over his mind, and the shock of that moment when he and Duval had faced each other still haunted him.

He waited now outside the secretary's guarded door, noticing how security had tightened since his last visit. They took away his blaster, then he was thoroughly scanned and even patted down for concealed weapons. When the guards missed the curved knife hidden in the top fold of his right thigh boot, he surrendered it angrily to the Marine lieutenant, underscoring the lesson harshly.

"You sonofabitch! You'd have let me go in there with this! It's your job to protect the President!"

"But, sir, I know who you are . . ."

"I don't give a damn, son!"

Jeezus, I've been planetside too long, he thought. On his return to Liberty eight months ago, Reba had met him, and that night they had whispered together in the semidarkness. She had seen the black descarring tabs across his chest and touched her finger to the twisted plex breastplate where the searing heat of the beam weapon had warped it and cold-melted the backing, and he had felt the shiver run through her.

"I hated to see you leave last time," she told him, dewy-eyed in the huge bed. "I looked at the containers loading up and the flags flying on the *Constitution*'s aerials and the plex rippling with colors and your men going through preflight checks, and I was sure your ship would hit a nexus cross-ways and you'd be killed and we'd never be together again like this."

"Ah, but there's a current only an astrogator knows," he had told her, putting his hand to his chest. "A current right in here. To know what to do. When to do it. How to do it. If a man feels it like I feel it, like John Oujuku feels it, and he takes good care to pay it respect, then he'll always be okeh."

"You really are one reckless bastard! They nearly shot you through!"

"I'm here, ain't I?"

"I hate those silly space superstitions you believe!"

"I'll tell you this, Reba, it's no coincidence that all astrogators believe the same thing. On the nexus the way is clear: we have free will, and when human beings live true to their inner feelings, then they action the universe instead of being at its whim. Humans are strange animals, y'know. There's nothing like us in the Known Universe. Maybe the ancient philosopher Carl Sagan is still gonna be right, maybe there are other planets where life started independently, but we ain't found them yet. We're unique, and do you know why? We make our own fate like spiders spin silk. No other living thing does that. And that's why I hate to have synthetic life servants around. Even your Matthew. They give me the creeps. They're intelligent and all, and you can get a conversation out of them all right, but by God they don't fit into the pattern of destiny, and they don't have fates of their own. To me that's like men without faces.''

She looked at him hopelessly, tears glinting at the corners of her eyes. "I know you believe all that stuff, Ellis, and I haven't loved you so long without feeling something of a current inside of you, but still you're going away, and that frightens me. I can't help it.''

"There now," he said tenderly, taking the breastplate from her. This is the proof of what I believe, he thought. The belief that has sustained me. He told her: "Anything but a ninety-degree hit would have refracted and had the power to burn right through the reflecting motes, and the fact that I had the thing on at all is a miracle.''

"Next you'll be saying it's a miracle the beam hit you.''

He shrugged. "That the beam hit me is a mystery. Perhaps it was never meant that I should take Duval off of Seoul.''

She buried her face in the pillow. "Promise me you'll never cruise away again. Remake your vow to me. *Please*.''

"I can't do that.''

"I love you." Her voice was suddenly lost.

"And I love you too.''

"Then promise me. You've done enough. Stay planetside.''

"That's not my fate.''

"Well, make it so, Ellis, you stiff-necked bastard.''

He had put his head back, studying the shades of moonlight on rippling leaves outside the window, feeling also the old wound in his shoulder, the one he had taken away from the Sado apron. "There's a battle coming to make all others that have gone before seem like a pump-room brawl," he said. "It's the Armageddon your father foresaw twenty years ago. I've got to cruise just one more tour, my love. One more, then I'll be yours.''

But he had waited out the winter planetside while his cracked ribs healed. The season had seen tremendous mobilisation, and by spring almost the entire eligible population of the Sector had been put under arms. Huge companies of men and women drilling with small arms and whatever could be found to arm them. Combat instructors had been marshaled together, briefed in booby-trap techniques, and then sent out to every vulnerable center. Units of very green troops, uniformed and trained but only marginally equipped, had been ferried to all the strategic places where a landing was suspected. And throughout that time Ellis had had frequent cause to wonder what the result would be when the drop landings began. There would be slaughter. Massive. Bloody. Obscene. Properly coordinated, the samurai veterans of the conquest of Cho Sen and Free Korea would smash these scratch soldiers to pulp if ever they were allowed to land.

He knew with a sinking heart that that prospect had been heightened by the dereliction he had shown at Seoul.

"I could not have killed him," he had confessed to Reba in torment at his failure. "I stood as close as we stand now, my blaster in my hand, and still I know I could not have pulled the trigger."

"You're the better man for that."

"You think so?"

"No man could kill his only brother and come away unstained."

"He wouldn't follow me. He *chose* not to come away. He deserved to die."

"Yet you didn't pull the trigger."

"Yes, but how many others are gonna die because of that?"

"That's Duval's fate, perhaps. And yours."

Now he had arrived at Cassabian's office, and as the door opened he saw the weary face of the secretary lighten.

"Great news, Ellis! Fantastic news!"

Ellis's spirits leapt. "How's that?"

Cassabian fixed him with a wonder-filled gaze. "It was no work of mine. It's just fabulous psi! Like a bolt of lightning zapping down onto Seoul, killing him just like that."

The rushing of air-cars in the lanes above and the sounds of marching men in the streets below filled the room. Ellis's voice rose. "What're you talking about, Mr. Secretary? *Who's been zapped on Seoul?*"

"The man we've most feared all along, Ellis. The cherry-blossom-assed sonofabitch himself. Oh, the shattering at Chongjin must have broken his heart like a polystyrene cup! Their admiral in chief, the great danger to us—Baron Harumi! He's dead."

44

"The daimyo is very pleased with what you have done, Duval Straker," Katsumi said, examining the artfully arranged *ikebana* of iris heads and willow fronds.

Duval faced him, hating him more completely than he had hated anyone in his life. To have killed him now would have given his soul the same satisfaction that the murder of Baron Harumi had given his mind. He remembered the day he had thrown Katsumi down in a Sado street, his hands around his throat, choking the life from him. How sweet that would be now, he thought. How sweet and how just. You're filth. I know why you want to find Michie, but you'll never find her now. Never.

"Yes, he's very pleased. A hundred singularity guns, and more to come before we light out. Enough to destroy the Amerikan fleet, don't you think?"

"Perhaps, Excellency."

He longed to fall upon the man. With Baron Harumi dead, what did his own life matter? Now there was no reason to live. No reason to carry on making guns for Yamato. He should have gone with his brother, but he had not known. *He had not known . . .*

He forced himself to make Katsumi the offer. "Excellency, might I ask a favor of Nishima-sama?"

"A favor?" Katsumi's surprise and amusement were rich. "I don't think he owes you any favors."

"Still, I should like to ask him."

"Ask him what?"

"I should like . . . I should like to go with you to Amerika."

Throughout the long wait, Duval had suffered the agony of knowing he had made a fatal mistake. Each day he had watched for his chance to gain entry to the citadel, but there had been no way to get close to Baron Harumi. One day he had glimpsed him coming into the shield installation, another time standing on the crete fortifications high above, but Duval was not permitted to leave the area of the laboratory and Baron Harumi never visited it, except once in formal attire to inspect the damage the Amerikans had done during their impudent raid.

The fires of that harrowing night had burned long and bright in Duval's memory. He had hidden his head, pressed into a star niche of the citadel wall, as the massive series of explosions had shaken the entire fortress to its plex roots. It had been thunderous enough to waken all of Seoul.

By noon, *sangokujin* slaves had damped the embers, and he had staggered among the smoking ruins, seeing the load-bearing members of the calibration machine, the optical alignment apparatus, the barrel-reaming lathes, everything busted out of kilter. The explosions had been the wrecking of the argentium tubes, fifteen hundred of them blown to murdering shards by a triple charge of plastic explosive and an oversized mortar bomb that had crashed through the unprotected window. The Amerikans had fled long before the inferno had touched it off.

It had been a brave jaunt, and a hero's gesture, but it had cost his brother his life, and for what? Duval knew now the loss of fifteen hundred argentium tubes was less than an incidental damage to the invasion effort. They would light out with ten thousand ship-mounted beam weapons now: the news had escaped that afternoon that Chongjin had been wrecked by John Oujuku and another year must elapse before they could mount the invasion.

A year to rebuild the research facility and the specialised manufacturing machines. A year to use his techniques in a dozen other labs. A year to make ten thousand singularity guns. With ten thousand singularity guns the invasion must succeed, and there would be no way to stop it. He could have thrown himself headfirst off the fortress wall, but it would have achieved nothing. The singularity guns would still be made. He had lived to kill Baron Harumi. Only that. And now Baron Harumi was dead.

"Amerika?" Katsumi said. "Why should Nishima-sama agree to that?"

"It is the Sector of my birth, Excellency. I would like to see it again before I die. I would like to be allowed to . . . help to liberate it. I am a trained gunner and no man knows better than I do how to use a singularity gun. Do you remember the day on your father's *han* when I demonstrated my skill?''

''Yes.'' Katsumi's smile disappeared. ''Yes. But you're Amerikan. And I don't trust you.'' I hate you, he thought. Because you defiled my sister and because you keep her from justice.

''Don't I deserve some trust, Katsumi-san? I offered my services to you. I did not go with the Amerikan raiders when I had the opportunity.''

''We have enough gunners,'' Katsumi said, toying with him. Privately he was trying to hide his bitter disappointment. The news from Kyoto had been a total calamity and his temper was close to breaking point. It had been made even more fragile by Nishima Jun's rage at the Emperor's decision, and Duval's asking for favors was the last straw. Nishima-sama might want the scum preserved, he thought, but I don't. I want to see him pay for his crimes. Perhaps it's time I began to distance myself from Nishima-sama. After all the favors I've done him . . . by the gods, there's no justice! I didn't poison Baron Harumi in order to see a nobody appointed commander in chief! Nemoto Chikara? *Who is he?* Samurai, of course. A black-toothed court chamberlain and a very high nobleman, yes. But what else? A military sheep, and hardly qualified to lead the invasion! The *bakufu* and the rest of the Emperor's government have gone completely insane.

He turned to Duval, visibly angry now. ''You gave yourself up in the hope of protecting your wife. The Korean, Choi, told me that before he died. And you were not taken by the Amerikans because they did not know you were here.''

Duval swallowed down the hard knot of bile in his throat and bowed his head humbly. He knew from Katsumi's reactions that as soon as the last mounting plate of the last singularity gun was in place he would have him Probed again, just as he had had Choi Ki Won Probed, to find out where Michie was. Katsumi's very presence inflamed and disgusted him, but he knew he had to try once more to get himself aboard the *Takeda Shingen*.

''Katsumi-san, please excuse me but you're wrong about the raiders. They came for me particularly. They knew exactly where I was because Michie-san told them.''

"*She told them?*"
"She's in Amerika. And only I know where."

45

LIBERTY

All morning the headquarters staff had struggled to keep their invasion simulations going, but the giant screens in the War Room burst with a fury of diagrams and codes that taxed Ellis Straker's mind, and he found there was no opportunity to digest any of it. From the command center the party of high-ranking brass could see the likely unfolding of the attack in sixty-four bright colors, distinct in four probability zones: to their left was the open assault simulation, dotted with ships like jewels, an emerald guard of Amerikan lookouts cruising the approach orbits and buzzing the ruby nexus points one after another; to the right the pale pearly arc of the favored approach, and, seventy degrees beyond, the sapphire interceptors stationed so as to prevent the Yamato commanders staging their invasion from the satellites of the gas giant Arcadia, currently on the far side of the primary star; straight ahead, the possibility of an appearance from the tricky hot nexus that sometimes irised open close to the star itself close by the tiny barren speck of Icarus and well within Liberty's orbit; behind them there flashed a planetside attack senario: landings on sparsely populated polar areas that were still frighteningly naked to the enemy.

All present felt that nakedness keenly. News had come today that, at last, and at full strength, the invasion force had lit out. And time and again the simulations had come up with defense failure after defense failure.

Ellis listened as Admiral Luban, saturnine, long-faced, and all in blue, thrust out his finger at the screens. "We can't afford that many ships! We'd leave the Arcadia option completely open to them."

"Amen to that." Deke Copeland, admiral and commander in chief, Amerikan Forces, bearded and in his fifty-third year, shook the fatigue from his shoulders. For almost half a year he had held supreme command for all military preparations. Now the decision was his how best to dispose the fleet. He turned to Ellis.

"I think the second plan's better. We gotta have two squadrons. Seagrave's at the main nexus to dissuade Yamaguchi, but our main force ought to lie at the Arcadian nexus to protect our most obvious weakness—the possibility of landings on those moons."

"Forget the moons!" Oujuku said, careless of the rank of the men around him. "Let's get our ships down to Yamato like we did before. In an open fight we'll massacre them."

"And if you miss them? What, then, you crazy sonofabitch? No, John, I can't risk that."

"Did we miss them last time?"

"Then they were defenseless, sitting on their aprons!"

"Jeezus! The invasion can only come one way!"

"What if they shoot the hot nexus? I can't risk it!"

"God save us," Oujuku barked bitterly towards the screen. "Because our ships won't!"

Ellis felt the worry that was eating at them all. According to Cassabian's spies, the fleet that Yamato had finally put up was vast, and with Duval's aid its armament was likely to be considerable. He repented his failure once again as he took the comander in chief's elbow. "I gotta tell you this: three squadrons. Oujuku's at Arcadia, yourself at Liberty, as you rightly say, and leave Admiral Seagrave to guard the hot spot. A compromise, eh?"

"I'll think about it."

"Better think fast, Admiral," Oujuku said from a distance, but the attack warning siren carried the words away as another defense scenario came up FAIL. FAIL. FAIL.

Ellis could feel his forebodings deepen. Another blast of psi-tingling ran through him.

"Will you look at it!" Copeland said bleakly.

"This is ox shit! The best we've been able to scenario all along is a zero-sum draw."

"You said it! A draw in the ball game."

Luban shook his head, his shoulders rising. "Sure, and I don't see how we're gonna get a single touchdown out of this one."

Copeland looked back stonily. "A draw's equally tough for them."

"Didn't they ever tell you in Navy school, Admiral? War ain't a ball game. In war you wanna fight on the other guy's home ground."

"All I can say is I hope God's on our side this time," Oujuku said.

"In God we trust, John. Remember that?" Copeland turned away, his responsibilities acid-etching his face. Ellis slapped his back heavily. He knew that a psi-storm big enough to scatter the Yamato fleet in hostile space as they tried to transit was the only real hope of averting disaster.

"Yep, Deke," Ellis said quietly. "You ever hear of the term 'kamikaze'? It means 'divine wind'—the wind that blew away the Mongol invasions of Old Japan over a thousand years ago. If God's an Amerikan, then we'll have the biggest psi-storm you ever saw, and for once we'll all be glad of it."

46

THE AMERIKAN BOUNDARY AT THIRTY DEGREES

The drumming to quarters began late on the afternoon of *kin-yo*, Friday, the twenty-ninth day of the month of *Shichigatsu*, by Kyoto reckoning. Aboard the *Oda Nobunaga* the commander in chief, Nemoto Chikara, had reverently unfurled the standard of the Emperor, a red and white flag of incredible age, depicting the rays of the rising sun, the same flag that the Showa Emperor, Hirohito, had saluted on the day Japanese forces had taken Singapore on Old Earth more than five hundred years ago.

The ceremony was broadcast to the entire invasion fleet. As soon as it concluded, the *Takeda Shingen*'s crew began flying to their stations, and soldiers packed the landing modules and took positions along the hatches fore and aft. Duval Straker ran to the gun blister, his pulse beating like the drums that summoned him. Ahead he saw what could only be the final nexus. On the other side would be Liberty. At last the invasion had come upon Amerika's capital world.

The fleet had departed Seoul on the last evening in May. That was eight weeks past, and Duval had watched the Shinto priests prepare their way with offerings and *sake* each day, and he had eaten and drunk with them, feeling each time he ate that a greater burden of guilt was upon him.

On the first day of their voyage, Nishima Jun, with Katsumi at his side, both dressed from head to toe in their ceremonial armor, had delivered them the diatribe. Only the fearsome face masks were missing.

"Soldiers of the Emperor, we ride to glory. We ride to overthrow a most vile Amerikan woman. We ride to release from her bondage those in Amerika who still hold to the Way. And we ride to establish once again the rule of the Emperor. Have no fear, then, but hold in your hearts the expectation of victory. For we are the Emperor's sword and we shall not be denied. Glory to the Emperor, who has kept faith! Glory to his government, which the *gaijin* have failed to bring down! Glory to the gods of Yamato, who go with us! Take heart, for you are the exalted warriors of the Land of the Rising Sun, and your reward shall be a thousandfold. Brave soldiers, Yamato shall have the victory. The gods are with us, and therefore we cannot fail. *Banzai!*"

"*Banzai!*"

"*BANZAI!*"

"*Banzai!*"

Duval had observed the *Takeda Shingen*'s soldiers throughout the harangue. He saw the way they drank in Nishima's words. They truly believed they were invincible and ignored the Cho Sen mercenaries who stood to the rear and who had barely understood the speech. There had been not a single word to encourage these *sangokujin*, but still they were prepared to fight for Yamato.

The *Takeda Shingen* was a great ship of nine thousand six hundred tons, vice-flagship of the Shinano Squadron. Great blue-and gold-phased horns rose up from her nose; eight turrets, like those of an apron fortress, overhung her flanks; a capacious gallery occupied the three sides of her stern. On her domed bridge

Nishima and his lieutenants strutted proudly in their burnished armor, and the flanks of the ships shivered with the colors of the *sashimono,* huge rippling flag-like hull patterns, bearing the *mon* of the chief officers in yellow and black and green and brown. Across the other ships, vast sunbursts, chrysanthemums, and *kanji* characters proclaimed the power of *bushido* and the nobility of the Empire; brilliant decoration crusted the stern and the long, elegant beakhead, and when the drums beat, colored flares and bursting fireworks lit up the spaces between the ships. But for all its martial pomp the fleet's outward show belied the truth.

The *Takeda Shingen*'s complement was six hundred and forty crew and thirty thousand assault troops. For most of the voyage her cargo of troops had slept between decks. They had been loaded in plex freezee tubes, smaller than coffins and in all ways similar except that they were designed to open and eject their contents alive after suspension. Of the invasion force, only the staff officers and samurai connected by blood to the foremost clans were permitted to remain sentient for the duration.

Duval, as nominally a member of the gun crew, had staked his claim to a space between the fourth and fifth starboard gun blisters in the cruiser's waist. Though open to the main corridor, the fire control bulkhead had given him some privacy and separated him from the noise of the crew's mess, and a rough, mutually protective friendship existed between the gunners. Because of the Yamato fetish for open structures, every sheet of plex on board the entire ship had been phased to maximum transparency. He knew, as did the rest of the crew, that quasi-nights under the star-filled sky would be preferable to the hell of opaque hull walls that would remind them all of the stifling overcrowding. He had sat quietly, his back against the bulkhead on those long, empty watches, playing his fingers over the calculator tattoo that still functioned on his hand, substituting different values for the constants in the equations of state of the cosmos. So many stars, so many worlds, so much of the universe beyond the blind confines of the hull, and he a prisoner of his dreaming syllabic poems.

> *A million-million,*
> *Fields of star-dust, infinite,*
> *Like stars, the galaxies.*

He had explained Olbers's Paradox to one of the gunners. "It's poetic license, you see? There are not really an infinite number of stars."

"How do you know, Hasegawa-san? Have you counted them?"

"No, Makino-san. But I can show there cannot be an infinite number."

"How? Only the gods can say."

"By reasoning. See, if there were an infinity of stars beyond the hull, then wherever you looked, whatever line of sight you chose, you would have to be looking directly at a star."

"Perhaps I am."

"But then the sky would be as brilliant as a star's surface, not black. Don't you see?"

The unwilling student had cocked his head. "Not really, Hasegawa-san."

"It's because the universe is expanding. Distant light is red-shifted, its energy is diminished."

"Astronomers always blame things they can't understand on the expansion of the universe. I don't believe it's expanding, Hasegawa-san. I don't believe it at all. I think the universe is the Void and that is why the spaces between the stars are black."

Six days out and Makino had snapped under the pressure of "homesickness." He had written his death poem, folded his kit issue neatly on his strap hammock, stripped off everything except a ring containing a lump of pure aurium, and thrown himself into a Dover hopper. By 0600 UT most of the crew had eaten his recycled remains. By 1015 UT the Dover generators were out of operation, their catalytic converters overpowered by the aurium nugget that scrambled the output into unmentionable offal.

By the time they reached the fourth jump the smells issuing from the ship's bowels had been stomach-turning:

"Better sitting inside your assault suit. At least you can get a whiff of fresh oxygen now and again, eh?" Saigo, chief gunner, had got up onto the power cables beside him. He picked a wad of onion fat off his dish and scooped up a mass of purple sticky rice with it before putting it into his mouth.

"You're quite right, Saigo-san."

"Want some?" Saigo had asked. He farted loudly and a rank

goat smell enveloped him. ''Courtesy of Makino-san and Kimura the quartermaster.''

Duval showed his surprise. Since the breakdown of the Dover machines rations were strictly limited, and he had seen Saigo eat once already today.

''Here. Take it.''

''Whose is it?''

''*Baka!* It's mine, of course!'' He shoved another cold lump, a hybrid of Chinese duck feet, wintergreen, and dry tea leaves, into his mouth. ''Why not? It's a bit mixed up, but at least it's better than yesterday. Almost palatable. And it all goes down the same hole, eh?''

''That's like saying we're all dead in the long run.''

''Well, so we are! Listen, they're down on the slate as Makino-san's rations, but he won't be needing them, or anything else, where he's gone.''

''Gone?''

''He's dead.'' Saigo shrugged. ''Yesterday. He threw himself into the hopper. That's what threw the food machines into chaos. It's all his fault.''

''By the gods! No one told me!''

''No one may discuss the incident. General Orders, eh?''

''It's General Orders to report a death.''

''You report it if you like, but I don't recommend it. Tanaka-san was beaten just for vomiting in an officer's presence.''

''Beaten for that?''

''It's true. I saw it myself. He was just clearing his throat, but Nishima-sama's man took it the wrong way.''

''Which man?''

Saigo swallowed another mouthful and inclined his head towards the bridge. ''That bastard Hasegawa Katsumi, of course. Come on, eat. And don't worry about Kimura—the quartermaster's in on it. Harada-san!''

The hatred Duval nursed for his wife's brother had bubbled up uncontrollably as Harada, the surly Hokkaido gun captain, came across and took a piece of octopus and blue cheese mush.

''What's the matter? You don't want any?'' Harada said.

''Yes. Take a lump,'' Saigo told him again, thrusting out the bowl. ''Those bastard officers steal what they like. Why not us, eh? Gunners need to eat—without us they'll get nowhere.''

"No one knows how long it will be before we make planetfall again," Harada said darkly. "Not even our generals."

Duval recalled the look on Nishima's face after his last meeting with Nemoto Chikara. The commander in chief had invited his commanders aboard the flagship, *Oda Nobunaga*, and sent them away tight-lipped and furious. Duval had speculated about the meeting, but it had been difficult to imagine what had been said. The following day, the crewmen had been even less willing to get in Katsumi's way; clearly, whatever had been decided, Nishima had not agreed with it.

Rumors had run riot through the ship: A landing on the Arcadian moons had been intended, and it was that which had been canceled. Nemoto Chikara had ordered a surprise attack on New New York by the Hizen Squadron to pay the devil Oujuku back for what he had dared to do at Chongjin. Even that the whole invasion was a gigantic ruse and they were going to land secretly on Iowa before hitting New New York. The Hokkaido man was right, he thought: no one knew where they were going.

Since leaving Seoul nexus, psi-waves had battered them. Strong fields had forced them to rethink their approach the moment the engines had boosted them to injection velocity and taken them beyond the point of no return. One of the heavy equipment transports, the *Tsunetoki,* was damaged and returned to the Seoul apron. By the middle of the month of *Rokugatsu* the psi-storms had blown themselves out and the Index and all the other probability factors had risen again. Aoki, the astrogator, told him they were still standing at less than forty percent, scarcely better than when they had begun. Nishima's temper had flashed white at their lack of progress, while at his back the *kaigun* naval astrogators he despised began to make disrespectful remarks over the speech he had delivered to them about the Emperor's will being done.

"If it's the Emperor's will that we invade Amerika, why don't we have a painless passage?" Aoki had grumbled, but under his breath so that none of the *rikugun* military men heard him.

During acceleration the communication ports were sealed tight, and no one could egress beyond the hull. Nishima, disgusted by the crew's inability to provide hot, clean bathwater, ordered a general punishment: the entire hull was phased to black, and the interior grew even more noisome. What feeling of light and space there had been was now gone, and those quartered sentient for the duration were packed tighter than squid in their jars. At least the crew, though daily abused, were now able to make good their dignity at the expense of the haughty, usually planet-bound men that a few rough transits had turned into groaning, green-faced *hinin*.

After two weeks they had begun to run true, passing through the Hawaii system without opposition. Orders had emanated from the *Oda Nobunaga* that the commander in chief wanted all nexus ships to clear for action, and so they had, jettisoning almost everything that was not strictly necessary aboard an assault ship. The crewmen had made no open complaint, though none had been able to understand the reason why the Nemoto-sama had made this order.

" 'We shall go from here as if we were in the presence of the enemy,' " Aoki had repeated, spitting out his scorn. "What does he think this is? A screen simulation?"

And Duval had nodded in agreement. "You think he's worried about the Amerikans intercepting us when we transit?"

"If he does, he's a fool."

"Why doesn't Nishima-sama come out?"

"He's sick as a puppy dog from the transits, like all the rest of them," Aoki grunted. "I can't wait to get at the Amerikans. They're the real cause of this war. I hate them and I want to see them all crucified."

Then, as soon as the probability indices had turned noticeably more favorable, Duval had gone down to inspect the lower freezee holds with Kimura, the quartermaster.

"Those *hinin* Koreans! Sorry, Saigo-san, but this is the last straw to break the peasant's back. Look at these seals! Half of them are leaking at the anterior end umbilicus. We're losing a ton of refrigerant a day already. And if the freezees are leaking, what are the men going to be like? If air gets in, they'll rot."

"Those *hinin* technicians in Seoul have shafted us."

They smelled the stench as one of the worst-affected freezees was cracked open.

"That's tainted flesh, all right!"

"Yes! Look, I've seen that before. Rot gas bubbles out of the muscle tissue and pressure bursts the skin. The dog-eating *hinin* must have sabotaged it deliberately."

"What if it's like this aboard the other ships?" Duval had said as they frantically unearthed more and more spoiled coffins.

"Oh, *ko!* The smell! The Nemoto-sama will have to put in at Guam now, whatever the Emperor orders."

"You think he'll disobey the Emperor?" another had asked in awe.

A group of crewmen had begun to crowd at the hatch, curiosity at the reek overcoming them.

"He'll have to!"

"He'll see us die first."

"I hope they all fester in hell! Especially Hasegawa Katsumi."

"Goddamn those Koreans."

"It wasn't the Koreans who said it was the will of the gods that we must invade Amerika," a maintenance technician said.

"What do you mean by that, *inu?*" Saigo said furiously.

"Just that I pity the Amerikans when we come upon them. They'll keel over at the stink."

"Get to your stations, the lot of you! Or I'll have your guts spilled!" Saigo had slapped down the freezee lid angrily and left them, and Duval had stared stoically at the rotted corpse. Though half the losses were due to the poor quality of the seals, the rest, he liked to believe, was the just vengeance of Choi Ki Won's friends and fellow saboteurs.

So, three weeks out from Seoul, and they had had to make planetfall at the intensely cold Guam apron, losing a whole month. The daimyo of Guam, Kido Chochi, had been informed and the fleet had gathered, half in the shelter of the ice mountains, half remaining on the exposed flash-over zone. But that night a violent snowstorm had hit the town, and the ships outside had been buried in ninety-foot drifts. The *Takeda Shingen* herself had put down in a sheltered area, but still the entire fleet had to remain there a whole month until the ships that had been iced in were burned out and recovered, and while new freezees were ordered and installed. It had taken a superhuman effort, but the targets had been achieved and the fleet was once more under way.

Now Duval watched Amerikan Space coalesce outside the observation blister, recalling the panic that had flooded Guam the night before their departure. Hizen salvagemen had come down with the absurd story that John Oujuku was bearing down on them with fifty ships a mere twenty astronomical units away. Perhaps that had decided the commander in chief to order the evacuation, Duval thought; perhaps he had been encouraged by the sudden leap in the Index, perhaps he had been frightened by the Emperor's urgent communiqué that the invasion must proceed as closely as possible according to the original timetable. It was then that Aoki the astrogator had told him that the rumor about the cancellation of the Arcadian moons landing had been correct.

When the *juniji* bell sounded at noon, Duval was still gazing at the massed fleet ranged around him, watching them form into their defensive disposition. Close by stood the *Hidetada*, named after the ship that had brought the Emperor to Amerika on his sole state visit, the huge transport *Iemitsu*, and the assault cruisers *Ietsuna* and *Tsunayoshi*. To the rear stood General Sumita's *Ieyasu* and beyond her the flag of the Shinano squadron, *Ienobu*. On the far side the *Ietsugu*, General Yonai's flagship, mightiest and newest of the Ise attack vessels, and the *Yoshimune* beside her.

Duval saw that the powerful warships were maneuvering into two groups, following what must have been Baron Harumi's original battle plan, tipping the cusps of the fleet with sword steel. Named mostly for the various supreme shogun of the Tokugawa clan, they made a tremendous sight. The *Ieshige* of General Cho's Kozuke flotilla, the ex-Korean ship *Ieharu*, and the four vast battleships of Nemoto's van: the *Ieyoshi*, the *Iesada*, the *Yoshinobu*, and his own *Oda Nobunaga*. Their combined radio black shields winked on simultaneously and the stars disappeared. The stealth technology was working. Despite all the setbacks and all the delays, all the shortcomings, the sabotage and the holocaust of Chongjin, the invasion fleet was still the most magnificent force, the greatest, that had ever assembled. Duval knew there was nothing in Amerika that could hope to stop it so long as the great ships attacked en masse and so long as they couldn't be detected until the last moment.

Above, on the bridge, Katsumi, shining in his family's ancient war gear, watched with an ecstatic expression as the ships grew luminous once more. They were passing inside the blackout, inside the vast coalesced shield of the fleet. Nishima was a distant figure, squatting austere and solitary on the highest point of the bridge with his war fan in his hand. It was black, shaped like a butterfly, and on it was a red spot with a gold *bonji* device, like the one the Japanese daimyo Takeda Shingen had carried into war a thousand years ago. Both men, in their way, were paragons of samurai virtue, haughty, proud, inflexible, completely indifferent to the suffering of their men and totally convinced of Yamato's coming victory.

Duval forced himself to look away, hating with an ice-cold anger the men who had shaped his life. I've waited to repay you for so very long, he thought grimly, turning his firing key over in his palm. I pray to my own God that the hour will come soon.

47

THE LIBERTY SYSTEM

At the break of the same day, in Amerikan reckoning the nineteenth day of July, Captain Tom Brophy, in a ship bought from the spoils of five years' marauding in the Neutral Zone under Ellis Straker, emerged from the Liberty nexus a quarter of an astronomical unit from the planet to discover a shoal of luminous shark hulls ranged in a loose formation, surrounding him.

Momentarily paralysed by terror, the Texan rubbed at his eyes and then told his helmsman to run swiftly out of the shield of radio black and make for Liberty. The backfire crackled their aerials to vapor, blacking them out, and they were unable to respond to orbit challenges when they injected above Liberty and were fired on. The crash landing was heavy, and Brophy broke his arm, but by four that afternoon his air-car was plunging across Philadelphia with a tale that the Yamato invasion force was no more than thirty million miles away, but pretty well invisible.

Behind him the news threw the city into uproar. Brophy found the city Defense Committee in a barbecue arranged by the mayor of Philadelphia for his Navy guests: de Soto, McKeown, Frastley, the Hawken family, all were present. Ellis Straker and John Oujuku, bearded and in dress uniform, stood out near the barbecue, a jug of beer and a heap of Dover pork ribs occupying them. They were in conversation with Admiral

Copeland and the tough Rhode Islander Curtis Frastley when Brophy burst in.

"It's the bogies! The bogies are here with a thousand ships! I swear to God!"

Ellis prepared to send his empty rib plate across the lawn like a Frisbee, but the commander in chief stepped across his line anxiously.

He called after him, "Well, now, Deke, I guess you just ain't hungry."

"My God, Straker! What you got in those veins, ice water? They're on top of us! They're trying to bottle us up in orbit and they've got the singularity guns to do it!"

The aghast silence became a storm of tongues, but it was Oujuku's voice that rose above them all when the waiter tried to pick up his half-empty beer glass.

He pushed his sleeves up his forearms and hissed, "Touch that beer, son, and I'll take your head off!" Turning to Ellis, nonplussed at Copeland's agitation, he said, "We got two hours yet. Even if Brophy's right, there's still time to eat." But the admiral was already hurrying away.

Deep inside, Ellis's anxiety at the prospect of an invasion fleet as heavily armed with singularity guns as the Amerikan fleet had reached its peak. He had persuaded Copeland to concentrate his own and Oujuku's squadrons together at Philadelphia, and in the weeks following, the admiral had put everyone on top alert, his temper quietly fraying. Then news had come of the invasion force's halt at Guam. Instantly both Ellis and Oujuku had pressed their case to the Security Council. Lubbock, now readmitted to the President's confidence and freed from all pretenses, had obtained from her an order to permit the fleet to follow the attack plan, and through most of July they had been cruising about in the Guam chain, hoping desperately to catch the great fleet unprepared once again. As he watched Copeland making for his air-car, Ellis recalled ruefully how the Amerikan fleet had got to within twenty astronomical units of Guam before a contrary Index had forced them to turn back.

"Wanna settle for a draw now," Frastley said drily, mindful of the wager that rode on the manner of the Yamato fleet's appearance.

"A draw? What's that?" Oujuku said. "There ain't no such a thing."

By a quarter after four the Philadelphia apron was on fire. Hundreds of ships and shuttles were lifting off. The orbital configuration of the main defense satellites favored the attack, and most of Amerika's trim ships had to be tractored offplanet under crude jet power.

Ellis had left the apron last of all, not wanting to miss the sight. The *Constitution* was already in orbit, but this was a moment a psi-talent could not pass over.

"Not so fast," he told the shuttle's coxwain, and climbed up onto one of the stubby air wings and sat down to breathe deep and drink it in. He felt the lubed plex under his hands, microridged and yielding like corduroy shark flesh and still warm from reentry. The engine cowls were smutty with unburned carbon. There was an acrid apron smell on the air and the jetting humming noises of a great fleet putting off.

The cox and his copilot watched him, kind of respectfully, kind of puzzled. Ellis Straker's psi-talent was legendary; maybe he was delaying them around some kind of foreseen disaster. They had heard tales of talents who just reached into inspection hatches and pulled near critically failed units right out on bare intuition. It was *spooky*.

"See that," he told them, staring into the gold and peach sky. It was rent by condensation trails as the big ships lifted off.

"Sir?"

"Moment of history, boy. Moment of goddamned history. Better believe it."

"Aye, aye, sir."

The big ships rose up like primeval gars and skates, bogling and vortexing swirls of air from their backs. Copeland's *Virginia*, renamed the *Chongjin* after Congress had used some of the profits from the Chongjin mission to purchase her, cruised out in a mass of boiling air, followed by the *Arkansas,* the *Illinois,* and the *Missouri*.

Ellis felt the blasts of warm air abrade him and the heady aromatic smell of the engines. He felt the vibrations shudder through the live wing he was sitting on, dying away as the squadron trailed into specks. Then came Mac Savage's *Georgia*, covered in insignia and revolving lights. The Aquila eagle adorned the hull, glittering in gold, Altair an eagle eye—and a weapons blister. In company were the three other presidential ships, the ones that had blasted their way into and out of Chongjin: the *Pennsylvania*, the *Colorado*, and the *Massachusetts*. They phased to midnight blue as they passed overhead, leaving only their landing lights winking and rippling along their trailing edges.

He saw Hawken's *Texas*, eight thousand tons and bristling with sixteen singularity guns, coming out to meet Oujuku in his *Kalifornia*. Dain Fenwick's *Ohio* and Glory Smith's *Florida* both making to accompany the *Constitution*. The sight of those big sharks made him sigh and gave him a strange fist-hard feeling in back of the sternum. Never had such a collection of Neutral Zone traders and Navy astrogators been brought together before, and the psi-currents in his mind surged at the incredible bond he could feel.

That's the strength of Amerika, he thought. Individuals, damn right, but a tight family when there's work to be done. A man'd need to be a stone . . . He rubbed a hand over his face and slid down off the wing.

"Okeh," he growled, giving them some of the affectionate Straker abuse he knew they prized. "Take her away, you psi-damned idle pieces of hogshit."

"Sir!"

He got aboard the *Constitution* at the height of the exodus and came alongside Fort Bush before local sundown. All around the stationary orbit belt vessels were sliding slowly into eclipse towards optimum defense stations.

As the tension mounted, the fleet of Amerikan nexus ships escaped Liberty orbit, reaching open space unseen by the invader's sensors, and during the passage round darkside Ellis Straker's squadron stole silently into a hyperbolic intercept trajectory, to begin tentatively snapping at the heels of the invader. Once they were certain they had been identified, the radio black screens came down and the awesome splendor of the invader was revealed at last.

When midnight UT rang out throughout the ship, Deke Copeland's shuttle approached the Yamato flag and gave the Yamato fleet his challenge as the Code required. Then Copeland led his line into battle against General Sumita's squadron. The fighting was reserved and cautious, Copeland's line never daring to close with the Yamato fleet. At one point, by chance, they managed to isolate the ailing *Iemochi*, and like a grizzly bear surrounded by vicious pit dogs, they sent themselves against her, putting a dozen holes through her, and the success gave Ellis leave to hope.

By the end of the second day it became clear to him that they were in great jeopardy. If they maneuvered to meet the main Yamato fleet, they would be destroyed, but if they returned planetside, the invader's stately progress into Liberty orbit would continue virtually unhindered. He thought of the *Iemochi* and decided he must press his attack more forcefully, risking himself within range of the heavy but short-range singularity guns and ship-smashers. One Amerikan ship, he reasoned, sailing alone and unattached, might drive into the enemy and detach a vessel for the others to fall upon. It was desperate, and it was suicidally dangerous, but something had to be tried.

He thought darkly of his promise to Reba as the third day began to dawn. Do or die, he had said, this would be his last voyage. And today was the day they would find out which of those forebodings had been correct.

48

Duval Straker had seen the small black and white insignia stippling the Amerikan ship's tail fin and it had filled him with a tremendous urgency. As the ship closed he ordered the gunners to don their pressure suits so that they could continue to fight if a singularity hit should suddenly rob them of atmosphere. The suits were made of micro-thin flexiplex, skintight and almost transparent. They had removable gloves and a snap-up bubble helmet to dome-in the head, neck, and shoulders; four connex hoses hung limply off the torsos like used blue condoms.

He told them to arm their argentium tubes, taking care to monitor the temperature readings carefully, and looked desperately for Harada's return. He was sure at last that his chance had come.

The Hokkaido man had gone below to the *Takeda Shingen*'s aft argentium tube store. He guarded the massive arming keys, while Saigo was fully occupied supervising the forward magazine, and Saigo had ordered him below to augment the argentium on the gun deck. He knew that if the coming attack was as sharp as those of the last two days, they would certainly fire off hundreds of rounds.

The same ferocious vessel that had attacked the *Iemochi* was closing on them now, and Duval looked again at her black-fin device, confirming the flaming hope that the first sight of it had raised up in him. Yes! There was no doubt. It surely was a black field upon which stood out a pure white skull. But Ellis's ship was heading straight down the barrels of the most dangerous singularity guns in the fleet.

Harada returned with the argentium. According to a safety procedure he himself had originated many years ago on Sado, Duval looked at the temperature setting and knelt down to examine it. He turned his back to cover his actions as he did so. In his gloved hand was a small bar magnet that would make the temperature control panel read haywire.

He slipped it under the panel. Then, as he set about opening the argentium flask, he took the first sample tube in his hand and felt it. His brows knit and he tilted the flask up, at the same time hiding the magnet in his hand.

"This argentium's hot," he said, standing.

"Hot?" Harada asked, his Japanese struggling under a thick Hokkaido accent.

"Yes, hot! You can't feel it? Take your glove off." He thrust a tube of first-grade refined argentium against the man's cheek. "And look here—the temperature reading. It's way off!"

"But—it can't be!" The humorless surprise on the Hokkaido man's face showed him at a loss to explain the facts. Argentium tubes had a very narrow operating tolerance, only 3 degrees either side of the critical 282.27 Absolute.

Praying that Harada would defer to his expert knowledge, Duval waved the tube at him angrily. "Can't be? But it *is*! By the gods, if you've been meddling in the magazine, Saigo-san will have you flayed!"

"Keep your voice down! You think I'm a fool? I don't take liberties with argentium."

"Somebody has. And there's only you and Saigo-san been in there since we left Guam."

"I . . . Maybe it's more of that Korean sabotage."

"You'd better find out. If Saigo-san finds out—" He pursed his lips at the consequences.

Harada was aghast. He cast about him secretively, turning the stares of the others away, then examined the temperature reading again and stared at the underside of the flask. He looked up, watching the onrushing Amerikan ship, shivered by the beam weapons that lanced out, testing the *Takeda Shingen*'s defense shields. Finally he said, "Come with me."

Duval felt a spear of exhilaration, remembering in lucid detail the terror of the kamikaze ship that had blasted the *Thomas J.* to pieces on that psi-drenched day so long ago. He picked up one of the huge arming keys, that for security reasons were as big as a hunting rifle, and followed, but when they were only halfway across the deck, alarms began in the forward scanners, and the despairing yells of the crew, like witnesses to a calamity, rose to a crescendo. Harada ran back, following the line of their eyes, and saw that the Amerikan ship had sheered away, forcing General Yonai's flagship, the *Ietsugu*, to take sudden evasive action, but she had crossed the bows of another Ise Squadron ship whose shields were of identical resonance. The shields interpenetrated instead of repelling one another, and there was a collision that carried away the *Ietsugu*'s bow horns. Meanwhile, Ellis's ship was tacking round to press home his attack. Duval darted an anxious glance towards Saigo, who was striding along his guns, urging his crews to greater efficiency, then to Katsumi and Nishima Jun, who had been brought out onto the bridge by General Yonai's accident.

"Harada!"

"I'm coming."

They went below, Harada besuited, but bareheaded and now without his gloves, carrying the suspect flask close to his chest. The guard admitted them both to the after restricted zone on sight, and they rattled down the zero-gee communication shaft to the gloom of the argentium store. The Hokkaido man twisted his ID smart in the big plex door. No one was allowed here, not even a first lieutenant, and the only illumination was the baleful red glare of operational lighting. It would make looking for a nonexistent temperature problem all the more difficult.

The magazine hatch sill was built up a foot or so and the door edge sealed with huge interlocking pins to prevent unauthorised personnel getting in. Its walls were of solid plex, half an inch thick. The Hokkaido man stepped inside and bent to put the flask down. "Show me where you think—"

Duval's arming key crashed down across the back of his neck. He hit him again with dispassionate force, this time on the crown of his head as he staggered, and then he lay still, bleeding from ear and nose. Immediately Duval took up the flask and began to calculate the time he would need to accomplish his aim.

He split open the plex cover of the *seppuku* pin. Inside, the self-destruct lock gleamed back at him. Firing it would blow the *Takeda Shingen* into tiny fragments, but to succeed he must first arm it. To arm it he needed a pair of keys, and any attempt to insert them would send loud warnings over the whole ship. In addition, the procedure could be overridden from the bridge at any time. It was an immense gamble.

He licked his lips nervously. He felt no fear for himself, but something inside was shouting at him. Five minutes ago it had all seemed so simple. He had committed himself absolutely to dying if it meant the destruction of the ship and all it contained, but now he realised that his commitment had been to suicide, to an alien ideal, to a Yamato ideal. The thought repelled him.

There must be a better way . . .

To get up the comm shaft. Ten seconds to be on deck and three more to get into the airlock, say a minute to egress the hull and accelerate clear of the debris. No room for error.

Could it be done? If so, how? His mind raced as he tried to accommodate the problem.

Another powerful concussion blasted the port shields, shivering the internal fabric of the ship. Soon they would be taking singularity hits from the Amerikan ship. What can I do? Any moment now they'll miss me. They'll certainly miss Harada. It's instant death to desert battle stations, so they'll be looking out for him.

He crouched low, hugging the flask tight to his pressure suit. Put it down, went into the corridor, stared up the companionway. The guard was still standing, arms folded, back to him, his pair of swords jutting. Please God, tell me what to do. Concentrate. Think. Think! What's possible? Ten to fifteen seconds is a minimum. The only sure way's to somehow activate the *seppuku* pin, but I've only got limited resources here. The procedure's too slow and it'll risk discovery, unless . . .

Jeezus, yes! If the bridge can override instructions, they must be remoted in the control circuitry! And you've got Harada's maintenance key!

He examined the panel just above his head. It was smooth and offered no means of access. The one set into the floor was more promising. He prised it open and the plex sheet sprang off. He took care: inside, dozens of colored needles of laser light jittered with gigabyte data blocks. They were powerful and would burn him. Their beams had to be wide enough to avoid data corruption by any microscopic dust that might float into the conduit, yet powerful enough to repulse anything bigger that blocked the information path.

He heard a thin squeaking coming from the conduit.

Ne . . . he thought, reacting immediately. Nothing in the cosmos has been able to stop them spreading. They go wherever men go. We have to put up with them . . . I hate rats.

His mind blanked as he read the coding on the plex grille. He searched frantically, the dagger-bladed characters knifing at his eyes and brain until he could hardly read them. Then he saw it, the *kanji* for "self" and "kill"—*seppuku!*

So! It was an interrupt system. A kind of booby trap.

How can I interrupt the optical pathways? What can I put in there that won't burn through? It must be foolproof. I've got to be certain.

The lasers were old technology, almost as old as the idea of hard wiring, invented just after the dawn of electronics, but they were used for a purpose. Old technology was tried and trusted. And no circuit on the ship had to be trusted more than the *seppuku* refresh line. It was part of the dead man's handle design: without regular heartbeat pulses sent from the central organism of the ship, the self-destruct would be set in motion, ensuring that no crippled ship could fall into the hands of the enemy. If interrupted for more than a minute, the refresh would be missed, the circuit would go into alert. Any attempt to restore the refresh without coded procedures would create an immediate detonation.

Suddenly the parameters of the problem were clear in Duval's mind: first, fix the alarm line; second, cause an interruption of the *seppuku* pathway; third, wait for one minute; fourth, restore the laser.

But how?

The microsecond the laser started up again the *Takeda Shingen* would be dust.

It was a big ship. There were three charges and three circuits, all separate. It would be sufficient to blow just one. And best to blow the aft circuit. He ripped out the alarm line transceiver.

Dead man's handle . . .

He looked at the motionless Hokkaido man and a hair-raising solution bloomed. Quickly he lifted the bloodied body upright and it fell down, with a ghastly groan as the last air escaped from its concertina rib cage. With grim curses on his tongue, Duval rolled Harada's corpse over, arranging the limbs straight, as if the body was at attention. Then he took the dead hand and plunged it into the laser.

Where the needles touched, smoldering began. The skin of the palm cooked and browned like paper under the brilliant focus of a magnifying lens on a summer's day. Greasy smoke billowed in the needle beams, and within two or three seconds the beams were emerging from the back of the hand.

Duval's neck hackled with a deep-seated fear. Everything he was doing flew in the face of the safe habits and prohibitions of a lifetime. The sweat steamed from him and his head filled with the grisly reek of charred flesh. He tried desperately to calm himself, knowing what he must do. The lasers were more powerful than he had supposed. The rat problem well catered for.

He pushed Harada lengthways into the conduit.

A sudden pang of terror overcame him and he began to tremble. My knees are going, he thought. What if my knees go? Harada's inert body smoldered horribly as he watched, then the universe blinked out. A bang had torn him away from the mesmeric sight. The vault door had been swinging as the ship yawed to escape the attentions of the attacking ship and the compensators reacted. It had slammed noisily, shutting out the corridor light. He twisted round in utter blackness. Only the smoldering needles were visible now; only those jittering multicolored lines existed in the whole universe, drilling their way inexorably through Harada's body, lighting him up from the inside with a ghastly and terrible Christmas-tree glow.

Where was the door? Where was it? As his hands groped out blindly they touched cold panes. He began to claw furiously at its edge in the jet blackness, but his nails could make no purchase.

The door was stuck fast. The roasting flesh spat and crackled, the stinking smoke making him retch.

"Jeezus Christ! Help me!" he shouted, giving way to panic. He pulled the arming key from his belt and then he realised that the door opened outward. He heaved his shoulder blindly forward and burst out into hellish red light. It was flashing—blasting an interrupt warning which should have been screaming around the ship, but which he had curtailed by pulling out the alarm transceiver. He slammed the vault and locked it. Gripping the handholds, he pulled himself up the comm shaft, but it was as if his body was made of lead and his feet were held fast on the treads. He forced himself up, painfully, one step at a time, and when he got to the gun deck men were peering down at him anxiously. He tried to make a reassuring face at them, but he was shaking and he was aware of how sick his smile must be.

The guard turned. "You! Where's the other one? Two of you went down."

Another deafening concussion crashed out from the screens.

"He's there, look."

Duval looked up to where Nishima Jun and Katsumi would be standing together on the bridge, many decks above. He took a deep breath and, when the guard bent to peer below after Harada, he took two steps towards him and brought the arming key down on his head. The guard's body pitched into the gloom of the comm shaft, falling soundlessly until he hit bottom.

Three men saw him do it. They broke away from their stations instantly, yelling as they came at him. He leapt for the comm shaft, hauled himself up the weightless tube, pulling desperately on the aluminum rungs, then onto the upper gun deck, and began to make for the airlock hatch.

"Stop him!"

"Somebody take him!"

"He's gone mad!"

His own gun crew was before him, barring his way into the airlock. Saigo's face was angry and uncomprehending. Duval snapped the bubble of his pressure suit up and threw himself at the man with all the force he could manage.

49

Ellis Straker pressed home the attack furiously against the *Takeda Shingen*. She was vice-flagship of her squadron, and almost three times the mass of his own ship. Her armament was heavy and accurate and the *Constitution* had taken deep wounds from her in her attempt to close.

Ellis gritted his teeth and held his course, heartsick that Copeland's formal strategy had not worked. His impatience had burst out yesterday. Twice Ellis's orbital pilot had warned him of the folly of cruising within range of the *Takeda Shingen*'s singularity guns.

"She's a big one, sir. And though we're pretty handy ourselves, we won't live long if you bring us under those guns again."

"Hold your helm steady, Lieutenant," he had shouted back, knowing that they had no choice.

As the vast bulk of the fifteen-thousand-tonner grew ahead, he ordered the skull ensign broken out across the tail fin. Doubtless there were enough Zone veterans aboard the Yamato ship to understand and respect it. Then he had seen the Ise Squadron leader, *Ietsugu*, sixteen or seventeen thousand tons of her, thundering in, and he had tied the enemy's course in a knot and thrown her into collision with two ships so that she lost her dorsal fin and stabiliser pods.

And so they ran on, the decks jumping with the shocks of their beam weapons as they closed for hand-to-hand. The shields lit up in fantastic colors as the bright beams slammed into them.

"*Five thousand yards and closing*," the ship's evaluator chimed.

This adversary's the equal of any in the fleet.

"*Four thousand yards and closing*."

I'll chop her to bits and show Deke Copeland the way home. *"Three thousand yards and closing."*

And if we die, we'll have died with honor . . .

Suddenly, at two thousand five range and just as they were about to come under the lethal singularity fire of the *Takeda Shingen*'s biggest guns, the watching Amerikans saw the fist of God appear over the stern of the enemy and hammer her to pieces. A second later the shock of a massive explosion peppering their shields with debris could be felt, visible as a ring expanding across the clarity of space. It shook them, and the watchers saw that what had seemed to be a titanic fist was a huge blossom of twisted fragments in a blaze of meson radiation.

Ellis looked to his gunner incredulously. There had not been a beam weapon close to making hull contact for over half a minute.

"Chief gunner?" he shouted in the stunned silence, but the gunner held up his hands disclaimingly over his still-loaded weapons.

The whooping and cheering began as the fragments cleared. They watched ragged lumps of plex and metal rain into the shields all around them as they were consumed in burning white embers. Some pieces hung there spinning above the *Constitution*'s deck, where they were pointed at triumphantly. The entire stern of the *Takeda Shingen* had been blown away and everyone who had been on her bridge was dead. The rest of the crew were trying desperately to recover and seal her bulkheads so that the oxygen-fed flames spurting out from her stern could be smothered and the leaking atmosphere did not make a vacuum of the rest of their ship.

Ellis barked himself hoarse, sending the ensigns and cadets round the decks with a hundred orders. The invaders had seen the *Takeda Shingen* explode, and several of their ships were putting about to help. There were too many for the *Constitution* to fight and Ellis put her head about too, suddenly iron certain that it was the right thing to do. The warble of an alarm by the stern screens comms bank made him turn.

"What is it?"

"There's a man outside the screens, Captain," a voice shouted below him. "He's alive!"

"A man?" he called at the scanner.

"Do we blast him, sir?"

"You sonofabitch," he shouted, angered at the man's moral

cowardice. "I won't have you shooting down survivors. Get a line to him. He may have something to tell us."

There was a pause. Then, "We heard they sometimes got booby traps strapped to them, sir."

"Bring him inboard, and that's an order!"

"Yes, sir."

They closed the shields down for a few seconds and tractored the lightly suited figure inboard, and moments later, with the *Constitution* accelerating planetward, the exhausted man was hauled up before the captain.

* * *

Those who watched were amazed at the way they fell into each other's arms. It was as if they had both been trying to hug the breath from the other's lungs, and for the rest of that dizzying afternoon brother had looked at brother again and again.

Ellis found himself drawn to stare at his brother's face and listen to the accent of his voice that was at once dearly familiar and yet completely foreign. And often as he looked, he found Duval was looking back through the gloom of the bridge's operational lighting, as if trying to fathom the changes worked by so many years. There was so much to talk about, but a battle was being fought, and Duval lent himself to the gunners.

They shared the *Constitution*'s bridge as Amerika's defenders broke off pursuit of the massive fleet. Watching Oujuku in the *Kalifornia* and Hawken in his *Texas*, both remembered the evil that had been done to them on Sado. Duval told him that Baron Harumi had been his reason to stay in Seoul and that the Sado daimyo had been blown to ions when the *Takeda Shingen*'s bridge disintegrated. Ellis, for his part, told Duval how his son and wife were safe in Amerika, and when Duval described the circumstance of Kenichi's birth, Ellis shook his head in wonder before admitting how it had been this very ship—*this very ship*—that had attacked them.

It would have been so easy to have destroyed their ship in revenge for the deception the Yamato vessel had practiced, Ellis thought. Yet he had not. And again, at Seoul, when they had met face-to-face only to be ripped apart by a stroke of chance. How many times had he wondered about that. Why? What unimaginable reason? And when, after Seoul, he had awoken aboard the *Constitution* and had thought his brother lost to the enemy, and there had been agonies . . .

His mind heaved with a strangeness that prickled his flesh, and the psi-currents swelled up his spine. He had never believed in blind chance, and it was as if a golden aura, rooted in his life but born of mystery, enveloped them both.

"You never told me about my father," Duval said, the strangeness of his accent fascinating Ellis. "You never said we were only half brothers."

And Ellis looked at him, tears in his eyes, and told him, "A brother is a brother. You either got one—or you ain't."

50

That night their joy at meeting was undiminished, but Ellis took his brother aboard the *Chongjin* to join in counsel with Amerika's admirals; he had not lost sight of the menace that still towered over them.

"The Yamato commander has orders from the Emperor," Duval said, passing on what the astrogator Aoki had told him. "Orders he was intending to follow to the *kanji*, that there must be no attempt at a landing until his fleet had secured a bridgehead in orbit and the army under General Yamaguchi was made operational. Tell your army that the moons of Arcadia at least are safe."

There was a flurry of activity as the admiral ordered an immediate communiqué to Lincoln sent out, then Copeland said urgently, "You say you know all about their guns and their disposition? Our fleet mounts in total around five thousand singularity guns, but of the big long-range guns designed to hit at three miles, we have less than a thousand. How is it with them?"

"They're mounting ten thousand new pattern singularity guns, but they're not of the Amerikan kind. They have heavy, short-range ship-smashers." He turned to Ellis. "Though I respect my brother's bravery, it's my belief that his ship would have been sunk had the *Takeda Shingen* not lost her tail, and that applies to the other big ships equally. To come within three thousand yards of the fleet shield will be suicide. They're relying on the Hakon Effect, what they call the Radiant Sun Strategy—all of their ship's shields coalescing into a mega-shield stronger than the sum of its component contributions. You must stand off from it at all costs!''

"That ain't our style!" Curtis Frastley said, rising. "We must break them before they reach Fort Bush."

"Sure," Oujuku whispered to Ellis as Frastley voiced his thoughts. "We *must* close with them, or we're lost! I don't give a damn about all this tactical bullshit, but I'll fight as I've always fought, according to my best feelings—in here!" He thumped his chest. "And if Admiral Copeland don't like that, then that's his problem."

"And if you're court-martialed for your disobedience?"

"Hell, you wouldn't shoot me. I'm the best goddamned astrogator you got."

"You're pretty sure of yourself, ain't you?"

"Yep. It takes a court to shoot a man, and a court's gotta have evidence. What me and my boys get up to is something I got five hundred sworn witnesses to. That's loyalty, mister."

Copeland tried to steer them away from the issue of Oujuku's individualism. He turned to Duval. "So, because of their singularity guns, if we get closer than three thousand yards we'll be minced up, but they're shooting beam weapons at normal range. And as we've seen, our own beam armament's not energetic enough to overwhelm so many ships in so tight a formation."

Duval said, "It's their hope to keep that 'radiant sun' made up, a formation which takes a lot of power and well-skilled orbit pilots to hold because their shield repulsion tends to squeeze it apart. If they can hold it, they can't be taken."

"It ain't enough to keep wild coyote dogs out," Oujuku said fiercely.

Hawken shook his head. "It ain't enough to follow them like wild dogs. We might be dogs and them a bunch of sheep, but we still gotta bring them to a fight in time to prevent their taking Fort Bush."

Copeland said, "He's telling us that if the guns on our ships can't bust a way through their defenses before they reach orbit

—and nothing else'll disturb their composure—then we're helpless."

"Helpless?" Frastley echoed, and Oujuku told them all, "I'll burn in hell before I'll let any man of them get planetside of me. When they're well herded into Seagrave's ships, we'll go in blazing as we have today, 'cept this time we'll be at pointblank. Sure! A couple of hundred yards' range where a singularity gun'll make so much Swiss cheese outta anybody—them or us!"

"There is a way," Duval said. All present turned to look at him. His voice was soft, almost distant. He was remembering the cargo deck of Jos Hawken's old flagship, the *Thomas Jefferson*, and the way fear had engulfed him as he saw the enemy approaching. Though it was almost twenty years ago, he was reliving the hell that had played about him on that deck: the same fires that had burned the ship into an inferno about him had made the guns stutter into uselessness. The stability of argentium tubes was very temperature-dependent, 3 degrees Celsius either side of the critical operating temperature of 282.27 Absolute and they wouldn't work!

But how could they heat up the tubes in the whole Yamato fleet?

The Olbers's Paradox . . .

"Yes," he said. He began to scratch-pad the back of his left wrist with his forefinger, and the keys of the calculator tattoo responded by appearing on his thumb. "Yes! There is a way!"

51

At the seventh hour on Sunday, July 28, the day *shichiban* in the month of *Shichigatsu* in the reckoning of Yamato, the Invincible Liberation Fleet finally ended its long planetward run. It had been successful, running the fearsome gauntlet of Amerikan attacks and achieving its objective of Liberty orbit, where it injected almost completely intact.

As his ships lay tight in their defensive formation thirty thousand miles above Liberty's equator, the commander in chief and his council met again. They were invulnerable inside their Hakon Effect ovoid. Never had the prospect of landing General Uehara's and General Ida's troops been so bright; never had the success of the Emperor's glorious design been so clearly assured. Then the scanners began to erupt with warnings.

Eighty foolhardy Amerikan ships in line-abreast came stealthily out of the shadow of Liberty. Every Yamato officer knew that so suicidal an attack mounted in the confining space of low orbit could only be a measure of the Amerikans' desperation. They started to train their guns on the approaching ships, then lights flared on the shields and pyrotechnic displays began as every beam weapon in the Amerikan fleet was trained on the tight globe of invading ships.

"What are they doing?" Nemoto Chikara asked his aide with incomprehension.

"Excuse me, Lord, but I can't understand their aim. It seems to me they are committing *seppuku*."

Nemoto's quizzical expression showed that he was mildly perturbed. "It is true that our shields can absorb beam weapon energy without fear of failure, is it not?"

"*Hai*."

"How long can they keep it up?"

"For several hours, at least, Lord. But that's of no advantage to them."

"And you say it can't harm us?"

"They can fire every beam they have, for as long as they want, Lord, and it would not penetrate self-compensating shields. Like a knot, the harder they pull on the ends, the tighter it becomes."

"And they know this?"

"They invented the self-compensating shield, Lord."

Nemoto made a tight little gesture of surprise and his long solemn patrician face creased. Under the neat warbonnet a face so flat that it was almost concave seemed for once to be about to crack into a smile. Nemoto's teeth were lacquered a perfect Imperial black. "Then this is quite extraordinary behavior."

Soon all eighty Amerikan vessels had maneuvered into place

around the Yamato fleet. Their weapons blisters had become torches of brilliant fire. Tongues of ionised particles lit up the invaders in a violet glow of Cherenkov radiation as the intense fields of the defensive shield shattered the beams harmlessly. But still raging energy continued to pour into the shield sphere until it closed around the fleet in a complete ball of radiance like a miniature A-type star.

Inside the globe, the radiation temperature began to rise inexorably. Though there was no conduction or convection of heat in the vacuum of space, the radiant surface enclosed them in four pi steradians—over forty-one thousand square degrees— each square meter pumping energy into the plex hulls like a hot, white sun.

Aboard the Yamato ships the captains received orders to phase their hulls to chrome, the most highly reflective surface available on the mote palette. Deep in the ships' interiors, refrigeration plants fought back and were then put into overload. Another round of general orders was issued. They began to de-suspend the remaining shock troops to save on refrigerant capacity. But still, hour by hour the temperature rose inside the ships, under the frightening onslaught of energy that matched the conditions of a contracting universe.

Soon the crews were sweating in their uniforms, breathing slow and deep with the lassitude of tropical heat. The temperature alarms began to pop. Computer tissue began to complain, then to stifle. Sauna conditions prevailed, turning everyone red in the face. And then the refrigeration plants began to break down. In the external engine pods, plex surfaces began to glow red, then orange, then white.

One by one, the ships experienced a slackening of power on their secondary engines, and the shield repulsion gradually began to force them outward. The perfect globe became blistered like a great fiery bunch of grapes, then the individual grapes started to break off and drift away.

Within minutes of the first separation the reluctant Nemoto's ships were scattered and in confusion. The defensive formation that had protected them was now utterly irrecoverable. The Amerikan attack was pressed home against ships whose argentium tubes were disabled by temperature instability and whose engines were failing.

Oujuku and Straker, Frastley and de Soto, Hawken and Copeland, all went in without mercy, each lesser captain following whichever admiral he pleased. And for hours the lumbering gilded giants of Yamato, hidebound monsters, their defensive globe shattered, their captains chained down with tight orders and the fear of the Emperor's wrath, were relentlessly searched out, smashed, holed, sent spinning planetside, annihilated.

An hour later, the ships' gongs chimed midnight UT. It was now the day the Emperor had appointed for glory, but the pathetic remains of the invasion force found itself driven steadily onto the lethal upper reaches of the E-layer of Liberty's atmosphere. Finally, Daimyo Nemoto Chikara, chamberlain to his Imperial Majesty the Emperor of Yamato, came out of his paralysis. The vision of future disaster that had held him in its grip was no longer a mesmeric premonition; with dawning horror he began to understand that it was now a nightmare from which there would be no waking.

As his remaining captains put away the last shreds of hope for a landing, Nemoto's fervent prayers were answered. The singularity guns and the engines began to work again, but it was not the looked-for divine deliverance.

On the assault decks of the transports, General Uehara's troops knelt in vast ritual lines, thousands upon thousands, filling the spaces from which they had intended to paravane like a rain of death onto Lincoln and Philadelphia. They composed themselves with the precision of the intersections on a *go* board. As one, following the actions of their commanders, they drew their short swords from their belts and made the first of the three lethal incisions in their abdomens that would spill their entrails agonisingly onto the decks.

Pulling out of orbit, the Emperor's proud invaders found themselves being harried away from the Liberty nexus by fierce attacks. Suddenly there was before them nothing but death and destruction on the ragged retreat to Arcadia. No Shinto shrine would now be erected on the ruins of the White House. The Emperor's dream had failed.

* * *

Low over the rain-soaked hill where the White House's east garden merged with the aspen trees, a flight of five ten-thousand-ton nexus ships roared, blotting out the sky with their immense cross formation. Their plex hulls had been phased into total transparency and their decks were dressed by Marine cadets in their white dress uniforms and chrome helmets. As one, they saluted at the moment each craft of the flight peeled off and headed for the Norfolk apron. A presidential rostrum had been erected, and below it, with great perseverance because of the downpour, a huge concourse was being readied for the crowds. Pharis Cassabian watched the erectors balefully through the acre-sized panes of the secretary's suite. He knew that this was no time for rejoicing—a war had just begun.

Across Pennsylvania Avenue, in the Treasury, Conroy Lubbock turned away from the window and received his prodigal daughter. He told her the news that the father of her children had been shot through the helmet by a samurai assault trooper during his attack on the Yamato flagship *Oda Nobunaga*, but that the beam had apparently only parted his hair, and against the orders of his admiral he was presently giving his assailant lone chase through the branch chain of nexi that terminated hopelessly in the Oregon system. The incident, Reba was told, had been reported to the President by Deke Copeland. Captain Straker's disobedience, she had said, was to be deplored. He must come and account for it in person at the White House, and she would see to it that he got his just deserts pinned onto his jacket.

Outside, Michie pulled her coat about her and stepped down from the air-car into the damp Lincoln night air. She had come at the treasurer's command and was met at the steps of the Treasury by the always poker-faced Jiro Ito. Incredibly the mood of the night had got to him and he was smiling. He informed her that her husband had been picked up from the Yamato star cruiser *Takeda Shingen* and was presently aboard the armed merchantman *Constitution*, which had been most recently reported in the uninhabited Vav-Six-Oh system—a lone star girdled by a vast cloud of gas—hunting down a fleeing Yamato ship.

Beyond the White House gates, the President's rose gardens began to fill with hundreds of thousands of half-uniformed, dancing, rain-drenched revelers. They raised jugs of liquor and torches and a bewildering assortment of street furniture and festive trophies they had been pulling up and carrying about all day. They chanted and chanted and would not shut up until their President came to give them thanks for their loyalty.

Alone on her rostrum, Alia Kane watched them with love and

deep gratitude. Her people were unique in all creation, a democratic people free and unfettered under God, their rights guaranteed, their freedoms maintained, and it was she whom they had honored and chosen as leader.

Already below her were ten thousand upturned faces, drenched by the rain. This was her Sector, her Amerika. One day the histories would call her the one hundredth President, a childless woman, but they would be wrong: she was mother to all those rain-lashed and unruly children—every last one of them. The Emperor had tried to take them away from her, and certainly there was a long road to travel and miles to go before they were truly safe, but at last Amerikans were up off their knees and walking tall again, as a free people must.

Alia Kane wanted to tell them so, but in her heart she knew that the pride of Yamato's martial spirit, though dimmed, was undefeated. The cherished dream of their "Amerikan Empire" had been extinguished, but they would never give up.

* * *

Eighty days later, a terror-stricken messenger landed on Kyoto's Chiyoda-Ku apron and crossed the moat of the Imperial Palace; there he waited terrified beside the placid carp pond. Below the surface immense genetically altered goldfish slid amongst reeds and slimy water. Each had a human face.

His Imperial Majesty was at his writing stand attending to state papers. He did not look at the man who groveled at his feet, but with inhuman self-control listened to the news without pausing his writing brush.

When the messenger was gone, the Emperor rose and stood alone before the shrine where the Imperial jewels were housed. He felt utter humiliation before the spirits of his ancestors. It seemed to the Emperor that he had betrayed their trust in him.

Icily he told his most constant companion, the chamberlain, Kido, "I give thanks to the gods that I can build another fleet greater than this I have lost whenever I choose to order it." Then he turned his eyes heavenward to contemplate the serene brilliance of the Nagoya event that continued to lighten Kyoto's daylight sky.